CEDARHAVEN

A Novel of the Early Northwest

BY PATRICIA CAMPBELL

THE MACMILLAN COMPANY, NEW YORK

FIRST PRINTING
LIBRARY OF CONGRESS CATALOG CARD NUMBER: 65-13593
THE MACMILLAN COMPANY, NEW YORK
COLLIER-MACMILLAN CANADA, LTD., TORONTO, ONTARIO
PRINTED IN THE UNITED STATES OF AMERICA

CEDARHAVEN

CHAPTER 1

On a fall morning in 1859 the schooner *Ladybird,* outbound from Richmond, passed into the Strait of Juan de Fuca.

Darrie Starkweather with her younger sisters Belle and Genia were repacking their trunks for the ending of the voyage when Papa opened the cabin door. "Come up on deck! I want you to see your new home—Washington Territory."

The wind was cold, with occasional stinging drops of rain, and Darrie held her cloak close about her throat. The younger girls clung to Papa's arms.

"Oh, look at the mountains!"

"The Olympics. Unexplored. No doubt rich which minerals—gold, silver, who knows what?"

"Where is Port Townsend, Papa?"

"We can't see it yet. We'll be there this afternoon."

"Where are the towns?" This was Belle's voice, with the suggestion of a quaver.

"There are no towns just here. It's a newly opened country. That's its merit."

"Oh—! Isn't it exciting to be here? After five whole months at sea!" Excitement and delight bubbled out of Genia like water from a spring. A spring at which Papa could refresh himself. . . .

Darrie drew a little apart and let her free hand rest on the *Ladybird*'s salt-dampened rail. She had become sea-wise enough to sense in her own flesh the schooner's weariness as it moved forward sluggishly, laden now with weeds and barnacles. By looking straight down into the undulating water she could see the streamers of brown weed whose backward flowing was the only proof of the *Ladybird's* progress. She had an odd reluctance to lift her eyes to the shoreline about which Papa and the girls chattered. The sea, the *Ladybird,* were familiar. Washington Territory was the unknown. But she looked up.

An endless wall of blue-green forest divided cloud-patched mountains and sullen gray-green sea. Not a single patch of cleared land broke the wooded shoreline. Not a thread of smoke rose into the overcast. Yet somewhere ahead of them, in some now-hidden inlet, was Port Townsend, their new home.

Darrie tried to imagine what Port Townsend would be like. Cousin Fayte had described it in his letters as a "jewel set in the forest," a "community of brave young dreamers." But there was the magazine article at which Papa had first frowned, then laughed. Port Townsend was, this author had said, "the sink-hole of Puget Sound, the last refuge of the desperate and the damned." "Ridiculous!" Papa had said. Washington Territory was a land of promise, a free and open country where "gentlemen would not be harassed and humiliated by their political beliefs." Darrie, twelve at the time, for that had been a year ago, had not known certainly what that meant; but she had known with awareness as precise and painful as a knife blade that at home in Richmond Papa did not believe in something called Secession, that his lack of belief had alienated Mama's family and had made him lose his position at City Hall. The motif of life's design had been Papa leaving the house each morning, hat at a jaunty angle, gold-headed cane swinging at his side. Suddenly threads of this comfortable texture were pulled askew, the pattern lost. Secession was the witch-word that had caused this. There was an ugly period when Papa stayed at home, and Mama cried. But comfort had returned with the name Port Townsend, where Cousin Fayte would see that Papa was restored to his rightful place in life.

It was a pity Mama had not lived to see their arrival in this new world. . . .

"Oh!" Genia cried, "I can hardly wait to see where we'll live!"

Belle said, "Without Mama . . . if God hadn't taken Mama. . . ."

Darrie saw the flesh shrink around Papa's eyes. He turned away, his shoulders drawing slightly together; it was a trick he had begun to use in the two months since Mama's death.

A gust of wind caught Darrie's scarf; she felt the sting of fresh raindrops. She took Belle's arm. "Come along," she said firmly. "It's beginning to rain again. Besides, we're not through packing. Papa . . ." She hesitated. "Papa, can you find one of the other passengers to talk to?"

Rain and a lowering sky made the hour seem later than it was when they came on deck again for their first view of Port Townsend.

The schooner rounded a low-lying point adorned by tumbledown shacks—an arm of land outstretched to shelter the harbor. The town itself was a string of frame buildings along a narrow waterfront.

"Oh, Papa!" Belle cried. "Is *that* Port Townsend? It's little—and it's horrid!"

Even Genia's lightheartedness was dimmed. In silence she slipped her hand under Papa's arm.

The business section of Port Townsend, Darrie saw through the curtain of early dusk, was crowded between sprawling wharves and a sharply rising cliff of yellowish clay. Along the crest of this hill a dozen homes clung precariously. To the south the ground sloped away to a beach crowded with weatherbeaten shacks and a jackstraw collection of canoes and small boats. Darrie heard one of the ship's officers tell Papa that was Kah Tai, the Indian settlement.

Twilight seeped downward from a darkened sky. Pinpricks of light appeared among the buildings on shore. Behind them voices clattered, lines rattled, canvas slapped; the schooner's sails were being lowered. From the shore small boats approached over water teased into white-tipped curls.

Confusion and disorder surrounded their leaving the *Ladybird:* men in the billed caps of Government uniforms were coming aboard; was there room in that boat for the Starkweather luggage? No matter, it could follow in another boat. The Holcombs, bound for Olympia, were going ashore too—or, no, they were not, the weather was too bad. Then they must say goodby now. "But we'll see you tomorrow—the *Ladybird* will be here another day or two!" This was better; goodby's were hard to say. "Careful there, young lady! That's a rope ladder, not a set of marble stairs!" Belle was trembling; "I'm so scared. . . ."

What's to be scared of? This is our new world waiting for us. And yet the seaman's oar pushing the small boat away from the stained and sea-worn curves of the *Ladybird*'s hull was bruising Darrie's own flesh. Five months of haven thrust away with the brass-bound tip of an oar. Darrie bit a knuckle until it ached and looked resolutely toward the little seaport that housed their golden future.

Strange the unsteadiness of solid earth under feet used to a sea-borne deck. Each step was a rejection. Genia laughed and clung to Papa's arm. "It feels so queer—the ground! And—oh dear!—look at that mud!"

Could this be the main street, this strip of trampled earth between board sidewalks so coated with mud as to blend unnoticed into the roadway? It was the main street. False-fronted wooden buildings faced each other sullenly across it. A sign, swaying in the wind, proclaimed "Pioneer Hotel." They moved toward it, picking their way carefully across the mire.

In the lobby a man was standing on a chair to light a hanging lamp above the desk. He got down to greet them. It seemed to Darrie that man and chair joined in creaky protest at the interruption. Yes, he had rooms. Two adjoining? With beds for three in one of them? Well, no, a big bed—big enough for three young ladies. They'd be comfortable. Clean sheets—he guaranteed that. All right then.

He lighted a lamp to guide them up the stairs. Weariness, and this unaccustomed stability underfoot, were making Darrie's legs tremble. To offset this she spoke with firmness to her younger sisters: "Papa will take the front room, of course. This one will do us nicely. Belle, put down your valise—don't just stand there!"

A kerosene lamp in a wall bracket was lighted for them.

Through the connecting door they saw Papa's lamp being lighted, money changing hands. The hotelman creaked away.

"Now, my dears, I'll leave you to unpack and tidy up. I'll find Cousin Fayte. It's odd he didn't meet us, but there's always a chance that letters have gone astray. In a town this size I'll have no trouble finding him."

Genia asked, "Won't Cousin Fayte be mad because we didn't go right to his house? Kinfolks would, I should think."

"We're not that close—second cousins, he and I. Oh, if he has room I'm sure he'll want us while we're looking around for a place of our own. But we don't want to impose. Let the invitation come from him. You're sure you'll be all right here, waiting?"

The narrow handsome face directed concern toward them. Papa's sea-tan was becoming, Darrie thought, bringing out the blue of eyes set wide apart under a finely shaped forehead. Even aboard ship he had contrived to keep his dark beard short and neat. Cousin Fayte would be proud to see him. . . .

He closed the door. His footsteps sounded loud and hollow in the hallway and on the stairs.

Belle pressed a handkerchief to eyes as blue as Papa's. She was the only one to have his eyes. Genia's were a clear golden amber in a rosy dimpling face. And Darrie's, Mammy Scofer had always told her, were yellow like a cat's.

Mammy Scofer! In a shattering flood of anguish Darrie relived the moment of parting or, more precisely, the moment she had known the parting was final. She stood again at the *Ladybird*'s rail looking toward the port of Richmond and waiting for Mammy Scofer to come aboard. The wooden rail was cold to her hand and damp with the same morning mist that cooled her cheeks and stung her nostrils with brine. Overhead gulls wheeled and screamed and struck each other as the ship's cook flung out scraps from the crew's early breakfast. Threads of smoke rose from a hundred chimneys like ravelings of brown yarn to blend into the overcast. Darrie tried to pick out a tendril of smoke that might conceivably come from their own home. But no longer their own. In strangers' hands now. And she waited for Mammy

Scofer; Mammy Scofer, the unchanging core of life whose presence would give continuity to outer change.

"All right," Papa said; "let's go to our cabins. We'll be in the way here when they make sail."

"But where is Mammy Scofer?"

A look passed between Papa's eyes and Mama's, a freighted look, a knowing look.

Awareness struck Darrie like a bludgeon: Mammy Scofer was not coming. Foreshadowing but unheeded at the time were a hundred revealing gestures: the too-tight handclasp, the almost smothering strength of last night's embrace, the final clinging, the heavy warmth of lips against her hand when she had stepped a few minutes ago into the waiting rowboat.

Darrie looked down at her narrow hand clasped on the ship's rail. The knuckles were white with the fierceness of her hold. A pain, actual and dreadful in its intensity, struck through the center of her being. The gray and undulating world grew black. Beads of sweat came out on her upper lip and turned cold in the morning air.

Belle had been whimpering; now she began to cry in earnest. For a moment tears trembled in Genia's golden eyes. Then she flew to Papa's arms. "How can we *live* without Mammy Scofer?"

When Darrie, holding the cup of herself with brittle care, turned away from the rail, Mama gave her a searching look. "I declare," she said, "look at that child! She could be going to the kitchen for a drink of water! Throw her to the lions—*she* wouldn't care!"

Mammy Scofer's strictures lived on: "You the strong one. You sisters count on you. You got to take care of 'em."

Offered in the safety of gracious rooms now three thousand miles away, the admonition persisted in this shabby hotel room. Darrie commanded, "Stop your sniveling, Belle, and unpack your valise. We can at least get our night things out, and tidy up, as Papa said. Look, there's water in the pitcher here, and clean towels. Well, towels. . . ."

Genia was at the window staring out. "I can't see the street from here. I'm going to look out of Papa's window."

"You'll do no such thing! A big girl like you, hanging out a window! Just you pull down that shade and get yourself freshened up. When Papa comes back we'll be ready to go out to supper."

"Where will we have supper—at Cousin Fayte's?"

"Maybe. Or maybe in the hotel diningroom. We'll see. . . ."

Time passed. Valises were unpacked, their contents hung in the wardrobe or placed in bureau drawers. Faces were washed, hair brushed. There was time to unpack Papa's carpetbag and put away his things. Both rooms were inspected thoroughly, both beds tested by bouncing and declared equally lumpy and unyielding. Minutely, iron bedsteads, varnished bureaus, and stringy window curtains were compared. "Papa's aren't quite so grimy, do you think?" Papa's room had a steel engraving on the wall: a cloud-swept sky threatening a lonely cabin. It was studied in detail.

Belle was on the verge of tears three times, and was three times comforted. Genia flew into a small rage. "I'm starving—I declare I am! My stomach is *caving in*!" Instantly she was contrite. "Oh, Darrie, don't look so worried! It's not your fault." Her arms were strangling tight; her heart could be felt beating, hard and quick, where breast crushed breast.

Darrie disentangled herself and smoothed Genia's hair. "You mustn't get excited, Genia. Mammy Scofer always told you it wasn't ladylike."

Belle's tears spilled over at mention of Mammy Scofer. "If she was here she'd see we got our suppers. She *would*! Something awful has happened to Papa—I just know it has!"

Darrie and Genia joined in comforting her, but Darrie, like Genia, felt close to starvation. They had had their last meal aboard ship long ago, and then it had been slighted from excitement. The trembling had begun again in her legs, and she felt giddy. She couldn't be getting one of her sick headaches, now, when she was so greatly needed. She told herself her weakness was from hunger. When she pictured a bowl of soup, some bread and butter, saliva came up in her mouth. She made a quick decision.

"We'll go out by ourselves. Papa will understand. He has been delayed somewhere. Now get your cloaks on, and your hats and mitts. We don't want to look like—" She had been going to say "like orphans," but the word stung her mind with its truth. She substituted "bumpkins."

Downstairs the desk was untended. Three or four rough looking men sat about in the lobby, their cigar smoke filling the shabby room. After a few minutes of awkward silence, Darrie asked of no one in particular, "Pardon me, but is there a hotel diningroom?"

There was not.

"A place . . . a place to eat?"

"You can't go out alone."

Darrie's chin lifted. She felt her eyes narrowing. Who was this stranger to tell *her*? She shepherded the younger girls toward the door. "Come along!" When the man rose and came toward her, she gave Belle a push—naturally Genia was already outside—and let the door close on his protests.

By a miracle the rain had stopped. To the west the sky was clear; a dark overcast squeezed out a flood of greenish light that made the street seem brighter than their lamplighted room. Perhaps it was not so dreadfully late after all.

Belle shivered and clung to Darrie's arm. "Where are we going?"

"I don't know. We'll just walk along until we find a restaurant."

There were few people on the street. Darrie surmised that most of the townspeople were at their suppers. The occasional passers-by were obviously seamen, some white, some dark-skinned but not the Negroes Darrie was used to seeing. She remembered that two other ships had been riding at anchor when the *Ladybird* made port. Sailors ashore in a strange town would know as little about directions as she did. She linked her free arm in Genia's and they moved along the board sidewalk.

The places of business they passed were dark, their doors locked. A few shopwindows displayed merchandise catering to the sea: coils of rope, brass findings, a compass and a telescope.

The block ended. They picked their way across a muddy street and found the buildings more scattered, smaller and dingier. They came then to a cluster of small houses close to the sidewalk. Here and there a red lantern hanging above an entrance gave a weird impression of Christmas-out-of-season. One door stood open. A woman leaned idly against the frame. She could not have expected anyone to see her for it was obvious she wore only a low-necked wrapper of rose-colored satin.

Darrie felt the awkwardness of speaking to anyone so unready for the public eye, but she was getting desperate and this was the first woman they had seen. She said, "Excuse me, I see you don't expect company—"

The woman's laugh rang out, loud and brassy but not unpleasant. Another door opened nearby and a frowzy head emerged. "What's going on, Lil—oh, my God!"

Darric kept her eyes on Lil's face; indeed she was too embarrassed to let her gaze wander. It was a kind face, really: rosy and goodnatured. "I am sorry to trouble you, but we're strangers and we're looking for a place to eat."

"Well, girlies, you're on the wrong street for that. You turn around and scat back uptown as fast as your legs'll trot. Don't you stop until you get across the street and up the whole next block."

"I see. . . . Thank you. And will we find a restaurant there?"

"Not one fit for young ladies like you, I'll tell you that. For God's sake, who let you out, anyway?"

Genia pressed forward. "Our father was delayed. We got so hungry. Our name is Starkweather. I'm Imogenia, and this is Isabelle and Darrelline. Darrie's oldest and she's named for Papa —Darrell Starkweather."

"Pleased to meet you, I'm sure. I'd love to gab, but believe me, girlie, you better not hang around. Now scat—the three of you! Quick-step, remember, till you're past the second corner."

Intuition told Darrie Lil was right. She thanked the woman and urged her sisters to "quick-step" back the way they'd come.

"We could have asked her more," Genia protested. "Where *can* we eat? I feel like I'm going to faint, I truly do."

A triphammer warning beat at the base of Darrie's skull: she was getting a headache, no doubt of that. Meantime there was the matter of getting food. At the second corner they turned onto a side street, for no particular reason, and found a door marked Bar and Grill. A delicious odor of frying met their eager nostrils. "Come on," Darrie said, and pushed open the door.

The room they entered was more bar than grill: its full length was taken up by a polished mahogany bar behind which shelved bottles glistened in the lamplight. Two men in shirtsleeves and white aprons busied themselves serving liquor from these bottles to their patrons. To Darrie's alarmed gaze it seemed there were hundreds of these patrons, all men, some standing at the bar, others at the half-dozen small tables against the opposite wall.

Her entrance, with her sisters, had an electric effect. As one after another of the men realized that aliens had appeared, they put down their glasses and turned to see what the others were staring at. All talk ceased. All eyes stared at the girls. From humming, glass-clinking conviviality the room froze into silence.

One of the barmen recovered first. He hurried to the girls. "Young ladies, excuse me, but you gotta be making a mistake."

His red-mottled cheeks were as bright as if waxed; his mustache rose in two spiked curls. Above this, round eyes protruded like marbles ready to fall.

Darrie's voice was faint. "We're looking for a place to eat. We're terribly hungry."

The words must have been magic. There was a scurrying about of both barmen, a stirring of customers; a table against the wall was summarily cleared of patrons, chairs were set, cloaks removed. Gradually the room's cheerful sound rose again, but muted. Food was brought. It was delicious—straight from heaven: fried potatoes, bread and butter, thick steaks. Belle winced when the blood ran beneath her knife, but Genia ate like a fieldhand. Darrie forced down a few mouthfuls after the first ravened slice of bread had cured her dreadful hollowness.

She had discovered, after sitting down, that her chair faced a larger-than-life painting of a naked woman who lay on a bear rug and stared at the world with sleepy smiling eyes. Strangely enough, although the woman wore no stitch of clothing, she seemed less exposed than had Lil leaning in her doorway. If Darrie had not been so tired, and so shaky from advancing headache, she would have tried to puzzle out the reason. But this was not the time for it.

Someone must have been sent to look for Papa. They were finishing their meal when he appeared, patently embarrassed, to reclaim them and to pay their bill. It was only then Darrie realized she had no money. This knowledge added to the growing sickness at the pit of her stomach, the soft hammering of congested blood.

Back at the hotel she lay shivering on the outer edge of the bed waiting for the waves of nausea that long experience led her to expect. When the gray dishwater light of morning began to seep in around the window shade, she groped her way to the washstand. The day would be lost, wiped out. Papa and the girls would have to manage without her.

CHAPTER 2

Darrell Starkweather walked down the flight of dusty wooden stairs to the lobby of the Pioneer Hotel, saluted Tad Holmes, the decrepit owner, manager, clerk, and sometimes chamber maid, laid his two-bits on the desk, and asked for a San Francisco paper.

At dawn he had heard a ship's anchor chain running out, and

the sound had blended into a dream that he was home, in Richmond, hearing coal poured down the chute into the storage bin. Wakening, finding himself alone in the lumpy, sway-backed hotel bed, he had found comfort in thinking that, later in the day, a new ship in the harbor would provide fresh newspapers.

Not that any newspaper was exactly fresh when it reached Port Townsend. He glanced at the dateline: March 12, 1860. And this was—what? The second of April? The date reminded him that he had been in Washington Territory half a year. It didn't seem possible.

Half a dozen men, sunk into the leather lobby chairs, were already reading their copies of the *Alta*. Stark pulled a chair around to face the window and opened his copy of the paper. The news was of gold and shipping, gold and abolition, gold and—yes, there was that ugly word again: Secession. He had left Richmond to escape it.

It had been the right decision, concurred in by Cynthia. Yet now Cynthia lay asleep off Cape Horn under fathoms of green water. The canvas-wrapped bundle had looked so small, as if it held a child. Would the canvas have rotted in eight months? A picture came to his mind of loosened hair wavering like brown seaweed in the still caverns of the ocean's floor. . . . He didn't want to think—would not *let* himself think. . . . Today's necessities, and tomorrow's, must hold his mind. Soon he would have to make some different living arrangement. He did not like to remember that first ghastly evening in Port Townsend when he had set out to find Fayte Starkweather only to learn that his cousin had left town. Even more galling was his recollection of the girls wandering about town and ending up in a saloon.

Within a day he had found a respectable place for them to board. Mrs. Duncan, a kindly soul if somewhat lacking in polish, had squeezed them into the log cabin she shared with her two growing daughters. The household arrangements were so primitive and so crowded, even though Mr. Duncan was off prospecting, that Stark avoided going there except from necessity. But he assumed his daughters were reasonably happy. After all, they were children, and children accepted whatever living arrangements their elders made for them. No doubt they missed their mother and Mammy Scofer. But there was nothing he could do about either of these deprivations. Meantime they had to be sheltered, kept in a home safe from the Indians who wandered Port Townsend's streets in a chronic state of inflammation from what the people here called "siwash whisky" or "tangleleg." Not to mention a shifting population of sailors who prowled the streets for whatever entertainment they could find.

Belle and Genia—how old were they now? Eleven, twelve?—were in school, or what passed for school in this frontier village. (Stark had given passing thought to applying for the position of teacher, but it had seemed a shade beneath his talents.) Darrie stayed at home with Sophie, the older of the Duncan girls. Sophie was, so Darrie had explained to him, "spoken for." What a common expression! Apparently this happy state put her beyond the need for further education: she and Darrie were—again the explanation was Darrie's—"learning to keep house." This was ridiculous in Darrie's case. Women in the Starkweather family had servants to do their work. Still, if it kept Darrie happy and out of mischief he had no quarrel with it. Experience had taught him that she could be difficult. . . .

As these thoughts, all springing in one way or another from the headlines about Secession, went through Stark's mind the newspaper lay unheeded in his lap. He stared out the window hardly aware that his eyes were trained on Port Townsend's main street, on yellow mud deepening under the spring rain, on passersby with their coat collars turned up, on a dispirited team from the country plodding along, heads down, rivulets of water slipping off their flanks.

In his bemused state, and staring through the rain-smeared window, he even imagined he saw Darrie coming down the street, a poker-straight little figure with a shawl held tight beneath her chin. It must be a trick of dull light and swirling rain. But, no! It *was* Darrie, heading purposefully toward the hotel entrance. His first impulse was to get out of sight, but it was too late: Darrie had her hand on the door.

Once inside she drew off her shawl and shook the raindrops from it.

Perhaps it was the attention of the other men in the lobby, who had frankly abandoned their newspapers, that made Stark look freshly at his eldest daughter. He found himself wishing she would wear her russet hair down as she used to instead of in a coronet of braids. They made her look older and gave a suggestion of hauteur to the way she held her head. Yet she was pretty in spite of that: her pale complexion—almost too pale for his taste—was flawless, her features delicate. Her eyes were her most unusual asset: light brown and shaped like melon seeds. Angered, they could narrow to slits of yellow fire.

She looked not so much angry now as intent. Her lips were tightly held, the lower one pressed outward in a determined little bud.

Getting to his feet Starkweather asked, "Is something wrong?"

"No. I just came to talk to you."

"We'd better go to my room."

Upstairs Darrie looked around his quarters with an attentiveness that made Stark feel defensive, as if he had to justify the room's shabbiness. When Darrie's eyes rested on the folding frame that held photographs of Cynthia on one side, Darrie and her sisters on the other, he began to imagine reproach in the pictured eyes. He went to the bureau and closed the frame. It was not so easy to escape Darrie's gaze.

After a time she said, "Papa, have you quite made up your mind about staying in Port Townsend?"

"Naturally! My mind was made up when we left Richmond."

"But you have looked around a bit, as if you might—"

"I've investigated nearby communities, yes. Not a comfortable thing to do, either, especially in winter. But I've visited Olympia, Seattle, Tacoma, even Victoria. The miles I've endured on that wretched little steamer, the *Eliza Anderson*! But I can say now with real conviction that Port Townsend is the most promising location."

"Why is that?"

"Really, Darrie, if you're questioning my judgment—"

"Oh, no, Papa! I'm simply asking."

"It's quite obvious, although one doesn't expect the female mind to—but no matter. The most hopeful outlook for any community on Puget Sound is to court the maritime trade. Each month sees more ships flying the American flag. With the Pacific area opening up, Port Townsend's location is invaluable. The powers-that-be have recognized this in placing the Custom House here."

"Are you going to get a job in the Custom House, Papa?"

"It's quite possible. If Cousin Fayte had stayed here—"

"Why do you think he left?"

"He's unstable. Always was. I should have known. . . . Still, everything he said about Port Townsend is true, you know. Superb location, temperate climate, scenic grandeur. Did you ever see a more magnificent view than on a clear day when the mountains are out on both sides?"

Darrie said matter-of-factly, "There are trees around the Duncan cabin. We can't see out."

"Ah, yes! The forest! There's another source of potential wealth."

"Were you thinking of cutting timber, Papa?"

Starkweather could not keep from smiling. "Not personally," he said. He saw no use in mentioning that the timber around here was damned hard to get out, and damned far from any market. It was true a few of the hardier locals were engaged in logging; Port Townsend's only present evidence of industry was the logboom in the bay. But Stark could not picture himself beavering spars and sawlogs out of the wilderness, using bulls to drag them to the waterfront, and chaining them into booms to wait for an out-bound schooner. In time, when more people had come to the Territory, and there were closer markets, dealing in timber might be profitable. From the broker's end, that is. But Port Townsend's real future lay with the sea. Why, in another year or two there would be six ships in the harbor for every one that dropped anchor now! Schooners would be fitted here to new suits of sails; dry docks would be established and bottoms scraped free of barnacles picked up as far away as Melbourne or Singapore. Slop chests would be filled, galley shelves stocked, water casks replenished. Already the people here who really prospered were the ships' chandlers, the mercantile houses catering to the maritime trade. Not to mention those dubious places of business that always flourished in a seaport.

All this was in his mind when he said to Darrie, in a voice intended to be reassuring, "I am sure you can trust me to make a wise choice when I do settle on a line of business."

"I'm sure of that. I only wondered if we were definitely going to stay here."

"Indeed we are!"

"Then you really shouldn't have to live in a place like this." Darrie's glance went back to the room's shortcomings, the faded and stained wallpaper, the bureau with one drawer that didn't match. "It's not good enough for you."

"I admit it's not what we're used to. I've been hoping to find a house for you girls' sake more than for myself. I daresay this is quite palatial compared to the room you share with the Duncan girls. Fortunately I've been spared the actual sight of that."

"It's dreadful, Papa. Even though Ma Duncan is kind to keep us, the room is really dreadful."

"Still, with her husband off on his wild-goose chase for gold, I imagine the board money is welcome."

Darrie had seated herself on the edge of the bed, and for a time she seemed to be considering his statement. She chewed her lower lip and looked at Stark in a peculiarly penetrating way. As always, he found her regard disquieting, and said, rather stiffly, "Naturally, I'm glad to be of service to Mrs. Duncan."

Darrie looked away from him almost, he felt, as if she wanted to keep him from guessing her feelings. She let her fingers wind about a cotton tuft on the not-too-clean bedspread. "Where," she asked, "is all our furniture?"

"In Bonner's warehouse."

"I suppose it's getting moldy and the rats are nibbling it."

Stark thought, Damn it! She's heard the Duncan woman say that. He walked to the window, clipped the end of a cigar, lighted it, and looked at his daughter through a haze of smoke.

Although the matter had been brought up before, and supposedly settled, he felt impelled to say, "You ought to be in school."

Darrie sighed and went back to twisting the cotton tuft, her head bent, her expression thoughtful. A face so delicate, a jaw so narrow, had no right to cry stubbornness. Those level eyes, that straight line of brow, must be the stigmata of obstinacy. It was a pity. Stark was not the only man who treasured softness in a woman.

Darrie had apparently decided not to answer him about school, except indirectly. "I'm learning other things."

"I can't imagine you learning a great deal from Mrs. Duncan. She's hardly my idea of . . . of . . ." What did he mean, really? She was good enough to take the girls in.

Darrie saved him. "Ma Duncan's kind, but I know what you mean. I'm afraid Belle and Genia are picking up habits that—well, they should be where they can copy you, Papa. That's why I'm so anxious to—" She broke off, biting her lip and looking at him quizzically.

Stark was mollified in spite of himself. It was gratifying to know that Darrie, young as she was, could make this distinction. He said, "My dear child, you are no more anxious than I am for us to be together in our own home."

"If that's really true—"

"Would I say it if it weren't true?"

"Oh, I *am* glad to hear that! I didn't want to think you were just—well, letting things go."

"Naturally I wouldn't do that. It's quite contrary to my nature."

"And you have found out there's no proper house for rent?"

"Indeed there's not!" Stark could speak here with real conviction. "There's hardly an empty shack, let alone a decent house. Why, there are families camping along the beach in tents! I wonder the tide doesn't carry them away."

"I was sure you'd looked into all this. So I suppose you've decided to build a house."

"I wouldn't say I had absolutely decided—"

"But there's nothing else to do, is there?"

Stark couldn't think of an immediate answer. When he started to say, "Well—well, probably, in the near future—" Darrie got up from the bed rather hastily and interrupted him to say, "I'm probably keeping you from something important. I'll run along. You'll see me out, won't you?"

Darrie was half out the door before he could say, "Yes, of course!"

As they passed the desk, she turned to smile and bow to Tad Holmes. There were times when she amazed Stark with her grown-up ways; she could have been thirty instead of thirteen. But, seconds later, his pleasure in her good manners was swept aside. "Good afternoon, Mr. Holmes," she was saying. "You'll be sorry to lose Papa's custom, won't you?"

"How's that? You leaving us, Stark?"

Before Stark could get his mouth open, Darrie answered for him. "My father is going to build a house. He's been waiting to make up his mind, but now he has decided." She nodded brightly at Mr. Holmes and continued toward the door. There she turned and smiled at Stark. "Thank you, Papa, for letting me know your plans. I'll tell Belle and Genia as soon as they get home from school. They'll be as pleased as I am."

Everyone in the lobby heard her parting remarks: her voice was well-bred but it did carry. For an unnerving moment Stark had the notion she'd carefully planned their entire conversation. Except that it was impossible—she was a *child*. . . . Before he could explore the thought, several of the men were crowding over to congratulate him.

"Going to build, eh? Well, good for you!"

"Say, my brother-in-law's a good carpenter. I'll send him around."

"Before you buy yourself a lot, Stark, let me show you one I own. Say, she is a dandy!"

He hadn't had this much deference since he had arrived in town. With the little group of hotel hangers-on moving with him, he returned to his chair near the window. "I'm not going to build any little old log cabin," he told his audience. "I intend to have a home suitable for my three daughters and myself."

"Sa-ay, man! You got some daughter! That high-headed little filly, yes sir!"

High-headed little filly . . . hm. . . .

CHAPTER 3

Leaving the hotel, Darrie walked with quick determined steps. She had an errand to do: Ma Duncan had asked her to stop at the Kentucky Store and get a spool of thread. Ma would be surprised to learn that Papa was going to build a house. . . .

She passed beyond a frame building and found herself on a board walk that ran, for a hundred feet or more, along the open seawall. A murky rain hid the farther shore of the bay; she might have been at sea again. Arrows of rain stung her face; when she closed her eyes against them, the wind tore at her hair and lashed her temple with a tendril of hair. It had been like this at sea; the wind was ever present, its voice keen against taut rigging, its pressure caressing, teasing, coercing, exasperating, or, at times, rising to a violence that closed out every emotion except the need to stand against it.

It had seemed to Darrie, in those months at sea, that any solid earth, any home with four walls, would be as sweet as heaven.

Each of the family had reacted in her own way to the voyage. Belle had withered in terror at the fluid and formless world.

Genia had met its challenge laughing, head thrown back to catch the wind's full force. Mama became inert, a thing of sparrow bones and wasted flesh. It was this pallid stranger who was sewn into canvas and buried at sea, not the laughing, teasing, dancing Mama whose continuing love-affair with Papa had been the bittersweet core of life at home. And Papa . . .

Darrie stopped, facing the wind-swept harbor, her hands on the wet railing of the seawall, and puzzled once more over changes the voyage had made in Papa, changes as imperceptible as the tides but no less certain. His diminishment evaded capture in words. But there had been, almost from the beginning of the voyage and surely from the start of Mama's illness, a subtle shifting of authority, a transfer never spoken of between them but known as the color of blood is known and the solid framework of unfelt bones.

Out of this bone-and-blood awareness of truths too subtle to be put in words, Darrie, with her face lifted to the rain-filled east wind, knew that Papa had not meant to build a house. The idea had been hers. She could still go back and say, "Papa, you mustn't let me influence you. You must decide. . . ."

The image gave her a rushing sense of release, as a gull might have when it rose on the wind. Even her breath stood still, arrested between what had happened and what might have happened. Or should have happened. . . .

"You alone, honey?" A shambling creature in a seaman's knitted cap stood beside her, broken teeth showing between slobbering lips.

She brushed past him and walked quickly toward the Kentucky Store. She never should have doubted the necessity of their own secure home in a town full of this sort of ugliness.

With the door pushed shut against the wind, Darrie was embraced by the unique richness of the store's climate—the background of shelved merchandise, the odors of leather, tar, yard goods, hemp, and tea mingled with a hundred she could not identify. Baron Rothschild himself came forward to wait on her. "Ah, Miss Starkweather, what will it be?" He was tall and blond, with the bearing of a soldier. Ma Duncan said his title was a courtesy, but it suited him. Darrie charged the spool of thread to Ma's account and went on.

When she opened the cabin door, Ma Duncan looked up from putting wood in the cookstove. Her sallow face was flushed with heat, her spare and wiry body, as always, tensed for action. "My laws! You're half drownded! You get those wet shoes off right now. Sophie, fetch Darrie's knitted slippers from the other room."

The fragrance of tea competed with the smell of wood smoke. The cookstove sent waves of welcoming heat toward Darrie. Sophie's hands were waiting to take her shawl. She found, with surprise, that it was possible to enjoy what no longer stretched toward eternity.

*

A site for the Starkweather house was chosen: one of several building lots on a ledge between the water-level business streets of Port Townsend and the bluff on which the best homes had been built.

A scowload of lumber had to be brought from the Discovery Bay Mill, bricks ordered from Allen's brickyard across the bay. Doors and windows were shipped by steamer from Utsaladdy. A carpenter was hired, and a helper. After what seemed to Darrie an interminable delay, work was actually started.

It was fall before the house was ready for occupancy. It was an impressive building, one of the best in town: a nine-room two-story frame structure, proudly white, with bow windows and a narrow, covered side-porch. The house faced away from the harbor and onto an embryonic street reached by four wooden steps. Beside this front entrance two tall cedar trees, stubborn and incongruous on the dry hillside, had been left at Papa's insistence. Now, when the house was finished, the trees darkened the front room but gave the building an air of permanence and dignity. Papa announced they would call their home Cedarhaven. He hired a man to carve the letters in relief on a panel which he placed above the front door.

Ma Duncan sniffed. "Uppity! But kind of pretty at that." Then she rolled up her sleeves. "Come on, child. We'll get your furniture uncrated and settled in. After that you can manage by yourself."

Darrie accepted the challenge with a surge of pure delight. Here was something she could get her teeth into after the frustrations, delays, and inactivity she had gone through.

Papa had talked vaguely of servants—"perhaps a good strong Irish girl"—but Ma's astringent realism had cured Darrie of such illusions. "Why would any good strong girl—Irish, Swede, or what-have-you—work in your Pa's kitchen when she could have her pick of a dozen men to set her up in a kitchen of her own? No, my dear, it's up to you girls. Which means, when all's said and done, it's up to *you*."

"I'll manage," Darrie said. If she had reservations she wasn't going to admit them to Ma Duncan, much less to any of the neighbor women who had been quick to offer help and advice. "Thank you," Darrie had told them all with cool civility, "but I don't reckon I'll need any help." The galling months when she had been a recipient were ended. A wild notion of becoming so efficient the neighbor women came to her for aid had to be shelved as unrealistic. But she would take no more favors from anyone.

If only Mammy Scofer were here she would have no misgivings. It was a dream of heaven to imagine Mammy Scofer in the kitchen of Cedarhaven, her strong hands coping with the perversities of stove and pump, her voice—deep and sweet as a bumblebee in honey—giving orders and advice. Lacking the physical presence of Mammy Scofer, Darrie conjured up her image: Mammy in the brick-floored laundry room at home, head bent over an ironing board, black hand pushing equally black iron that nosed like a questing animal into ruffles of cambric and linen. A voice as authoritative as the voice of God saying, "You face up to what you got to do. Else you . . . is trash." The iron thumped emphasis. No Starkweather was trash.

Very well, then, Darrelline Starkweather would face up and do what she had to do, which was to somehow manage this household and take care of her two younger sisters. Belle and Genia would have to help, of course. She would outline certain tasks which they would have to do. They wouldn't want to, but she would make them. There was a trick to it—she'd seen Mammy Scofer manage that, too. "Do this!" one said, and pretended not to imagine for one moment that it would not be done as ordered.

"Belle, you carry those blankets out and hang them on the line to air."

"Oh, Darrie, they're heavy."

Ignore the protest. Assume it will be done. "And, Genia, you fill the woodbox."

"Oh, Darrie—!"

But this was easier; Genia really wanted to please. Dimples emerged from what had been almost a pout. "All right! I reckon I can."

Yes, Darrie saw, this was the way it had to be done.

CHAPTER 4

In the early afternoon the bar at Tibbie's was almost deserted. Stark ordered a bourbon and water and told himself he would make it last a good long time, at least until someone came in to share a drink with him.

It was really too early to come in here, but the wind outside was bitterly cold for May. If he had stayed out on the street he would have ended up with pleurisy or, at best, a chest cold.

Without a wife to look out for him, a man was subject to all sorts of hazards. Now Cynthia . . .

But this was water under the bridge. They had had to leave Richmond . . . hadn't they? If he had it to do over again, would he take the Southern position on States' Rights, he wondered? Even if that meant fighting? But this was nonsense! The Southerners, proud and hot-blooded as they were, would not carry it that far!

President Lincoln seemed a tolerant man, and wise. He could be trusted to arbitrate these minor differences.

Perhaps it was small-minded of Stark—he tried not to think so—but he had not cared for some of the new President's appointments. Take Salmon Chase, for instance. Things had been going very well here in the Puget Sound Custom District and Stark had felt sure he was going to get a deputyship. Now Collector Phillips was out, and a new man, a newspaper editor from Cincinnati, appointed in his place. Stark meant to approach this Victor Smith as soon as he reached Port Townsend; meanwhile he was back in that limbo of marking time.

Stark noticed that his glass was drained. He held it for a while, looking into its emptiness, thinking he ought to leave. The barman, catching his eye, raised an inquiring brow. Stark sighed and nodded. When the barman approached, Stark flicked his glass with a thumbnail. "Put this on the cuff, will you?"

There was a perceptible pause before the man said, "Okay." Not "Yes sir," mind you, but "Okay."

Stark took an uneasy glance over his shoulder, but he was alone in the bar. The truth was—he let himself admit it—he needed a steady salary and he needed it quickly. The capital which had seemed so generous when he left Richmond had dwindled to near zero. The passage from Virginia, the expense of boarding once they were here, the new house which had cost more than he had dreamed possible—all had taken their toll. Could he have managed better, he wondered? Perhaps a few dollars had slipped through his fingers while he had lived at the hotel. He really was no poker player, but it didn't do, if one wanted to become a member of the community, to sit back and refuse a friendly game. And one really had to treat at the bar once in a while. Maybe he had made a few more such small gestures than were actually necessary, but after all he was new in the community and he wanted to make a good impression. It would be absurd to say now, at this late date, "Look, my friends, I am not a rich man at all. In fact, I have, so to speak, shot my bolt." Now more than ever he needed a reputation of affluence.

Damn it! he thought. This was getting to be as unpleasant as those last months in Richmond. What a relief it would be to talk it over with Cynthia! She had always known how to comfort a man. Her warm flesh . . . Was it less than two years? Yes, yes, two years this August. Those last weeks she had been nothing but bird bones and big eyes. She had already been—he realized that now—slipping from his reach. That was why—but he would not think of that. There had been *no* connection. Anyway, her eyes had warmed to his, her fragile hand had lifted. . . .

Through the prism of sudden tears the amber liquid in his glass spun like the design in a kaleidoscope. He drained the glass and set it down.

Two men had come in and were standing toward the center of the bar. Stark imagined they glanced at him hostilely. He thought he caught the whispered word, "Copperhead!"

He knew the men slightly. They had a small gristmill at the mouth of Chimacum Creek. He lifted his now empty glass toward them. "Join me in one?" he invited.

"No time," muttered one. "Got to get back." Still he made no move to leave. There was more talk, impossible to ignore, of yellow-bellied Seceshes and dirty slaveholders.

Stark could feel the color coming up slowly, warming his throat, his cheeks, his forehead. He edged along the bar, cleared his throat, and said, "If you are talking about the Southern—"

"We was."

"Then let me say, as one who comes from Virginia, the Southern people as a whole are as loyal to our government as you are yourselves. They may resent some actions of Congress. They've held conventions to discuss the possibility of Secession. I regret this—as I am sure they will also, in the fullness of time. However, you may be sure they will never lift a hand in violence—"

One of the men interrupted him: "Guess you ain't heard, then?" He let fly a yellowish stream, missing the spittoon and creating a round tobacco-colored stain in the sawdust floor.

"Heard? Heard what?"

"The dirty Seceshes have fired on Fort Sumter, that's what! They's a war goin' on."

A joke, Stark thought, a stupid joke. But the man's grizzled face denied that. "How do you know?" Stark asked.

"Feller just came down by launch from Victoria. They've had the Frisco papers there. It stands in black and white."

Stark managed to get up with dignity and walk out. He heard the bartender and the two men sniggering behind him.

Civil war! It was hideous—*hideous*! But it would soon be over. A few hotheads had got control, but the saner ones in the South would bring them back in line. Perhaps it was an exaggeration. Perhaps they hadn't really fired on Fort Sumter, only threatened to do so. In the deepest part of his mind he knew this was folly.

If he were still in Richmond . . .

There was a kind of fatefulness about the whole thing. As if he had been guided away from the scene of conflict. But there was always a price for being spared.

He had turned toward the hill. In his mind was a vision of home, of Cynthia to draw this needle-tip of poison, to reassure him. . . .

He had gone half a block before he realized Cynthia was not there. But he had no place else to go.

Darrelline was washing the front steps when he arrived. Her skirts were pinned up, and an apron offered some protection, but in spite of these precautions she looked bedraggled and damp about the edges. He noted that her dress was short in the sleeves and that, down the front, the buttons were straining at the buttonholes. Even in his preoccupation the sight startled him.

His little girl was growing up! A girl of her age was marriageable, sought after. He put the implication out of his mind and said, "My dear, you oughtn't to be doing this sort of work. It's for servants."

Darrie emptied the bucket of water and shook out the brush.

He smiled at her, but she turned away and entered the house. He followed her, his eyes on the narrow back, ramrod straight, that strained the covering of calico. If her nubility, in terms of an asset, was an unworthy thought, to think of her marriage as a means of escaping from her—such an ugly idea could not have entered his mind.

Driven by the need to discuss the day's news with someone, he followed her into the kitchen. There she unpinned her skirts and sat down at the table with a bowl of potatoes to be peeled. He said, "I was wondering if I couldn't have a cup of coffee?"

Darrie started to get up, then sat back in her chair. He noticed then that her face was rather drawn. He hoped she wasn't getting one of her disabling sick headaches; they made the household quite impossible, not to mention the pain to her. He said, "Maybe I could make the coffee?"

"Do try."

He went into the pantry. He had seen this process carried out a good many times. He found the coffeepot, ground a handful of beans for it, added water, and put the pot on the cookstove.

"Open the damper," Darrie advised.

Stark sat down at the table to wait. He still needed to share the knowledge so recently acquired. "There's big news downtown," he said. "It appears that war has broken out between the States."

Darrie looked up from her potato peeling. "What states?"

"The Southern, or Secessionist, states and the Federal government, the Northern states."

"Does that mean back home?"

It might have been her tone, or some connotation of the phrase itself: Stark felt tears burn along his lids. They had been waiting there, he thought, all afternoon. He said, "Yes, the Old Dominion will have its share of trouble."

"The Old Dominion?"

"Surely you know that name for Virginia!"

"Maybe. I've forgotten. It seems so long ago." Strips of peeling began to fall again from her fingers.

What a cool little thing she was, her father thought. Her occupation, or her attention to it, added to the impression of maturity that had always been her trademark. What went on, he wondered, beneath the neatly coiled russet braids? Her eyes had lifted momentarily, as if to appraise him, but they were screened again by dark lashes. Unnatural child, he thought. Yet there was this need to placate her. . . .

The coffeepot began to whisper on the stove, but at once the sound was lost in a rush of footsteps on the back porch. The door opened to let in cool air and sweet, light voices. Belle and Genia were home from school.

Stark's mood rose at once. The little girls were so sweet, so affectionate, so—what was the word that set them apart from Darrie? Undemanding? Perhaps that was it.

Genia poured a cup of coffee and bore it to him as a slave girl approaching her master. The saucer was half full, and drops fell to his brocaded waistcoat, but that was a small price to pay for such engaging service.

"Papa, can I get your slippers for you?" This was Belle, leaning on his arm and breathing toward him the milk-sweet breath of childhood.

"*Dear* Papa!" Imogenia beamed at him, her dimples flashing, her eyes bright with affection.

It seemed unkind to go into the other room, to leave Darrie here, but she shrugged acceptance of the arrangement.

Genia clung to Stark's arm, hampering his efforts while he lighted the fire already laid in the grate. It smoked, and he found a paper to fan it. This wretched coal brought from Bellingham across the inlet—what wouldn't he give for a scuttle of the clean hard coal they used to have back home! And an obliging darky to tend the fire. This war so newly broken out—if it were truly a war—how would it affect slavery, he wondered? He had never quite believed that one man should have ownership of another. Yet how else accommodate these simple, dark-skinned people? They could scarcely cope for themselves in a world so difficult that he, Darrell Starkweather, was hard put to care for his family. In a way the darkies were fortunate to be looked out for, weren't they?

The fire was drawing now, flames licking upward through the coal and sending a minor warmth into the room. He drew his chair closer, and Genia ran to get a stand for his coffee cup. But the coffee had grown cold. It had been weak to start with. Cooking was not a man's work.

Belle wandered to the piano, spun the stool a few times, and began to pick out one of the little pieces she had been learning back in Richmond. She did very well, he thought, for having been two years without a lesson. When he got established, when there was an income again, he would find a teacher for her.

Genia drew a hassock to his side, and caressed his coatsleeve. She said, "Isn't it a shame for Darrie to work so hard? Why didn't we bring someone from home to help her?"

"I've told you a hundred times, we couldn't bring our people here. This is free soil. Slaves are not allowed." The reminder of Darrie, alone in the kitchen, was not pleasant, and he was aware his voice had hardened.

Genia pouted for a moment then, in a lightning change of mood, showed her dimples in a disarming smile. "At home you always said I was your little princess and I wasn't to lift a finger. Am I still your princess?"

She was irresistible, and knew it. He tried to sound stern when he said, "You must act like a princess, and a polite and well-mannered one, if you want to be one." His sternness dwindled under the coquetry of amber eyes that looked at him, wide and adoring, then disappeared behind fans of feathery lashes. He laughed. "You little minx!"

Imogenia leaned away from him. He reached after her. His hand enclosed a small soft arm.

"Papa!"

She was a born flirt. He could swear he felt her flesh tremble. She drew against his hold. Her voice heightened. "Papa! What are you going to do?"

"I ought to spank you!"

Laughter, and something else rising behind it in deepened color and quickened breath—fear? Surely not! This child—this adored child—this never-actually-to-be-punished darling . . . Roughly now he pulled her into his arms. "You little silly, you!"

For a moment she was a wild thing struggling to be free. Within the tender casing of her flesh he felt the rapidly beating heart, the tangled breath, the quivering nerve. Then she was limp in his arms. Her moist and rosy mouth lifted for his kiss. The moment—mad and inexplicable—was past. She was again his dear, his tractable little girl. Lying in his arms, panting from the brief but violent struggle, she looked up at him adoringly. Astonishment caught at his breath when she said, "Then you will get us a slave, or at least a servant, won't you, Papa?" It was, he thought, almost as if she were exacting tribute.

He laughed down at her. "I'll have to get a fine position with a nice big salary first."

"Oh, yes, Papa! You do that real soon, won't you?"

*

No one, Stark told himself, could want a worthwhile position more than he did, or try harder to find one.

Victor Smith, the new Collector of Customs, reached Port Townsend in July. Stark approached him at once, but met with evasiveness. Half the men in town were after jobs and, although he knew he was better qualified than most, Stark realized Smith was in a delicate position.

Before anything could be settled, Stark began to have serious doubts about the new Collector, who was no sooner established in the Custom House than he began to talk about removing it from Port Townsend. Rumors flew about like starlings: Victor Smith owned property in Port Angeles and wanted to sell the Government a lot there for a new Custom House; Victor Smith was going to close down the Marine Hospital, one of Port Townsend's small but steady sources of revenue; Victor Smith believed that England, encouraged by the Civil War, was getting ready to attack the United States by way of Victoria. This last premise required the fortification of Port Angeles and the virtual abandonment of Port Townsend which, according to Victor Smith's reputed comments, had a worthless location, a poor harbor, an inadequate water supply, and an uncouth citizenry.

When, on top of these rumors, doubts were expressed about Smith's loyalty to the Union cause, Stark had reason to hope the Collector's days with the Custom Service were numbered.

All the better, he told himself. He had influential friends in the capital—at least they had been influential before all this trouble started, though goodness knows who was on whose side now. He wrote several letters, implying as delicately as he could that if the local Collectorship should become vacant, Darrell Starkweather was eminently fitted to occupy the post.

It took forever for letters to go back and forth, but he had set things in motion. There was nothing for it now but to wait and see what would happen.

This particular interval of waiting came to an unpleasant punctuation on an afternoon in early winter; when he returned home, Darrie greeted him with bad news. "Papa, when I was in the Kentucky Store today Baron Rothschild said he was sorry but he couldn't give us any more credit."

"Why, the idea! I'll speak to him tomorrow."

Darrie looked at him.

Damn it! he thought. How did she create that effect of not looking at him but through him? Her yellow eyes took on a cat's disdain. He had to somehow escape that look, to make her realize he was doing all he could—all anyone could—under the circumstances. Angrily defensive, he said, "We shouldn't be here! We ought to be back home where it's civilized, where a gentleman could find an opening suitable to—suitable for—"

"You'd find some problems there too, now, wouldn't you?"

Six months ago, he thought, she hadn't known what the war was about. Now it obsessed them all to the point where even a child could put her finger on the exposed nerve. But Darrie was no child. . . . He said, going back to their original subject, "I'll see the Baron tomorrow."

"You do that," she told him. At the kitchen door she turned. "Lacking beef for supper, we're having an omelet."

True to his word, Stark called next morning on Baron Rothschild. He hated to go in a suppliant's role, for he regarded the Baron as one of the few men in town who possessed cultivation and breeding. Straight as a soldier, beard golden against fair skin, nose thin and high-bridged—he looked every inch the aristocrat. Stark would have liked to deal with him on a basis of equality, not to open the conversation as he was obliged to do by saying, "I'm sorry about our account. I understand you spoke to my daughter about it."

"Unhappily, yes. She is the one I see. Had you come in—"

"Oh, it's all right! Naturally! I only wanted to say—to make a suggestion—"

"Yes?"

Even while his mind was saying, 'I can't do this—I'm not a clerk, a counter-jumper' he heard his own words: "I expect a good position, something permanent, very soon. Meantime, I *am* experienced with accounts—all that sort of thing. Possibly I could work out what we owe." "We," he thought; that was an odd way to put it. Did he mean himself and Darrie?

If he had not intended to involve his daughter, it was clear the Baron did. After a moment in which the shrewd blue eyes searched him with uncomfortable thoroughness, the Baron said, "Unfortunately I have just hired a new clerk-bookkeeper. The young man arrives this week from San Francisco. But his coming will assist you. He has asked me to find him a pleasant family where he can board. And Miss Darrie agrees to take him into your home. This will not be a great deal of money, but a small steady amount, no? Perhaps later she finds others. She tells me you have plenty of room."

Stark's humiliation was a physical thing: blood swimming behind his eyes, gall on his tongue. His lip, when he tried to speak, actually trembled so that he had to wait for self-control. "Of course," he said. "Very kind of you."

He could not, in the stress of the moment, decide whether to pretend knowledge of the plan—in which case the Baron might know him for a liar—or to admit the surprise, the shock, he felt.

The Baron chatted on: "Miss Darrie! What pride you must have! Like a little old lady, eh? So solemn. So capable. Permit me to congratulate you."

Stark said, "Thank you," through carefully firmed lips, and left the store.

The saloon at Dog Corner, that gathering place for outcasts and bums, was the nearest place for refreshment. Stark walked to the bar and ordered bourbon and water. Time enough to speak of credit after he had downed the never-more-needed drink.

A few evenings after his conversation with the Baron, Stark arrived home to find a strange young man sitting in the parlor. He had been telling himself to expect this, and at the same time imagining a shipwreck, a scourge of smallpox, an earthquake, or some other disaster that would liquidate the interloper before he could move into Cedarhaven.

None of these had happened, and now here he was—an ugly black-browed fellow (it seemed to Stark), smooth-shaven except for dark sideburns, and with an Irishman's spadelike upper lip.

The man promptly got to his feet when Stark came in, bowed with his heels together, and said, "Pompey Ryan, at your service, sir. You'll be the man of the house, Mr. Starkweather?"

There was nothing for Stark to do but put out his hand. He thought of several polite things he might say: Glad to meet you—you're welcome here—hope you'll feel at home. None of them was true. He managed a "How do you do?" and went on to his room. The door to the back entry was open and he could hear, from the kitchen on the other side of the entry, the chatter of his daughters' voices. They were higher than usual tonight, more animated.

"You'll be the man of the house," Ryan had stated. Stated? No, it had been a question, and the answer was "No!" A man was alone with the women of his household, the master of the home, or he wasn't. There was no halfway ground. A hundred times since the Baron had talked to him, Stark had opened his mouth to say to Darrie, "I forbid this! You will *not* take in a boarder . . . a stranger . . . another man. . . ." The phrases ate like acid. The words had stayed within him, the more galling for being held back. He had known what Darrie's reaction would have been. He had tasted in imagination the cool appraisal, the slight narrowing of eyes. "We need the money," she might have said. Or, "Someone has to pay the bills." If she had not spoken the actual whiplash words, they would have hung there between them, unspoken. Their potential had kept Stark quiet. Now it was too late.

When an unusual burst of chatter and laughter came from the kitchen, he crossed the entry and said through the open door, "I have a headache. Perhaps I could have a cup of tea, here in my room."

The girls turned and stared at him. For a moment he saw three strangers. Then each became herself by making the response that only she could make. Darrie, cool and guarded, said, "Very well, Papa." Belle tossed her curls in petulance. "Oh! The table's already set, *specially*." Genia came to put her arms around him. "Oh, Papa, is it bad? I'll get you a headache wafer."

He withdrew from her embrace. "That won't be necessary. A cup of tea. And no supper, please."

Back in his room, he assessed the location of Genia's bangs as she had hugged him: at his chin, no less. And she the youngest! No wonder they had not seemed like his little girls.

Their voices rose again. Someone laughed—Belle, he thought. Belle, caring only that she must change the table-setting. Never mind his pain! His mind followed her: he saw the table, his place at the end vacant. Darrie behind the teacups. The man, the interloper—where would he sit? Good God! Not in *his* place!

Stark recalled what a brazen eye the young man had. It would travel from one to another of the little girls . . . the big girls . . .

the almost-young-women. That bold Irish tongue, what might it not say to three unprotected virgins?

Stark took off his coat, washed his hands and face at the basin, brushed his hair and beard, and put on his coat again. He opened the door to find Genia there, teatray in her hands. He said, "I've decided to come to the table. I ought to be there, headache or no."

Behind Genia, Belle's voice rose in a wail: "Oh, Papa! I've already changed the table!"

"Hush your mouth!" Darrie's voice was sharp. She came to stand before him as Genia, balancing the tray, withdrew. Her eyes were nearly level with his. She pulled his lapels straight and brushed an imagined speck from his shoulder. "I'm glad you're feeling better," she said. "Why don't you go in and talk to Mr. Ryan? We'll call you both in a minute."

*

Reluctantly, Stark had to admit it was stimulating to have another man at the table.

Pompey Ryan—"Call me Pomp—everyone does. 'Tis the best you can do with such a fancy name!"—had reached Port Townsend by way of Boston, Illinois, and San Francisco, where the Baron's agent had arranged for his position at the Kentucky Store. He was young, admitting to twenty-two but looking older. Due, he said, to hard usage along the way.

When Stark mentioned that a good many men his age were in uniform these days, Pomp said that neither side suited him well enough to risk being shot at. "No true Irishman would fight on the side of vested interest, so that lets out the Union. But then no true Irishman would fight to keep his fellow-man in slavery, so that lets out the Rebs. Sometime I might go home and risk me skin for a free Ireland. Till then I'll be saving it."

Naturally Stark himself was not in uniform. There was his age, and he had three motherless daughters to look out for. Still, he hesitated to press the issue with young Mr. Ryan. Instead, he questioned the use of the word "home." "You don't intend to become a citizen? Ireland is still home to you?"

"Now who can say as to that? In Boston I said to meself, 'My boyo, you'll never get your roots down here.' In Illinois I said, 'No, not yet.' In Frisco I said, 'Sure and this is getting a bit better now, but things move fast here for a boy out of the Irish bogs.' Now that I'm here in Washington Territory—well, let's put it that I'm more reminded of home. The green of it, and the blue water, and the mists cat-footing down the valley and leaving shreds caught in the treetops. 'Tis more like County Donegal. This might be the spot I stay."

Stark was amused and yet annoyed. Pomp was hardly the country boy type. His assumption of naivete hid a sharp mind. Stark had never liked the Irish, they were too theatrical. Too bad about their troubles—the potato famine and all that. But maybe the worst of it was this influx of Irish to the United States.

Before he could sort out for reply one of the several elements in Pomp's speech (that was another fault of the Irish: too eloquent for their own good) Genia came up with a saucy remark: "You won't find things moving too fast for you here, Mr. Ryan. I declare they simply and perfectly stand still here."

"Do they now? Or is it that you're a bit above town and don't see what goes on? I'm told you can find excitement downtown, after night falls to cover it."

Genia pouted prettily. "We're not allowed downtown after night falls. Hardly even in broad daylight. I wish I could see some of the excitement."

"Genia!" Belle disapproved. "You don't know what you're saying!"

Stark, too, felt he must offer reproof. "A conversation hardly suited to our dinner table. A well-brought-up young lady, Genia, doesn't look for excitement."

A moment later she was twinkling in his direction. "I'm sorry, Papa. I was having a little fun. I must apologize for my manners."

It was impossible to remain annoyed with Genia, even though he had to acknowledge her high spirits sometimes worried him.

Hard enough to control them without encouragement from some riffraffy outsider. The very minute he had a worthwhile position, he told himself, out Pomp would go. Meantime, of course, the board money would help.

Once the privacy of Cedarhaven was broached—one stranger within its gates, as it were—the actual number of intruders made little difference. Pursuing this line of thought, it was Stark himself who brought Alonzo House, the Indian Agent, to spend a few days with them. Mr. House was, after all, an educated man, a gentleman. His cousin, it was discovered over a drink at Tibbie's bar, had gone to the University of Virginia with Stark. Moreover, House was a person of political influence, very close, he hinted, to the present Administration. *Very* close.

CHAPTER 5

Darrie had been astonished when, at the end of Pomp's first week at Cedarhaven, he had handed her the $5 gold piece and the bank notes that made up the agreed amount for his board. She had supposed he would give the money to Papa, and Papa would give it back to her—or some part of it—to buy food. Instead, here was Pomp putting the money in her hands.

" 'Tis you will be spending it no doubt, so why don't we keep it between ourselves and not bother himself at all?"

Before she could stammer out a protest Pomp went whistling off to work.

It was wonderful to have the money in her hands, to think of the meat and milk and flour it would buy. Papa would be angry . . . but she hardened her heart. It had become apparent in a hundred ways that whatever money Papa had brought with him was as good as gone. If the Baron had not suggested sending Pomp to them—but he had suggested it, and that particular moment's peril had been skirted. There would be other perils. And it would be up to her to find a precarious way around them.

Pomp's board money was not mentioned between her father and herself. When Papa announced one afternoon that he was bringing a Mr. House to stay for a few days, he added casually, "He gave me $10. I thought that would be about right for the time he's here—a week, or maybe a little more. I hope you'll have something especially nice tonight. A roast of beef, perhaps."

Darrie finished filling the teakettle and put it on the stove. She wiped her hands on her apron. Conflicting thoughts were whirling in and out of her mind. As a general knows by some quickening of corpuscle and gray brain cell—though sometimes too late—that his forces face a moment of truth, so Darrie knew this was the crucial instant between her and her father. But she knew it in time.

Her hands were quite dry now. There was no excuse to go on wiping and inspecting them. She made herself look up. Sickness rose in her when she saw on her father's face the mingling of eagerness, ingratiation, and uncertainty. Her voice was harsh more for herself than for him: "Give me the money."

"Now, my dear—"

"If you want him fed—and with a 'nice roast' at that—I'll have to have the money."

For a naked moment he looked at her with hatred. Then his still handsome face softened, weakened, disintegrated. He reached in his pocket, pulled out bank notes, and handed them to her. "I spent a few cents. The least I could do was buy the man a drink."

Darrie smoothed the bills in her hands. There was $8. In silence she took two dollars and gave them back to her father.

"No—no! It's for you—for the table—" But his hand was already moving forward.

The final defeat was shared between them. Darrie would have touched the bearded cheek, clasped the aristocratically thin fingers now fumbling with the notes, pressed her father's arm, made some gesture however slight of consolation or comfort. But her own hands, occupied with the money, were stayed by that, and by something less tangible but more prohibitive. Her father turned and left the kitchen.

When he was gone, Darrie went to mend the fire under the teakettle. For a dizzying moment she was tempted to throw the money in the fire. Her mind's eye saw it curl and flame, burn to ash and disappear. Then she thought of the Baron refusing credit, of Genia's shoes with newspaper filling the holes, of the nearly empty coalbin, and of tonight's supper table set with six places. Resolutely she thrust the money in her apron pocket.

As she prepared dinner Darrie wondered vaguely what an Indian Agent was doing in Port Townsend. The Clallam Indian village of Kah Tai, sprawled across the tide flats at the opening of Happy Valley, seemed quite self-sufficient. Indeed it seemed to Darrie the Indians got along better than the white people, if only because they required so much less. Their shacks were made of split cedar or driftwood; they ate mostly seafood, ducks, and wild fruits; their clothes were a mixture of their own woven fabrics and cast-offs from the white people. If they got sick they practiced their tahmahnawis and either got better or died. She couldn't see what an Indian Agent needed to do for them.

But within five minutes of sitting down at the table she, and they all, had been informed: the Clallams were to be transferred from Kah Tai to a reservation on Hood Canal.

"High time they were moved, too. In fairness to both races, there should be complete separation. The situation here will be greatly improved by my work. Greatly improved."

Genia said, "Do the Indians want to go?"

"They must. Their transfer was implicit in Governor Stevens' treaty signed at Point No-Point. Your Chetzamoka was a cosigner, you know."

"Do you mean the Duke of York?"

"Amusing name! Oh, very! But one and the same man."

Papa said, "I doubt if that one will leave Port Townsend. He seems pretty well entrenched. Four of his sisters are married to—" There was the slightest of pauses; "—to leading citizens."

"Unfortunate. Most unfortunate." Mr. House signified his disapproval by puffing out his cheeks. When he did this his short red beard spread in a half-circle to give him the look of a sea egg. Darrie raised her napkin to hide a smile.

" 'Tis the talk around town the Clallams won't stay on the Reservation." Pomp's eyes were bright with something that Darrie thought was amusement. She was still not sure how to take Pomp. Papa said all Irishmen were contentious and made trouble whenever they had a chance.

"They'll stay," Mr. House stated. "I've made it clear they must. And if I may say so, I am very persuasive."

Pomp looked as if he were going to say something more.

"Another biscuit?" Darrie offered.

He took the plate she held toward him, winked at her, and kept still.

Mr. House went on talking about his "charges." "We aren't really kind in the long run when we leave the Indian outside the Reservation to compete with the white man. He is congenitally unfitted for the competitive life. Then, too, there is always the unscrupulous white man who is willing to play on his weakness, to sell him whisky or if he has sisters to—"

Darrie, her hand outstretched toward the teapot, felt a moment of electric silence.

Then Mr. House cleared his throat. "Ah, yes . . . to be sure."

There had been a warning look, no doubt, from Papa.

"More tea, Mr. House?" Darrie asked, as if nothing had happened. As, of course, it hadn't.

"Yes, thank you. Delicious!" Stirring sugar into his tea, Mr. House continued with his theories: "As long as you have renegade white men preying on the Indian's weakness, you'll have trouble. I happen to be a rather shrewd observer. Another man in my place might not have noticed all that I have. But I assure you that I will be able to place certain information before the United States Commissioner. In due time action will be taken, and I think you will be surprised when it is taken against some rather highly placed individuals. The selling of whisky is *not* going to be tolerated."

"And is *that* against the law, now?" Pomp was as wide-eyed as a schoolboy.

"Selling to the red man, naturally."

Genia dimpled and looked up from beneath her lashes. "Are red men and Redfellows the same thing?"

The gentlemen all laughed at this, as Genia must have known they would.

Pomp answered her: "Not at all, at all! And aren't some of our leading citizens Redfellows? Redblooded Redfellows, sworn to uphold the Union, their secret constitution, the honor of womankind, and the right of every male to a weekly night out wearing his badge of freedom."

Genia looked at him with admiration. "What is their badge of freedom?"

"In this case, a headband set with chicken feathers. A leather apron it may be, or an elk's tooth, but 'tis the same thing."

"Really, Pomp, you manage to make it sound quite childish." Papa looked displeased. "As a matter of fact, the Masons—"

Pomp held up a warning hand. "All right! I withdraw any comment at all on the Masonic Order or any of its members. The Redfellows it is, then. The Royal and Benevolent Order of Redfellows, Port Townsend Longhouse, Exalted Sachem, and loyal blood-brothers—"

Genia laughed and clapped a hand over her mouth.

"And is it amusing now?" Pomp assumed a mighty frown, but under the down-drawn black brows his eyes glinted with mischief. "This solemn confederation of our finest citizens, sworn to pay all funeral expenses and a bit to boot for the widow—"

Apparently Mr. House did not care to lose the center of the stage. He interrupted: "An unhappy choice of symbols, if you ask me. The Indian is not noted for his forethought. For him, tomorrow does not exist. We must accept the red man as if he were . . ." He hesitated, groped for a phrase, and came up with: ". . . what he is."

Genia giggled.

Mr. House gave her a reproving look and went on: "The very name Redfellow implies something which is, in fact, false." He stopped to clear his throat, or possibly to wait for further inspiration.

Darrie, her eyes on her plate, thought, How utterly stupid he is! How can men pretend to be the superior sex when they drivel on like this?

Having got back the spotlight, the Indian Agent seemed unsure what to do with it. He took a drink of tea, and wiped his beard with careful little pats of his napkin. "You will see a great improvement in the Indians' state when they are on the Reservation and being given the paternalistic care they need. Like children—simple children. I have made a study of them, you may be sure. They themselves—" he held up a finger for emphasis, "they will be happier in their new life."

"Let's hope 'tis themselves that know it."

Darrie took care not to meet Pomp's eye after he had said this.

A few mornings after this, as Darrie washed dishes at the kitchen table, she glanced through the window, gave a second startled look, then went onto the back porch. A long line of dugout canoes, tied bow to stern and drawn by a side-wheeler, moved across the harbor. Each canoe was laden nearly to the waterline. The heads of passengers rose unevenly above the mounds of luggage. The strange fleet had crept to Marrowstone Point and partially disappeared around it before Darrie thought to count the canoes, but she guessed there might have been thirty of them.

There can't be any Indians left, she thought. Who'll bring us clams, and mushrooms, and huckleberries? Then she was ashamed of her selfishness; hers was a minor loss compared to being uprooted and taken far away to a strange new home.

It was not until she turned to go back into the house that she saw the billows of smoke rising from Kah Tai. The village itself was hidden by the shoulder of cliff, but she could see the reflection of flames bright on the smooth harbor.

Usually she was little concerned with what went on beyond the walls of Cedarhaven: the demands there were enough to keep her occupied. Yet now a morbid curiosity took hold of her, a need to go and see what was being done. It was a quarter past ten; she could run to Kah Tai and back and still have midday dinner on the table. If she hurried.

She caught up a shawl and ran down the back steps.

When she reached Water Street she found other people hurrying toward the tide flats of Kah Tai. She nodded to acquaintances but kept to herself. At the livery stable corner she could see a wall of smoke and fire rising from what had been the Indian village. The prevailing breeze, sweeping across Happy Valley from the Strait, was laden with smoke made acrid by leather and old cloth. Most of the curious stopped here, discouraged by the smoke, but Darrie needed to do more than simply look at the fire from a distance. With her shawl across her face she followed a path that skirted the hill and came out behind the village. Now the wall of smoke stood between her and the town.

To the east the low ground of the valley, the old Indian portage, was free of smoke. The fields and cabins of the valley's few scattered farms lay awash in autumn sunshine. Darrie felt an almost physical pain in the contrast between the peaceful valley and the burning village. Against reason she had a sense of participation, of guilt for the burning. It had been discussed at her own dinner table—no, not the fire, although Mr. House must have planned it even then. Suppose she had protested? It would have done no good. But shouldn't someone have opposed such cruelty?

Even as she watched, the fires were dying down. After all, she thought, the village had consisted of cedar buildings, few of them larger than a single room. With time, and continued cooking fires, they would have been tinder dry. By now roofs and walls had collapsed, but the smoke continued to boil upward as strongly as before. The earth itself must have taken fire, earth that for generations had been soaked by a slow seepage of fish oil, the fatty drippings from scraped hides, the accumulated residue of living.

Alone here behind the curtain of smoke, Darrie had a feeling of complete desolation; still she could not turn back and join the people who had done this. There was a footpath over the hill, one she had often followed with Sophie Duncan. She made her way toward it now. The ground here was marshy. She was aware of heavy grass clinging to her skirts and ankles and of the dampness that soaked through her shoes. It would have concerned her more if her mind had not been filled with the enormity of what had been done to the Indians. Careless of her steps, she tripped on something in the tall grass and plunged forward. Her hands, thrust out to break her fall, were stung by the sharp grass. After a stunned moment of surprise she saw that she was not alone: beside her on the marshy ground, and obviously the cause of her fall, was a young Indian woman, her lower face hidden by a scrap of gunnysacking.

Darrie scrambled to her feet. "What are you doing here?" she demanded.

There was no response. The woman half crouched, half lay, in the tall grass. The brown hand that held the sacking across her face was trembling. This surprised Darrie; Indians were supposed to be without emotion, or too stoical to show it.

She said, "Are you hurt?"

There was no sign she had been heard.

She had an impulse, strong as hunger, to go up the trail to Cedarhaven, to forget this woman. It was no concern of hers. But the creature was homeless . . . *homeless.* That knowledge rooted Darrie's feet in the wet ground.

She had noticed by now that the woman's faded calico skirt was soaked with marsh water. With a start she saw something else: burned-out holes in the fabric.

"Were you in the fire?" she asked.

This time, although the woman did not answer, Darrie felt that she responded by a slight drawing together of her flesh.

"Don't pretend you can't talk! Tell me how you got away."

After an interval of silence two words came, somewhat muffled, from behind the sacking: "I hide."

"What are you going to do now? The others have gone, you know."

A sound—a grunt or groan—was the only reply.

Darrie fought against her feeling of involvement. Anger presented a solid hold. "You needn't keep that old rag across your face—I'm not going to hurt you!" She leaned over and tugged at the sacking. There was a whimper of pain. The woman drew back, losing her balance. In righting herself she let go of the cloth.

It was Darrie's turn to cry out. Her hand went to her throat. Her eyes had closed instinctively, and she fought against the necessity to reopen them. When she did force herself to look, the gunnysack was back in place. But seared on her mind was the image of a face young and smooth on one side, the other burned and ashmarked like a piece of meat retrieved from live coals.

There was need now for positive action. Darrie took hold of the woman's hand, pulled till the cloth fell again, and forced herself to inspect the injuries. They looked the worse for being full of ashes. Someone running, and falling headlong into fire, might receive just such burns.

Mutely the woman held out her free hand; its palm was blistered and crusted with ashes. Darrie saw, too, that one side of her hair rose in an untidy fringe of curled and reddened ends.

The young woman simply looked at her. Her eyes were like polished brown stones under the triangular Indian lids. She made no more demand than a beaten dog.

"I'm going to take you home and fix those burns. You hear me?" She pulled on the undamaged hand.

Awkwardly the woman scrambled to her feet.

"Thank goodness you can stand up. You aren't hurt except for the burns, are you?"

"No."

"There, now! You can talk, can't you? We're going right up this trail to where I live. You come along after me. And hurry, because I have work to do." Darrie kept on chattering as if her voice made some kind of bond between them. Even so it was a bond she hardly dared trust, and she kept looking back over her shoulder to see if the woman was following. When she finally reached Cedarhaven she felt as if she had dragged a heavy burden the whole way.

Flying about the kitchen, determined to have dinner on the table by twelve-fifteen and thus avoid any questions, Darrie wondered if the Indian would stay in the attic where she had hidden her. She had dressed the burns as best she could, cautioned the woman to keep quiet, and had flown downstairs to prepare the noon meal. Thank goodness, she had cold beef, and potatoes ready to fry! It wouldn't take long.

Dinner was ready to serve when the men came in—Pomp first, with Papa and Mr. House close behind him.

The talk was all about the moving of the Clallams.

"A dirty job, if you ask me," Pomp called it. " 'Twas enough to rout them out. Why burn their shacks?"

"Because if their shacks—and you're certainly using the right word—were left, the Indians would sneak back to them."

"You might have waited till they were out of sight. The wail they set up! It made me blood run cold."

"They have to know the village is burned. Now they'll be content to stay at Skokomish."

"Will they now?"

The discussion was obviously heading toward trouble. Darrie interposed a question: "Did the Clallams all go?"

"All but one."

She hoped she was concealing her surprise. "And who was that?"

"An old man. We'd have had to use force. At the last minute he sat down on a log and said here was where he'd been born and here he'd die. But he'll get lonely and follow the others."

"And there was no one else?"

"No one. I think we can say, truthfully, it was a most successful undertaking."

"Well," Papa said, "the town won't be the same without our red brethren."

Pomp's black eyebrows had a life of their own, Darrie had noted. Now one of them rose slightly and drew to a peak in the center, but he made no more comment on the moving of the Clallams. Instead he made a remark about the war: there'd been no important news for some time, but it was still a topic the men found endlessly absorbing.

Darrie lost track of what they were saying—it all seemed remote to Port Townsend and to Cedarhaven. Meantime, there was that woman upstairs. What was she going to do about her? Feed her, of course, after the men were gone. But after that . . .

"Darrie!"

Startled, she realized it was not the first time her father had spoken her name. "Darrie! What are you daydreaming about? That's not like you. We're ready for our dessert."

"Oh—dessert!" In her excitement and haste she had neglected to provide one. "I'm sorry, Papa. I'll bring some fruit. That will have to do."

As she went through the swinging door she heard Pomp say, " 'Tis a miracle, no less, and she a mere—" The door closed on the rest of the sentence, but the tone had been approving.

During the afternoon Darrie had plenty of time to wonder how she had got herself into this situation and—more important—how she was going to get out. When the girls came home from school she took them into her confidence.

Belle was outraged. "A filthy old siwash in *our* house? You can't keep her here—Papa won't let you!"

But Genia said, "Oh, the poor dear thing! Is she badly hurt?"

"After I'd cleaned the burns up they didn't look so deep. But they must hurt her terribly."

Belle shuddered. "How could you touch her?"

"Come on, Darrie, let's go see her!"

"*You* can go," Belle said. "I don't want anything to do with it."

Genia proved to be an ideal ally. She was delighted with the notion of keeping a secret, and brought various wiles and pressures to bear on Belle to prevent her from speaking to Papa.

She was willing, too, to help care for the Indian, making countless trips up and down stairs to wait on her and to make friends with her. This, in fact, was a story Darrie had seen played out a hundred times before: something engaging in Genia's nature, something spontaneous and unguarded, melted the coldest heart. In no time Genia had discovered about the Indian all that Darrie had tried, and failed, to learn. Her name was Cheechawitza—"We'll call her Cheecha for short, she doesn't mind,"—and she had indeed fallen into the fire while running away from the herding together of the tribe. "She thinks she's about twenty years old. She had a husband once, but he didn't like her and put her away. I think she's cute, truly I do."

Darrie tried not to think how hard she had tried to win the Indian's confidence. And it was impossible to hold a grudge with Genia, who threw both arms around her and said, "Oh, Darrie, you were so brave to rescue her! I declare, it's just like a story!"

Cheecha's burns healed by first intention. She must, Darrie thought, be very healthy. After a few days in the attic she began to grow restless, especially during the day when Genia was not there to chat with her. Several times on going upstairs Darrie found the girl poking around the second floor.

"You must stay in the attic. You must stay hidden," she warned.

"Awright. I hide."

But an hour or so later Cheecha would again creep, barefooted, down the stairs. It was only a matter of time, Darrie realized, until Cheecha would show herself at the wrong time and be seen by Papa. Then out she would go. Unless . . . unless. . . .

She was surprised at the core of resistance that formed in her mind. Unless I said she *had* to stay. What then. . . ?

CHAPTER 6

Stark was sorry when Alonzo House went back to San Francisco. They had had a good deal in common, not the least of which was a shared disapproval from the townspeople. The fuss some of them had kicked up over the moving of the Clallams had been ridiculous. It was no credit to the community that some of the so-called "leading citizens" had married Indian women. Naturally, it had been embarrassing to see their in-laws hustled off like cattle, but they should have thought of that. Stark's own sympathies were with the Indian Agent: Port Townsend was a more attractive place without the Indians.

Alonzo had agreed with Stark, too, that Victor Smith was a dangerous person, and had promised to make discreet inquiries when he got back to San Francisco. It was consoling for Stark to remember the way Alonzo had pressed his hand and said, along with his goodby's, "I'll have a bug to put in official ears about who *ought* to be Collector here."

Meantime there was nothing to do but wait—as if he hadn't been doing just that for better than three years. Now, however, some of the town's dislike of Alonzo had rubbed off on him so that the waiting was, if possible, more onerous than before.

One afternoon a week or so after Alonzo's leaving, Stark left Tibbie's bar early and climbed the steps to Cedarhaven. It was a fine thing, he thought, when a man had to go home in midafternoon because his own home was the only place he could escape hostility.

When he got inside the back entry he was surprised to hear voices from the kitchen. The younger girls would not be home from school yet, would they? And Darrie did not "neighbor" with the other women on the street. Puzzled, he opened the kitchen door, and fell back with a shock as positive as if someone had slapped him across the face. Standing in a tub in the middle of the kitchen floor was a naked woman. A brown woman. A shameless woman who continued to goggle at him—as he must be goggling at her—without making the least effort to cover herself.

It was Darrie who cried out, "Oh, Papa! My goodness—!" It was Darrie who got a towel around the creature.

"What in heaven's name is going on here?"

The brown woman continued to stare at him across the shielding towel. He saw now that one side of her face was covered with newly healed scars.

Darrie, with her usual perversity, put the blame on him—as if Cedarhaven wasn't *his* home! "You never come home this time of day! Please go in the other room."

The kitchen had been pleasantly warm, fragrant with a browned-meat-and-onion smell connected, no doubt, with supper. On the parlor hearth a coal fire whispered cheerfully. Everything was in order—except for that creature, of course. A temporary intrusion, he supposed. Yet in a way the annoyance pointed up something Stark (he saw this now) had been taking for granted: warmth and order, meals tastily cooked and tastefully served, the general comfort of a well-run household. All this in the hands of a teen-age girl. Perhaps, grateful for Darrie's efficiency, he had been giving her too much leeway. A man unappreciated by the community should at least find peace and authority in his own home. He would take a firm position with Darrie. "Get that creature out of the house at once! I will not tolerate this sort of—" It was a pleasant image, but ephemeral.

He leaned over and poked the fire. An acrid whiff of coal smoke struck his nostrils. He sneezed. Was he catching cold? He mustn't—a man was helpless when ill, as dependent as an infant on his womenfolk.

Darrie came into the room behind him. He heard her, but he did not turn.

"Papa?"

"What is it?"

"About Cheecha—about that woman—"

"What in heaven's name is she doing here?"

"I was giving her a bath. She needed it."

"You mean she just dropped in off the street and you proceeded to scrub her?" Sarcasm was an unworthy weapon, but he had to say something.

Darrie, defensive, as he had intended, said, "She's been here since they burned the village."

"Here? In my house?" Astonishment brought Stark around to face his daughter.

"Yes. I went out that morning to look. Everyone did. She was lying in the bushes. She had fallen and burned herself."

"Why did you bring her here?"

"There was no place else. She was hurt and frightened. The other Indians were gone."

"And she'll have to go along after them!"

"She wants to stay here, with us."

"That's impossible!"

"Why?"

"It's unsuitable."

"Why?"

"Really, Darrelline, you're being damned impertinent."

Darrie simply looked at him.

Mentally Stark rallied his arguments, then stated them coolly and logically: "We have no place for her. She'd be one more mouth to feed. She'd never fit into the household and—this alone should decide the matter—we'd be in trouble with the authorities."

Darrie, who had been listening thoughtfully, pounced on the last statement. "Authorities! Papa, don't make me laugh! The same authorities that let men fight like dogs in the street and lie there untended afterward? That look the other way when whisky's smuggled in—yes, and buy it when it's here? The authorities that let a man be robbed blind in a poker game and knocked in the head if he makes a fuss about it? Are *those* authorities coming to take Cheecha away?"

Such questions from a sheltered young woman, from his own

daughter, stunned him. People had been talking to her—Ma Duncan—Pomp—someone who should have known better. He managed to speak calmly: "The other reasons I mentioned are enough. We can't keep a dirty half-civilized siwash in—"

Darrie's quiet fury stopped his tongue. He had never seen her so angry. Her lips were tight and ugly. They opened in the merest slit to say, "Cheecha is staying." As if that settled it, she turned and left the room.

After a moment Stark sank into a chair. He was used to Darrie's quiet persistence, of her having her own way in the end. But rebellion, an open flouting of his authority—this was something new. Something intolerable. He could not—he would not put up with it.

Cautiously he let his mind explore possible alternatives. He could tell Darrie—but he had already told her. He could tell the woman herself to get out. But suppose she followed Darrie's lead and refused to go? If Alonzo were still here . . . but he was in San Francisco by now. He could have the sheriff come in and—and what a joke that would be around town! Darrell Starkweather calling the sheriff to get an Indian woman out of his house! The interpretation people would put on that! No, that wouldn't do. Perhaps a waiting game. . . . In time Darrie would tire of the creature, or the woman would tire of being here. Of course! Something of that sort was bound to happen. He would have his way in the end. Still, he felt diminished by having to wait for it.

A new element came into the situation when the younger girls came home from school. He heard their rush of voices in the kitchen: "Cheecha downstairs! Why, whatever—?" Then a sudden hush, and whispers. Stark didn't need to be told that Darrie was giving an account of what had happened.

Presently Genia came into the parlor carrying a tray with a pot of tea and some little cakes. "Dear Papa!" she said, smiling at him. "You're so sweet to let Cheecha stay. Won't it be wonderful to have a slave—or at least a servant?"

Here, if you please, was idiocy! They'd be waiting on the creature, not she on them. But the inference that he had chosen this course soothed his pride. While he poured his tea, Genia smoothed his hair, pressing it back and kissing his ear where it was exposed. "Do you love me, Papa?"

"Of course I do!"

"The best?"

He did, but it was scarcely politic to say so. "I love you all the same," he told her gruffly. "You're all my daughters."

Within a month Stark was able to think he had advocated keeping the Indian. She was anything but attractive—the poor thing's face would always be scarred, he supposed—but she was strong and she tried to be helpful. She fetched wood and coal, swept and scrubbed, and rubbed out clothes on the washboard. It took some of the heavy work off Darrie's shoulders. She was worth her keep. After all, he had only objected because he had thought she might be an added burden to Darrie.

Meantime, although the fact seemed of little interest to Cheecha, the other Clallams were back on Kah Tai flat. They had slipped in, a canoeful at a time, under cover of the dark. A driftwood shack appeared, rising phoenix-like above the ashes of the old village, then another and another. The white residents of town thought it a great joke. The church women went down with their little baskets, doling out castor oil and Sunday School cards. The old pipelines were restored: whisky flowed as before into the village. The Indian girls managed their assignations with visiting sailors, with some white man always in the background. The Duke of York resumed his station in the Pioneer lobby, and on Saturday night Squinty Sam was to be found lying in the street reeking of cheap whisky. The information which Mr. House had placed with the United States Commissioner seemed to have been mislaid. Nothing was really changed.

CHAPTER 7

Genia was sure that, up to that point, nothing in her life had been as exciting as the event that people called the "Battle of the *Shubrick.*"

For weeks there had been a fever of preparation. Papa had brought a young Mr. Chalmers, a Custom House employee, to board with them. They two, along with a rather sullen Lieutenant Merryman, spent hours closeted in Papa's bedroom. It was impossible not to know, from words dropped and from the general air of excitement, that the dreaded and dreadful Victor Smith was finally going to get his comeuppance. He had gone back to Washington—everyone knew it was to persuade President Lincoln to move the Custom House away from Port Townsend—leaving Lieutenant Merryman in charge here. It was then that Papa—he was so clever, really!—had shown Mr. Chalmers and Lieutenant Merryman how to go over the Custom House records and find things called discrepancies. The one Papa and the two young men liked best was a flaw in Victor Smith's bond of office. They had sent a letter about that off to Washington (Papa wrote the letter in his lovely copperplate hand, but Lieutenant Merryman had to sign it) and were confident that Victor Smith would not even be allowed to come back to Port Townsend. But there was a simply frightful delay in getting letters back and forth; Papa said their letter and Victor Smith must have crossed one another, for he was returning to Port Townsend after all on the cutter *Shubrick,* and Lieutenant Merryman was not going to let him in the Custom House.

Oh, it was exciting! And so much at stake, because if Victor

Smith was unmasked Papa would undoubtedly get his position and everything would be rich and wonderful and she and Belle would have new dresses and Darrie wouldn't have to work so hard.

When the *Shubrick* was seen rounding Point Hudson people began streaming downtown to see the fun. Genia saw them from her bedroom window, and slipped out the front door while Darrie wasn't looking. In the street she began to run, with the heat of the August afternoon bringing drops of perspiration out on her forehead. By the time she arrived at the dock she was out of breath, and shaking from running down the hill, but she managed to push her way to the front of the crowd.

The *Shubrick* had come alongside the dock, and Genia was in time to see Mr. and Mrs. Smith, followed by several men, come down the gangplank. The Collector looked pleased to see so large a welcome; he bowed and smiled at acquaintances as he neared the closed door of the Custom House. When he took hold of the doorknob and nothing happened, his face took on a look of silly surprise. He turned to the crowd. "Why is the office locked at this time of day? Where's Lieutenant Merryman?"

Someone sniggered. A voice said, "Guess he's inside there, guarding the Government funds."

Smith cast a look of contempt in the direction of the speaker, but Genia saw color come up into his freckly face. Goodness! When a redhead got red in the face he was really on fire!

Someone pushed her rudely from behind. She looked up to see Mr. Hastings elbowing his way toward Mr. Smith. The two men shook hands and moved toward a corner of the building for privacy. Genia would have loved to hear what they were saying; their faces were alive with feeling, their mouths jerking over their low-spoken words, their gestures quick and tight. Oh, they were mad, those two!

When they had talked for a few minutes, Victor Smith came back to the door. He struck it with his doubled fist. "Merryman, open this door! I demand it in the name of the United States Government!"

Silence answered him.

"By God, Lieutenant, you'll be tried for treason! Let me in here!"

This time there was an answer from inside. Muffled by the door, only a few words carried to Genia's ear: ". . . your commission . . . heavy defalcation . . . no proper bond. . . ."

"Don't be a fool! You know I'm the duly appointed Collector for this District. I'm in authority here. Now open up!"

Again the answer was silence. Victor Smith, his head lowered, turned to glare at the crowd. Mrs. Smith looked unhappy, and seemed to be shrinking within herself as if in that way she might withdraw from a scene that obviously distressed her. But Mr. Smith was like an angry bull, his head down and rage giving a reddish glow to his eyes. Oh, how Genia adored excitement! Her heart was truly shaking against her ribs. She wouldn't have missed this for anything.

"You—!" Smith was gritting the words out: "You—all of you!"

To find herself included in his rage only heightened her excitement. Perhaps he even saw her in the crowd and recognized her. She pressed closer. He must know that Papa was against him, which would put her among his enemies, wouldn't it? She wondered if Papa was inside the Custom House, helping to keep Victor Smith out. She did hope so!

She saw now, to her regret, that Mr. Smith was leaving. He was going back onto the *Shubrick* with Mrs. Smith leaning on his arm and the other men from the ship tagging along. There was laughter and, shrill above it, a catcall. Smith stopped as if a hornet had stung him, stood tense for a moment, then yelled over his shoulder, "You haven't won, you know!"

The crowd jeered his progress up the gangplank and aboard ship.

"Hello, Genia!"

She turned to find Julie Duncan at her elbow. "Oh, hello, Julie! Isn't this wonderful?"

"Well . . . I dunno. . . ."

Genia could see now that seamen were working on the cannons

the *Shubrick* carried, A man near her said, "My God! They've drawn the shot and are ready to use shells!"

Another man said, his voice squeaking in excitement, "They wouldn't dare!"

"Little Napoleon would do anything to get his way."

Julie pulled at Genia's sleeve. "Let's get farther away."

"Oh, poo!"

"Aren't you scared?"

Genia considered this. Her blood was fiery hot, her heart beating so fast in her throat that it was hard to breathe. Was this being scared? At any rate, she didn't want to leave. She said again, "Oh, poo!"

Julie's face, she saw, had grown pale. She said, "Genia, if those are shells it's like they use in the war. People get smashed to pieces. Bits of them lie around afterward, bleeding and drawing flies."

A green sensation developed in Genia's stomach, revolved slowly, and spread outward. Now, more than ever, she would not leave.

A file of men was forming on the deck of the *Shubrick*. They wore guns at their belts, and an officer with a sword shouted orders at them. They moved to the gangplank, down it to the dock, and marched still in orderly procession to the steps of the Custom House. Their leader shouted "Halt!" Toward the end of the file one childish-looking marine stumbled into the man in front of him, recovered, and stood erect. The officer snapped his heels together as he turned to face the door. He yelled, "Open up in the name of the United States Government!"

Someone near them yelled, "Where's Little Victor? Is he afraid to come back?"

The officer-in-charge turned to glare. A nervous titter echoed through the crowd. A stout woman touched Genia's shoulder and said, "Child, you can't stay here. There may be shooting. Come on away."

"Yes, let's go," Julie urged.

To throw them off Genia began to move with them, but as

they brushed against a group of men she made a quick turn and went back toward Fowler's Wharf.

"Little girl!" she heard from behind her. "Little girl, where are you?"

The crowd had separated them, and she was not going to miss the excitement.

In sight again of the Custom House, she saw Mr. Pierson, the butcher, come stumbling out of his shop next door to it. Lengths of plank clutched to his portly front teetered and impeded his progress. Even from across the street Genia could see that his eyes were bulging with fear. Sweat glistened on his fat cheeks. In front of his display window he dropped the planks. Their clatter brought the heads of the uniformed men in his direction. The officer reached for his pistol, then converted the gesture into a silly readjustment of the gloves at his belt.

The crowd had thinned but the few who remained, mostly in doorways or peeping around corners as Genia was, laughed heartily at the officer's discomforture. Genia could see his neck reddening.

Mr. Pierson, paying no attention to the armed patrol, took a hammer out of his back pocket, nails from another, and attempted to nail a plank across his window. His hands were shaking and the loose end of the plank kept slipping down while he tried to nail the other end. Poor man, Genia thought, he's so frightened! She crossed the street and held up the end of the board while he rat-tatted with his hammer in the direction of the nail. It bent under his attack. "Och, Gott!" he cried, and struck sweat from his forehead with a shaking wrist.

Now a funny hollow-sounding voice came from the *Shubrick*. Above Pierson's clatter Genia could not make out the words. "Be quiet!" she told him. He stared at her, slack-jawed in astonishment and terror. "I can't hear what the man's saying."

When Pierson banged again with his hammer, Genia let go the plank and moved away from him. A man at the *Shubrick*'s rail had a megaphone to his mouth. Genia was in time to hear him say, ". . . give you exactly five minutes!"

The file of marines marched smartly away from the Custom House and lined up beside the gangplank of the cutter.

They are going to do it, Genia thought. They are really going to do it! If I stay here I'll be blown to bits, like Julie said. Reason told her to fly, but a delicious languor held her captive.

The officer on the *Shubrick*'s deck had a watch in his hand. When he put it in his pocket and drew out a pistol—he would signal with that, she supposed—the door of the Custom House burst open. There were a dozen or more men close inside it: Lieutenant Merryman, Mr. Chalmers, Mr. Plummer, and Captain Fowler. When she saw Papa among them she made herself small against the wall of the butcher shop and began to edge away.

They had surrendered. They had spoiled it all. Tears sprang into her eyes and spilled over, blinding her until she stumbled over one of Pierson's planks, scraping her ankle and nearly falling from the sudden pain.

Already informed by some magic of mass communication that the battle was over, people were converging again toward Fowler's Wharf. Genia stemmed the tide. By the time she reached the switchback steps below Cedarhaven she was spent, drained of excitement. Her ankle began to really hurt. She sat down on a step to inspect it. Blood had dried in a brown stain on her new striped stocking. When she tried to pull the cloth free, pain stung her into saying, "Damn! Oh, damn!"

"Well, we do have a casualty after all! And I thought it was all bluster and no bloodshed."

Genia looked up at blue eyes sparked with amusement, and teeth flashing white against tanned skin. She lowered her skirt, watching through her lashes to see whether this young man eyed her ankles or her face. Men, she had discovered, could thus be divided quickly and neatly. She did not object to admiration in either category.

She took a handkerchief from her skirt pocket, wiped the sweat and tears from her face, and smoothed her hair. "Who are you?" she asked, letting her dimples show but not quite smiling at him; after all, he was a stranger, though he had carefully not looked at the striped stocking.

"My name is Eric Bond. Yours?"

"Imogenia Starkweather."

"That's a mouthful. And, unless I'm fooled by your accent, you're from the South."

"Virginia. But—" She hastened to add this: "—we're not Secesh!"

"Good for you!"

"Do you live here?" She was sure he didn't, but it made a reasonable question.

"No. Just arrived today, in time for the excitement."

"Oh, it was exciting, wasn't it? Only I wish they hadn't given in. I hated that!"

"You didn't want to see your town blown to bits, did you?"

Genia sighed. "I'm not sure. What are they doing now?"

"Emptying the Custom House like a file of ants clearing the nest. While the City Fathers rage. I don't imagine this is the end of it."

But in Genia's mind the excitement was over. It was the end of it, and a sad end. "Are you going to live here?" she asked.

"Not now, unhappily. I'm on my way to join the Army. But I own some land here. When the war's over I'll come back."

"Do you have to go to war?"

"If you mean, am I conscripted—no. But, well, there the war is, and you go. Afterward, if you hadn't gone, you wouldn't like yourself."

"You might get killed, you know."

"So I might."

Genia stood up. "I have to go home now. I live right up here." She nodded toward Cedarhaven, white and austere above them. In case he wanted to know, later. . . . Then, feeling she had gone too far, she added, "My family is real strict with me. I sort of ran away today."

Standing, she had a better view of Eric Bond. He wasn't as tall as Papa. In fact, she came right to his eyes. But he was compactly built, strong-looking. There was an air of sureness about him. And smiling, as he was now, he looked young and pleasant, with thick eyelashes that turned up at the tips, and light feathers of sideburns. Genia found herself smiling. . . .

"I'm glad to have met you, Miss Imogenia. When the war is over I think I'll come back and marry you. You wait for me, will you? You have plenty of time."

He had to be joking. Yet, in spite of his smile, there was something in his face that made her wonder. Usually, with men, she knew just what to say, but now she could think of nothing. The way he was looking at her—

She lifted the front of her skirts and ran up the switchback stairs without looking back. She was ready to disappear behind the lilac bush before he moved—she could see that with the tail of her eye.

The silly great thing, she thought! Was that really a proposal? If so, no one would believe it.

CHAPTER 8

Darrie was horrified to see her father stumble on the back step. She ran to him, trying to get him up. His face was flushed, his eyes glassy. For a moment she thought he was ill, then, getting the full force of his breath, she realized he was drunk.

If she had seen him standing stripped before her, obscenely naked, she could not have been more revolted. All her life she had watched him drink in varying degrees of moderation but always with self-control. Now, in mid-afternoon, he was drunk—sodden, blind, staggering, filthy drunk.

Darrie screamed for Cheecha. When they had, between them, got him inside the house, into his own bedroom, deposited on the bed, Cheecha burst into cackles of laughter.

"Get out!" Darrie took a step toward her.

Cheecha, still shrieking with mirth, backed through the door.

Darrie's thoughts were murderous. She had not suspected, until she saw him helpless, what a fury of protectiveness he could induce. She got his shoes and coat off, poured water in the basin and sponged his face. He had been sick, she saw; traces of vomit were in his beard. How much he must have drunk, or what rotgut, to do this to him!

When she had him clean, covered with an afghan, and as comfortable as she could make him, she went back to her kitchen-work, leaving the connecting doors open. After a time he stirred and groaned, and she took him strong black coffee.

Sipping it, and avoiding her eyes, he muttered something about that "blackguard Smith—it's all his fault!" and would say no more.

At the supper table she learned the latest chapter in the Smith story. Lieutenant Merryman was under arrest in Washington. Young Mr. Chalmers, disgraced and penniless—he still owed Darrie a board bill—had left town. The Custom House and the Marine Hospital were, at this very moment, in the process of being transferred to Port Angeles.

"A great pity, all of it," Pomp said. "The town has lost its two good payrolls. The talk is going 'round—and mind you I don't believe it—that Smith would not have brought it off except for the Battle of the *Shubrick*."

Belle said, "But wasn't there a hearing in Olympia? People went down from here as witnesses—important people. Papa, for one."

Mr. Winly, the surveyor who had come some months before to occupy the good east room, answered that: "You're right, Miss Belle. A Grand Jury hearing, it was. Smith was found guilty of everything from treason to sucking eggs. But a Special Agent from the Treasury overturned the findings."

Darrie gave up trying to understand it. Nothing that went on downtown made sense. Papa had been so optimistic when he went to Olympia: "This is a civilized country! Even Smith can't get away with threatening to blow a peaceful town off the map." Yet apparently he had got by. She knew that Papa had borrowed money for the trip. In time the Government would reimburse him with witness fees. Meantime he must be galled by owing Captain Fowler money, and by knowledge that he had contributed to the downfall of young Chalmers and Lieutenant Merryman. Contributed. . . ? Was that the precise word for the part he had taken?

She must have missed some part of the table talk, but her attention was brought back by Pomp's voice: "A crying shame it is about Merryman. I hear talk downtown about getting up a fund for his defense."

"Hanh!" Mr. Winly's scorn was withering. "Talk is all! Merryman, nor Chalmers either, was never 'one of us' in this town. They can be tossed to the lions without the blinking of an eye."

Genia said, "But Papa—! Are they mad at Papa? He was only trying to help." Her eyes met Darrie's, and awareness ran between them. Genia faltered, her usual gaiety dulled by something new and alien. "Of course Papa did think he'd get a job—a really good one, I mean, if . . . if . . ."

Darrie broke in harshly. "Papa did the best he could. Let's hear no more talk about it."

*

As the weeks crept by Darrie saw that Mr. Winly had been right: the town accepted its defeat with the two young men as a vicarious price for it. Unfortunate, people said, but there it was. . . .

The creeping atrophy of war was intensified now by removal of the Federal payrolls. Ships seldom put in to Port Townsend since it was no longer the port of entry. If a few hopefuls came to town, a few disgruntled left. The town stagnated.

Cedarhaven did not escape the general hard times. Mr. Winly left and his room remained empty. It seemed to Darrie that she was continually engaged in balancing income against outgo: $40 a month from Pomp, 40¢ a pound for beef, $1 for a bushel of potatoes, eggs purchased from a farmer for 22¢ as opposed to 24¢ at the Kentucky Store.

They managed somehow to survive. Darrie became adept at stews and sausage loaves and economy desserts. She set a good table, but it was one where every penny counted.

Just when it seemed the war and its accompanying hard times would last forever, it came to an end. The news, cabled to San Francisco, reached Port Townsend in mid-April: Lee had surrendered to Grant at Appommatox Court House. It was over!

Port Townsend merchants closed their stores for the day. The cannon on Fowler's Wharf was fired in what was intended to be a 21-gun salute. In the excitement someone spilled the powder and the project was given up after six shots had been fired. A bonfire was built on the Point. Whisky flowed with abandon. Some women danced in the streets, while others clucked their disapproval: even the end of the war hardly justified such a casting-aside of gentility.

Darrie watched the festivities from the back porch of Cedarhaven. Reluctantly she had allowed Belle and Genia to go downtown, but only because Pomp escorted them. As for herself, she had bread rising and could not leave it; the ingredients of bread cost money. Remembering how she had run through smoke and cinders the day she had found Cheecha, she had to smile at past youthfulness. She was 18 now, a settled mature woman.

A few days after news of Lee's surrender had reached Port Townsend, it was learned that Lincoln had been assassinated. Shockingly, he had been dying at the very time they had held their celebration. The town was plunged into gloom. Hardly anyone here had seen Lincoln, or known him personally, but now his death was a symbol of broken hopes. The brighter times they had looked for would never come. Through all these anguished years the war had been fought—for what? What had been gained?

Men mustered out of the army slipped back into the community showing the harsh truth of war in scars, a dragging foot, an empty sleeve. And there were no jobs for them. Where were the good times they had expected?

The months of early summer dwindled away and were no different, Darrie thought, than the months of war—the years of war. There should be, by rights, something splendid, something dramatic, to mark the change.

Then, on a warm August evening, her father created the dubious drama of once more getting drunk.

For several days he had been trying to cash the Government warrant for Grand Jury witness fees that, after unconscionable months of delay, had reached his hands. Its face value was laughable—no one would give him that. Finally, bowing to the inevitable, he had accepted a discount of 50 per cent, receiving barely enough to repay his loan from Captain Fowler.

On the very day that Papa cashed his discounted warrant, news of Victor Smith's death reached Port Townsend. Returning to Washington Territory from the Capital, and carrying $3 million in gold, he had taken passage on the *Brother Jonathan* for the last leg of his journey. The *Brother Jonathan* had struck a reef off the northern California coast. There had been only a handful of survivors, and Victor Smith was not among them.

Darrie learned of the disaster when Pomp, arriving for supper, showed her the account in a San Francisco paper.

"Holy Mother of God! The man's worst enemy couldn't have wished him such a fate, now could he?" Pomp's square Irish face was pale.

Darrie was more shocked than she cared to admit. "Does Papa know?"

"If he doesn't, he'll be the one ignorant man in town. 'Tis the talk of every bar from Dog Corner to the Silver Safe."

It was too cruel a coincidence, Darrie thought: Papa unable to collect the paltry witness fee he had earned in trying to unmask Victor Smith, while the man himself was being trusted with three millions in gold—three millions now lost as completely as he was. The irony would not have escaped her father.

When dinner was over and Papa had not yet returned, Darrie made no protest to Pomp's going downtown for a "look around, just for luck."

Pomp's idea had been sound, but not put into execution soon enough. When he got Papa home later in the evening it took his and Darrie's combined efforts to get the older man to his own room and into bed.

Papa was not speechless this time—it might have been better if he had been. Angry words, accusing words, complaining words dribbled and slobbered from his slackened lips. An experienced public servant humiliated . . . no place for real merit while scalawags were put in high places. . . . "Sherve 'em right," he said. "Gone now—gold and Victor Smith too. And where's my stinking li'l old forty-two dollars and fifty cents, where's that?"

Darrie was scalded by shame. Pulling at Papa's shoes, she told Pomp, "I'll take care of him. You go on."

"Better for you to go. I'll get him to bed."

But they struggled on together.

If only her father had not kept on talking. His condition was bad enough, but he had further humiliation to offer. " 'Is town's dead and done for—dead as Smith. We'll all rot here—starve to death. He finished the Town. 'S like I knew he would. I warned 'em! Nobody'd lissen. But we can't get out now—not us! All my money sunk in this whi' elephant house. Stay here till we rot, yes sir! My li'l daughter Darrelline she fixed her Papa—she got him to buil' this li'l old whi' elephant. Hope she's satisfied—she and Victor Smith. Yes sir!"

The injustice of it, the cruelty, bore Darrie down with its weight. She could not meet Pomp's eyes.

They both worked in a fury of effort to get through and leave the room, leave this dreadful but at the same time pitiable creature. When they had him clean and in bed at last, Darrie was exhausted and degraded. Blowing out the lamp, she crossed the entry and stood in the kitchen doorway leaning her head against the jamb.

"You set," Cheecha told her. "I make tea."

Pomp helped her to a chair at the work table. It seemed only natural that he should sit down beside her, that Cheecha should set two cups on the table; only natural that he should be here in the kitchen taking tea from the cracked pot no longer considered fit for the diningroom.

If he had not been here, Cheecha would have sat with Darrie; as it was she perched on the woodbox sipping noisily from a cup nursed between her palms. Darrie noticed how carefully she kept the scarred left side of her face out of sight.

For a time no one spoke. Darrie's arms ached from the handling of her father. Even lifting her cup was an effort, but she needed the hot fragrant comfort of the tea.

It was Pomp who said, "By morning he'll be right as rain. Everybody gets a drop too much now and again. Don't you be taking it to heart."

Darrie shook her head. "It's not . . . just that."

"No? What is it then?"

She looked up from her tea, found Pomp's blue eyes brightly discerning under the quirked brows, and looked down again. She could not tell him. Her thoughts were so chaotic she could not even formulate them in her own mind. There was humiliation, weariness, despair at the dissolution she had witnessed. And beneath all this, like the hot eye of an ember buried in ashes, was the sense of her own part in it. Papa had said . . . but it was not true. It *wasn't true*.

After a time Pomp said, "When I came here you should have been playing with your dolls. I have to remind meself it's been four years. What were you like, I wonder, when you were a child—and knew it?"

What had she been like. . . ? It was hard to remember a world so unrelated to this, a world of service rendered rather than given, and of deference; of Mammy Scofer dependable as a black rock, of Mama with her rustling silks and cascading laughter, of Papa leaving, jaunty and self-assured, gold-headed cane in hand, for City Hall. . . .

The same Papa who now lay across the entry in a drunken stupor.

No, he was not the same. Nor was she. This was the concept her mind was struggling to formulate: life was change. There was no going back, only a choice of lonely paths forward.

Pomp might have been following her thoughts for he said, "You carry too much on your shoulders, Darrie girl. The load's too heavy."

For a tempting moment Darrie savored the idea of togetherness, of teapot and cups on a table between two—a man and a woman. She said harshly, "I can manage."

She saw that he was rebuffed. Had she intended that? She wasn't sure.

"Some thrive on bitter fruit," he said.

She allowed herself a smile. "Is that an Irish saying?"

"A Ryan one. Oh, 'tis full of wisdom I am!"

Cheecha cackled. There was no predicting what would strike her as amusing.

Pomp emptied his teacup and declined more. "It's been a day. For you, too, acushla." But he did not leave the table. His mind had gone back to Victor Smith, for he said, "To think the man's dead and gone after all the flithering and flathering he brought to Puget Sound. Gone to a cruel and watery grave—God rest his soul!"

"Does that make you forgive him for all the trouble he's caused?" She was thinking of her father, and realizing even as she spoke the unfairness of that. Her father had dug his own pit.

Pomp said, " 'Twas only those ripe for betraying that he led astray. And isn't that always so, now? But he found good pickings in this town. 'Twill never be the same again."

When Pomp stood up he paused for a moment behind her chair. She thought he might be going to lay his hand on her shoulder, or perhaps touch her hair. But he only said, "Good night," and went through the diningroom and toward the hall. His steps died away there, on the padded stairs.

After he had gone Darrie sat for a while wondering how little, or how much, he had meant. And how little, or how much, she could accept. Or trust. Under her breath she said again, "I'll manage."

It was 'I,' the singular. The lonely pronoun.

The most guarded loneliness, the most cherished independence, Darrie found, could lose its value. One person out of a world of people could make the difference. One person. . . .

The war had been over for six months, the trickle of returning soldiers had dwindled, when Eric Bond returned to Port Townsend.

Darrie had never heard the name—it meant nothing to her. But Genia and Belle came home from an errand downtown accompanied by a young man in a shabby blue uniform. As he crossed the back parlor toward her amid a rattle of explanations and introductions from the girls, Darrie noticed that he walked with a slight limp, a limp that he tried with the most careful balancing of his stocky body to minimize.

Her first thought, even before the shock of seeing the girls bring home a strange young man, was that he had the most delightful face she'd ever seen on a male creature. Its shape was round, giving him an effect of childlikeness that was enhanced by thick fair eyelashes of the sort that seldom survive the seemingly angelic innocence of childhood. Yet it was not a child's face: the mouth was strong, the eye knowing beyond youthfulness, the expression alert and shrewd.

"He's looking for a place to stay," Belle explained. "There's the room Mr. Winly had, isn't there?"

The introduction of a new masculine face was, Darrie saw, following its usual pattern: Mr. Bond's attention was on Genia, and Belle's on him. Genia allowed him a sidelong smile, a glancing look half teasing, half promise. "I met Mr. Bond—oh, a long time ago! Imagine running into him just when he was looking for a place to stay!"

As a rule Darrie examined both character and resources before accepting a boarder. This time she surprised herself by saying, "Yes, we do have the room. I suppose Mr. Bond is welcome, if the room suits him."

Darrie thought another glance was exchanged between him and Genia before he said, "It'll suit me, sight unseen."

"I'll show you where it is." Genia was already on the stairs, looking back over her shoulder.

She meant nothing by this flirting, by the seeming boldness of her suggestion. It was her way, as natural to her as the drawing of breath. And she was a child! Darrie hoped Mr. Bond would understand this.

It seemed he did, for before he made a move to follow Genia he looked directly at Darrie and smiled. "Thank you, ma'am, very much. I appreciate your hospitality."

A flood of pure delight swept through her. It couldn't matter that a strange young man, lamed by the war, was going to join the household. It couldn't matter—but it did. She turned away to hide the pleasure in her face. "When you've washed up we'll have dinner. At six."

Laying an extra place at the table, she thought, He won't stay. I won't let myself expect it. There's nothing to keep him in Port Townsend.

Eric Bond stayed three months. He had a small amount of capital saved from before the war and, contrary to the current opinion, he swore that Port Townsend was the place to invest it. Now the war was over, he said, the town—indeed the whole Territory—was bound to go ahead. As proof of his own faith he invested in a team and spring wagon, hired a boy to drive it, and set up a stageline between the town and Keymes Landing. Later he put a launch in service connecting with the stage and running from Keymes Landing to Discovery Bay. When these ventures were well established he left for the Coast, where he had been told money was to be made in setting up sealing towers to be manned by Indians, who had the patience to sit in the towers where a white man didn't.

Pomp said, "The man will work himself to death!" And, with

a speculative crooked-browed look at Darrie, he added, "I can see you admire beaverish qualities in the male sex."

This remark threw Darrie off her guard. She tried to make light of the charge. "It is nice to see a man who works instead of talking about it." It was apparent Pomp had trapped her into unintended criticism. She said, "I didn't mean you!" When her father gave her a reproachful look she saw she had made matters worse.

Pomp said, "Let it rest. Anyway, Sir Beaver is gone for the moment."

But Eric out of the house was not out of Darrie's mind. Images appeared before her mind's eye, preposterous but delicious: Eric in a banker's silk hat stepping down from a gleaming carriage, offering his hand to a companion still inside; the doors of Cedarhaven held open by a liveried servant—no less!—as the master and mistress returned from the Governor's Ball; inside, alone, his voice shivery with emotion: "A little bauble to remember the occasion—a diamond bracelet. Hold out your wrist. . . ." Her slender milk-white hand thrust forth—

Darrie closed her eyes, and opened them. There was her hand holding the paring knife, the fingers stained and roughened from housework, the back darkened by a newly healed burn scar. You fool! she told herself. You fool! But she could feel a smile tugging at the corner of her lips.

Dismissing nonsense from her mind, she counted potatoes already peeled: three, four, five. The young Reverend Newton had arrived that afternoon to conduct a series of evangelistic meetings. There would be Pomp, the girls, herself, and Cheecha. She counted six, and reached for another potato. Papa was already home, lying down in his room. He had told her rather thickly that he "wasn't feeling well" and would not be at table. Cheecha could take him a tray. She wondered if young Mr. Newton had a great appetite; preachers were rather noted for that, as if their devotional fires burned up an excessive amount of energy. Yet Howard Newton had looked unfleshly—delicate, really. Sometimes that kind were the hungriest. Count two potatoes for him —there, that ought to do it.

She would get them on to boil and set the table. Usually Belle or Genia did that, but they were at a linen shower this afternoon for Mary Hammond. Mary's wedding was set for June. She was only six months older than Belle. Startled, Darrie thought, That makes her younger than I am! And I've never thought . . . But hadn't she?

"You sick?" Cheecha's voice broke in. "You look—look, nothing there."

"Oh—! No, I'm fine. The potatoes are ready. I'll set the table."

They had sat down at the table before the girls came home from their party.

"Mr. Newton, I should like to present you to my two sisters, Miss Isabelle and Miss Imogenia."

He was on his feet at once. He had nice manners, Darrie thought, but no poise. His dinner napkin started to fall, he clutched at it, rattling the silver at his place. Blushes raced across his boyish cheeks and were gone, leaving him paler than before.

"An h-honor," he stammered over a leaping Adam's apple.

Good heavens! Darrie thought. What will he do in the pulpit—have a fit? "Do sit down again. Truly, we're not so formal here."

The girls, Darrie could see, were reacting according to pattern: Genia with smiles and dimples, Belle with blushes and lowered lids.

She touched the bell and waited with her usual apprehension to see how Cheecha would respond. After a sound of shuffling footsteps and heavy breathing, the kitchen door swung open to reveal Cheecha's ample rear. A revolving motion brought her scarred face into view, and her brown hands in a threat-of-death grip on the handles of the soup tureen. Darrie closed her eyes and held her breath until the tureen was in place before her.

The Reverend Newton spoke: "I see that you have spoken a personal grace over this food, Miss Starkweather. Would you mind if I pronounced one for all of us?"

Darrie kept her gravity though it was not easy. She nodded permission, and closed her eyes again.

Newton's voice took on a roundness, a resonance, it had lacked before: "Our Heavenly Father, we humbly thank Thee for Thy bounteous grace in placing this repast before us. Help us, we beseech Thee, to appreciate Thy watchful care, and guide us to put to Thy use the strength obtained by partaking of this blessed food. We ask this in Jesus's name, amen." Lifting his head, he added, "Thank you, Miss Starkweather."

For a moment Darrie felt she had been placed on a level that would make it unsuitable for her to ladle out the clam chowder. But Mr. Newton was eying the tureen hungrily. She took the silver ladle and started to serve.

CHAPTER 9

For lack of their own building, the congregation held their services in the Court House. After the evening service, when the handshaking and congratulations at the door were over, Julie Duncan and Alice Graves continued to dawdle. The Reverend said, "I have to lock up now." It seemed to Belle his eyes sought hers for help.

They all went outside, the Reverend coming last after blowing out the lamp inside the door. The key rattled in the lock. There was a moment of indecision, an awkward moment when anything that was said or done would be wrong. Then Mr. Newton said, "You young ladies mustn't be alone on the street, any of you. Miss Belle and I will be glad to see you to your doors."

Miss Belle and I . . . Miss Belle and I. . . . The words made a joyful chorus above the drumbeat of footsteps on the board sidewalk. Grace notes of giggles from Julie and Alice sounded only a suggestion of disharmony.

Four abreast they walked, arm in arm where the sidewalk was wide; then, when it narrowed, she and the Reverend falling behind, her hand still nestled within the curve of his arm. Through her silk glove she could feel the harsh fabric of his coat and, beneath that, the strong male flesh. Male flesh! Oh, dear God! Had her mind contained those words? "The pure in heart . . ." The very words of his text, and she had already violated them. The footsteps in their rough cacophony were now the drumbeats of vengeance. Oh, wicked girl! If he could see inside your mind!

Lest their tenuous contact through layerings of silk and wool communicate her thoughts, she tried to take her hand away from his arm. He pressed his elbow tighter. She could not escape.

"Miss Belle," he chided. "It's dark here. You must let me guide you."

Did he mean only that—or more? If she could say, if she could ask him—but no delicately reared young woman. . . Her heart was beating like a steam hammer. If he felt it, if he suspected, she would *die*.

"We're here!" It was Julie's voice, harsh and positive. "I'm going to stay the night with Alice. Goodnight, and thanks for walking us."

"Yes, thank you, Reverend. Goodnight, Belle."

The Reverend lifted his hat. "Goodnight, ladies."

To the end of the block and turn right. Now it was darker than ever, no houses here with lighted windows to send their yellow paths into the street. A dark grove of alders. Beneath them the board walk was damp. Cold struck through the soles of Belle's shoes. She willed herself not to shiver. He might think —anything. Yet, in spite of herself, a fine tremor began to stir her flesh.

Their corner at last, the few steps downward, their yard and walk completely darkened by the cedar trees. Belle broke away and almost ran across the porch. The door was unlocked.

On the hall table a lamp burned, its wick turned low. She moved to turn it up, then drew back the hand that would have betrayed her by its trembling.

The Reverend, behind her, locked and bolted the door. He took, it seemed to her, a long time about it. Shouldn't she say a quick "goodnight" and "thank you" and run up the stairs? She didn't. She stood, instead, with her hand on the newel post. Now Mr. Newton turned up the lamp wick, and lifted the lamp. Its oblique rays made caverns about his eyes, elongated the smooth-shaven chin, revealed nostrils meshed with minute hairs.

"Miss Belle—please! Would I be presuming if I asked you to stay with me a few minutes? If we could go into the parlor . . . there is something . . ."

A delicious weakness flooded Belle's limbs. Without trusting herself to speak, she glided into the parlor ahead of him. When he had set the lamp on a stand, he went back and closed the sliding doors.

"I thought," he said, with a terrible and simple earnestness, "that we might pray together. Will you join me?"

Her mood altered with nauseating suddenness. The stark necessity of failing strength brought her to her knees. Giddiness sent her head forward over hands clasped on the seat of the horsehair sofa. I must not be sick, she thought, and swallowed the taste of salt.

She heard the soft thump of his knees on the floor. There was a quiet moment. It was to be silent prayer then, she thought. I must collect my wits. I must think of what to say. Her mind cried, without direction, "Dear God! Dear God, help us . . . dear God. . . ."

"Our heavenly Father, we beseech Thee, look down upon Thy two humble creatures. Give them, if Thou wilt, some sign of grace, some hint of Thy divine intent. Thou hast created man in Thy image yet Thou hast given him a human heart full of frailties and capable of human desire. Thou hast given him a fleshly body subject to the temptations of lust as well as the divine fire of consecrated love. Man's judgment is not divine. Father, he needs at times some sign of Thy intent for him, some beacon that will guide him to the . . . to the . . . right marriage. . . ." With an uncertainty that was not like him in the act of prayer, the Reverend's voice faltered and stopped.

In the silence the hall clock ticked off passing seconds. Tick . . . tock, tick . . . tock. He must . . . go on. He must . . . he must. Tick . . . tock.

"Dear God!" Her voice was a bludgeon shattering the silence. "Oh, dear Father—" She pushed the words out to fill the dreadful void: "I add my voice—I beg Thy help! In Thine own Word it says, 'It is not good that man should be alone. Let God join them together,' the Word says, 'and let no man put them asunder.' " The enormity of what she was saying came over her. She bit her lip till the sharpness of pain could not be borne. "Heavenly Father," she said, and her voice shook on the words, "I ask only to do Thy will."

If this was not a sign the blind could read while running. . . .

"Our Father in Heaven, we are almost persuaded . . . If this tender virgin heart is willing—"

"Oh, it is! It is!"

"And if it is indeed Thy will then give us, we pray Thee, a sign of Thy approval. In Christ's sweet name, amen."

Oh, bolt of lightning strike! Now! Oh, heaven burst with some omen—something—

The touch of his hand on hers was shatteringly sudden. His flesh was warm but hers was on fire. Low-voiced he said, "Dear Isabelle, let us wait a moment with open hearts and open minds."

The minutes ticked by again. Belle kept her eyes screwed shut. I'm leaving it to God, she thought. Her hand turned in his. She had not willed it—truly, she thought, I *didn't*! Her fingers slipped upward on his wrist, inside the cuff, along the sinewy arm, found—within the curve of elbow—flesh tender as a woman's. His other arm was hard about her shoulder. His lips were hot and questing on hers. She fell sideways against the sofa, and let him have God's way with her.

It was God's way. He did nothing wrong, nothing to violate

her. It was a matter only of hungry mouths, and of hands hovering over rather than possessing.

Shaken, breathless, blinded, they pulled apart. He helped her to her feet. She leaned against him, unable to stand alone. When he tried to say something, she laid a finger on his lips. But he put her hand aside, after kissing it, to say, "We must never forget ours is a holy union, sanctified by God."

"We won't forget."

"Still, I think—with God's work waiting to be done—we should be married soon."

"Whenever you say."

"I must never betray you." His voice shook on the words. "I am a man of God, but I am a man. Now, in wisdom, we must go to our rooms."

"Yes, we should . . . dear." She hardly more than breathed the last word.

Again the Reverend took up the lamp, and gestured for her to precede him. At her door she stopped and motioned for him to lean toward her. "How did you really know?" she whispered. "What was the sign?"

"God's voice," he said. "I'll never hear it more clearly. 'Take this woman' He told me."

Belle's fingertips pressed her lips. She felt her eyelids widen, looking up at him. It was almost as if Genia were acting through her. "Reverend Newton, you make it sound so . . . so carnal!"

"Oh, never that! I respect your innocence with my whole heart and soul! Believe me, I do!"

"The lamp—you're tipping it!"

As he looked, startled, at the lamp in his hand, she slipped through her door and closed it behind her.

CHAPTER 10

Belle Starkweather and Howard Newton were married on a bright June day with the Reverend Tillinghast from Olympia to perform the ceremony. The bride was admirably pale in white satin and net, with Mama's long lace wedding veil that had been brought with them around the Horn. Howard Newton had the slightly stunned look of most bridegrooms. Papa was handsome in black broadcloth, giving the bride away with exactly the right blend of regret and pride.

It all seemed so suitable and so proper that Darrie kept having the notion she was reading about it in a romantic novel rather than seeing it happen in her own parlor. To test reality she dug her nails into her palms, and looked about the flower-filled rooms. Belle's gown had been created, at a shocking price, by Mamie Van Hoffen. The bill for that was real enough. Ma Duncan had, to use her own expression, "hammered out" Genia's and Darrie's pink bridesmaids' dresses.

There had been so many tryings-on, so many fittings and refittings, that Darrie felt her dress was an old acquaintance. Friend would not be the word, since no color could be less friendly to her than pink. When the dress was being made, according to Belle's stipulations, Darrie had not felt that it mattered. No one would look at anyone but the bride. There was no one Darrie cared to please. Then, two days before the wedding, when it had been too late to do anything about the bridesmaid's dress, she had known there would be someone who mattered.

A ring at the doorbell—answered by Darrie herself, since

Cheecha was in one of her starey do-nothing days—revealed Eric Bond on the porch, valise in hand. "Good morning, Miss Starkweather. Do you have a place where I can hang my hat for a few months?"

Darrie had told herself she would take on nothing extra until after the wedding—goodness knows she had enough to keep her busy! But this determination passed from her mind as completely as if it had never existed. She said, "We'll manage. That is, if you don't mind things being a bit upset. My sister is being married day after tomorrow."

"Miss Imogenia?" The question was like a shot.

"No, Isabelle. She's marrying the Reverend Newton."

"Well, I'm glad to hear the news. But you don't want extra work now. I'll stay at the hotel—"

"No—no! I won't hear of it! Your room—I mean, the one you had before—there's no one in it. You won't be any trouble." She, who was usually concise, was babbling like an idiot. What is the matter with me, she thought? Aloud, she said, "Do, please, come in. I see you have your valise with you."

"If it's no intrusion, then . . ."

"It isn't, I assure you."

After he had gone upstairs she had thought of the pink bridesmaid's dress, and, for the first time, with misgivings.

". . . I now pronounce you man and wife."

There was a flurry of kissing and good wishes. Darrie had no time to think: there was the wedding breakfast to be served; plates of food to be replenished; coffee to be kept hot and in good supply. In what seemed to be the midst of that, she ran upstairs to help Belle into her going-away costume.

Darrie thought her sister had never looked prettier—her face, flushed now with bliss, becomingly framed in the blue-satin lining of her bonnet. For this moment, at least, she outshone Genia.

Belle breathlessly hugged and kissed them all, including Eric and Pomp, and set off for the dock on the Reverend's arm. The wedding guests, to a man, accompanied them. Darrie had not planned on this; actually she had not projected her mind beyond getting safely through the wedding. When everyone left the house she had a devastating sense of letdown. To be sure, Eric had called to her from the porch, "Come along—we're all going to the dock!" But Genia was already clinging to one arm while Alice Graves closed in on him from the other side. Darrie had simply shaken her head and gone back to the shambles of the suddenly emptied rooms.

The diningroom table with its soiled dishes and remnants of food was a nauseating sight. Someone, she noted, had spilled coffee on the tablecloth. Napkins were crumpled and thrown aside; one, stained with jelly, lay beneath a chair. The room stank of food now stale, dregs of coffee, the hard-to-define but distasteful odor left by too many people breathing too little air.

Darrie's revulsion was complete. She felt for a moment that she was going to be sick. Her flesh shuddered in reaction. This silly old pink dress, she thought—it wouldn't keep a mosquito warm. She wanted to be rid of it, to escape this trapping of an event in which she had taken part yet had never been a part of. She ran up the stairs, her shaking fingers pulling at the dress-fastenings even before she reached her room.

There disorder met her eye. Belle's wedding dress lay across the bed, her slippers were toe-to-toe in the middle of the floor. The veil trailed from chair-back to carpet. The corner, Darrie saw, had been torn, caught perhaps in a slipper heel.

For a time Darrie stood in the middle of the room looking about her. She became aware of an underlip held hurtingly tight between her teeth. She released it. This was it, then. This was the pattern of her life. Someone to keep the family going, look out for Papa, get the girls safely married. The girls—was she not one of them? Nineteen. Scarcely an old maid. Belle was a young bride—too young, perhaps, at seventeen. Still the directness of her intent had carried the impact of accumulated ages. As well breathe against an arrow already shot as to divert Belle after Howard Newton had committed himself. What steps, Darrie wondered as she had wondered before this, had led to this commitment? He had been a young man interested in his work, devoted to his God, mildly pleased by Belle or by any young woman with a concern for this small and struggling congregation. Then suddenly, overnight, he was an ardent suitor, touchingly anxious to please, staring bemused and adoring at an essentially unchanged Belle. How had it been brought about?

Darrie put the problem aside as one that might, conceivably, be solved later. At the moment it was obscure. She folded the veil and put it away for future mending, shook out the wedding dress and arranged it on a hanger. She dressed herself in a sensible tan percale. The downstairs rooms must be set to rights, and something prepared for supper. There would be—she counted up—Papa and Eric, Pomp and Genia, Mr. Hall and herself; supper for seven, counting Cheecha. No one ought to be very hungry, though she could hardly skimp on Mr. Hall who had been at work and missed the wedding feast.

Downstairs she found the kitchen empty. Cheecha sat on the back steps. "Ho, Miss!" she greeted Darrie. "Everybody go, heh?"

"Everybody but us."

"Hanh!"

The mournful whistle of the *Eliza Anderson* sounded, a long toot and a shorter one; they were leaving the wharf now. Isabelle and the Reverend would be aboard, the wedding guests waving from the dock. A minute later the ear-splitting shriek of the Captain's calliope, made bearable only by distance, brought them the strains of a wedding march.

Cheecha, Darrie supposed, missed the subtle flattery in the choice of tunes, but she said "Hanh!" again, and stood to catch a glimpse of the little sidewheeler as it headed toward Marrowstone Point. "On boat, man he get at Belle, you 'spect, maybe? Or wait till night?"

Darrie gasped. Disapproval would be wasted. She said matter-of-factly, "I imagine he'll wait." Then she added, "Come on, Cheecha, we have piles of dishes to do."

Stacking plates on the kitchen table, she bethought herself of a warning, and said firmly, "Cheecha, when the others are here, don't talk about . . . about his getting at her. Do you understand?"

"No?"

"No!"

Cheecha's heavy shoulders lifted, and fell. "Awright, you say so."

*

It was nearly a month before the newlyweds returned. They came on a Friday night so that Howard could conduct Sunday services.

A gentle bloom lay over Isabelle. It could be the difference, Darrie thought, between a peach picked green and one that had hung in the sunshine till its flesh was delicately filled out, its skin velvet soft, responsive to the lightest touch. Yet fruit left too long could wither and be flung aside. . . .

Belle embraced them all, clinging a little longer to Papa than to her sisters, as if in learning to appreciate one man she had revalued all men.

The presence of the bridal couple produced a new mood at Cedarhaven. Supper was a gay meal. There was a laughing report of Belle's attempts at housekeeping. She had boiled the breakfast eggs for half an hour. "Fortunately," the Reverend said, "I had a heavy mallet in the woodshed and managed to crack them." Her first piecrust had been a pitiful attempt, though she was learning. "It makes me truly marvel at the way you managed things here," she said to Darrie; "Just a little old child, really, but you ran things as if you had been doing it for years."

"It was sink or swim," Darrie said.

But Papa told them, "Darrie is one in a million." Made expansive by the return of a successfully married daughter, he enlarged on the theme: "I declare, I've told myself more than once, Darrie can do anything she sets her heart on."

Darrie looked up to find Eric's eyes on her. His expression was not so much admiring as speculative.

"Yes," Papa continued, "I do believe Darrie should have been a man."

Keep on, Darrie thought; you're killing me. To Belle she said, "Do tell us more about your life in Olympia."

"It's really *sophisticated.* A friend of the Reverend's who lives next door to us is a judge." Belle could not resist a hasty glance around the table at this announcement. "He and his wife are truly refined people. We've gone to several parties—some in our honor. I tell the Reverend if we are going to pay back our social obligations we'll need a larger house."

Papa said, "If you should decide to move, find a house with an extra bedroom. I intend to run for the Legislature next year. I could save expenses by boarding with you."

When supper was over, Howard left for a meeting with the church elders. Belle accompanied him to the door where they parted in the manner of people who might, with good fortune, be reunited within the decade.

Helping Darrie with the dishes—a month ago she wouldn't have offered, Darrie thought—Belle wore a little secret smile. Darrie had been wondering how a confidential chat could be managed. Belle was ahead of her. When the towels had been scalded and hung on the back porch, she said, "Come upstairs, Darrie. I want to show you something."

The newlyweds were occupying the room the younger girls had once shared; Genia had cheerfully moved to a cot in the attic. It was a pleasant room with windows facing east across the harbor where two sailing vessels, their sticks bare, nodded at anchor. The afternoon wind had died down leaving the water oily smooth, touched now by the saffron overflow of a sunset invisible from this window.

When Belle raised the sash, for the upstairs rooms were warm in the afternoon, the harbor scent of salt and tar and hemp and long-wet canvas seeped into the room.

"Sit down, Darrie."

"What did you want to show me?"

"Oh, nothing! That was just an excuse. I thought we could talk. . . ."

"I see."

Darrie seated herself on the bed. Belle took the window seat where she could look, half-smiling, across the bay while her fingers toyed with the cord of the window shade.

"Are you happy, Belle?"

"Oh, rapturously happy! It's heaven to be married to a man like Howard, to know that you are carrying out God's will. I can't tell you. . . ." She shook her head.

"How do you know it's God's will?"

"He says so."

For a moment Darrie was in doubt as to "his" identity. Did Belle mean the Deity or—but obviously Belle meant her husband, for she went on quickly: "Howard makes it so understandable that marriage is God's design."

"Is it a . . . pleasant design?"

"Oh, Darrie, you'll never know!"

The implication was not flattering: would she never find a husband, or would he when found lack the necessary piety? She said tartly, "Don't be too sure, Belle."

"But, Darrie, there just aren't men like Howard."

"You call him by his first name to his face?"

Evidently Belle felt not the slightest prick of irony. "It does seem a little disrespectful. Of course I'm always careful to call him 'the Reverend' when people are around."

"I'm glad to hear that."

Belle chatted on: "You know, Darrie, I never really prayed till after I met Howard. Oh, I got down on my knees and said the words, but it took Howard to make me feel the presence of God. You were always so sure of yourself, and you *were* Mammy Scofer's favorite—we all knew that! And Genia, of course . . . I don't suppose Papa could help. . . ." There was the slightest pause, the suggestion of a caught breath, then the creamy complacence flowed on again: "I'll never be alone again. There's Howard—and God. I want to tell you, Darrie, about our wedding night—"

"Really, if you—"

"I must! It was so precious a thing! I want you to know what it can be like—marriage, I mean, as God meant it to be."

Twilight had filled the room while they had talked. Now, framed in the window, Belle lifted a profile of sweetest clarity against the evening sky. "That night, when we had gone to our bedroom, Howard left me to . . . to get ready. I was simply shaking when he came to the bed. But he did the loveliest thing. He knelt by the bed and asked God's blessing and guidance."

Hands were clasped beneath a profile delicately raised toward heaven. There was no mistaking Belle's sincerity. She went on: "I'd always had a dreadful *suspicion* there was something—well, carnal in what men and women *do*—you know. I thought that women—nice women—submitted. For babies, or because their husbands insisted. But when you realize that God does truly sanctify this act—that it's part of His divine plan—then there's such rapture in it, such utter joy!"

Darrie swallowed past a swelling in her throat. She was grateful that darkness concealed her naked face. Emotions she had not dreamed of possessing sang in her blood. She could not have spoken, but speech was not required of her. Belle had more to unfold.

"You can't imagine what it does to a man to be . . . to be with a pure women. In that way. Afterward, *nothing* is the same. Or ever will be. It was as if . . ." She paused, searching for the exact shade of meaning; ". . . as if he could truly die of gratitude. He was so humble. 'The rest of my life,' he said, 'I'll be your abject slave.' "

Frightened by her own emotions, Darrie sought defense. Irony was her weapon, preshaped and ready. "Will God like that?" she asked.

There was a moment of shocked silence before Belle said, "God comes first with both of us, of course."

The pinprick of sarcasm had destroyed Belle's mood. Darrie felt as if, at the very gates of Paradise, she had made some uncouth inquiry about adequate sewage and been forever damned.

Belle rose from her seat at the window and moved, a shadow figure in a room now full of shadows. "Where are the matches?" she asked. "I don't like this gloom."

The dusk would have been right if sisterly confidences were to continue. The mood had been shattered. Regret and relief mingled as Darrie struck a match and lighted the lamp on the bureau. She and Belle had never been close. Now, caught between fascination and revulsion, she had destroyed, stillborn, their possible rapport.

Other sisters might embrace and separate for the night with fond expressions. But she and Belle—

"Well, goodnight," she said. "Sleep well."

"You too, Darrie. Goodnight."

She had to go back downstairs to see that the doors were locked, the curtains drawn, cigar ashes emptied.

Genia had already gone to her attic cot. On her way downstairs Darrie had heard her youngest sister humming one of the songs the war had made popular—"Tenting Tonight" it was called. A mournful-enough ditty, but Genia had been making it sound cheerful. Now, climbing the stairs again, Darrie noticed that silence had fallen over the house. A thread of light showed under Belle's door. Behind it she would be daydreaming of the Reverend's return, of the fleshly but sanctified coupling that would undoubtedly follow.

Logic had given Darrie a good idea of the mechanics of sex; the emotional aspect was not so clear. Once you were married to someone and "with him" in that way—unconsciously she used Belle's circumlocution—everything was different between you. He became your slave, Belle said. Why should it really make any difference if you were married? Before, that is. Afterward, when he was your slave, he would be only too eager for marriage, wouldn't he?

Darrie undressed quickly without lighting her lamp. The sheets were shivery cold. What would it be like, she wondered, what *could* it be like, to share her bed with a man? Visions came to her mind: attitudes, positions. Sheets, so recently cold, were a warm embrace. When, exhausted by her imaginings, she began to slip downward into the velvet pit of sleep, window curtains stirring in the breeze became a bridal veil. Words dreamed, or imagined, repeated themselves: I, Eric, take thee, Darrelline . . . thee, Darrelline. . . .

The weekend passed quickly.

On Sunday Papa and Genia went to church to hear the Reverend's first sermon as a married man and a member of the family. Darrie had her old reason—or was it an excuse?—for not going. She had dinner to prepare.

At the table, over the chickens she and Cheecha had stuffed and roasted, she heard the favorable report: the hall was full, extra chairs borrowed; Belle, at the organ, had played like an angel. Never a better sermon—splendid text: Blessed are the pure in heart. . . .

"By Jove, Son," Papa said, flourishing the bone-handled carving knife, "you made them sit up and take notice. 'Unto the pure all things are pure, but unto them that are defiled and unbelieving . . .' "

Darrie caught Eric's eye. He looked amused. Quickly she looked away from him. Was she blushing? Perhaps she only imagined the warmth in her cheeks. But concern increased the rising of heated blood. "How warm it is!" she cried, and got up to open a window.

"You've been over that old cookstove," Genia said, flashing her dimples at Eric.

His attention, drawn to Genia, remained there.

I could be as red as a pair of flannel drawers, Darrie thought, with smoke coming out of my ears, and he wouldn't notice—*now*!

Darrie was ashamed of the relief she felt when the Newtons departed again for Olympia. Their connubial presence had created a sultry atmosphere she was glad to see abated. She assumed their leaving would reduce life to its acceptable if dull norm.

This was not the case. She found herself still thinking, shamelessly, about their marriage, its "sanctification," its "utter joy," the "slavish devotion" of a man initiated into the ritual of mating with a "pure woman." She might have doubted the extent of these changes, but there was the sweetened, gladdened, fulfilled Isabelle to prove her claims. And there was the fatuously devoted Howard.

Genia had not been unaffected by her sister's visit, but she reacted differently from Darrie. Preparations were being made for her to attend a girls' school on Whidbey Island that fall. As she and Darrie worked over the dresses and underclothes she would take with her, Genia asked, "What do you think of the Lovebirds?"

"They seem very happy."

"I think it's sickening."

Darrie looked up, surprised, from her sewing. "Why?"

"Oh, Howard's so sort of humble about it all. I saw him kissing Belle's hand and gawking at her like a moonstruck goonybird."

This was odd: "humble" was the very word Belle had used, though with a different connotation. "Is there something wrong with that?"

"It wouldn't suit me—not one little tiny bit."

"No? What do you want?"

"I want—I need—" Something rough and uncontrolled in her sister's voice made Darrie look up again from her work. Between narrowed lids Genia's eyes glinted bright and hard as gold pieces. "I want someone to *make* me love him—to force me—to beat me, maybe—"

"Imogenia!" It was a gasp of genuine dismay. "You don't know what you're saying!"

"Don't I?" The change was so instant that Darrie could believe she had imagined it. Honey sounded now in Genia's tones. Her eyes widened, and a smile that could only be described as knowing softened her lips into their usual dimpled charm. She laughed at Darrie but without malice. "It's you that doesn't know. You'll be an old maid. You're too bossy to get married. But I reckon that's what you want, 'cause you could have anything you set your mind on. We all know that."

The words stung Darrie more than she could have dreamed they could.

That night, after she had gone to bed, she turned them over in her mind. She remembered too—indeed she had not for one waking moment forgotten—her other sister's words. After a time, when sleep had proved completely beyond reach, she sat up in bed hugging her knees. She could have anything she wanted . . . and she wanted Eric for a husband. No one else would do.

There never would be anyone else she felt this way about—never. After they had been . . . together . . . he would feel the same way. He would be humbly grateful. He would kiss her. . . . When she tried to imagine the location of these kisses her breath and her heart became entangled. She thought for one moment of the anguished rapture that she was going to smother.

"If I stop to think, I'll be afraid to do it."

She had actually whispered the words out loud. She groped beneath the bed for slippers, pulled her robe about her shoulders, opened her door with shaking hands.

Eric was in his room. She had heard him come in and up the stairs—impossible to mistake his still slightly uneven step. Suppose he had locked his door! But he hadn't. The knob turned in her hand. A quartering moon shed its pale light into the room, revealing a mounded bed, a blond head pressed into the pillow.

She touched his shoulder. "Eric," she whispered.

He was instantly awake, sitting up. "What's wrong? What's happened?"

She pressed her fingers to his lips. "Ssh! They'll hear you." For one devastating instant she felt herself running, running, running, while there was time, escaping this alien madness before it engulfed them both. But she had not moved. His lips stirred beneath her fingers, warm and alive. The moment of running was passed. She raised the covers and slipped into his bed.

Wakening in her own bed in the morning, she remembered vaguely that she had returned to it as dawn had lightened the eastern sky.

Oh—! It had been everything Belle had said, and more! More! The twain shall be one flesh. . . . How she adored him! This, then, was the meaning of humility—a word despised before but now acknowledged to be the only one defining this sweet weakness, this longing to be absorbed, this fiery need to be made, by magic fusing, less one's self than an adjunct of another and infinitely more precious self.

After a time of ecstatic stillness, of reliving last night's miracle, she moved—to feel a physical hurt. Her body, lagging behind a soaring spirit, carried the reminder of its limitations in actual pain. But, after the first startled moment, she gloried in this proof of her fulfillment. Poetry, she thought; music, the symphony of nature itself—everything sweet and desirable in the universe moved toward this exquisite moment when two were made one. Now I believe in God. The words spoke themselves so clearly in her mind they seemed to have been said aloud.

Smiling, she slipped out of bed and dressed herself.

In the kitchen, with Cheecha, she felt herself to be on tiptoe, breath held back, waiting in suspension for that moment when Eric would appear in the diningroom, when their eyes would meet. . . .

Mr. Hall came down first, then Pomp. She served them coffee, and applesauce, carried ham and eggs and hot biscuits from the kitchen. Papa came out, yawning, from the downstairs bedroom. She kissed his cheek.

"Well, well! We're feeling cozy this morning!"

"I love you, Papa."

He stared at her, for once without a ready answer, and took his place at the table.

Pomp and Mr. Hall left for downtown. Papa retired to his room to shave. Genia came downstairs and, finding the diningroom deserted, set herself a place at the kitchen worktable.

Still there was no sign of Eric.

Darrie could wait no longer. She went upstairs, tapped at his door. "Eric?"

Silence.

"Eric!" Her ear to the panel she could hear no sound, no stirring of bedclothes, no drawing of breath. Dissolved in sudden panic, she threw open the door on emptiness. There was the tumbled bed, the unused pitcher of water that Cheecha must have brought earlier. The wardrobe door stood open to reveal empty hangers.

He was gone. *Gone.* The enormity of that added to the just-escaped terror that he was ill—or worse—were too much for Darrie. She clutched at the bedpost for support, half fell onto the bed, and clung there stunned. It was impossible. But it was true. He was gone. Why? *Why?*

After what seemed a long time, Darrie went back downstairs, "Cheecha, when you took hot water up this morning, was Mr. Bond in his room?"

"He gone."

"You didn't say—!"

Cheecha's polished-stone eyes rested on her with no hint of comprehension. "He gone a'ready," she repeated.

Darrie's fingers curled into her palms, their sinews tightening with the impulse to strike out—to hurt the impassive brown face so well within her reach. To think that Cheecha had known, all this time, while she had lived on in her fool's paradise. . . .

"What's wrong, Miss? He owe money?"

The animal instinct to hide a fatal wound from alien eyes made Darrie turn away. "Nothing's wrong. I'm . . . I'm surprised, that's all."

Genia spoke up, "Where did Mr. Bond go? He didn't say anything."

"I'm sure I don't know." Darrie took the broom from its hook. "I'll do the bedrooms," she said. In the shambles of her mind escape was the single coherent thought.

It was a week before Darrie saw Eric again. He appeared at the door one afternoon. His presence reminded her of the old *Anderson*'s whistle, heard not long before and noted but vaguely at the time.

She could not have spoken if her life had depended on it. She gestured for him to enter.

In the front parlor, led there perhaps by some instinct for formality, they took seats. Darrie had not yet spoken. Eric's efforts to communicate were obviously difficult. He looked uncomfortable, ashamed. But he struggled with the necessities of the occasion. "You must have thought I was a first-rate skunk—sloping off like that, I mean. I just couldn't think straight, at first." He took out a handkerchief and dabbed at his forehead. "Warm, walking up here."

"Yes, it's warm." Darrie winced at the cracked sound of her own voice.

There was a long and weighted silence. Then Eric spread both hands in a gesture of helplessness. "My God, Miss Darrie, what is there to say?"

Darrie's fingers were laced together now, the knuckles white from pressure. Her last ounce of moral and physical strength was bent toward maintaining self-control. Words repeated themselves in her mind: I will not weep. I will not accuse. I will not weep.

"You must know how you honored me—"

A short ugly word that Darrie had seen chalked on fences but had never in her life heard spoken came to her tongue. She tasted its contemptuous filth.

"If you expect something of me—maybe I should say, if something becomes necessary—"

"Necessary!" She breathed the word aloud after him. Against the enormity of their love-making and of his flight, she had not once thought of the possible consequence. She said harshly, "Nothing is necessary."

Again he pressed the handkerchief to his forehead. "Can you be sure, so soon?"

Clearly he knew more about the mechanics of these matters than she did.

She found now that in the past days and nights of anguish pride had formed a scab over her wound. "If there was a baby," she said, "I'd tear it out of myself and stamp it to death."

Pain tightened the flesh around Eric's eyes. He looked away from her. "You shame me. This whole thing hit me so suddenly. . . ."

His very decency enraged her. It was so meager a substitute for what they had shared. Shared . . . ? She reconsidered that concept. They had shared nothing. She had been swept to heights of unimagined bliss while he had performed an animal function in animal response to her uninvited embrace. It was as simple as that. His subsequent humility, his gratitude, his eternal cleaving to her after the act had been pure figment of her imagination—or of Belle's.

She had avoided looking at him. Now she made herself regard him with full attention. He was just an ordinary man: stocky and strong-looking, cleaner than most men kept themselves. No Greek god, certainly. If anything made him stand out from the common run, it could be only an aura of alertness and purpose. He was a man who would get what he wanted from life. But he didn't want her. That was the bitter truth he had come here to offer.

He went on speaking; he must have realized his words were not going to mend matters but they were all he had. "I tried to figure it out. At first I thought I must have dreamed it. If there'd been any reason to think—before that, I mean—that you were even interested in me—"

Fool! Oh, fool!

"But like that—out of the blue—" His stumbling embarrassment gave way to a sudden burst of truth. Almost in petulance he said, "It was a damned queer way for a nice girl to act!"

Later, Darrie thought, I may be able to laugh over that. Not now. Oh, definitely not now! But his obvious lack of ease had given her a slight feeling of command, enough to make it possible for her to say, "Perhaps you don't understand women. Men seldom do. The . . . the impulse came over me. It might as well have been anyone." She made a gesture of disinterest.

Now, reversing their positions, she imagined his mind saying, Fool! *Fool*!

Darrie stood up. "There's nothing more to say. To be frank, I didn't expect—" She weighed that, and changed it: "I didn't want to see you again."

He could not refuse this dismissal. But at the door he turned to say, "I'm sorry all around. Honest to God I am."

"Don't give it a thought."

"There's a particular reason, though. You see, I happen to be in love—"

The word pierced her—sweet, wild, improbable, but clearly spoken. "Love?"

"Yes. I've been waiting to get my affairs lined up. To have something to offer. And of course she's young yet."

"She?"

"Miss Genia. I was hoping to speak to her, soon now."

"Save your breath," she told him, and closed the door.

She groped blindly toward the stairway. A gust of laughter bent her double. A stairstep, reached for, was not there. She stumbled, striking her knee. Tears sprang from a wounded depth, colliding with false mirth. Her voice rose, keening like a lost dog's.

Barely visible below her, Genia's face appeared, milky with fright and wide-eyed. "Cheecha, come quick! Darrie's having hysterics!"

CHAPTER 11

Between them, Genia and Cheecha got Darrie up to her room and quieted.

It was so unlike Darrie, Genia thought, to carry on that way. Belle, now, had gone into hysterics more than once. But Darrie, the self-possessed, the cool, the—well, when it came down to it, Genia thought, Darrie didn't *feel* things the way she and Belle did. Darrie's only concession to weakness was the occasional day spent in bed, her room darkened, while the poor dear waited out the passing of a sick headache. For Darrie to weep and scream was a reversal of nature.

Searching for a cause, Genia asked, "Did that silly old Mr. Bond say something to you?"

Darrie, sitting up in bed now, reached for the salts bottle and passed it before her nose. "Of course not!"

"But he'd just left. What else was there?"

"I don't know what set me off. Maybe I've been working too hard."

Genia was sure Darrie was concealing something, yet in her dull and uneventful life what was there to conceal? But already she was getting back her habit of command. "You run along, both of you," Darrie said. "I'm perfectly all right. I just want to rest."

Cheecha, who before this had got as far as the door, slap-footed along the hall and down the stairs. Darrie lay back on the pillow and closed her eyes. Except for being a bit greenish she seemed all right. Genia lowered the window shade, stood for a minute wishing she could be of more genuine comfort, then tiptoed out after Cheecha.

In the kitchen she asked doubtfully, "Do you need some help?"

"Those hands too white—pah! Go on!" The look of adoration that accompanied this took away any possible sting.

We all impose on Darrie, and Cheecha too, she thought lazily, going down the back steps to stand in the warm bath of August sunshine. The sun was too warm, really, and Genia moved across the grass to where the hammock swayed invitingly in the shade of a willow tree.

Darrie's fit had had something to do with Mr. Bond, Genia was sure. But what? Had he made an "improper advance" to her? That wasn't likely. He'd never paid her any more mind than a fly buzzing. In fact—Genia could feel the corners of her mouth lifting in a shared-only-with-herself smile—in fact she was sure Mr. Bond was smitten with herself. She'd never quite forgotten that meeting—oh, it was years ago, before he'd gone off to the war—when he'd told her he was coming back to marry her. Actually, she wasn't interested in him. He might not be the milksop Howard Newton was, but he wasn't the dashing lover either.

It must be exciting, she thought, for a man to want you so terribly—to *need* you so—he could not curb himself. This might happen. . . .

A curtain of memory parted on shadows. She saw, softened by

time, the endless rise and fall of green seas, the pattern of rigging against a cloud-filled sky; she felt again the never-ending motion of deck and bunk and chair. She heard Mama in the bunk beneath hers, retching, moaning, retching. She saw her, gray-faced, against the pillows. Earlier and prettier memories of her mother were overlaid with this hazy but unpleasant image of persisting illness.

Yet there was a memory, small and bright, cutting the haze; a night when Papa begged, "Please, Cynthia! I'm only human, and it's been so long!" His voice was shaking. "Take pity—if it's only that. I need—I need—" Then the soft animal sounds. Old Brownie with pups at her teats had sounded so. And Papa's hoarse gasp of relief.

The next morning Mama had been dead.

Remembering, Genia found her throat tight, her mouth dry. She moistened her lips with her tongue tip. To rouse such need, such maddened need, that even death was not too great a price. . . .

But I would fight, she thought, and fight! Imagining it, her slender body arched upward, bow of young flesh taut against the arrow of attack. My honor at stake, I would hold him off. But in the end—! The straining arch could not be held. She relaxed, slowly at first, then with a sudden dissolving of tight-held muscles that left her small and formless in the curve of the hammock. Through parted lips her breathing was rapid and shallow, as if she had been running . . . running . . . running for her honor. For her life.

The westering sun had found its way beneath the willow branches. Lying in a bright band across Genia's body, it made her warm and drowsy. She closed her eyes. In two weeks, she thought, I'll go to Whidbey Island, to Miss Allen's school. Anything can happen there. Anything. . . .

It had been arranged that Genia, chaperoned by Darrie, would cross to the Island on Jed Holmes' plunger. They would hire a rig, if one were available, or walk the mile to Miss Allen's school.

On the morning they were to go, Darrie was down with a sick headache.

Ma Duncan, a little grayer, a little more wiry, than when the Starkweather girls had stayed with her, had arrived at Cedarhaven early to take charge in Darrie's day-long absence. Genia ignored the evident misgiving with which Ma Duncan saw her start off alone. "Remember to act the little lady, and you'll have no trouble. But mind! You watch yourself with that Jed Holmes! Give him an inch and he'll take an ell."

When Genia reached the dock, panting a little from carrying her carpet bag, Jed was standing on the dock above his sloop, leaning against a warehouse wall and smoking a dirty old pipe. She had taken care to be here in plenty of time—they weren't due to leave till nine o'clock.

Jed asked, "You going alone?"

"Yes. My sister is ill."

"Okay then. Hop aboard." He took the bag from her, tossed it into the cockpit, and helped Genia down to the tar-daubed afterdeck of the sloop. Then he cast off the mooring line, leaped nimbly onto the forward deck, and pushed away from the dock. When they were free, he hoisted a stained and well-patched canvas, secured the lanyards, and came back to take the tiller. This was the first chance he'd had to say anything. He grinned at Genia and said, "Make yourself comfortable. Cabin there."

It was a cabin by courtesy only, enclosed forward and to the sides but open aft. There was a blanket-covered bunk along one side, a bench along the other. In the forward end was a small cast-iron stove with a frying pan and a long-handled cooking pot swinging against the bulkhead above it.

Genia took the two or three steps down to the cabin level. In spite of its openness the room smelt of unaired bedding, tobacco, and old cooking grease. It was, she thought, a bachelor smell. She chose the wooden bench as being cleaner than the bunk, and sat down gingerly.

After a time, when they had cleared Point Hudson and started across the Inlet, Jed lashed the tiller and joined her in the cabin. She had not realized how tall he was: inside the cabin he had to stoop slightly to avoid the overhead.

"How about some coffee?" he asked.

Genia pondered this and answered indirectly: "I thought there'd be other passengers."

"If they didn't get here on time—" He shrugged.

Genia was certain they had left early. Obscurely, the idea excited her.

Jed put shavings in the stove, broke some scrap lumber in his hands. They were exceptionally strong hands, Genia noticed: long-fingered, wide in the palms, knotted with muscle. Adding the broken lumber to the shavings, he struck a match. Now the pungent smell of woodsmoke was added to the mixture of odors in the cabin.

Jed poured water from a can into a chipped graniteware pot, added coffee with his hand, and set the vessel on the stove.

Smiling faintly, Genia said, "That's cute—that little fence on the stove."

"Keeps the pot from falling off. Watch it, huh?" He went outside again, looked around the horizon, made some correction in sail and tiller, and came back. "Only a hatful of wind. It'll take us a while to get there." He poked at the fire through a lifted stove lid, shook the coffeepot, and sat down on the bunk opposite Genia. When he put his feet one on each side of hers, pressing them gently together, she was not surprised. She sat perfectly still waiting to see what would happen next.

What happened was that the coffeepot boiled over.

"Damn it!" he said good-naturedly, and got up to push it back on the stove while he got tin mugs from a locker. When the coffee, black as tar, had been poured, he said, "Let's take it out on deck. Nice out there."

Genia had to fold a glove around the handle of her mug before she could hold it and follow Jed up the short companionway to the open cockpit. There he lounged on a bench by the tiller leaving her to find a seat for herself on an upturned box.

The coffee, once the wind had cooled it, proved surprisingly good. Genia sipped, and looked around her. The Inlet, often an ugly stretch of water, was today only mildly disturbed by the south wind that was taking them at a slow tack toward Ebey's Landing. Small waves raced along beside the sloop; an occasional one crested white when a gust struck it. Point Hudson was behind them now, the town itself hidden from view. Before them, but still a long way off, were the cliffs of Whidbey Island, notched by low ground at Ebey's Landing and again further to the south. Far off, bearing down on them from the Strait, was a sailing ship. From this distance and angle of vision it looked like a great wide-breasted bird. Except for this ship, they had the Inlet to themselves.

"How long will it take to reach Whidbey?"

Jed gave her a speculative look. She noticed that, between his parted lips, his teeth were strong-looking and slightly pointed like an animal's. "Long enough," he said.

Blood rose in her throat till she could feel its pulse against her collar. For a time she kept her head down. Then she looked up, and smiled the honey-sweet smile. "If you touch me," she said, "I'll kill you."

Jed threw back his head and laughed. "I'll bet you would, you vixen! If I left you strength enough."

She stood up, tossed overboard the dregs of her coffee, and said, "Let me steer."

"Okay. But hold her steady. Else the boom'll come around and knock us both silly."

He stood up and she moved in beside him. "Show me how."

It was only a pretense. Her hand, beneath his, exerted no strength on the tiller. Her shoulder fitted just beneath his arm. When her bonnet flew off and fell to the deck they both laughed and left it there.

"It could have gone overboard," he said.

"I know."

A loosened tress of hair whipped against her temple. She could feel blood drawn upward by the sting of salty wind beating on her cheeks. She felt tremendously, exultantly, alive. When the little plunger bowed suddenly to a wave larger than its fellows, Jed's free arm went about her. It was an awkward position: there was no place for his hand to rest. "Can't let you fall, eh?" His voice had lowered and thickened. Now his fingers were beneath her arm so that the curve of big hand followed the curve of a small but forward-thrusting breast. When he caressed her gently a flood of exquisite feeling ran through her body. For an instant she closed her eyes, luxuriating in the delight. Then she quickly drew away from him.

He moved after her. The tiller shifted, wind cracked in the canvas, the boom started swinging toward them.

"God damn you!" he cried, and brought the tiller back with such angry force the boat swung hard a'port and heeled beneath the wind.

Laughing, Genia caught at the bulkhead to keep her balance. Over her shoulder she saw Jed lashing the tiller with unsteady hands. When he came at her she began to fight.

His surprise was ludicrous.

Beneath his clumsy catch-as-catch-can hold she felt herself to be springsteel, quicksilver, flame, springsteel again. When he pinned her at last against the corner of the cabin bulkhead, she bit his bare forearm.

He roared with pain and anger, and struck back. She felt as if her neck had snapped with the weight of his open-handed slap. For a moment stars wheeled across a blackened sky. But she was free. Jed stood apart from her, rubbing his injured forearm.

"You God damn little chippy, you! I ought to—" He gritted his teeth and left the threat unspoken.

Genia's head throbbed from his blow. It was over now, the excitement, the ecstacy. She felt sick at her stomach. Above all, she despised this animal. She could feel scorn burning in the look she turned on him. He must have stung beneath it, for he said, "Some day you'll get hold of a feller won't let you off so easy."

"I said I'd kill you if you touched me."

He spat toward her on the deck, rubbed it with his shoesole, and turned his back.

Genia picked up her bonnet. Miraculously, it had escaped being trampled. She brushed dust from it, smoothed her tumbled hair, and put on the bonnet. Then she went inside the cabin. She wanted only for the trip to be over. Her feeling for Jed was utter contempt.

When they had tied up at Ebey's Landing she picked up her

carpetbag and scrambled to the dock, disdaining a hand Jed offered for her assistance.

"Hey!" he called after her; "Where's my pay?"

Genia turned in a fury. "Papa paid you!"

"The hell he did!"

A couple of men lounged on the dock. They chuckled in appreciation of the exchange.

Genia saw now that bloodstains darkened the sleeve Jed had pulled down to cover his wound. The sight pacified her. After all, he had been the first man to try. . . . She let her smile build slowly, grow heavy with sweetness. Turning from Jed, she drew it like a trail of honey across the two onlookers. One of them stood up from his lounging position. The other fumbled with his cap. "My father *will* pay you," she told Jed.

"You can't carry that bag—a little thing like you!" Both of the bystanders started toward her and, sensing competition, both quickened their steps. Still smiling, Genia set down her bag. "I truly thank you, both. I'm going to Miss Allen's school."

Half an hour later Miss Allen was greeting her with concern. "Dear child, you look so rumpled! I had thought the crossing would be fairly calm today."

"For a little while it was quite, quite rough."

"Oh dear—! But you are none the worse—"

Delight twitched the corners of Genia's lips. "No, Miss Allen, I am none the worse."

The winter that might have been dull in a girls' school was made endurable by Genia's speculation. She tried her slow sweet smile on the man-of-all-work, knowing full well he was beneath her notice—an old man, timid, toothless, but a male. She got in return a slavish devotion that made her fellow students laugh, but proved nothing.

Then, in the first sweetness of false spring, the school had a chaperoned hayride and bonfire party, with boys. One dark and dashing young man, older than the others, singled out Genia for attention. There were whispered pleas for another meeting. Genia could not leave the issue unresolved. There were other, and secret, meetings. In the end there was violence, primitive and ugly, beyond her power to stem.

It was a little death, courted with dread, obtained with pain and pride. By Easter vacation Genia was tired of the game. She knew her worth, and demands turned to pleading did not interest her.

CHAPTER 12

In Port Townsend the summer of 1866 was full of hope. The Custom House was being returned at last, re-established where it should have been all the time. Now good times were not only possible, they were predictably at hand.

Darrie felt she would soon escape the doldrums of vacant rooms, delinquent rent, overdue grocery bills. She did not know how she had scraped together the money to keep Genia in Miss Allen's school, but next winter—surely!—it would be less of a burden.

She even allowed herself to think of the wild luxury of a bathroom inside the house. She could ask more room rent, then, and be more choosy about boarders.

Perhaps because her mind was full of these concerns she almost had to be clubbed over the head with proof before she realized that Genia was with child. Then, looking back, she saw that evidence had been mounting: Genia's growing disinclination to eat breakfast, her greenish pallor at the sight of certain foods, her brief spells of giddiness. On a morning when Genia stayed late in bed, pleading illness, Darrie—suddenly and wildly alarmed—began to question her. Reluctantly Genia admitted even more conclusive evidence. Her usually bright face clouded over with awareness of something unnatural, something as yet undefined. "What could be wrong, Darrie? I thought perhaps I had . . . caught cold."

Darrie simply stared at her. Did she actually have to say the brutal words: You are having a baby? Could it be that her sister, in this condition, was this innocent?

Perhaps her expression was revealing enough. Genia's golden eyes widened, stared deeply and dreadfully into hers. The soft lips drew in childishly, and fingers went up to hide their telltale quivering.

These signs of vulnerability in the self-sufficient Genia were more touching than a cry for help. After a long moment, while their eyes held each others, Genia turned her face away. "I suppose I did . . . sort of know." Her voice dwindled. "I didn't want to."

"You mean you were *forced*—"

A quick-drawn breath told Darrie that Genia had not meant that, but she pursued the line of escape inadvertently offered. "Oh I *was* forced," she said. "I fought and fought! Afterward I was so black and blue I had to undress in the closet so the other girls wouldn't notice."

Knowledge of her sister modified this picture for Darrie. She had a twinge of guilt at her disbelief, and asked, "Who is the boy?"

"We-ell, I went home with Lissa Holman for the Easter weekend. You *said* that was all right, you know. If Miss Allen approved, and she did."

"It happened at the Holmans'? One of their family?"

"No-o, not exactly. Well, maybe he was sort of a cousin. He just came there. I was at the barn looking at a new colt. We sort of talked, and he . . . he went crazy. He was sorry afterward. He groveled." A change, subtle but unmistakable, had come into

Genia's manner. Pride giving way to contempt? That hardly seemed credible.

"He should have groveled! He should have been horse-whipped."

Genia lifted a shoulder. The gesture was slight, offering an overtone of indifference.

"He'll have to marry you, of course."

"He has a wife."

Darrie knew her legs were not going to hold her up. She groped her way toward her sister's bed and sat down.

Genia said, "Oh—ouch!" and pulled her feet out of the way. But she smiled at once and said, "You didn't really hurt me."

This reaction, so quick and charming, so like the child Genia, made ugliness unreal, impossible. For a brief sunlit moment it had not happened. The words had not been said. Then Genia made it real again. "What are you going to do about it, Darrie?"

"I? What am *I* going to do?"

"There's no one else."

"There's you! You got into it."

"Well, yes. . . ."

Even through her anger, through a conviction that a way out was neither possible nor deserved, Darrie's mind had begun to explore. "The Easter weekend . . ." This was June. Perhaps three months. . . . Genia's condition would soon be visible. The first thing was to get her away somewhere, out of sight. But there was no place to send her. No place to hide. Oh—! How could Genia have done this stupid, this wicked thing! Darrie fought, unsuccessfully, against a memory of herself slipping along a darkened hallway, opening a door, flinging herself—

It was a recollection she never consciously allowed herself, yet never truly escaped. At a certain level of her mind it dominated all else, waiting for that unguarded instant just before she fell asleep, or as she wakened in a velvet midnight, to ravish her with its unique mingling of arrowed sweetness and unbearable shame.

Now its simple existence in her life denied her the comfortable reproach of "I don't see how you could have!" She saw only too well. Except for sheer undeserved good luck she herself might have faced the same consequence. Even now, nearly a year later, the danger she had passed through sent a cold finger of fear along her spine.

Genia put a trusting hand over hers. "I thought you'd just about kill me. That's why I didn't tell you when—when it happened. But now if you're on my side it'll be all right. You can take care of everything. I feel better already, with you knowing."

There was no hint of remorse in Genia's manner. In fact, she seemed almost pleased with herself. Something here baffled Darrie, but she put it aside. Still she could not quite resist the impulse to prick Genia's so easily restored complacence. "What do you think Papa will say?"

"Oh, Darrie! He mustn't know! He couldn't stand it—you know that!"

"Not know! Good heavens, he can't help but—"

"No, he mustn't, truly! We'll have to go away someplace, don't you see?"

Darrie simply shook her head. "You make it sound like going to the store for a pound of sugar."

Genia's confidence was undimmed. "You'll manage," she told her. "You always do."

How effectively Genia had made it Darrie's problem rather than her own! "You'll manage—you always do." It was the very trick, in reverse, with which she had gained obedience from a younger Belle and Genia. Expect compliance, allow of no other course. Now the other side of the coin was presented for payment. There was something too apt in this turnabout. Darrie put that aside too, as something to be puzzled over later. Meantime, there was the immediate problem of Genia.

When a solution did occur to her, it was so perfect she was afraid to trust it. Some months before, a Mr. and Mrs. Armstrong had stayed a week at Cedarhaven en route to the Indian Reservation at Neah Bay, where Paul Armstrong would manage the government farm. Neah Bay was the loneliest of lonely outposts on the northwest tip of the Territory. Claire Armstrong had been appalled at the idea of two years in virtual isolation and had urged everyone within the sound of her voice—including the

Starkweather family—to visit her when possible and stay as long with her as possible. At the time, a visit to Neah Bay had seemed as remote to Darrie as a visit to Mars. But now—now, where could she find a more perfect hideaway?

She wrote to Claire at once, reasoning it was better to have Genia's condition known in advance than offered as a later surprise. She worded the letter cautiously: Genia raped by a villain—a married villain at that; Papa kept in ignorance "because of his health." "We must turn to someone we can trust." The closing line, at least, was unvarnished candor.

Mail to Neah Bay was a hit-and-miss affair. By the time Darrie had a reply she could see the first signs of thickening in Genia's slender waist. To her dismay, the letter was far from cordial. Frequent underlining of words conveyed a sense of unwelcome pressure. "Of course I can't *refuse* help, especially when I did invite you to come. As you reminded me. However, I did not anticipate a *prolonged* visit." Darrie closed her eyes to shut out the grudging words, then opened them again to know the worst. "Mr. Armstrong, who had to be told, of course, is very upset. He will be extremely busy for the next weeks with the fall harvest, and I assure you I have all *I* can do with my household chores in this *primitive* situation. However, we do have room, and under the circumstances I will not refuse you shelter. I assure you, I am thinking particularly of your father. I know his *splendid* Southern pride, and I can understand your wanting to protect him *at no matter what cost to others.*" That entire phrase was underlined.

Darrie realized her teeth were gritted. She made herself relax, physically at least. Clearly she and Genia would pay for any favors received from the Armstrongs. But where else could they go? If money were no object—if pigs could fly! She had figured to the penny what she would give Claire to cover the actual cost of their food. Where else could they live for that? And where else be so thoroughly hidden? She went ahead with the necessary arrangements.

To Ma Duncan she said, "Genia's not a bit well. I think she needs a change." Immediately she regretted that word—Genia would have a change all right! She started over: "I'm a bit tired myself. And the Armstrongs at Neah Bay urged us to visit them." Defiantly she told herself, They did urge it—till they knew we were coming.

Ma Duncan was not displeased with the prospect. "I'll be glad to look out for things. Cheecha's getting so she can handle most of the work, isn't she?"

"Oh, yes, she cooks and washes dishes, and cleans. It's chiefly that you'd have to plan the meals and order them, and help with the cooking sometimes."

"I'll take care of it. What I can't do I'll fob off on one of the girls. You go and have a good time, and don't you worry."

Don't worry—the irony of that!

"How long you think you'll be gone? Couple of weeks, maybe?"

"Oh, all of that! More like a couple of months. Or . . . or longer. . . ."

Momentarily Ma looked nonplussed, but she rallied. "Stay as long as you like." She made an airy gesture. "I and the girls will take care of things. And we won't overcharge you."

"I know you won't. I appreciate it." An impulse stirred to put grateful arms about Ma's shoulders, but habit forbade. Darrie contented herself by saying again, "I do appreciate it."

And still Papa had to be told—something!

Darrie chose an evening when they were, by chance, alone in the parlor. This was so unusual as to suggest prearrangement: as a rule Papa went downtown in the evening; if he did stay home it was in the company of Pomp or one of the other boarders. Darrie felt that fate had played into her hands. She must take advantage of it.

"Papa?"

"Hmmm?" He kept his eyes on the San Francisco paper someone had brought him.

"Papa, have you noticed that Genia is . . . not too well?"

The paper came down. "I have, at that. Though I've thought recently she looked better."

This was true. With morning sickness past, Genia had positively bloomed under her condition. Darrie hastened to say, "She does look a little better, but I happen to know she's not really improved."

"Oh? Some woman-thing, I suppose?"

"You could say that."

"She ought to see the doctor."

"She has." Darrie crossed her fingers inside her apron pocket. She wasn't saying when Genia had seen the doctor. She went on hurriedly, hoping a connection would appear where none existed. "She needs a change. To get clear away. Sea air, perhaps."

"Sea air? Good Lord! Unless she went under water she couldn't get more of the sea than she has right here."

"Well, yes, but she needs a change too. The Armstrongs who stayed with us last winter asked us to visit. I think we'll go out there for . . . for a little while."

"If you want to get away for a bit, why not Olympia? Belle would love to have you, especially when she is . . . ah. . . ."

Darrie stifled the hysterical impulse to laughter. Belle was not the only one who was . . . ah. . . . She said firmly, "Genia *wants* to visit the Armstrongs. And so do I."

Papa was frowning. "As a rule Genia comes to me with her little wishes."

So many answers occurred to Darrie that they seemed actually to clog her throat: Genia's little wishes—yes! But a big life-and-death wish, she knows better than to turn to you with that. *I* am the one now, sparring with you for her sake, while you prattle on about her "little wishes." I, who could strike you down with a single word of truth.

Even thoughts, it seemed, were dangerous. Papa gave her a searching look. "There's nothing really wrong with Genia, is there? I mean, nothing serious?"

Darrie willed calmness, self-control. "She'll be her old self soon."

Cautiously then: "How long would you be gone?"

"Oh, we might make quite a little visit. It's no easy trick to get out there and back, you know. We'll make the trip worth-while."

"Do you think Cheecha can manage?"

"Ma Duncan and the girls will help."

Papa never looked happy at the mention of Ma's name. "I do wish you wouldn't always turn to her! You have closer neighbors who are . . . well . . ."

"Would you like to ask Mrs. Fowler or Mrs. Nesbit to cook your dinner? I wouldn't."

"I'm sure they'd be glad to help, but you're so stand-offish. . . ."

Darrie let that rest. She couldn't say, "This is no weekend absence we're talking about, nor a ten-day one, nor even a month." This knowledge would come to Papa later, and gradually. She said, "It's a business arrangement with Ma. That's better than asking favors of a neighbor. She'll collect the board money and buy the food."

"Oh, come now! The men had better pay me."

Darrie forced a smile. "Papa, you know the men don't think of you that way. Anyway, Ma has agreed."

Her father gave her a look of reproach before he disappeared behind his paper. From its shelter he said, "You might give me a little consideration before you make decisions."

She waited a minute, wondering if she could have won so easily. She had expected this to be her biggest hurdle. But no doubt Papa's mind was filled with dreams and schemes built around the return of the Custom House. These plans, she was certain, would come to nothing, but she was grateful for their existence now. He would be furious later, when they stayed away as long as they would have to—but that was in the future.

Pomp, reluctant, and protesting that they ought not to take the trip at all, worked out their transportation to Neah Bay. They could not wait for a coastal steamer whose skipper would be obliging enough to set them ashore at Neah Bay: it was September, and only by the tightest lacing was Genia able to conceal her pregnancy. They would go to Dungeness by Indian canoe, from there to Neah Bay on a plunger.

The trip did not go according to schedule. The Indian paddlers beached their canoe on Protection Island to inspect a duck net, and spent considerable time sorting out edible ducks from those too long dead. When the voyage was resumed, Darrie suspected their choice had been liberal: even in the fresh salt-stung air a gamey odor rose from the ducks piled at her feet.

Genia, who had every excuse to be ill, was undisturbed. She chatted with the Indians about how the ducks would be cooked, and gravely discussed with one of the men the suitability of his taking a second wife.

Darrie, fighting off nausea, paid little attention to the conversation until she heard one of the men say, "You make baby, huh?"

She roused herself to answer for Genia, "Certainly not!"

Genia merely looked amused.

Sudden fury, unreasoning, violent enough to set her to trembling, possessed Darrie. How calm Genia was about all this! How—yes, complacent was the word. It was she, not Genia, who had scrabbled a way out of her difficulties, who had humbled her pride to accept grudging refuge, who had counted pennies, recounted them, and now scarcely hoped to emerge solvent. It was she who was revolted and half-sick from this miserable trip while Genia enjoyed—yes, enjoyed!—herself with these savages. For a wild, blood-racing, mind-blackened moment she thought of overturning the canoe. They would both drown. That would be the end of it. The Indians too, perhaps, and no matter. Let the world come to an end—it would be no real loss.

Now nausea did indeed grind through her. She leaned, defenseless, over the gunwale. Genia crept to her over the evil feathery cargo, and held her forehead. "Poor darling! Oh, what a shame! Here, let me clean you up. . . ." Genia's cupped hand brought seawater to cleanse her face. Darrie was able to lift a handful of water to rinse her own mouth. After that she leaned, spent and shaken, on Genia's shoulder. Her eyes were closed, but she heard the men laughing, felt the violence of Genia's reaction as she shouted, "Shut up—all of you! Shut up!"

The canoe rose and fell, and rose again. A great lassitude numbed Darrie's limbs. She thought, I'll sleep, just for a moment, now there's nothing more to do. Now that it's taken care of, and we're on our way. . . .

It was after dark when they reached Dungeness. Darrie and Genia were carried by their boatmen over what seemed like miles of tidal flat, and set down in sand so soft and thick that Darrie had trouble keeping her balance. A lantern bobbed toward them. A bearded white man, well bundled up against the half-mist half-rain that had begun to swirl through the air, said, "You the Starkweather gels?" and led them off through the clinging sand.

Darrie's exhaustion was so complete she could barely mouth the necessary polite words to the man's wife when they reached his cabin. She stumbled into bed, not sure whether she had undressed, and not caring, and woke to gray daylight and the whipping of rain on a small window above the bed.

Genia was already up. Her gay light voice came from the cabin's main room in counterpoint with the heavier tones of their hostess:

"Poor Darrie—I'm glad she's sleeping in."

"Your sister ain't well?"

"She works too hard. She needs a change—a rest."

"Looks like a worker, I'll say that."

"She's been a mother to me and my sister." A serious note crept into Genia's voice. She said slowly, as if weighing the words and evaluating them: "She has never let us down. Never."

Throughout a stormy day and night they waited for the weather to moderate, then resumed their journey on a dirty looking sloop already overcrowded with crates, boxes, bags, oil tins, and barrels. Again it was dark before they reached their destination. Again there was a bobbing lantern, beach sand slithering away from feet numbed by inaction; again a rain-filled wind tore at their hair and clothing.

Feeling rootless and alien, Darrie stumbled along behind a guide's unsteady lantern.

"This here's the Armstrong house," they were told.

Against a night sky she saw the outline of a two-story frame dwelling. Because it was there, within her reach, because it was indeed a house rather than a crowded cabin, because she had—by using the last ounce of her reserve strength—brought them this far, she began to weep. Genia put both arms around her. "Don't cry, dear! We'll be fine now, truly we will."

Darrie had no time to speculate on this reversal of their roles. The door before them opened. In the fan of lamplight that spread about them, Darrie was acutely conscious of the sorry picture they must present: two waifs, straight out of melodrama, tearful and storm-battered. She drew herself up. Defiance, which she had not intended and which she instantly regretted hardened her voice when she said, "Well, here we are."

Claire Armstrong, lamp in hand, looked at them for a lengthening moment. "So I see," she said.

CHAPTER 13

To be away from Cedarhaven was a constant hunger ravening within her. Darrie could not escape the thought that Genia's swelling body was being nourished by her own mysteriously transposed tissue, and that by the time her sister's child was fully formed she herself would be a hollow and strengthless shell. The notion was ridiculous but it persisted.

At Cedarhaven she was mistress of the house. Here she was reduced to a cipher, and an unwelcome one.

Claire immediately ordered the making of a layette. The need had not occurred to Darrie. Even now, with the necessity pointed out, Genia was indifferent. "I simply cannot understand your sister! To act as if this . . . this situation was something to be proud of. . . ." A hundred times a day some variation of this refrain was dinned into Darrie's ears.

She couldn't understand Genia either. The old excuses she had used in her mind were threadbare: Genia's young—she was sixteen, scarcely a child; Papa always catered to her—so did they all, as if her very nature demanded and received deference; she will be different when the child is born—there would be two problems then instead of one. None of it made sense. Life now was simply a procession of inexplicable days to be endured till pardon came.

A few days after their arrival at Neah Bay, Edward Lord, the Resident Agent, had called on Darrie. Through Paul Armstrong he had been presented with the careful fiction that she and Genia were Claire's cousins from Portland, Genia a widowed Mrs. Brown, Darrie her unmarried sister Miss Hansen.

"I am responsible for everyone here, red and white," Edward Lord told Darrie. He stood in front of the Armstrongs' fireplace, coat tail turned upward, steam rising from the combination of wet shoes and hot brick hearth. "If there's a situation that might develop into trouble, I have to know about it."

Darrie chose not to meet his eye—a difficult task since he was concentrating on her the nervous attentiveness of a terrier. Indeed, she thought, he was rather like a terrier in appearance: small, wiry, bright-eyed, with wild little tufts of red emerging from the gray of hair and beard. Now, fencing for time, she said, "I don't expect any . . . situation . . . to come up. As Mr. Armstrong must have told you, my sister—she's a widow—is going to have a child. But she's very healthy. I'm sure there'll be no trouble."

"Why did you choose a place a hundred miles from a doctor?"

"As I said, my sister is healthy—"

"And unmarried, I take it."

Darrie turned away. In a voice she hoped was indignant, she said, "That is an insulting suggestion."

"Your assuming I wouldn't see through this is the real insult."

Darrie decided she must, once more, bow to the inevitable. After a little thought she said, "It isn't possible for her to marry. I wanted to get her to some out-of-the-way place."

"I see. . . . Well, taking one point at a time, why isn't it possible for her to marry?"

Darrie wished he would leave her alone. None of this was any concern of his. Yet the Indian Agency was rather like a ship and he its captain. Whatever he wished to make his business was his business. She told him, "The man is married."

"Hmmm. . . ." Then, with a darting look from beneath his shaggy brows, "Another man might have been found. Wives are in scarce supply in the Territory."

"Are you suggesting—" Darrie's indignant reply died on her lips. Yes, this would have been a possibility. The child would then have had a legal father. She simply had not thought of this way out.

Lord must have noticed her belated qualms. "Am I to understand you handled this thing alone?"

"We have no mother."

"And your father—?"

"He doesn't know."

"How old are you?"

"Nearly twenty." She added, "I've been in charge of the household for more than six years."

"And those six years have given you certain delusions of omnipotence."

Darrie bit back an angry defense. This little pipsqueak! She had got Genia out here, hadn't she? Could he have done better?

"I didn't mean to criticize. You did something, rather than sit and wring your hands, which would have been the usual reaction of a twenty-year-old girl. Unhappily, having lived through more than twice twenty years, survived two marriages, and brought up four children, I have more awareness than you of the pitfalls in your plan."

"For example?"

"For example, not counting the Indians, there are four white men here on the Reservation and one white woman—Mrs. Armstrong. From time to time there are traders, seamen, visitors of one sort or another. Any one of them might put two and two together, recognize you or your sister at some later time, and give the show away. Not to mention Mrs. Armstrong, who must know quite a bit more about you than I do. Don't you see, you are placing yourself in hostage to any chance encounter that might take place in the next ten years, or twenty, or a lifetime?"

Darrie was at a disadvantage, and knew it. She said, "I couldn't think of anything better to do."

"I see. . . . Well, then, for better or worse, this is the step you've taken." He looked at her for a time, his little terrier eyes bright and hard. Then he said, "We'll do what we can to protect you both."

His use of the word 'we' made Darrie start in surprise.

He shrugged. "You're here. It's too late to make other arrangements—if there were better ones. Perhaps there weren't. Will you and Mrs. Armstrong be able to see your sister through this?"

"We'll have to."

Edward Lord gave a wry smile, his first since the beginning of the conversation. "I am supposed to be, among my other talents, a sort of pinch-hit veterinarian, doctor, and priest. But I hope you can get along without me. An accouchement is hardly in my line."

He gave the word its French pronunciation and for a moment Darrie did not recognize it. Then her mind's eye saw it spelled out on a page in the doctor book she had read with avid attention before leaving Port Townsend. She had wanted to bring the book with her but its sheer bulk and weight had prevented, and suspicion might have been aroused by its absence from the bookshelf. Still, she had read and reread half a dozen times the chapter on what she had called, exactly as it was spelled, the a-couch-ment. Now she said, pretending to a confidence she didn't feel, "Mrs. Armstrong and I will manage."

"I hope so."

Nothing remained to be said between them. Lord had served notice that he saw through her deception. Still, he lingered on in the square ugly parlor of the farmhouse. Sufficiently warmed by now, he moved away from the fireplace. An odor of wet wool moved with him, along with the faintly sour smell of too-hot leather. At Neah Bay, Darrie had observed, everything smelled:

salt water, rotting seaweed, whale oil, clams, filth—there were degrees of stench but never an absence of it. On an impulse, she said, "Mr. Lord, why did you come here? It's not a pleasant post."

He tipped his head. It was the terrier's wary, sideward glance. "Some day, a hundred years from now, what I do here may have value. My predecessor, Judge Swan—maybe you know him?"

"I met him in Port Townsend when—" Her hand went to her mouth. Lord had been too clever for her, or she too stupid. He knew now where they came from. But he chose to ignore her slip.

"Smithsonian is full of stuff Swan sent them—Indian tools and garments, knickknacks, stuffed birds, pressed flowers. I couldn't name them all. Besides that, the Indians trusted him. He helped them. In short, he did a good job here. I'd like to keep it up."

"How can you truly help the Indians? They live the way they want to. Why not leave them alone?" In her imagination she saw again the burning village of Kah Tai.

"It's true, they're the immovable object, and—" Lord gave his wry smile; "—I fall short of being the irrestistible force. Still, I keep trying."

"Aren't you afraid, sometimes? Mightn't the Indians rise up against you, against us all?"

"It's conceivable, although unlikely. I pride myself I have sold them on the idea that it wouldn't work—for long anyway. If they did us in, there'd be other white men in "fire canoes," and punishment enough to offset all their gains. That happens to be true. When all's said and done, Miss . . . ah . . . Hansen, truth is man's best weapon."

They were back now to the falsity of Genia's and her positions here. Darrie offered an excuse, even while she disliked herself for it: "Men run the world. Women have to manage by the rules they set. It drives us to deceit."

"You have a point there. Still, in the particular spot your sister is in, women would be your real enemies, wouldn't they?"

Darrie sought for a nonexistent rebuttal, and looked up expecting to find triumph in Lord's eyes. Instead his expression was regretful. Instantly on guard again, he said, "Well, Miss Hansen, I came here to find out what I could. And to say you needn't expect help from me. Instead . . ." There was a pause. "Instead—well, if I can be of service, call on me."

She found his hand thrust toward her. Taking it, she was surprised by its tough resilience. Something constructed from odd bits of old harness would have been softer to the touch.

After this meeting, Darrie saw little of Edward Lord. A slave-driver for himself as well as for others, he was constantly at work improving the Agency, visiting nearby Indians, entertaining those visitors who braved the difficulty of the long journey here or who came ashore from passing ships. He had no time for an unwelcome, perhaps threatening, visitor to his domain.

Darrie, too, was occupied—Claire saw to that. In truth there was plenty of work for all of them: washing, ironing, baking, taking in the harvest and preserving it in one form or another. Genia, clumsy now—with need for concealment past she had grown big as a woodshed—tried to help. But she was inept at best, and made nearly helpless by Claire's sneering criticism.

Darrie knew she was paying the actual cost of their keep and earning it twice over again in work, but there was no help for it. That the price would be so high was an unpleasant surprise, but one that had to be accepted.

She had been equally unprepared for the fall climate at Neah Bay. Rain drifted in from the Pacific in an endless curtain of monotony. From the windows of the farmhouse, through a glass distorted by rain, she looked out at gray sky, gray ocean, gray beach, gray buildings of agency and school, gray barn with gray oxen huddled against its side. Beyond her vision but known to her mind's eye was the even more dismal cluster of shacks occupied by the Makah Indians. If there had ever been color here it had been leached away in this endless rain.

Darrie seized with delight those days when a lighter-than-usual rain drifted in wavering ribbons across the beach and village, days when she could put on her mackintosh and boots and—sometimes with Genia but more often alone—take walks along the beach. She kept a watchful eye always on the tide, sure that if she were caught by it she would perish before she could fight her way through the knife-sharp spruce, the poison-needled devil's club, the barbed salmonberry bushes that walled the seacoast.

When Genia accompanied her, she tried to make some sort of ordered plan for their future. But Genia seemed to feel no need for this. "We can't change things, can we?" she said. And this was true. They were caught, inexorably, in the slowly revolving days that would bring the end of her pregnancy. Nothing could shorten that, nor alter its direction. But after that—what then?

"Maybe," Genia had said once, half-smiling in the way she had of seeming to know something hidden from others, "maybe the baby'll die. Or be born dead."

"Would you be glad?"

"It would be easier, wouldn't it?"

"Do you mean—" Darrie had been going to ask, "Do you mean you have no love, not even concern, for your unborn child?" But it was no use to ask. Obviously Genia did not care. And I, in her place, with a fatherless child and all my life before me . . . It was the old disarming awareness of what it had been like—what it must be like now for Genia.

"Maybe Claire and Paul would like to take it," Genia offered. "Claire can't have a child, you know. That's one reason she doesn't like me."

That, thought Darrie, and the way you look meltingly at Paul. Not that you can help it, I suppose. It's simply in your nature. . . . She said aloud, "It's safe to say Claire won't want *your* child."

They had reached a jumble of great rocks which marked the limit of their walk since, beyond them, they would be out of sight of the Agency. Darrie stopped, leaning against the cold side of the tallest stone. Damp sand, sucking at their feet, made walking a burden, and Genia stopped too, breathing hard. When she pushed her rainhood back, moisture gathered in her hair and tightened the dark-gold tendrils at her forehead. Her creamy skin had never glowed so brightly, her eyes had never been so radiantly clear as now.

She's not being punished, Darrie thought. Do I *want* her punished? What *do* I want?

Genia reached out and drew a finger along Darrie's forehead.

"You're so frowny! I'm sorry I'm such a worry to you—truly I am! And you've been so good to me."

"I wouldn't mind so much—at least I think I wouldn't—if I felt that you had learned anything."

Genia's dimples flashed. "What should I have learned? You tell me, and then I'll know."

"The penalty for being—" Darrie hesitated before the ugliness: "—promiscuous."

"I've told you, I couldn't help its happening."

"I know you've said that."

Momentary dismay clouded Genia's face. "Don't you believe me?"

Doubt of Genia's complete innocence, which had teased Darrie's mind this long time, kept her from an immediate answer.

"Oh, Darrie—please!" The full underlip trembled. Tears filled the golden eyes. "I don't want you to be—"

"Sorry? Is that the word? Perhaps if you felt even the least bit sorry I wouldn't be so concerned."

"I *am* sorry! Truly and truly I am! It's awful, being so pooched out and ugly. I hate it! But I just don't let myself think about it. It'll be over soon and we can forget it."

As well try to capture the sea mist in a cupped hand or preserve the cry of the gull that wheeled above them in the wintry sky. Genia had her own logic. At no point did it make contact with Darrie's. Feeling suddenly old and weary, Darrie said, "We should get back." She turned away from the rocks and started back along the double line of footprints.

A breaker larger than its fellows spread muddy lace along the sand, wiping out the tracks where they had detoured to inspect a melting jellyfish. In an hour, or less, the tide would have obliterated all signs that they had walked here. The beach would be as it had been a thousand years ago, and would be a thousand years from now. It did not matter that they had passed this way. It did not matter that ten years ago, just beyond the rocks that made their turnabout, the Indian Obi had killed a white man. Paul Armstrong had told them the story, smiling at this safe distance over the simple Indian ways. It had been a senseless killing, all but forgotten; the white man's body, washing, drifting in the tide, had been carried at last to the sea's final and mysterious grave. Obi had gone about his Indian ways of life. The murder had been made known at last only when a relative of Obi's, quarreling with him over a slave woman, had denounced him to Edward Lord. And when long-delayed justice had loomed, Obi had vanished into the forest, unpunished, unregretting. "It simply happened," Obi must have reasoned. "I could not help myself. Now, when it no longer matters and the intruder's bones are bleached white as moonbeams in the sea, they talk of punishment."

"What are you thinking, Darrie? You're not still mad at me, are you?"

There was nothing to answer. Genia, like Obi, might be supremely innocent or supremely evil. Who could say which one it was? One point was clear: she did not belong in the halfway house of innocence and evil intertwined, where men picked their way carefully along the neatly marked paths they called virtue, sharing a common shame when one made a misstep.

In November the farmwork slacked off. The harvest was all in and the earth, in Paul's words, "put to bed for the winter."

Housework could not occupy them all, even with Claire's make-work projects. Darrie found herself with time on her hands. She had wanted to know Lord better; she offered, now, to help him with correspondence and records she had heard him complain of having to neglect. Her aid was gratefully accepted and she began to spend an hour or so a day at the Agency, in the crowded fusty room that Lord called an office. There a plank writing table held a jumble of papers, records, forgotten memos, letters to be answered, letters half written and put aside, broken pencils, empty sand-shakers, and nibless pens. A larger worktable contained, when Darrie first saw it, books, tools, drying starfish, two human skulls, a bird's nest, some poorly cured otter hides, one boot, and a broken copper lantern. The contents of this table varied from day to day but maintained at all times an air of raffish confusion.

Lord had been in the habit of copying into a ledger, and not too accurately, his own correspondence. Darrie found a letter press, neatly copied the Agency letters in ink and left their impression in the tissues of the press. As she had time, she sorted the old correspondence and filed it in a cabinet that must have been intended for that purpose although she had found it full of shoemaker's tools. Gradually the writing table took on a semblance of order.

"The woman's touch," Lord called it, and hastily added, "Not that I'm not grateful!"

"It keeps me busy, so I'm grateful too."

They were having one of the stolen moments of leisure and conversation that Darrie enjoyed; Lord had brewed some coffee, brought it in a blackened coffeepot, and poured it into the chipped mugs that apparently constituted his household chinaware. Darrie had often wondered what sort of mare's nest served him for a kitchen or, for that matter, a parlor. Convention kept her from entering the living quarters of the Agency, but imagination had created a setting similar to the worktable.

Lord sipped his coffee, eyeing her over the mug's rim. "You're a great one for work, aren't you?"

"I declare, I'd have to be. Ever since we moved out West there's been work waiting for me."

"Your father might have married again."

"He'd have liked to, I think. But there aren't too many women in Washington Territory."

"No, I've found that out myself. I'd get married in a minute if I could find a pretty young woman, well educated, of independent means—oh, and a nice disposition, naturally!—who'd enjoy living in an Indian Agency."

He said all this so gravely that Darrie studied him for a moment, wondering if it was meant for irony. The spark of amusement in his eyes gave him away. Equally grave, then, she pointed out, "You forgot to say she'd have to be a good cook."

"Yes, she must have a light touch with clams—that goes without saying. And if she can half-sole boots, all the better."

"When I get back home I'll keep my eye open for someone."

Lord didn't answer. She looked up to find him gazing at her

with an odd intensity that both flattered and disconcerted her. "The way you said that: 'When I get home . . .' You are homesick, aren't you?"

"Homesick? I don't know." Studying the matter, she added, "It's funny—when I was scheming to get us here I never once thought of what it would be like when we were here, or how we'd manage. It was just a matter of getting here, getting out of sight. Now that I'm here—I don't know how to say this, really, except that I feel as if I'm being nibbled away—used up. I'm not real any more. I ask myself, 'Is this me, copying your letters, or walking on the beach, or whatever?' Does that make sense?"

Lord had set down his coffee mug and was scraping at an ill-smelling pipe to which he was devoted. After digging out the bowl he pressed in tobacco, struck a match, and drew vigorously. Only then did he say, "It makes sense for you. It wouldn't for me, because I live in my hat. Women are different—some women anyway. My first wife. . . ." He seemed to be having trouble with his pipe.

Darrie made no move or sound to alarm him; she was intensely interested. The pause grew embarrassing in length before Lord cleared his throat and said, "My first wife lived all her girlhood in a little town on the Ohio River. She went with me to Arizona Territory. It's supposed to be a very healthful climate, except that hunks disappear from otherwise healthy scalps. At least it's warm and sunny, you know? But she never lived easy there. 'I keep waiting for something,' she'd say. I'd ask her what, but she didn't know. She . . . she sickened and died. For no reason. No reason the doctor could find anyway."

"I'm sorry. . . ."

"Oh?" He looked up as if surprised to find Darrie there. "Well, thank you. There were children. I married again. A widow. She was—" A smile quirked his lips; "—let's say more prosaic. The doctor had no doubt about her death. She was thrown from a horse and her neck was broken. You'll admit I'm doing all I can to cheer you up."

"I don't know why you're telling me these things."

"Damned if I do either. I'm not leading up to a proposal."

Darrie laughed in spite of herself. "Thanks for warning me."

"That sounded egotistical. Well, let's face it: all men are egotists where women are concerned. But I'd know better than to approach you. You've got a fence around you." He picked up the coffee mugs. "I'll drop these in the kitchen and go along to see if Manabuti's squaw has dug up his grandpa's leg."

"*What*?"

"Yes, didn't you know? They've been rooting around all morning, Manabuti's squaw and her friends. Manabuti broke his leg and he won't let me splint it till he's got grandpa's legbone to do it with."

"Are they crazy?"

"Depends on the viewpoint. Makes sense to them. Of course, if they don't find an old shinbone pretty quick, Manabuti's leg will set crooked. Probably have his toes pointing backward. But it's his leg. Well, so long!" He raised a finger in farewell and strode out through the back door of the office.

Darrie sat on at the writing table thinking about their conversation. Edward Lord made her think. There was something eager and questing about his mind that started her own curiosity. Could she, as his first wife had done, sicken and die away from Cedarhaven? In flights of fancy she had pictured herself as a bride, but never as a bride leaving Cedarhaven. She had pictured herself living on there, with Eric. . . .

If, even for a moment, she relaxed her guard the old searing humiliation flamed through her blood leaving a bright residue of mingled ecstacy and anguish. How could she have lived through it . . . how could anyone. . . .

She rose with sudden awkwardness from the desk, needing only to escape her thoughts. When she took her mackintosh down from a peg on the wall and slipped into it, she shivered at the touch of cold fabric. Suddenly the cold, the rain waiting for her beyond the door, her whole rootless existence here, swept over her in a flood of longing for Cedarhaven. Long-held-back tears burst from her. She leaned against the doorframe and waited for the storm to pass.

"You're so fond of keeping busy," Edward Lord told Darrie on a morning when there was nothing further to do in his office, "why don't you do something with the Indians?"

"What could I do?"

"Offer them whatever you can, if it's only friendliness."

"I haven't even that—to spare."

"Interest, then. To feel that others are concerned with you is a pretty common need, isn't it?"

"Suppose I'm not interested?"

Edward Lord smiled at this. "You're crowding me. I can only say, they might be interested in you."

Repeating the conversation to Genia, Darrie met with instant response: "That's a good idea! Let's visit the school—talk to the children. It would be fun, wouldn't it?"

"In your—" Darrie didn't finish the sentence; her eyes traveling downward spoke for her.

Genia said, "Why not? The Indians don't fuss over having a baby. They won't care."

Claire's protests, of course, had to be overridden. "I've lived here all these months and don't know one siwash from another. You can't mix with them."

Perhaps as much in defiance as anything else, Darrie announced that she and Genia would visit the school, after all.

The schoolmaster was an ill man. He coughed, spat blood into a handkerchief, and then—as if the effort had been too much for him—leaned on his desk with sweat beads shining on his forehead. He had neither the strength nor, apparently, the desire to cope with the dozen or so Makah children who sporadically showed up for class.

The village was full of children. There must be thirty or forty, Darrie guessed, of school age. Of those who did attend only two or three could read, a few more could speak English. It was a sorry excuse for a school.

Genia, who had been thoroughly bored with life at Neah Bay, was enchanted with the Indian children. She went to the school each morning, while Darrie divided her time between the school and Lord's office. Genia found a pitch pipe, and got the children to singing simple airs. Darrie, not to be outdone, wrote the words of songs on the blackboard in the hope it would inspire the children to read. Gradually the children's timidity, or their stolidity, thawed. They began to smile at the sisters and make small overtures of friendship. Sometimes their mothers appeared at school to stare impassively as the children sang or recited. Outside the schoolhouse, the older Indians studied Darrie and Genia with dark, unsmiling eyes. Perhaps they were more puzzled than unfriendly, but they offered no encouragement to socialize.

This interest outside the Armstrong household, minor as it was, made the days pass more quickly. November dwindled away.

December began with a flood of rain, and then turned cold.

On Christmas Eve there was to be an Agency party: a Christmas tree at the school, carols in which Genia had painstakingly coached the children, candy and cookies for any Indians who would attend. Claire spent the day popping corn and making it into balls for the party. Even Genia had been willing to help at this task, consuming a good deal of popcorn in the process. When, in the late afternoon, she began to complain of discomfort, Darrie put it down to overeating. Later, when Genia said she was too ill to attend the party, Darrie became more concerned, and over her sister's protests, remained at home with her. Before long she realized the baby was going to be born. In a panic she got Genia into bed and raced to the schoolhouse for Claire.

It was not a difficult delivery, but Darrie was not prepared for the final spasms of pain which left Genia pallid and bathed in sweat, or for the bloody untidiness of the process. When a small, squirming girl-child, red as a lobster and ugly as a frog, was bathed, wrapped in flannel, and bedded down in a clothesbasket, Genia gave a great sigh of relief and went to sleep. In contrast, Darrie was so shattered she felt she would never sleep again. Moreover, she was convinced her sister had given birth to a monster.

To her astonishment, Claire bent the face of an enraptured stranger over the clothesbasket. "Oh, what a little love! What an adorable doll!"

"Do you mean that?"

"Of course I do! Her is lovely—lovely—lovely!" Claire must have realized she was stepping out of character. She straightened up. "She's certainly beyond anything Genia deserves."

Doubtfully Darrie said, "She seems awfully red. And sort of . . . bent."

"They all are, at first. This one has lovely features—not that she won't need every advantage."

Darrie could not believe the long wait was over. Even after she had gone to bed, with the clothesbasket on a chair within arm's reach, her dreams pursued the familiar pattern of creeping hours. There was to be—there was to have been—a Christmas party. Darrie stood alone by a bedraggled tree in the Agency schoolhouse. Paper chains drooped from wilting branches, withered popcorn strings were entangled with cobwebs. Beneath the tree dry pine needles lay in a crazed pattern on the wooden floor. Despair thickened Darrie's heartbeats and stopped the breath in her throat. She had waited for Christmas, and waited, and somehow it had slipped past her so that she must go on waiting without hope. A door opened behind her. A cold wind touched her cheek and stirred the dead branches of the tree. Her father's voice said, "I told you it would be like this, but you have delusions of omnipotence."

"Don't say that!" Darrie cried. "It isn't fair!" A part of the unfairness, though she did not mention this, was that Edward Lord and her father were the same man.

With a dream's illogic, a doll—new and beautifully dressed—appeared among the dusty pine needles on the floor. Darrie snatched it up. "I'll show you!" she cried to Papa-Lord. But when she turned only Genia stood there, smiling that secret knowing smile. Darrie thrust the doll into her sister's arms. Genia's hold on it slackened. The doll fell, face down. Genia, still smiling, turned away.

The dream dissolved and reformed.

Now she and Genia waited on the beach. The tide rose slowly, inch by inch. When it reached the black rocks they would be free to go. Each wave hissed toward the rocks and, rattling pebbles, withdrew again, leaving its shape for a brief moment in a pattern of froth on the sand. Something small and red washed toward them in the waves, retreated, drifted in again. Dear God! It was a baby, newlyborn. "I'll save it!" Darrie cried, and tore at recalcitrant shoelaces. Genia only smiled and shook her head. "It's no use," she said. "Can't you see, the tide's going out? It's being carried off to sea."

"No—no! It can't be!" Darrie stared into the waves. But Genia was right—the child was gone. "You wicked girl! Unnatural—*wicked*!" The slow sweet smile, the knowing smile, curved Genia's lips. "I'll go," she said, "if that's what you really want." She moved toward the sea, her steps slow as death. Waves ruffled about her feet. Billows raised the edges of her skirt so that it stood out, flowerlike, from the slender stem of her waist. The water rose. Mist rolled in, now hiding, now revealing, the dwindling figure. "Come back! Oh, Genia, I didn't mean it—I didn't!" But she was gone. A faint cry came from across the water. "A-ah! A-a-ah!"

Instantly Darrie was awake. Sweat cooled her palms. She slipped out of bed and leaned over the clothesbasket. When the child continued to stir and cry, she took it out of the basket and got back into bed, holding it in the curve of her arm. It quieted then, and slept. On her other side, Genia too slept peacefully.

She could hear, in the night silence, the sleep-thickened breathing of Paul Armstrong in the room across the hall. Of all the household, she thought, in this predawn of Christmas Day, she was the only one awake. But she would rather lie wakeful than to dream again.

Claire proved to be right about the child: quickly it lost its look of rawness and distortion. It had a finely shaped head, wide misty eyes fringed with long lashes, delicate features, tiny starfish hands with nails like bits of enameled jewelry.

Claire could not keep her hands off the little girl. She insisted, on the basis of past experience with nieces and nephews, on bathing and caring for her. She boiled and diluted milk, sweetened it, and held the baby for hours coaxing her to drink.

Genia, who refused to nurse the baby, paid for it in discomfort. Before Darrie and Claire between them had managed to dry her breasts, she lay ill for several days, at one time sinking into a feverish stupor that left Darrie weak with fright. Then suddenly, miraculously, she was well again. Color came back into her face, sparkle to her eyes. She got up, shaky at first but eager to be at life, and came downstairs on Darrie's arm to eat her New Year's Day dinner.

The baby did not interest her. "I don't feel she's mine. I can't pretend. . . ."

"She *is* your's! She's adorable! A lovely, perfect little thing—"

Genia only laughed. "I didn't expect you to go to pieces over any baby, Darrie. You, so self-possessed—"

"She's not just any baby—she's yours! Your own flesh and blood. You *can't* be so indifferent—"

For the briefest moment something alien, something implacable and feral, looked out of Genia's eyes. It was a flash of steel touching warm flesh, a sudden icy wind gone before it could be assessed. "Not mine alone," Genia said. Then she was her warm smiling self again. Darrie thought she must have imagined the fleeting change.

In one way, Genia's insight proved to be more sound than Darrie's: Claire, once she had held the baby and tended her, wanted it for her own. She was as able as Genia to forget who was the true mother. Tight-lipped, she told Darrie, "You can't take her back with you—you know that. You *have* to give her to me."

A month ago—ten days ago—Darrie would not have dared hope for so easy a way out. Now, with the baby a human entity —warm, helpless, irresistibly appealing—Darrie's feelings were the exact reverse. She refused to consider any course other than keeping the baby with them. How that could be accomplished was another matter.

At least she need not be hurried into action. She had been prepared for Claire to say, as soon as the child was born, "Get out! There's no further excuse to stay on with us!" On the contrary, Claire now made every excuse to keep them at Neah Bay, as if time must inevitably play into her hands. Genia, she said, was not well enough to travel; the baby was not yet settled on a proper mixture of milk and water; now, in January, the weather was too bad for a trip to Port Townsend.

This last excuse did have some validity. Gales blew in daily from the North Pacific. The very violence of the wind raked the sky free of clouds, and the sun shone brightly but without warmth. When Darrie tried to take advantage of clearing skies to walk along the beach, she found the wind knife-cruel, chilling her to the bone in spite of any wrapping.

Waiting for the child's birth—a definite and inevitable event—had been hard enough. Waiting for a solution to a problem that could not be solved, hoping for a miracle when no miracle could be expected, was worse. Darrie's feeling of rootlessness, of drifting, became obsessive. Sometimes when she wakened in the night she felt she was entering a dream state rather than escaping it. She would slip from bed to stand above the clothesbasket where the baby's head was a dimly seen but reassuring shadow on the pillow. By leaning close she could hear the faint whisper of the child's breath. The infant lived. She was truly there. But her very existence added to Darrie's sense of unreality. She had struggled, schemed, and fought to bring Genia to Neah Bay, Genia and some imagined projection of Genia's self. Or, more accurately, some projection that had been impossible to imagine. Now they were three, where two had come here.

All Darrie's life she had heard the common phrase, "the miracle of birth." It was not birth itself that made the miracle, it was the coming into existence of a new being, a personality whole and alive and bearing the tremendous potential of growth and life, of happiness and despair, of good and evil. All these possibilities existed in the small but perfect envelope of flesh lying here in the Armstrongs' clothesbasket.

Once these thoughts, overwhelming but alive with challenge, began to turn in Darrie's mind, she would find it impossible to go back to sleep. She woke oftenest in the very core of night when darkness was complete. She would try to recapture the trick of sleeping, pressing her eyelids shut, willing her mind to emptiness. The effort seemed only to drive sleep further away.

Reconciling herself to this she would let her eyes remain open to explore the room. In the darkness its corners disappeared. It became a sphere obscurely revealed in the faint light that seeped through the single window. Sometimes this sphere shrank until she could feel it drawing about her as cruelly as the Indians' close-hauled fishnets closed about their catch. It seemed impossible then that the baby sleeping so close beside her, or Genia within the touch of her hand, could share this straitened space. She must be solitary in a shrinking cocoon whose meshes would, in a moment, shut off her breath and heart.

Again, when it seemed this illusion could not be borne a second longer, it gave way to one more terrifying: the emptiness of the sphere widened and spread outward into space. There were no walls, no window, no limits of any sort. No use to call or reach out; there was no one in this empty world but herself. She floated utterly alone in endless space. Yet nothingness itself could exist in action and in motion. The darkness around her rippled and pulsed, carrying her with it so that she rose and fell, swayed, and returned, and rose again.

A dreadful dizziness more of the soul than of the flesh would seize Darrie then. She would clench her teeth, sink her fingers talon-like into the covers, and will herself to be still, to resist this cosmic undulation, to recapture her own sense of identity. If only she were back in her own bed at Cedarhaven, if only these last months could be wiped out of memory. . . . But there was the child, the tangible and irrefutable proof that the months had passed.

Genia grew restive. "Why don't we go home, Darrie? It's so dull here."

"Have you figured out what to do with your baby?"

"It's not my baby!"

"You brought her into the world!"

Genia shrugged. On this subject she was adamant: she accepted no responsibility for the child. Now, with only a mild show of interest, she said, "Claire wants her—what better can we do?"

Darrie set her teeth and turned away. Over her shoulder she said, "If there was nothing else against it—and there is!—Claire isn't the right kind of person to bring her up. She's selfish and unkind."

"Don't be cross! I'm only thinking of an easy way to—"

"An easy way! You little bitch!" Darrie didn't know where the word had come from. She had never spoken it aloud in her life.

Genia stared at her. The full lower lip trembled. Two crystal tears formed, quivered, and dissolved on her cheeks.

It is incredible, Darrie thought. She's crying because I called her a bad name—and well deserved!—but she has never shed a tear over having a fatherless child. It was beyond comprehension. "Don't cry—I'm sorry." This was ridiculous, for her to apologize to Genia.

"I can't bear it if you're mad at me. Truly I can't. You're all I have."

"All right. I won't be mad. But the baby is going home with us. We'll find a way. And I've been thinking about a name. We can't go on saying 'she'. We'll call her Elaine."

"Elaine What?"

"That I don't know—yet."

It was one thing to announce with firmness that the child was going home with them, another to find a reasonable excuse for appearing at Cedarhaven with an infant. Darrie was almost relieved that, as January wore on, continuing storms made it possible to put off action.

CHAPTER 14

The Makahs took the weather to be a bad omen. It was unnatural for the sun to shine so brightly in what ought by rights to be a wet moon. The strong wind was a punishment, perhaps the breath of an angry spirit. It would do great harm before it left them.

One morning the storm brought a dead whale close to shore where it wallowed in the breakers in grisly simulation of living motion. The Makahs were elated. This was a good omen, possibly good enough to offset the evil weather. The entire village turned out to salvage this gift from the depths. Naked men waded into the breakers and attached lines by which the monster was pulled inshore on the rising tide.

When the sea began to ebb, the whale was left high and dry. At once the village burst into frenzied activity. Darrie and Genia walked to the schoolyard where they could watch.

The Makahs knew they had only brief hours before the sea would again claim their prize. The men attacked with knives, slicing off blubber in great blood-flecked slabs. With each new opening in the carcass the smell grew worse. When the whale's interior was breached, spilling blood and entrails into the sand, the stench became so nauseating that Darrie and Genia had to move upwind, finding a new vantage point on the steps of the residency.

From there they watched the Indians hack out the choicest part of the whale, a saddle-shaped piece of blubber from behind the head, and carry it on a long pole to the Chief's house.

During all this cutting and chopping the women of the village scrambled about barefooted in the slime and gore. They used clamshells to dip into pockets of the animal's flesh or hollows of the sand, transferring to cans or pots or waterproof baskets the oil they collected. Apparently they enjoyed being covered with blood and filth, for all the Indians, men and women alike, pushed one another, fell down in the slime, scrambled up again, slapped one another with strips of blubber, and, in general, acted as if they were engaged in the jolliest possible game.

It sickened Darrie, but when she suggested going back to the farmhouse Genia protested: "It's exciting! If it weren't for the smell I'd go closer. Do let's stay!"

Perhaps, Darrie thought, excitement was keeping Genia warm. She herself was chilled to the bone. Presently she walked back to the house, leaving Genia alone.

It was an hour or more later when Genia burst into the Armstrong kitchen, her cheeks scarlet with excitement, or cold, or both. "Darrie, you should have waited! The mother of that little boy at school—the cute one they call Nooga—came over and asked us to the whale party tonight. I said we'd go."

A potato that Claire was peeling dropped out of her hand and splashed into the pan of water. "You wouldn't dare!"

"Why not? They invited us. You could go too if you wanted to."

"Spend an evening with those filthy savages? I should say not! You'd bring home fleas—or worse."

Genia was undisturbed. "Leave the washtub in the kitchen, and a fire burning. We'll take baths when we get home."

Uneasy about the prospect, Darrie ran through quickening twilight to the Agency. When Lord answered her knock she asked if it would be wise for Genia and herself to attend the whale party.

"Wise? Hardly! You're not apt to be harmed, if that's what you mean. But you won't have a comfortable time."

"Genia's set on going."

"Hmm . . . suppose I escort you?"

"Oh! I didn't mean to ask that!"

"No, of course not. But it's a good idea. I'll come by for you after supper."

"Well, thanks, then. I will feel safer."

When they reached the center of the village later in the evening, the whale party was in full swing indoors and out. A huge bonfire lit up the great curved cage of ribs, stripped white, all that was left of the honor guest. Makahs sat by the fire, or moved about, eating boiled whale meat. Lord said they had been eating constantly ever since stripping the whale. Occasionally someone, reaching complete saturation, wandered onto the beach, vomited, and came back renewed to the feast.

For a time Lord and the two women stood about near the edge of the circle of firelight. They were thoroughly uncomfortable. The fire was blisteringly hot on their faces while the wind at their backs felt like so many icicles being thrust under their collars and around their shoetops. The din was frightful: dogs barked, people yelled and sang, drums throbbed.

Some of the Indians came close, looked at their white guests out of the sides of their eyes, and went off without speaking.

Darrie said, "We shouldn't have come."

"They're just being polite," Lord assured her. "Giving us time to decide whether we want to stay."

"I already know—I don't want to."

"Oh, Darrie! Don't be stuffy! It'll be fun."

Darrie started to protest again, but it was too late. The required interval for decision must have passed: an Indian approached them and said, "You come. Good! House now."

It might have been an invitation but it sounded very like an order. Lord answered, "Very well, Ubatsk." Meekly they trailed after the Indian into one of the houses.

A fire burned in the center of the room. Some of the smoke escaped through a hole in the roof, more remained inside where it blended with the smell of whale meat in various stages of rawness and decomposition. On a bench sat three children who had been smeared with something sticky and daubed with feathers until they looked like large ill-used birds. Darrie supposed one of them was Nooga, but in the smoke-filled, fire-lit room she could not be sure.

There might have been a dozen people in the house, all in such good spirits their number seemed to be doubled. Hospitality, in the ordinary sense of the word, was lacking: members of the family grinned at the visitors, spoke unintelligibly among themselves, and went on about their affairs. Apparently the guests were expected to join in the fun, but it was like coming into the middle of a game where both rules and objectives were unknown.

They had been inside the house only a few minutes when something struck the door with a splintering crash. This caused intense delight and merriment. One of the feathered children was especially moved, hiding her head in her arm and going into a paroxysm of giggles.

Even Lord looked startled, and exchanged some words in the Makah tongue with their host. They had scarcely finished speaking when another crashing blow was dealt to the door. Under cover of renewed laughter Lord explained to the girls. "Nooga's sister—in the middle there—has reached marriageable age. A suitor and his friends are banging on the door with a harpoon to show honorable intentions."

"Will they let him in?"

"Oh, not tonight! It's not good form to be too willing."

In spite of the general confusion, Darrie noted that Ubatsk, who had brought them here, kept close to them. Apparently he was head of the household, father to Nooga and the marriageable sister. She studied him further. He was rather good-looking—tall and well-built, with the wedge-shaped face and bladelike nose common to Coast Indians. In his case however there was symmetry to his features that set him apart. His mouth was well-formed, his teeth beautifully strong and even, his eyes brilliant and less heavily lidded than most of the Makahs. Darrie remembered that a Spanish fort had been established here a century ago. The shape of Ubatsk's eyes and a certain lightness of his skin suggested the infiltration of another blood.

Each attack on the door seemed to delight their host. He responded to it by crowing and slapping his sides, meanwhile watching his guests for their reaction. Darrie managed a faint smile which she hoped was approving. Genia clapped her hands and shouted, "Oh, wonderful! This is fun!"

"For heaven's sake, do you want them to break in?"

"They won't break in," Lord assured her. "They'll leave soon. There's a ritual to all these affairs."

He was proved right. Soon the noise outside the door ceased, while the hubbub within the room mounted. A wooden plate of food was brought to the guests. Lord, to whom it was offered first, took a morsel in his fingers and appeared to eat it. Darrie too helped herself, but when she raised the food to her lips she let it slip into her palm and later dropped it on the floor. Genia took a bite, choked, converted the sound to laughter, and apparently ate her share of the offering.

Simply thinking of the food was sickening. Darrie swallowed, kept swallowing, and pondered escape. Lord must have seen her difficulty for he said, "We'll get out of here," and addressed Ubatsk in the Makah language.

The man's brows drew down in a menacing scowl and he barked a reply that, without being intelligible, was clearly angry. He stepped between his guests and the door, and gestured toward someone else in the room. A squaw waddled up to them, her manner placating. "You stay, please?"

Lord said something Darrie did not understand, but his manner was decisive. Ubatsk apparently realized he was not going to detain his guests. The squaw became his scapegoat. With a cry of rage he struck her across the face. She cowered away, but he struck again, and again.

Under cover of this diversion, Lord got the door open and shepherded the girls outside. "Come on," he urged. "Let's get a move on."

When they stepped away from the shelter of Ubatsk's house the wind struck at them, whipping Darrie's skirts and making her clutch at Lord's arm to keep from falling. From there on he kept his arm firmly about her waist.

At the Armstrong door he said, "Come over in the morning, Darrie. I want to talk to you."

She was too spent to do more than nod agreement.

Darrie assumed that Lord meant to give her a scolding for attending the whale party. She was no more than awake in the morning than she began to speculate on what form the reprimand would take, and found herself rather looking forward to reproof as if it might be pleasant to have someone else take a position of authority.

"Genia," she said; "Genia!" and touched her sister's shoulder.

"Oh, please! Let me sleep."

Sighing, Darrie turned away from the bed, reaching quickly for her clothes in the icy room. Now that the baby was born, Claire didn't care how late Genia slept. It gave her that much more time with little Elaine. This morning the bed-basket was not even in the room; Claire had made Darrie's and Genia's attendance at the party an excuse to keep Elaine in her own room for the night.

When Darrie reached the kitchen, Claire, with the baby on her arm, was heating a bottle on the newly kindled fire. The stove still snapped and groaned at the sudden change of temperature.

"Go ahead and fix breakfast," Claire ordered. "I'll feed Elaine."

Darrie stopped to slip a finger inside the scrap of flesh that would some day be a hand as large and strong as her own. Claire pulled the baby away. "Her's starved, poor dear! Her doesn't want to play, does her?"

Darrie had to turn away to keep from making an angry retort. She ought to snatch Elaine from Claire's arms and shout, "*You* get breakfast! This is *my* child—I'll see to her." But the truth was that Elaine was no more her child than she was Claire's, and they were all here by Claire's sufferance. The necessity to get away filled Darrie's mind while her hands stirred oatmeal, ground coffee, sliced bread to toast in the rapidly heating oven.

Paul came in, yawning, scratching at an overnight stubble of beard. "Where's Genia?"

Claire's disapproval flashed in a glance that assessed tousled hair, shirt open at the throat, the general puffy untidiness of an outdoors man temporarily confined.

It was Darrie who answered him: "Genia's sleeping in."

"Yeah? How was the whale party?"

"So-so." Actually it had been awful at the time, and was worse in retrospect. Last night Darrie had been too concerned with getting away from the village to think about the blows Ubatsk had given his wife. Remembering them now, she winced, and wondered how badly the poor creature had been hurt. No doubt she was used to this sort of knocking about. No one had seemed disturbed by it, the squaw least of all. Darrie remembered that soon after they had come here one of the Makahs had struck a slave woman—harder perhaps than he had intended. She had been thrown outside the house unconscious and had died there. Even Edward Lord had agreed no action needed to be taken; the man striking the blow had meant no harm. Oh! she thought, what an abominable place this was! Lord's presence was the only thing that made it even remotely endurable.

Still too queasy from the night before to enjoy her breakfast, she put aside her emptied coffee cup and got her heavy shawl from behind the door.

"Where are you going?"

"Mr. Lord wants to see me."

"The dishes—"

Darrie closed the door firmly on Claire's protest.

Rounding the corner of the house, she fell back for an instant under the impact of the wind. Then she tightened her hold on the shawl and went on. Even the storm, she thought, was preferable to Claire's company.

Edward Lord admitted her to the Agency and led her to the office. Even here the wind made itself felt: from the hearthfire, tongues of flame roared upward to disappear into the chimney; the house timbers creaked under a sudden gust; salt encrusted the glass of the seaward windows.

Lord had drawn two chairs before the fire. He motioned for Darrie to be seated. "I asked you here to talk about your sister."

He spoke with an emphasis that dispelled all thought of Claire and the Armstrong household. She stared at him, her mind wiped clean. "What about Genia?"

"You'll have to get her out of here. She's trouble."

"That's unfair! She hasn't done a thing—"

"It's not what she does. It's what she is."

Darrie's anger flamed. To think she had just been telling herself what a good friend he was! Words of defense for Genia came to her mind, and were discarded.

It was Lord who broke the silence that was growing awkward. "There's a term in law for anything dangerous but enticing—an open pit, a treacherous pool. It's called, legally, an attractive nuisance. A man is not allowed to keep such on his property."

Low-voiced, Darrie said, "You're cruel."

"I am, and I regret it. But I am responsible here. I blame myself somewhat for last night. When Ubatsk's squaw invited Genia—that was ridiculous, if I had stopped to think. She'd never have done it on her own. Ubatsk had sent her."

"What difference who asked her?"

"A great difference. Ubatsk would be interested in a white woman—in any woman—for one reason only."

"I don't believe that!"

"Why not? The Indians are casual about sex. They accept the fact that whites have certain tabus about it. But they're not fools. They have surely reasoned that Genia has already broken these tabus. The condition that protected her at first is—" He shrugged. "Now, obviously they are thinking of her as a woman, and available. If she stays here there'll be more trouble. And I won't have it."

"What can we do?"

"The moment the storm lessens I'll send you by canoe to Port Angeles. You'll be able to manage from there."

"But Elaine—the baby! How am I to explain her?"

"That, I am afraid, is your sister's problem. Not mine, nor yours."

"Genia wants—"

"Go on."

It was a shamed whisper: "To leave Elaine with Claire Armstrong."

"That might be wise."

Darrie was standing. "I expected better of you!" she blazed. "I won't allow it!"

"Is the decision yours to make?"

"I'll make it mine! By God, I'll keep that baby!" The oath had slipped easily off her tongue. A thought flashed, bright as a passing arrow: What am I turning into?

Lord said, "You couldn't, I suppose, consider yourself at all? What if you should want to marry—"

"I *don't.*" The emphasis was very nearly an affront, but Darrie made no move to soften it. Anger against him was still hot in her blood. She snatched up her shawl. "We'll go as soon as you make the arrangements. I'm sorry we've been such a trouble to you."

Lord looked at her without answering. His little terrier face was sad, but she knew he was not going to say that she had been no trouble, or that she was a good girl to take her sister's part, or that everything would work out all right in the end. Feeling obscurely betrayed, she went out of the office without a farewell, and he let her go.

The wind, like a great hand on her back, hurried her along the path to the farmhouse.

CHAPTER 15

After lunch Darrie went upstairs to the cold bedroom and crept between the covers. She expected to try to think, to puzzle out the inevitable next step after leaving here. Instead she fell instantly to sleep.

She wakened feeling she had slept for hours. There was no clock in the room. She hurried downstairs to find that it was four o'clock. Winter twilight was closing in.

Except for the baby, asleep in her basket, Claire was alone in the kitchen. She sat by the window to get the last daylight for her sewing which, Darrie knew instinctively, would be something for Elaine.

Darrie said, "Where is everybody?"

"Paul's at the barn."

"And Genia?"

Claire's expression spoke the contempt she kept out of her words. "She said she wanted to find out 'how badly hurt that squaw was.' I suppose you know what she meant—I'm sure *I* don't."

Darrie was already on her way out of the door. The wind was wickedly cold and strong, but she did not stop for a wrap. As she approached the beach, particles of sand stung her cheeks already stunned by cold. Her eyes watered till she could scarcely see the path. She was aware of pins slipping from her hair, braids loosening, and finally a wild russet mane whipping about her neck and shoulders. She was beating with her fists on Ubatsk's door and shouting, "Let me in!" before she realized how wind-torn she must look, and how wildly foolish if Genia was not here. Or, perhaps, if she was here.

But it was too late to reconsider: the boy, Nooga, opened the door and grinned a welcome. "You come. Sister here."

Irrelevant—the comic touch to bring drama down to earth—were last night's tufts of feathers still sticking to his ears. "Come," he repeated, pulling Darrie by the arm so that he could close the door.

Genia came toward her, smiling. There were others in the room: Ubatsk's squaw lying on a pile of mats, an Indian crone bending over her, Ubatsk himself standing by the fire and eating from a shell. Nooga seemed, no doubt by virtue of his dubious English, to be master of ceremonies. He gestured toward the squaw prostrate on her mats. "She hurt. Get fixed. Ready now."

Genia clutched Darrie's arm. Whatever her other emotions might be, she was obviously excited. "They're going to cut it open—the bruises! Can you imagine? Oh, the poor thing—!"

Darrie was beginning to recover her wits. "You're insane to be here. Come away right now."

"No, I want to see it." She pulled away from Darrie and went closer to the Indian woman.

Repelled, yet fascinated, Darrie too looked at the injured squaw. The firelight, poor as it was, revealed the swelling of purple bruises on her cheeks. The other woman, bending above the patient, was shriveled with age, her hair as gray as hanging spruce moss. Her hands hovering over the injured woman's face were as fleshless and unclean as a bird's talons. She thrust a knotted corner of blanket into the squaw's mouth and picked up a short-handled knife. There was a flashing movement. The blade caught the firelight. Then, from the squaw's cheek, blood began to ooze in thick, dark drops. The victim made no sound, but Darrie could see her jaw muscles knot as she clenched her teeth on the blanket.

From the fireside Ubatsk watched, groping in his clamshell dish for some choice morsel, and licking his fingers after he had transferred it to his mouth.

Darrie moved toward Genia, took her arm. "Come on!"

Ubatsk cried out something in his own tongue. He set his food dish down and came toward them. In a single flash of motion, and before Darrie could protest, he had dipped a finger in the squaw's swelling blood and smeared it across Genia's cheek. In a peremptory tone he instructed Nooga, pointing at him his red-stained finger.

"He says, 'Our klootchman now—our woman. One of us.' He likes her."

For an instant the red stood out on Genia's cheek, startling against her pallor. Then the flood of her blushes rose to drown it. "Oh—!" she gasped, "Oh—!" and backed away from Ubatsk. He followed her, half-smiling, his movements cat-smooth and sure.

"No!" Darrie screamed, and stepped between them.

This time when she said, "Come!" her sister obeyed. They found the door, fumbled for the latch, and stepped into the salty freshness of wind-swept air.

They were nearly to the farmhouse before Genia spoke. "I only went to see . . . to see if she was badly hurt. Truly, I didn't know. . . ."

"When we get to the house, we start to pack."

"You said we couldn't go home yet."

"You *want* to stay, now that—" Now that you've scented danger—was that what she meant? "We're starting home the minute this storm lets up. Meantime, you're not to set foot outside the house. You hear me?"

Upstairs, in the room they shared, Darrie poured cold water into the bowl and scrubbed Genia's face. Her sister stood docile as a child. When the towel and washcloth were hung away, Genia came and laid her head on Darrie's shoulder. "Don't be mad at me, please! How could I know?"

Darrie put her arms around Genia and held her close. They seldom exchanged caresses—it was not Darrie's way. This moment was unique, heavy with emotion shared and emotion carefully guarded from sharing. You were frightened, Darrie thought, for the moment. But you deliberately sought out danger. Don't you know that, my little sister? Or don't you care? Who will it be that keeps you from destroying yourself? Must I be the one because I know you best? But that wasn't entirely true: Edward Lord had seen Genia with eyes clearer than her own. If only Papa could be made to see, to understand . . . but even as her mind formed the wish she knew that was impossible.

"You aren't mad, Darrie?" Genia was smiling, now that she was safe again, the honey-sweet disarming smile.

"I'm not mad. But we are going to pack—*now*."

That night, as the hours crept by without bringing sleep, Darrie told herself it was because she had slept too long in the afternoon. Again, Elaine's basket was in the Armstrong's room. "It's warmer," Claire had claimed, "with the chimney running through it." This was true enough, and Darrie had let it pass because so soon they would be taking the child away. Now she missed Elaine's presence, the tiny sound of her breath. Darrie turned and twisted on the pillow. Beside her, Genia breathed softly, her lips curved in the memory of a smile. Elaine was the least of Genia's worries.

The gray light of winter dawn was touching the bedroom window when Darrie imagined she heard sounds foreign to the night. She sat up in bed. A shout—at this hour? Listening intently, she heard the sound again. She slipped from bed and went to the window. There was a light offshore. At first its significance escaped her. Not infrequently ships put in here for water, or some needed item of supply. Although the roadstead was exposed . . . Exposed! Her heart gave a hard and sudden beat as realization struck her: now, in this storm, no ship should be in Neah Bay. To enter it, running before a gale, was to enter a bottleneck and face the bitter choice of Bahad Reef or the breakers of the open beach.

She saw now that lights were moving along the shore from the Makah village. The shouts would have come from there. Like vultures, the Makahs waited for the death of a ship to strip it as clean as they had stripped the bones of the whale. No Makah shack was too mean, Lord had told her, to be without a chair or chest, a lantern or a bit of sail, salvaged from some past shipwreck.

Knowing this, Darrie strained her eyes toward the light offshore. It seemed now to be nearer the reef. She closed her eyes and prayed, then scorned herself for praying. If God could save the craft by the lifting of His hand, could He not do so without her puny intervention? More to the point that people should do something. Herself, perhaps? She could try, she thought. She could offer.

She dressed with shaking fingers, put on her warmest clothes—they had been laid out for the trip home—and crept downstairs.

A few stars still burned in the lifting sky, but day was nearly here. Darrie ran along the path to the Agency. In the yard, at the base of the flagpole, several men were staring so intently seaward they failed to notice her approach: Lord, Cutler, who ran the trading post, and the schoolmaster.

The ship, a barkentine, was caught now in the trough of waves that rolled beachward one after another like an endless and moving range of mountains. Sometimes only the tips of her masts were visible, writing wild messages on the pale sky. Again, her hull rolled into view as she lay over sickeningly on a rising wave.

"Can't you do something? Can't anyone do anything?"

Lord looked at her and shook his head. "They've got their anchors out, of course. But they won't hold."

"And no one could go out to them?"

This time he looked at her in silence, as if the question deserved no answer.

The schoolmaster said, "If there was a lifesaving station here, trained men, the right kind of boat—" He coughed rackingly into his handkerchief, and Cutler told him, "Fred, you ought to go in. You'll catch your death out here in this wind."

"I've got my death," he said. "It's only a matter of time."

Darrie shuddered with more than cold. He could be speaking for those on the doomed ship as well as for himself.

Dawn had come as they watched. The eastern sky flowered in red and yellow, and a winter sun thrust fingers of cold light across the mountains behind Neah Bay. It caught the brass masthead light on the barkentine and made it, for an instant, bright as a diamond.

Now, in the daylight, Darrie could see figures moving on the ship, clinging, as they moved, to rail or rigging.

"By God!" Cutler said, "They're going to launch a small boat."

"The fools!"

"They might get in closer to shore."

"And be broken up in the surf!"

They all watched in sickened fascination as a lifeboat was raised in its davits and put over the rail. The Indians, Darrie saw, had gathered at the shoreward end of the reef, and were watching with the same intensity.

"Dirty devils!" the storekeeper muttered. "Ready to grab anything that goes adrift, on the reef or off."

The ship's boat was out over the side now, with perhaps a half dozen people inside it. As the barkentine rolled down with the wind the small boat licked the top of a wave, lifted again with the opposite roll of the ship, lifted . . . lifted . . . and crashed into the ship's side. The crunch of broken wood carried to them on the wind along with a faint cry of terror. When the next wave separated ship and boat, men fell like rag dolls into the sea.

Darrie could stand no more. She turned and ran back to the farmhouse.

Throughout an endless day she refused to look again at the dying ship. An air of morbid excitement pervaded the household and, she had no doubt, the entire Agency. Paul Armstrong came and went, reporting events as they occurred. For a time, as the tide was turning, it had seemed the ship's anchors might hold. But when twilight closed in it was seen that she was again moving inexorably toward the breakers. Two people, one of them a child, had been lashed to empty casks and lowered into the sea in the hope they would be washed ashore alive. Both had drowned. An effort had been made to launch a Makah dugout, but it had quickly swamped and the Indians had refused to try again.

"No use pushing the idea," Armstrong told the women. "Couldn't get alongside the ship if they did go out. It's just the notion of doing something—anything. . . ."

This was the real agony shared by all—the standing by idle and helpless while death closed in.

There was no attempt to sleep that night. Paul joined the men in their futile watch at the Agency Residence. Darrie, Genia, and Claire sat about the farmhouse silent, almost stunned, by the tragedy unfolding beyond their reach.

Just past midnight a sudden change took place. The wind, whose unrelenting pressure on the walls of the house had seemed almost an assault on their own flesh, was gone. Now they heard a sound the wind's screaming had concealed before: the steady thunder of surf breaking on the beach.

Darrie's instant thought was that the ship would now be safe. She caught up her shawl and ran outside to see the miracle. Paul met her on path. "She's gone," he said. "She's on the reef. I couldn't stand to see it."

When Darrie tried to pass him he caught her by the arm, too overwrought to realize the cruelty of his strength. "Don't go—don't look!"

"But the storm—the wind! It's stopped!"

"The sea won't go down for hours. She's *gone,* I tell you!"

Darrie swayed and would have fallen except for his hold.

*

In the cold dawn the quiet was so unnatural as to be itself a threat. It had become normal to walk bent against the wind, to thrust oneself against a ceaseless opposing force. Now Darrie's body seemed almost weightless as she walked toward the Agency.

There had been an attempt at rescue work after the wind had ceased. She knew a few crewmen had been saved, more had perished. Some bodies had washed ashore. The tragedy was so great her mind no longer attempted to cope with it. It had happened. She had been powerless to change events. Later, perhaps, she could assess the facts and relate them to herself. Now they were pushed into some recess of her mind. They were remote from the moment, too awful to be faced.

Giddy with sleeplessness and exhaustion, she clung to one solid fact: the storm was over and they must leave Neah Bay.

Entering the Agency hall she saw, through an open door, several blanket-wrapped bundles lying on the floor. It took her a moment to realize they were bodies. Bodies! Yesterday live and sensate, terrified certainly, no doubt scenting doom, but alive. Now, in a gray dishwater dawn, it was all over. No more struggle. No more pain. No more hope. . . .

She took hold of the doorframe to steady herself before she walked into the office and closed the door on the sight of the wrapped bundles. Time had lost its normal rhythm; ten minutes might have passed, or an hour, when the door opened.

Edward Lord said, "They told me you were here."

"We're ready to leave."

"Leave? Oh—oh, yes!" Apparently he had forgotten his own dictum, laid down so forcefully—when was it? Yesterday? The day before? Last week?

Darrie shook her head, but there was no clearing of her thoughts.

"There'll be people here soon to investigate the wreck, identify. . ." He let that go. "You should be gone before that. Tomorrow morning, at the change of tide—the Makahs won't launch a canoe except on high tide, you know. It'll be an early start."

"That doesn't matter."

"And, Darrie, there's an explanation I've thought of for the baby. The *Arabella* sailed from a Mexican port. Probably no one here will ever check the passenger list. There were two families aboard—all lost. They tell me one was an infant."

Darrie stared at him, trying to relate his words to herself. Some essential point of contact was missing. She mouthed the word, "Drowned?"

"Yes. Don't you understand what I'm telling you? If you say this baby of your sister's was rescued somehow from the shipwreck, no one will challenge you. It's the best chance you'll get. Take it!"

Darrie forced her mind to the issue. It seemed unimportant. More to quiet the Agent than because she saw merit in his plan, she said, "Yes, I see. I'll do that. . . ."

The storm, the period of threat without action, had given Darrie a sense that nothing would change. Yet now in the fresh rain-filled dawn they were wrapping Elaine in shawls, their carpetbags were by the kitchen door, Paul was bundled into a greatcoat waiting to take them to the beach.

"You coming, Claire?" he asked. "Wrap up good if you are."

Claire had been holding the baby. She looked at her hushand across the swathed bundle with hatred in her eyes. It occurred to Darrie suddenly that Claire might blame him for their childlessness. Could a *man* be at fault?

"Well?" Paul urged.

"I'm not going."

He shrugged and went out the door. Genia had already gone ahead without a farewell. Perhaps she had expected Claire to accompany them to the canoe, or perhaps she didn't care as long as she made her own escape.

Darrie and Claire were alone in the kitchen, with the child still in Claire's arms. The advantage was hers. She knew it, and blazed defiance. "I won't give her up! Your sister doesn't care—why should you? Go on! They're waiting for you!"

Darrie was afraid to struggle over Elaine lest the child be hurt. She forced herself to act with coolness, sat down at the kitchen table, with a steady hand poured coffee still hot from breakfast into the cup at her place. "I can wait," she said, "and so can they."

Claire's face was withered, bloodless. "You can do *anything*, can't you, Mrs. God? Here—in my own kitchen—" Her throat seemed to close. She pressed Elaine so tight the baby whimpered. Claire was instantly contrite. She drew the shawl from the child's face and crooned, "I wouldn't hurt you, Precious! No, I wouldn't

—not ever, ever, ever. . . ." Under the soothing voice and the gentle swaying of Claire's arms, the baby quieted. Claire's face, bent above Elaine, was alive again, warm with adoration.

She lifted brimming eyes to Darrie. "Haven't you any pity? Leave her—oh, please leave her! I love her so—I *need* her! You don't know what it is to want a child, year after year."

Darrie was used to seeing anger, hostility, contempt, in Claire's eyes, but not tears. Tears made them childish and vulnerable. She said, "I'm sorry. I'm terribly sorry. But I have to take her."

"Why? *Why*? How can you explain her? What chance will she have? Think of her, if you won't think of me."

"She'll be all right."

"If you expect help from that—that—from *her mother*—"

"I don't."

Claire said again, with a sort of helpless stubborness, "I won't give her up."

Various possibilities went through Darrie's mind: Paul might grow impatient and come back. "Don't be a fool—give the child up!" he'd say, with a man's impatience with feminine illogic. Edward Lord might be called in to arbitrate. Would he be on Darrie's side? Of course he would, from moral right if not from sound judgment. Or suppose she walked, empty-handed, to the waiting boat and said, "Genia, I've left your child behind. You'll never see her again." No use to think Genia's response would be other than relief and delight. "Oh, Darrie, I'm glad—truly I am!" After a time, Darrie thought, I would forget her too. Papa wouldn't need to be disturbed. . . .

With the image of her father, Darrie's resolve hardened. A stubborn contempt for the easy way out made her say, "You have to give her up, Claire. She isn't yours to keep." She rose from the table, buttoned her coat, and held out her arms. "Give her to me."

For a long moment pale eyes glared defiance. Then Claire's face crumpled like a child's. "You've got everything!" she cried. "You *take* everything! You came here, used us, played on my pity —everything—anything to have your own way, you—you—"

The baby might have fallen if Darrie had not been there to take her.

In a flurry of sobs and flying footsteps, Claire was out of the room and up the stairs.

Elaine flexed herself in Darrie's arms and stared upward with eyes as blue and unfocused as a kitten's. Darrie had won, yet she had no sense at all of victory.

When they reached Cedarhaven, after a return trip made more difficult by the baby's presence, Papa was so glad to see them that he made no protest over Elaine. Word of the shipwreck had come ahead of them, and he was inclined to think the sheltering of the "Spanish orphan"—as Elaine immediately was called—was a pretty thing for his girls to have done. In any event, concern for the baby was swallowed up in delight at having his adored Genia back at Cedarhaven—and Darrie too, of course. "Mrs. Duncan did very well, but we did miss your hand at the helm, my dear!"

It was only after a week or two had gone by, and the household had settled into routine again, that Papa challenged the baby's presence.

He had come home early one afternoon to find Darrie in the parlor, cradling Elaine on her arm and coaxing her to finish her bottle. Papa stood before the fire, his coat tails turned up for enjoyment of the heat, and said, "You'll be hearing soon from the baby's relatives, I suppose."

Darrie felt her flesh tighten with surprise and the need for caution, and hoped the sudden tensing had not been noticed. She spoke with careful casualness: "I don't believe she has relatives."

"Nonsense! Everyone has relatives! I understand her parents were lost, but—"

"No one who survived the wreck knew anything about her family." Darrie was able to say this much with a clear conscience.

"But inquiries can be made—will be made. There's a list somewhere of the ship's passengers."

"In some Mexican port, maybe. I understand they keep poor records."

"You certainly aren't deluding yourself that no one will claim the child!"

Elaine had finished all but a few drops of milk. Her eyelids lowered so that lashes more delicate than silk floss lay on her cheeks. Her small mouth was open, the lips stirring with her breath. Darrie wiped away a filming of milk and the pink lips drew together as the rosy fringes of a tiny sea anemone might close when touched by a rude finger. The child was utterly adorable, and hers. *Hers.*

She stood up, moving carefully. "She's asleep. I'll put her in her cradle."

The cradle stood, during the day, in the back parlor. Papa followed Darrie as she moved toward it. "I asked you a question—"

"*Ssh!*"

When Elaine was in the cradle, and covered, Papa said in a low voice but a firm one, "Come back to the fire. I must insist on—"

They were far enough from the cradle now for Darrie to say, "Insist on what, Papa?"

"Something definite. Yes, that's what I mean! You can't keep that child here. You surely know that!"

"Why not?"

"It's obvious! Good heavens—the care, the worry, the expense—"

"A cup or two of milk a day? Oh, Papa, you don't begrudge her that!"

"No—no! Of course not! I'm not a monster! But—well, I'm really thinking of you. A household like this, even without an infant to care for—"

"She's very little trouble. Such a good baby! And I enjoy everything I do for her."

"But it all falls on you. Oh, don't think I haven't noticed that! I would have expected Genia to fuss over the child more than you. But she's such a child herself, maybe her nose is out of joint."

"Maybe."

"In any event, you can't saddle yourself with a child to raise. Why, you'll be getting married one of these days. No man wants to take on a ready-made family."

"Papa, if you'll excuse me, I must see how Cheecha's getting along in the kitchen."

"We haven't finished discussing this." Color came up into Papa's temples when he was annoyed and his handsome nose seemed to tighten and thin down at the nostrils. A fleeting picture, unrelated but painful, crossed Darrie's mind: a Jovian Papa with beaver hat to one side and gold-headed cane grasped like a scepter. Rage, sourceless and undirected, washed away the picture and the pain that accompanied it. Her lips felt tight and ugly as they paid out the words: "There's nothing to discuss."

"After all, my girl, I *am* the head of this house!"

Darrie was sure that nothing could equal the cruelty of her silence, but she could think of no words that would not wound. When she made herself, finally, look up into shamed eyes, their shame was her own. She wanted only to escape. "I'm sorry, Papa, really. I—I have to get dinner."

Again it was a victory without pride.

On her way to the kitchen she stopped to lean again over Elaine's cradle. She knew by now every fold and dimple, every delicately articulated joint, every sea-shell scrap of toenail and fingernail, almost—she felt—each single hair. There was, for example, an especially long eyelash in the corner of Elaine's right lid that curled endearingly upward. A single eyelash more precious to her now than the whole of her own body. She sensed that this was no comparison at all: it was too late to make peace with her own treasonous and despised flesh. But that no longer mattered. Here was Elaine, utterly innocent, utterly vulnerable. A human infant could not survive an hour naked to the winter world. This knowledge trembled through Darrie's flesh in a warm flood of protectiveness. No cruel wind, no whisper of danger, no needle-prick of pain would be allowed to touch this child of hers. No mouthing from Papa of futile threats . . .

She could, and would, protect the child from pain, but she could not protect herself. Her knuckles, pressed to her teeth, stung from sudden pressure. She turned quickly and went into the kitchen.

CHAPTER 16

Before long Stark was able to believe that he had approved, from the start, of keeping Elaine.

She was a good baby, causing little trouble, and besides that she gave them a certain status in the neighborhood. Matrons who, long ago, had given up making friends with Darrie now came bringing clothes and toys for little Elaine. Darrie was submerged in good advice and—Stark was first to admit this—she accepted it with better grace than in the past.

What a generous thing it was, everyone said, giving this orphan a home! And how devoted Darrie was to her! Odd that Genia was not more interested in Elaine—or Lainie, as they had begun to call her. Stark could only conclude that Genia needed a child of her own on whom to lavish her wealth of affection.

The same thought must have been in Darrie's mind because, only a few weeks after the girls got home from their ridiculous vacation, Darrie came to him and said, "Papa, I want to talk to you about Genia."

"Genia? My goodness, *she*'s not in any sort of trouble!"

Darrie gave him an odd look. Being away hadn't made her any easier to understand. "I'm thinking about her future. About getting her married."

That was a queer way to put it. Darrie must have meant "about her getting married." It was a pity the girls' educations had been cut so short. There was nothing he would have liked better than sending them all to some fine finishing school back East where they could have learned the diction and the graces suitable to their station in life.

"Papa, you aren't paying attention."

"Oh? Well, really. . ." His attention had wandered for a moment, it was true. It was only because he was tired. He was tired so often these days. . . . With an effort he recalled what Darrie had said, and told her, "Genia is still very young, my dear. When she finds Mr. Right—"

"Will she find Mr. Right—by herself?"

"Most girls do."

"But Genia is so—" There was a tightening of Darrie's lips; she had always been a little jealous of Genia, Stark thought, as who wouldn't be? Darrie went on: "Genia is so affectionate, so trusting, aren't you afraid she might commit herself to Mr. Wrong before Mr. Right comes along?"

"Oh, I don't think so."

"Well, *I* do. I lie awake nights thinking—"

Stark tapped Darrie playfully on the wrist. "Now, my dear Darrie, you aren't responsible for the whole world. Since the subject has come up, I've been wanting to tell you men do not find a strong-minded woman as attractive as they do a gentler one. You might, in your own interests, give this a little thought."

They were in Stark's bedroom. Darrie had come in bringing a cup of cocoa to his desk as he worked at copying a brief for Lawyer Tripp. Now she turned away from his desk and walked to the window. It had a magnificent view of the harbor, and she stood quietly for a few minutes enjoying it—or so he could only suppose. He began to wonder if he had hurt her feelings. It was not fair, or at least not kind, to measure Darrie against the incomparable Genia. He ought to remember that. He cleared his throat.

As if that had been a signal, Darrie came back to stand beside him. "Papa, won't you—for Genia's own sake—try to arrange a suitable marriage?"

Stark closed the inkwell, blotted his work, and put it in the folder before he allowed himself to speak. "You displease me *very much.* I have never, in all these years, permitted myself to think of any gain to myself—"

Darrie's lips parted. Her eyes widened until russet lashes lay flat against her upper lids and her irises were round as pennies. She gasped, "But I didn't mean—" She had to stop and swallow before she finished: "—*that*!"

Stark was mollified in spite of himself. "I assure you many a man in my position would have taken advantage of the—the situation here—" Looking up, he saw that Darrie had recovered from her first surprise. Her eyes were themselves again, the thick lashes concealing whatever emotions might lie behind them. He thought of telling her that calculation, along with strong-mindedness, was not a desirable feminine trait, but she broke in before he had his sentence formulated.

"Believe me, Papa, I gave you credit for thinking only of Genia's good. Of course you wouldn't want to gain from her marriage. If someone insisted—but no, I don't want to think about that, and I'm sure you don't. Let's think only about Genia. She's quite old enough to marry—"

Stark could not keep from interrupting: "Some girls do marry at her age, I know. But our Genia is so childish, so sheltered—"

"You're right! That's what we have to think of! She's exactly the kind of girl to throw herself away on some ne'er-do-well, some adventurer who would appeal to her generous nature and then break her heart. Oh, really—" It was surprising to see Darrie's genuine concern for her sister. For a moment her hand covered her mouth and her shoulders quivered. "Really, we must protect Genia!"

"We-ell, I must say I hadn't thought of it in just this way."

"Then do, please, think of it. A spring wedding, Papa—wouldn't that be lovely? And Genia would be happier. I'm sure she would. And safer. Although she'd miss you, of course. But better to have her marry someone here in Port Townsend than to go away, like Belle."

That was certainly true. Stark had allowed himself to think of the years going on and on at Cedarhaven, with the mixed blessing of Darrie to run the household and Genia to warm his heart with her charm and her affection. But it wouldn't last forever. Perhaps it would be as well to exert some sort of control, or at least direction. . . .

Darrie was talking on. Really, he couldn't remember when she'd been so wound up. "You know all the important young businessmen in town. You meet them every day. Why not think about who has the most to offer—of course I mean in character and principles! Genia needs a strong, honorable man. You know, Papa, she'll be looking for someone a little bit like you."

"Oh, well—not really. . . ."

"Yes! Yes, she will! You think about this, Papa. Bring some young men home to dinner. Or we could have an evening party or two. After all, Genia's been away at school or—or on vacation. The eligible bachelors haven't had a chance to meet her."

Darrie did something then that was almost out of character. She stooped and kissed him on the top of his head. In this way, her final words were hardly audible, spoken as they were into the thatch of whitening hair that Stark felt gave him a look of real distinction. It sounded as if she said, "Help me, for God's sake." But he must have been mistaken.

He reached for the cocoa Darrie had brought him at the beginning of this strange conversation, and made a little face when he saw the ugly scum that had formed across it. She might have let him enjoy his drink before starting the discussion. Yet her proposal did have merit. Hadn't he, in fact, told himself more than once how happy Genia would be with a child of her own? That did require a husband. Now let's see. . . . There was Abraham Bauer. He had come out from Philadelphia with some money to invest in farmland. And John Tower, who had opened an insurance office and was dabbling in real estate as well. Too bad Eric Bond had left town again—that man was a comer. Last heard from up in Canada. Speaking of Canada, there was Jason Corbett. He came into Port Townsend two or three times a month on business, and was talking of settling here and taking out citizenship.

Oh, there were a dozen young men in town right now who would jump at the chance to marry a lovely young woman like Genia. By God, he thought, there were aspects of marriage that would make any father's gorge rise. But a decent young man respected the innocence of his bride, cherished it as the treasure it was, didn't he. . . ? Stark would certainly have a good talk with anyone who seemed to be getting serious about his little girl. He straightened his shoulders. The young upstart would have to prove himself.

To find a suitor for Genia proved ridiculously easy. After a couple of well-cooked meals in the gracious and orderly Cedarhaven, and after even the briefest exposure to Genia's sunny charm, a young man was panting to be led to the altar.

John Tower was the obvious final choice: well-bred, good appearance, genial, and well-liked. He attended church regularly, belonged to the Masons, and had recently joined the local Long House of the Redfellows. Moreover, he had a good business head. He was interested, along with Judge Swan and others, in plans for the coming railroad, and was reputed to have options on much of the property along the proposed right-of-way.

When John asked for Genia's hand, after Stark had brought the conversation around to his own perfectly natural concern for seeing his daughter safely married, everything seemed to be settled. Everything, that is, except Genia's concurrence.

To his dismay, Stark found her quite disinterested. "Oh, Papa! Truly, I don't want to get married."

"Of course you do! All girls want to get married. You don't want to be an old maid, for heaven's sake!"

"Mmmm . . . I suppose not. But John Tower! Why, he's an utter milksop! It would be no fun to marry him."

"Fun! Well, I must say that's a strange reason for getting married."

"I'm not in love with him, anyway."

"You can't possibly know anything about love. With a good man, love will come—later."

Genia could pout, and did so now. It quite eclipsed her natural beauty and gave her a sullen heavy look.

Stark hardly knew where to go from here. "Wouldn't you like a nice wedding, pretty white dress, lots of flowers, wedding gifts—all the rest of it?"

"You can't afford a big wedding."

"Well, as a matter of fact, John knows our circumstances, and he's offered to advance a little something. It's a loan, of course. But it shows a nice attitude on his part. You'd be safe with him, and happy." Stark was beginning to feel annoyed with Genia and his annoyance warmed to something stronger when she said:

"That's exactly the trouble! He's safe—and stuffy! I'm not interested in him. So there!" She actually flounced out of the room, leaving Stark, who had never before found any reason to discipline her, feeling at a complete loss.

When the conversation was repeated to Darrie, she said, "Don't worry. I'll talk to her."

It was amazing, Stark thought, how women understood each other in matters of this sort. Genia might have wanted only to be coaxed a little, or to have some girlish fears allayed. The next morning she came to him sweet as honeycomb and said she was truly honored with Mr. Tower's attentions and that she would be happy to marry him.

It was a beautiful wedding.

Stark was not completely happy, of course, in losing his adored Genia. Cedarhaven would never be the same without her. But she was moving into a delightful little home that John had purchased for them, only two blocks down the street. As Darrie had pointed out, Genia might have left town when she married. And she was getting a fine husband. . . .

*

Stark had no way of knowing that, while these thoughts were going through his mind, Genia, in her new home, was saying:

"When Belle and Howard were married, they left on the *Eliza Anderson* on *their* honeymoon. The Captain played a wedding march as they left the dock. It was so romantic. . . ."

"I thought, Genia, it would be nice for us to start our married life here in our own home."

"But we'll always be *here*."

"I'm sorry you're disappointed. You didn't tell me any different."

"It wasn't my place to."

"Genia, sweetheart, from now on all I want in life is to please you. If you'll just let me know what you want."

There was a rather long silence before Genia said, "That's kind of you."

"*Kind*? Don't you understand, I love you! I want to make you happy. I'm the luckiest man in the Territory to have won you, I know that. I can still hardly believe it."

"Oh, it's true enough."

"Are you—please be honest with me—are you a little bit afraid of . . . well, of being married?"

Genia looked up through her lashes at her new husband. He had been rosy with blushes during the ceremony and the wedding supper at Cedarhaven. Now he was so pale as to appear ill. His upper lip glistened in the lamplight, and she saw that his hand, on the chair arm, was not quite steady. The beat of her heart quickened. She whispered the words, "I am . . . a little bit . . . afraid."

"Oh, my darling! My little frightened dove! I've wanted to tell you, but it seemed . . . indelicate. Before, I mean. I promise, nothing will be forced on you—nothing! You'll find me the most patient husband in the world. And time—time and patience—will make everything all right. You'll see!"

Genia stole another glance at him. He looked so earnest, so agitated, so determinedly noble she could have laughed. Except that it was, somehow, pathetic too. She rose and smiled at him. "Come on, let's go to bed."

Genia did her best to care for her house, to prepare suitable meals, and to be a good wife. In the first two areas of her married state she received covert assistance from both Darrie and Cheecha. In the relationship with her husband, she sailed uncharted seas. His forbearance aroused only anger, his fumbling and puppy-like anxiety to please stirred her to contempt. He soon realized, as only a fool would have failed to do, that she tolerated his caresses out of the kindness of her heart.

Knowing that she loved small luxuries—the Starkweather household had been of necessity austere—he wooed her with gifts, beginning at first with what he could afford and progressing rather quickly to what he could not afford at all.

A young Mrs. Trevelyan who lived next door became Genia's intimate. On fine afternoons they dressed in their best and went downtown to finger bolts of silk brought from the Orient, tortoise shell combs from the South Seas, fur pieces from Alaska. They tried on feathered bonnets at Mrs. Dearborn's Millinery Salon, and boots at Proctor's. Inevitably they bought items that appealed to them, using, in Genia's case, her husband's credit.

On the first Christmas of their marriage John gave her a sealskin jacket, and talked of building a larger house to please her.

As well as being Christmas, it was Lainie's birthday. Darrie got around the fact that she would not have known the baby's actual birthdate by saying that Christmas was such a splendid time to celebrate they would establish it as Lainie's birthday. No one had reason to dispute the choice, and the family gathered at Cedarhaven to light the Christmas tree and to share a towering three-layer cake crowned with a single candle.

Belle and Howard came from Olympia with little Howie and three-month-old Marian. The Towers, of course, were present.

The surprise of the holiday was the arrival of Eric Bond.

CHAPTER 17

Darrie had put in a long and busy day-before-Christmas.

After a supper early enough to allow for the tree-lighting and exchange of gifts afterward, the family left for Christmas Eve services at the still not-quite-finished church. The services were to be conducted by Howard himself. The boarders were about their affairs, and Darrie was alone in the house with the children—Lainie, and Belle's two babies asleep upstairs.

She put out the candles on the tree—enough must be saved to burn tomorrow night when they would celebrate Lainie's birthday—undressed the child, and put over her nightgown a quilted pink robe she had made for a Christmas gift. In it, she thought, Lainie looked like a very young angel. Holding the child in her arms, she sat down by the dying hearthfire.

A year, she thought. . . . For a whole year she had possessed this unique treasure of living, loving flesh and blood and bone, of quick laughter, of tears as quickly dried, of wide-eyed wonder and growing comprehension.

At first there had been speculation among the neighbors that Lainie's relatives would appear to claim her. "Don't set so much store on that child," Mrs. Nesbit had warned. "It'll be all the worse to give her up—when you have to."

"I'll cross that bridge when I come to it."

"Well, remember what I say—I warned you!"

They might have said so much worse than this. During the first weeks and months of Lainie's life at Cedarhaven it had seemed to Darrie that words and questions filled the air like static electricity. They waited only for that chance stroking of glass rod on cat's fur, or comb on hair, to spark into danger: "Who *is* that child?" "Isn't it odd you girls were gone so long?" "There is something about Lainie's mouth. . . ." If the words were whispered at all they did not come to Darrie's ears, although she waited for them, head high, defiant answer ready.

The drama and effrontery of the Spanish orphan story had stopped the mouths of gossip. Darrie remembered a childhood adage: If you tell a lie, tell a big one; if you tell a big one, make it stick.

Their lie had stuck, and Lainie was hers.

In retrospect she acknowledged gratitude to Edward Lord. He had written to her in midsummer. Holding the envelope in her hands, she had speculated on the exact point at which he had known her identity—long before he had revealed the knowledge to her, she suspected. At first there had been the casual use of her first name, and now this letter. . . .

Well, no matter. He would never betray her. The letter gave that assurance. The schoolmaster had died, predictably. The Armstrongs had been transferred to a post in California. "I recommended this, with strong references to Paul's value," Lord had written. Obviously the transfer had been a deliberate calculation on the Agent's part, another move to make their secret safer.

I could not have managed it without Edward Lord, Darrie told herself. And he had asked nothing in return. Or had he? Had he, by implication, asked the one thing she could not give? In closing the letter he had written, "We won't forget each other, my dear. Although we will not meet again, each has left a mark that time will not erase. For this favor, accept my gratitude."

Now, remembering the letter, Darrie was grateful too. Lainie's future was secure. Without Lord's help she might not have managed that. And Genia was safe now too, though she had handled that alone. John Tower was rising and respected in the community, devoted to Genia. Too devoted. . . ? Could a husband be too devoted? Of course not! It was an ideal marriage. A situation intrinsically difficult and dangerous had been surmounted. There was nothing to worry about.

Looking down at the child in her arms Darrie saw that the rapt gaze of Lainie's dark eyes had clouded with sleep. She recalled her astonishment when these eyes had begun to darken from their cloudy infant-color. But now, as softly brown as melted chocolate, they gave authority to a Spanish heritage. Even as she watched, the lashes quivered above them, and fell to rest on curving cheeks. Unconsciously her hold tightened. The shadow of a smile sweetened Lainie's lips in response.

When the doorbell ground out a summons Darrie was tempted to ignore it. But the east room was vacant and, unlikely as it seemed on Christmas Eve, the caller might be a prospective tenant. With Lainie sleeping in her arms, she went to the door.

Light from the hall lamp shown on the lower half of a face whose upper part was concealed by the shade of a hat brim. Yet even the small revelation—the strong jawline, the firmly held mouth with a slight fullness of lower lip—was enough to stop Darrie's breath. She stepped backward. Her hold on Lainie must have tightened, for the child whimpered and stirred in her arms.

Eric's hat was off now. He too stepped back, his eyes white with surprise.

Darrie could find no greeting. "Good evening" was a banality —a nothing. There must be a right word, but it was beyond her reach. She became aware that Eric was staring not at her but at the child. Sheer nervousness made her laugh. She said, "No—no!" and "*No*!" on a note of rising hysteria.

"It—it isn't—?"

"Of course not!"

The situation was becoming grotesque. Darrie said, "Since you're here, come in."

He came in, closing the door behind him, and followed Darrie into the parlor.

"Take off your coat—you'll be too warm by the fire." Behind these words something mad and irresponsible was saying, "He's *here*—he's come back! It must mean something. . . ."

The child obviously fascinated Eric. Even as he followed Darrie's invitation to remove his coat, his eyes were on Lainie, concerned, speculative. When they were seated he said, "She's not—yours?"

Lainie had fallen back into sound sleep, her body curled toward Darrie's breast. She realized she had been holding the baby in a grasp too rigid to be comfortable. She loosened her hold and let the child relax in the cradle of her arm before she looked at Eric across the fledgling down of sunny hair. She said, "She's not mine the way you mean, but—yes! Yes, she's truly mine."

Eric continued to look at her, and at the child in her arms.

It was an old dream come to life, a dream within a dream: a hearthfire, a man, a woman with a child in her arms—eternal symbol of fulfilled love . . . tonight of all nights when the world celebrated the virgin birth. . . . She thought, Suppose I had said, "Yes, your child and mine! Be glad—rejoice! A child was born!" Could she have truly possessed him then for an evening, an hour, a moment—until he learned the truth? She thought, Did I forego the one chance to reach out and touch you, Eric? The true and secret *you*? Oh, Eric, Eric, why did you come back?

Control was slipping from her. She got to her feet, willed herself not to sway, to fall, and said, "Excuse me. I must take Lainie upstairs."

In her own room it took a while to control the trembling that possessed her like an illness. Eric might grow impatient and leave. Yet even as she told herself this, she was acting on the opposite premise. She bathed her face, ran a dampened comb through the hair on her temples till the wave deepened, pinched color into her pallid cheeks. She started to put on the pearl eardrops that had been her mother's, then threw them down so angrily that one fell from the bureau onto the floor. She wouldn't make a gesture so ingratiating. Yet every move she made, every breath she drew, was supplication.

When she got back to the parlor Eric rose and waited for her to be seated. He had mended the fire, she saw: new chunks of coal glistened through the flames, and the room smelled of fresh smoke.

"I'm sorry to have kept you waiting."

"Don't apologize."

"Could I get you something—coffee, brandy?"

"Nothing, thank you. I can't stay."

Darrie looked at the mantel clock. "Everyone will be home soon from church."

"I'll pay my respects another day."

Then go—go before I say something that can never be unsaid. . . . Her lips were pressed together. Only her mind said the words.

"That child—a niece? Belle's child?"

The statement with its careful blending of truth and less-than-truth had been made so many times the words spoke themselves: "Genia and I were at Neah Bay when the *Arabella* was wrecked. The passengers were all lost, except for a baby. It was a miracle. . . ."

She stopped abruptly. If he could be the one she spoke to, the one she could trust with the truth. . . . But every person lived in his own secrets, locked within his own lies. . . .

Eric was speaking: "Yes, I heard about the wreck. A terrible thing—terrible! About a year ago, wasn't it?"

"Yes."

"It was good of you to take the child."

"I did what I wanted to."

Eric lifted his hand. He was half smiling. "All right, then. Take no credit. I don't want to quarrel over it."

Darrie asked, "What do you want? What brings you back?" Her mind added the words: "—back here, of all places."

"Oh, I've been in B.C., Oregon, California, but I always meant to come back here."

"You've come to stay this time?"

"I hope so. I've bought the Winston house—or had an agent buy it for me. I knew the place, and always liked it."

Darrie's mind pictured the Winston house, one of the more imposing homes along the hill. A man alone. . . ? "Y-you're married?"

"Not yet." He smiled at her. "I hope to be, soon."

"And you came here to make sure I wouldn't—what? Denounce you? Make some claim on you? Is that it?"

Eric got up and moved about the room. He turned a vase on the mantel, and ended fingering a book on the marble-topped table. Darrie told herself, His manners never were good—he was too sure of himself, too forward. At once another part of her mind offered an excuse: He lived here, why should he not feel at home? Didn't she actually *want* him to feel—

Abruptly he clapped down the cover of the book and faced her. "The past is—past. I'd hoped you wouldn't bring it up."

We are talking, Darrie thought, as if he had seduced me, as if he had been the betrayer. Why don't I take the blame? But neither logic nor justice could be applied to what had happened; it must be without precedent. She made a great effort to speak coolly, and said, "But you did come here—to this house. I wonder why?"

"You can't guess?"

"No, I can't."

"You must have known how I felt—how I feel—about Genia. I want to marry her, now that she's old enough."

Darrie's lips moved to repeat, "Marry Genia?" but her mind remained blank.

"Come! You can't be that surprised!"

She thought she had known awareness of him in every possible way: voice answering voice; eyes moving possessively over features known in the very tissue of her memory; the dark secret knowing, brief and explosive, that had changed her life. But here was a stranger. That mouth with its endearingly full lower lip had said words that could not—*could not*—be said. He had become a monster.

Pain was beginning to be felt now, an ember burning within her breast. Her hand, tight-clenched, was pressed to that fire. She made herself release the fingers, spread them in her lap. Eric's face peered down at her, round and moony. I'll kill him before he touches her . . . kill him . . . kill him. . . .

"Miss Darrie, are you ill?"

Get hold of yourself—don't let him see. . . . Her sense of

identity became stronger: Darrelline Starkweather, mistress of Cedarhaven. Eric was the outsider. This was her home, her parlor, her hearthfire. A kind of sanity crept back. He couldn't have Genia. Why not. . . ? Ah, for the best of reasons!

Darrie looked up directly into Eric's eyes. She was possessed by the cruelty of her weapon. A wild exhilaration rode her words: "Genia is already married. Well married! Happily married! *You can't have her*!" The venom of the last words was sweet on her tongue.

Triumph was no sooner tasted than it began to slip away. Her mind searched for words of comfort. There were none. Like a single jewel-bright drop of gall had been the knowledge that he loved Genia. But everyone loved Genia. Papa adored her. Belle and Howard—not as they loved the Lord, of course, but dearly, dearly. John Tower spread his abject devotion at her feet.

"John Tower. . . ." Darrie had spoken the name aloud.

"Her husband?"

"Yes. Since May."

"John Tower!" Eric lifted his head, shook it as if to escape this final irony. "He is the agent who bought the Winston house for me."

Into the silence a coal whined with pent steam and burst apart. The clock cleared its throat and announced the half hour with a single note.

Eric drew what was left of his pride around him and said, "Give Genia my good wishes. My respects to the rest of your family." He took up his coat and hat and was gone.

After a time Darrie became aware of a chill in the air. She went into the hall and found the front door open. Eric, the self-possessed, the well-controlled, had left it so. His life, she thought, is shattered, just as mine was. The knowledge no longer gave her pleasure.

When John and Genia came in with the others for a cup of cocoa before returning to their own home, Darrie reported on her visitor.

Papa seemed most moved. "Eric Bond? You don't say! I always liked him. Why didn't he stay till we got home?"

John, his back to the fire, a cup of cocoa in his hand, was quite the picture of the rising young businessman. "I bought a house for him recently. He's going to settle here. Be married."

Genia showed only a mild interest. She looked up from stroking the soft fur of her sealskin jacket, held across her lap. "Who is he marrying? Someone from here?"

"His letters didn't say."

"Didn't he tell you, Darrie?" In a moment Genia repeated, "*Darrie,* didn't he tell you?"

Darrie felt the old thick-blooded throbbing at the base of her neck, a throbbing that shut off normal sounds, making Genia's question a mere whisper, a throbbing that soon would drive mallet-blows of pain into her temples. She frowned, concentrating on what Genia had asked. "No," she said at last. "No, he didn't tell me."

"Getting married!" Papa said, his voice expressing jovial interest. "High time too!"

Belle had been upstairs to inspect her sleeping children. Entering on the last comment, she asked, "Who's getting married?"

"Eric Bond."

"Well! Is he back?"

Darrie could not endure the normal but inane repetition. With care she put down her cup. Her arm was weightless, as if it were immersed in water. She said, "Will you all excuse me? I don't—feel well."

Genia's voice floated after her, diminishing as she mounted the stairs: "Oh, poor darling! She looks as if she's getting one of her sick headaches."

CHAPTER 18

Genia pulled a chair close to the cupboard, climbed up on it, and felt along the top shelf. There had been a bottle of brandy there yesterday. Now her questing hand found only two empty candy boxes, a ball of twine, and a cracked vase she might as well have thrown away. On tiptoe she felt into the farthest corner. "Oh dear!" she murmured. And then, "Oh damn!" John had found the bottle and taken it away. Without saying anything. Without chiding her. Pretending all the time he didn't play these sly little tricks. Still-waters John, she called him in her mind. Well, there was nothing she could do about it. The bottle was gone.

The chair teetered just enough to make her grab something for support. That stupid vase! She had put it away, cracked as it was, because it had been a wedding present from the Rothschilds and therefore must have been expensive: Chinese porcelain in shades of red, with a dragon winding its golden tail about the base. She held it at arm's length and inspected it. It had been a lovely thing. But now— Deliberately she opened her hand. The vase dropped and broke into a hundred pieces. She stood for a time looking down at the bright jigsaw bits on the kitchen floor. Why did I do that? she asked herself. There was no sense in it.

Presently she climbed down from the chair and went into the parlor. A bonbon box stood open at the end of the sofa. She curled up with her feet tucked under her and fingered through the candies. The kind she really liked were all gone. Belle had told her, "You shouldn't eat so much candy. You're getting a tiny bit—well, you know. . . . Besides, it's so self-indulgent."

The latter was Belle's real objection. Or perhaps back of Belle's stated reason was the springboard of all her reasoning: the Newtons could not be self-indulgent. A minister's salary had to be so carefully eked out to cover shoes, and flour, and doctor bills that nothing was left over for bonbons. The young Newtons' eyes gleamed with an ungodly eagerness when they visited their Aunt Genia and spotted the boxes of candy with which John kept her supplied. She took care to have a large box ready to send home with them when they visited from Olympia. Bella found no objection to *that.*

Well, Genia thought, perhaps she *was* putting on a tiny bit of weight. Having failed to find a tempting candy, she put the box aside with a feeling of virtue and tested to see whether she could span her waist with her hands. Her fingertips failed to reach. She laughed. They never had reached. It was John's larger hands which had been able to encircle her waist. It was a test he had not made recently.

She had tried—truly she had tried—not to let him see how repugnant his caresses were. But emotions of this sort were hard to conceal. He suspected her reluctance, he grew more suppliant, she grew more revolted. There had been that ugly night last week when he had wept—yes, wept!—with his face distorted with tears. "Five years of giving you . . . everything—everything! And you . . . despise me. For God's sake, what more do you want?" The words had been broken apart by gasps and hiccups. Lainie, in a childish pet, might have sounded so.

Genia had tried to comfort him. God knows she never wanted to be unkind to anyone. On a sudden impulse she had pulled away her nightgown and drawn his tear-wet face against the warmth of her bared breasts. How shocked he had been! Electrified, even through his sniveling, into springing back and drawing the sheet across her nakedness. It was the kind of thing, he told her when he was able to speak coherently, the kind of thing a Bad Woman would do. She, in her innocence, could not know this. But in the future, even with him, she must be more circumspect lest the beast lurking in every man . . .

In her innocence . . . He had used the same phrase when he

had noticed the attrition of his liquor supply. "I know, dear, you only taste it occasionally, out of curiosity. In your innocence you cannot know what liquor does to a woman."

Gradually he had ceased to keep liquor in the house, except for the occasional part-bottle left after guests had been here, such as the brandy Genia knew quite well had been on the top shelf only yesterday. Oh, well, she didn't want to get the name of being a tippler. Papa would be so hurt. And Darrie, too. She did try to please Darrie.

She smiled a little to herself at the image of Darrie, admirable against the background of a superbly managed Cedarhaven, devoted foster-mother to a delightful child. Yes, Lainie had become a charming creature. Now, when Genia visited Cedarhaven, Lainie would run to her, gay and quick as a sunbeam, with outstretched arms and fluting voice: "Dear Auntie Genia! I'm so glad to see you!" No one could resist her, least of all Genia.

The once-terrifying image of a squirming red-faced little beast, symbol of pain endured and danger lurking, could not be superimposed on a picture of the sunny-haired laughing child that Lainie had become. The earlier image, once deliberately thrust away, had dimmed with time. Now it could be recalled without pain, as an old nightmare may be conjured up, remembered not from the dream itself but from its later retelling. Lainie's relation to Genia herself, believable only when she stopped to think it out, was one of life's small caprices, to be smiled over or used as a teasing weapon.

That was the true irony: exposure had been a potent threat in Darrie's hand; now the blade was reversed. There was throat-catching excitement in those dialogues whose audiences remained innocent of the sword's keen edge.

"Lainie reminds me of myself when I was little. Truly, she does."

"I don't see the likeness."

"Maybe not so much in looks, but there is *something*. . . ."

Harshness would creep into Darrie's voice: "You're imagining things."

"Lainie's hair is lighter than mine. Isn't that odd for a Spaniard?"

"We don't know she's Spanish."

"Perhaps we will know . . . sometime . . . about her family."

"It's hardly likely."

"It would be interesting, though, wouldn't it, to learn the truth?"

Tight lips paid out the words: "The past must be left alone. *Alone.*"

It was a duel, exciting and dangerous, brought to a halt only when storm warnings in Darrie's eyes could no longer be ignored. Afterward, in privacy, Genia would say, "Don't be mad—I didn't mean anything, not really."

"Take care Lainie doesn't hear you. If you hurt her—!"

These small triumphs, recounted now in Genia's mind, brought no satisfaction. She never wanted, really, to hurt anyone. No, truly she didn't. Or did she now . . . at times . . . did some evil alien thing possess her tongue. . . ?

Genia moved suddenly as if pain had run through her, and pulled the candybox toward her. Those cherry centers, though not her favorites, were not bad. She let the chocolate dissolve sweetly on her tongue. She did love chocolate, but the sticky sweetness of the cherry center was always a disappointment. If it had been maple fondant, or coffee cream—but no matter.

It was better, it was safer, not to let her mind play with thoughts about Lainie. If she and John had had a child—but the formless vagrancy of her thinking was arrested by the utter nonsense of that! To be shapeless again, ugly, trapped in thickening flesh—it was a thought so horrid she looked about for a refuge from it. There must be something to do—but there wasn't. It was too far now to visit Minnie Trevelyan. This new house was blocks and blocks from her first tacky little old home. And the house was spotlessly clean, for Cheecha had been here yesterday to scrub and sweep and dust and to take the Towers' soiled linen back to Cedarhaven for laundering. There was not even dinner to prepare for tonight, for they were attending the Redfellows'

Autumn Banquet. It was supposed to be a secret, but word had reached Genia's ears that John was to be named "Redfellow of the Year."

He would be pleased, she thought, by the recognition.

Ah! This suggested a possible activity. John's good broadcloth suit might need a bit of brushing before such an illustrious event. She could check on her own costume, too. She would probably wear her gold brocade, but she would look at the rose satin too. Cheered by the prospect of something definite to do, she turned toward the stairway.

The Redfellows' banquet was, Genia thought, like a hundred others she had attended since becoming Mrs. John Tower. They were not always given by the Redfellows; there were the Masons, the Volunteer Firemen, the Ladies' Aid, the Elks. But the cast was the same—Port Townsend's leading families in the inner circle, and people like Ma Duncan and Mrs. Gentchell and the Warren sisters who were always in the kitchen, or carrying wood for the heater, or fetching borrowed chairs at the last minute.

The John Towers, Genia reflected, were almost among the leading families. She sometimes had the feeling that if she herself made just a little more effort, they would be "in." Often at night she put herself to sleep with plans for a series of little dinners, or afternoon teas, or of church work—all of these as suitable follow-ups for John's successful efforts in Port Townsend's business community. But when morning brought cold daylight and clear vision, these same plans sounded so dull and unrewarding that she pushed them into a comfortable and indefinite future.

Some of her shortcomings along this line were brought into focus as she and John entered the Redfellows' Hall and were greeted by Mary Whiteson. "Good evening, Mr. and Mrs. Tower. My dear, where is your cake?"

"My . . . cake?"

"You were pledged to bring one."

"I declare, it slipped my mind. I'm sorry."

Mary Whiteson's face, in disapproval, reminded Genia of a pincushion. She didn't know why. There was no physical resemblance, but the image sprang into her mind. She giggled, hastily put her muff across her face, and produced a cough.

John, speaking to Ben Pettygrove, had not heard the exchange. He turned back now, beaming impartially at Mrs. Whiteson and Genia. "I imagine you good ladies have been hard at work producing a feast for us tonight."

"*Some* of us have."

Ira Bascomb, Grand Sachem of the Port Townsend Long House, laid hold of the Towers and escorted them to the center of a horseshoe table. "Want you folks to sit here tonight," he boomed. "Want you close to me."

John smiled blandly and Genia wondered if he knew he was being singled out for honoring. It was no matter. No situation could catch him off guard—none except those relating to herself. It was not fair, she thought, this burden had been placed on her. Simply not fair. . . .

She slipped into the seat Ira held out for her, smiled across John at Ira's fat wife, turned to her left, and said, "Why, hello there!"

"Good evening, Mrs. Tower."

Eric Bond was the town's most attractive bachelor, Genia thought. He wasn't handsome, like the pictures of Edwin Booth, the matinee idol; he was too stocky for that. Still, he was half a head taller than herself, while his very stockiness gave him a look of strength. He was—she searched for a term—he was virile-looking, that was it. Smooth-shaven except for sideburns, a full underlip that hinted at sensuality—the thought made her shiver slightly. And those thick tipped-up lashes . . . What fun to see them blackened with that stuff actresses used! She smiled in spite of herself.

Eric smiled in return. "You seem happy tonight."

"I was thinking of something amusing."

"Why not share it?"

"I'm afraid it would sound disrespectful. And personal."

"Both at once? Now you have aroused my curiosity."

"Have I?" She let her own lashes fall slowly, separating herself from the expression of warmth and interest that she accepted as the natural masculine response to her existence. Funny, she thought, that Eric Bond had never married. He could certainly afford to! He had built the fine stone Bond Building on Water Street, and had an office in it from which he conducted all sorts of successful sidelines. They said around town that everything he touched turned into money.

It was nearly five years since he had come back to town to marry someone; he still owned, but now rented out, the house he had bought for his prospective bride. Obviously something had gone wrong. He had never, so far as she knew, offered an explanation. Perhaps his betrothed had died.

The idea of a broken heart, bravely concealed, gave a fillip to her imagination. Had he *kept away* from women since then? Men usually didn't: their appetites were too lustful to permit that. Still, it was hard to picture him in one of those dreadful but exciting places where—oh, dear! She oughtn't to let her mind drift into such channels. But Eric did seem too clean, too fastidious. . . . Her eyes rested on his hand, its fingers lightly turned about his water glass. It was a large hand, long-fingered, but thick with muscle through the palm. The nails were as clean as a woman's, but no woman's fingers would have those little islands of hair. . . . Genia laid her own hand on the tablecloth. It did not quite touch his, but she imagined she could feel the warmth of his flesh transmitted to her own.

He turned toward her.

"Excuse me," she murmured, and drew her hand away.

"Yes?"

"I thought I had . . . touched you." No one else could possibly have heard the words. Perhaps he had not heard them, for he made no answer. A second later they leaned apart for the waitress to place a steaming plate before Genia.

The magic of the moment was gone—or had never existed. Eric was talking matter-of-factly now to someone on his other side. She had never noticed his voice before: it had the resonance that must come from a deep chest. She'd read somewhere that all sounds were really vibrations. Certainly voices vibrated in the chest and throat. She put her hand against her own throat. If it rested against Eric's she could feel—

"Darling, what's the matter? Have you a sore throat?" When John's hand, under cover of the tablecloth, touched her knee she could have struck it off.

"Leave me alone!" she whispered furiously, and was instantly contrite at the pain in John's face. She forced a smile. "I have a little headache."

"I shouldn't have dragged you here. You didn't say anything—"

"It's nothing—nothing! Eat your dinner, John." She picked up her own fork.

For the rest of the meal she studiously avoided Eric Bond, keeping up her own cross-fire of conversation with John and the Bascombs. But even as she mouthed pleasantries her mind made furtive excursions: Eric had always liked her, hadn't he . . . ? Why years ago, when the war was just getting started, he had said, "I'm coming back to marry you." He hadn't meant it, of course, for he had come back—actually to Cedarhaven itself—and had never mentioned marriage. If he had, in small subtle ways, paid her court, so had every other male sheltered by the Cedarhaven roof. And then, abruptly and without reason, he had left town and she had forgotten him—or almost forgotten.

Since he had come back (changed and hardened by success, she thought) the very nature of society had kept them apart. He was a bachelor and she a married woman. Occasionally at some ball they danced together, or shared a table at progressive whist. Her mind went back over the times of meeting: had there been a special attentiveness across the card table, a closer-than-necessary embrace on the dance floor? In her own peculiar climate of admiration it was impossible to say. But now! If he should lead her in the coaxing strains of a waltz, her hand nestling small in his larger one . . . Oh, God! she thought. How easily I could be a Bad Woman! She forced her gaze resolutely on her plate.

Now Ira Bascomb was getting to his feet. He made a safe target for her glances.

"Friends, Redfellows, and their Squaws—"

Laughter rose to this sally, and Mrs. Bascomb struck at him playfully with her napkin.

"We are gathered here tonight on this auspicious occasion to have, first, the financial report of the Port Townsend Long House of the Royal and Benevolent Order of Redfellows. In the past year two of our members have had occasion to be grateful for the benefits accruing from membership in our order. Carl Seaborn, who has since transferred to the Anacortes Long House, broke his leg and was incapacitated for several weeks. During this time he received benefits of $46. Our late respected member Lafe Burrows, who was unfortunately drowned in Scow Bay, received the maximum, or death, benefit of $500. Neither of these members would have enjoyed these generous allotments were it not for our able Keeper of the Wampum who has handled the financial affairs of the Long House during this past year."

Genia, picturing the form which the late Mr. Burrows' enjoyment might have taken, stifled an impulse to giggle. She pressed her napkin to her mouth and stole a look at Eric Bond. His face was carefully impassive. She had missed a few words of Ira Bascomb's speech. He was saying, "—to give you the report himself, our loyal Keeper of the Wampum, Mr. John Tower."

There was a ruffle of applause as John got to his feet.

Red-faced, he had a brief struggle with his collar, gulped a time or two, rattled some papers, and stumbled into a salutation to Redfellows, friends, and ladies. . . .

He had, Genia thought, less than his customary aplomb. No doubt awareness of his impending honor embarrassed him. She didn't try to follow his financial report. It sounded impressive, and confusing: money invested there, invested here, on call in an Olympia bank. A total in the thousands. When he sat down the handclapping was lively.

Ira Bascomb was on his feet again, first leading the applause, then motioning for silence. "We come now to the second purpose of our meeting. Each year, as you know, we select one of our members who has made a special contribution to the good of the Long House, and acknowledge him as Redfellow of the Year. This year we have—I have here—that is, I did have—" Ira groped frantically under the table's edge. His cheeks pinkened with excitement and effort. "Now where the dev—ah!" He straightened up clutching an Indian headdress toward which his wife's Plymouth Rock hens had obviously contributed. Recovering his poise, he announced, "This year we have a young man who, without the slightest fear of contradiction, has earned the title of Redfellow of the Year. John Tower, Keeper of the Wampum, I hereby place this eagle-feather symbol of appreciation on your deserving head."

Out of breath by this time, and possibly dizzied by the eminence of the occasion, he thrust the headdress down on John's dark hair with the tailpiece in front. Both he and John snatched to rearrange it, and a Plymouth Rock feather floated out across the table.

There was a flurry of clapping. "Hear, hear!" "Good old John!" "Speech!"

John rose, the feathered headdress tilted dangerously over one eye, and said, "Thank you all very much."

Genia noticed that his earlier flush had died away; she did not remember ever seeing him so pale. To think this recognition meant so much to him! When he had sat down she impulsively leaned toward him and said, "John, I'm so glad for you. Congratulations!"

His look of dog-like gratitude made her turn away. Turning, she met the steel-sharp eyes of Eric Bond. They were looking past her, however, and were fixed on John with a peculiar intensity. Hostile, curious, speculative—before she could make up her mind Eric was smiling at her and saying, "You must be very proud of your husband."

"Indeed I am."

"Genia, darling? *Genia?*"

"Oh—! What is it, John?"

"You weren't listening."

"Yes, I was."

"What was I saying?"

"That—that—well, perhaps I did miss a word or two."

John wiped his lips and put his napkin aside. It was one of those rare mornings when Genia had risen to prepare his breakfast. Now she said, in a cross between apology and justification, "Truly, John, it's so early I'm not awake."

John rose, and paused beside her chair. "It is early for you. But sometimes, no matter what time of day, I get the notion that what I say to you doesn't matter."

"Now, John! I declare, you know better than that!"

"Do you want to know what I said?

"Of course I do!"

"I said I had ordered a carriage, and I have my eyes on a pair of chestnut mares out in the country. In the spring we'll be driving our own carriage to Keymes Landing, or the Fort, for picnics or what have you."

"You're very generous. Really, you are, John." She was aware that John waited at her shoulder for some more tangible gesture. She measured half a spoonful of sugar into her cup and stirred it carefully. It would be nice to have her own carriage and pair. But expensive, too. She hadn't thought John could afford that, really. A carriage house would have to be built, too, and pasturage arranged for. John would need to hire someone to care for the horses. It seemed a rather prodigal gesture, although recognized as one aimed at her pleasure.

Well! Her own carriage! She pictured herself on a sunny afternoon, driving through the Cut to Adams Corner, then down the length of Water Street. A stop at Katz's to match embroidery silk, then to the Kentucky Store to see what, in the way of fancy groceries, had come in from San Francisco. Some boy—or man, perhaps—would offer to keep an eye on the team. Suppose . . . just suppose it happened to be Eric Bond. He might say, "This is a mettlesome pair. I'd better drive you home." "I wouldn't think of troubling you." "A pleasure rather than a trouble. Here, let me help you up." His hand was firm and strong. Some mysterious force held hers clasped within it though she tried to draw away. Seated in the carriage, her eyes looked downward into his, their gaze locking over the still-clasped hands. . . .

"Genia!"

"W-what? Oh, John!"

"Who did you expect—President Grant?"

"I declare, I thought you'd gone."

"Without kissing you goodby?"

She lifted her face. His lips on hers were soft and moist. She turned her mouth away, felt the tickle of his mustache on her cheek, and said, "Goodby, John. You don't want to be late at the office."

Dressing for the Thanksgiving feast at Cedarhaven, Genia told herself she didn't really care any more for these family dinners. When we were all girls together we used to laugh and have fun in a way we never do now. Some vague thought of innocence once lost, never to be regained, passed through her mind and was thrust aside. It sounded too much like one of Belle's platitudes.

Belle. . . .

She and Howard and the young Newtons had arrived yesterday from Olympia. Little Howard would have outgrown his jacket sleeves again, Marian would be missing a front tooth. David would have the sniffles. The baby—but the baby would not be at table yet. Genia could see the others in her mind's eye: Lainie, effervescent with delight at being with her little cousins. The Newton children, excited, overeating—they always did. Marian was sure to be ill afterward. Belle, with her air of tears bravely held back. Howard—ah, but Howard was truly sweet! I declare, Genia thought, he is the *best* man that ever walked. It was hard to remember why she had once thought him dull. Perhaps at first none of them had appreciated him. But time had proven him to be cast in the image he had set for himself: a man of God. If she had married someone like Howard, Genia thought. . . . The idea was both illusive and disquieting. For Belle, though, Howard was perfect. Without him Belle, by now, would have drowned in her own tears.

Pomp would be at dinner, of course, as much a member of the family as any of the Starkweathers. Pomp with his quirking eyebrow, his occasional bright rapier of wit, his quizzical yet affectionate regard always on Darrie.

Darrie herself would sit regally at the foot of the table, exercising the control that Papa, from his place at the head of the table, relinquished to her. Dear Papa! There were times now when he seemed truly old. Genia did some mental addition and thought, Heavens above! Papa's in his fifties! He *was* old. Her mind glanced at the thought that she herself would age, her eyes grow dull, her hair gray, her flesh withered. . . . I couldn't bear it! The thought was so fervent Genia felt her lips forming the words. She brought her mind back to the family gathering for which she was, even now, hooking the tightly-fitted rose satin dress. It was necessary to not only hold her breath, but to breathe out *hard,* and hold it. Panting slightly, she felt the last hook slip into its matching eye. The lining of the dress must have shrunk a bit. But no matter—it was fastened now. She took a last smiling and approving look at herself in the mirror, picked up her sealskin jacket, and started downstairs where John had been waiting patiently for the last hour.

The day turned out quite differently from what Genia had expected. They were hardly at table—Papa had just begun to carve the turkey—when someone came for Howard. There had been an accident at the dock; some heavy machinery had fallen while being unloaded. One man was killed, another dying and in need of Howard's good offices.

Lainie began to weep.

Belle announced, with a great display of righteousness, that men had no business to work on the Lord's Day, and had to be reminded that the Pilgrims rather than the Deity had set this day apart.

When John heard the victims' names, which meant nothing at all to Genia, he grew pale as pot cheese and hurried out after Howard. Papa, himself badly shaken by the unhappy news, opined the men were Redfellows and that John must be concerned by his responsibility for them.

The day was truly blighted. The dinner might as well have been sawdust for those who were left at Cedarhaven to eat it.

Howard came back after a time to announce that the injured

man, too, had died. The only grain of consolation in the whole tragic affair was that the widows would receive death benefits from the Loyal and Benevolent Redfellows. John, it was assumed, was detained with paper work attendant on such payment.

At dusk, when John had not returned, Howard walked Genia to the Tower home. As they picked their cautious way between mudholes, she found herself confiding in her brother-in-law: "In the spring John is getting us a carriage and pair. The carriage is already ordered from Sacramento."

"John must be prospering indeed."

"Oh, he is! He makes lots of money."

"You're fortunate."

Genia assessed this statement carefully for irony; none seemed to exist. Howard accepted without rancor that other men, other heads of families, had more than he of worldly goods. Impulsively she squeezed his arm. "You're really sweet, Howard. I declare you are!"

"I'm lucky, Genia. I have work that's important, a wonderful wife in Belle, and fine healthy children. What more could anyone want?"

"We-ell, money, perhaps?"

"We have enough. Money's not important."

The statement lodged in Genia's mind: Money's not important. As she waited through the evening for John's return, and finally made her preparations for bed, she thought about it. If money wasn't important, what was? "God's will," Belle would say. But wasn't it hard to know God's will? Or, if you suspected it, to stay within its confines? Obviously God's will was not that His children be . . . she sought for a pleasant word: unchaste.

She turned the lamp wick low to wait for John, and slipped between the sheets. I couldn't help myself, she thought. I fought—I really fought! Every time! Oh, that dreadful bruise where he threw me down against a rock—he would have killed me—

She realized she had the sheet twined about rigid fingers, a corner between her clenched teeth. She forced herself to relax. That was in the past—forever in the past. John was never stirred in such a manner. A hint of resistance stripped John of his very manhood. Their ordered and furtive coupling, with the sheet drawn high against the eye of night itself, was as tepid as the joining on a plate of two poached eggs. And for sharing in this essentially shameful rite, John gave her obsequious gratitude and whatever material prizes he could lay at her feet. What could such a man give his wife except the fruits of money? And yet . . . she was growing drowsy now . . . and yet money was not important, unless you had nothing else.

She slept, uneasily at first, then as deeply as if the nested blankets were solid earth and she a part of it.

Eric Bond came toward her in a wooded place. "Do you want money?" he asked, and held out a closed hand. She drifted forward in effortless dream-languor till their hands touched, his strong and thick-muscled, with the little islands of fair hair. His hand was empty—he had been cozening her. Yet not empty when it closed like iron on her wrist. A scream, fearful and yet delicious, rose in her throat. She struggled. Her wrist—her *wrist*—! A final frantic effort wakened her to milky half-light. A corner of the sheet was twisted around her arm, growing tighter as she pulled against it.

Morning, and she alone in the wide bed—it couldn't be! She stumbled out of bed and pattered, bare feet shrinking from the cold floor, to inspect the clock. Nearly eight. The lamp had burned out, leaving a stale and smoky odor in the closed room. It was morning, and John had not come home.

Unreasoning panic seized her. Dreadful things took place when Port Townsend was dark. Men's throats were slit for a mere handful of change, let alone the substantial sum of insurance benefits. Or men were set upon from darkened alleys and carried unconscious to some ship shorthanded for a voyage to the Sandwich Islands, or Singapore, or Melbourne.

Genia began to cry. Fumbling with chilled fingers for her underclothes, she struck away the tears, childlike, with her palms. The bitter aftertaste of self-loathing rose in her throat with the tears: how often she had thought, If only John were dead she would be free. But not now—not this way. It would be as if she had willed him to his death.

Dressed at last, in clumsy haste, she ran out the front door—dear heaven, it had been unlocked all night!—and along the deserted morning streets toward Cedarhaven. Halfway there she remembered that it was winter—a cold mist laced with raindrops drifted up from the harbor—and she had forgotten her coat. Pain pierced her chest from the cold, and from her breath shortened by the unaccustomed running.

Her bare fists beat the cold wood of Cedarhaven's front door until it gave way—it had not been locked. Darrie was hurrying toward her. "Genia! What's wrong?"

She flung herself in Darrie's arms. "It's John," she sobbed. "He's gone! It's just as if I'd killed him."

"There, there, there. . . ." Darrie's hand soothed her shoulder, and steadied it. Darrie's arm was strong, supporting her. Against her cheek Darrie's cotton dress had the familiar smell of fresh-ironed starch. It would be all right now. Whatever dreadful thing she had conjured up could not reach her past Darrie's strength.

Cheecha's scarred face appeared behind Darrie's shoulder. "Something bad? Somebody else get killed, huh?"

"Go back to the kitchen, Cheecha. Finish serving breakfast. I'll take Genia to my room."

Upstairs, the bare facts were hardly fearful after all: simply, John had not come home all night.

"Men do things like that," Darrie pointed out. "I wouldn't have thought John—but he's a man."

Wiping her cheeks with the handkerchief Darrie had given her, Genia said, "He might be dead—or shanghaied."

"What nonsense! You lie down on my bed—here, I'll cover you —and we'll find out what's happened. Pomp can look for him."

With that transference of thought, sometimes frightening in its accuracy, that passes between those long familiar, Genia recognized Darrie's mental image of John—victim of too much to drink, or even of Those Women. Such worldly possibilities would be better explored by Pomp than by Howard, the logical messenger.

This new picture of John, superimposed on her earlier one, was less frightening. Indeed, now that she was here at Cedarhaven with Darrie, her alarm at waking in an empty house had leached away. But because she did not want to face Belle and Howard, nor to hear awkward questions from the children, she obediently snuggled down under Darrie's coverlet and prepared to await developments.

The sounds of the household went on around and beneath her. She heard Pomp's voice with Darrie's in the hall; she heard the distant clatter in the kitchen. Smiling faintly to herself, Genia recalled that Cheecha could make more noise with a coffeepot than someone else could make with a brass cannon. Presently she heard the children on the stairs. It sounded, she thought, as if they were dragging a sack of coal, but it was likely nothing more than two empty spools on a string. That's the trouble with my house, she thought: it's so quiet all day. But I won't be going back to it. Now that was a ridiculous notion! Why wouldn't I go back? Continuity eluded her, and she dozed.

She wakened to find, standing over her, a Darrie so pale and shaken that earlier terrors rushed back over her. But it was only for a moment; Darrie's first words were reassuring: "John is all right."

Obviously something was less than all right. Genia sat up in bed and pushed the hair out of her eyes. "You look so scared—what's wrong?"

When Darrie turned away, Genia slipped off the bed and followed her. "If John is all right, then what—who—?"

"It depends on what we mean by 'all right.' He isn't hurt. Or drunk. Pomp found him in his office."

"He'd been there *all night*?" Genia realized she was shaking Darrie's arm, as if she might force information from her.

Darrie took a deep breath. She put her hand over Genia's. "John has been—well, speculating. There are no Redfellow funds. There's *nothing*. He owes thousands of dollars. Even your house is mortgaged for all he could get."

Genia's first thought was, Well, business—it doesn't touch me. Her second was, The carriage! I'll never get it now. Then a dreadful hollowness began to spread through her. She said, "Poor John! He did it all for me—you know that! I've got to see him right away. I've got to tell him he musn't worry. We'll start over again—with nothing."

Darrie gave her a look of mingled annoyance and compassion. "You don't understand! He'll go to prison. It's not just bad debts—he has embezzeled the Redfellow funds."

"Prison? Oh, no! They couldn't do that!"

"They can—and will. Don't you see, all this talk about investing the funds so wisely—he was investing in his own affairs. And he has *nothing*."

Genia groped her way to the bed and sat down. "Poor John," she repeated. "Where is he now?"

"Pomp took him home—to your house. He thought it was best to keep him out of sight."

"Will there be a trial?"

"I suppose so."

"Then I'll get up in court and tell them it was my fault. He kept trying to get things for me. Don't you see, Darrie, he thought things like—like the new house, and my piano and fur jacket would make . . . everything . . . all right." She faltered on the last words. Darrie could not possibly guess the utter wrongness of their marriage. Perhaps it would be no clearer to judge and jury.

Darrie was fingering her lip. "The only chance—if there's a chance at all—would be to make up the shortage. None of us has money like that. Cedarhaven is already mortgaged. No . . . no. . . ." She shook her head. "It would be money down a rat hole. Nobody would do it."

Genia seized on this hope at once. "Maybe several people together. Maybe Pomp—he seems like one of the family. Or Eric Bond . . ."

Darrie whirled to face her. "Eric! Why did you name him?"

"We-ell, I . . . I don't know. He *has* money, hasn't he?" The real reason lay in the subterranean knowledge that Eric was concerned with her. Or she with him. This could not be spoken to Darrie, but perhaps it needn't be. Again there was that subtle and wordless communication of knowledge: Darrie knew as well as she that Eric had some special interest in her. This particular awareness drifted in on a cold wind of deeper and more profound emotions. The air in the room became charged with unspoken thoughts. For a long moment they looked at each other with that mingling of loyalty and hostility that could only be described as a "family look." Then Darrie turned away and went to adjust the window shade.

"The sun is coming out after all," she said, as if she must take hold of any matter-of-fact straw that floated by.

Genia thought, There is nothing more to be said. We both know Eric will help. He has money enough, and he'll be willing. Darrie will go to him. I don't need to worry.

CHAPTER 19

After Darrie had left Genia with instructions to stay in the bedroom and talk to no one, she went back downstairs.

Alone in the hall, she paused, pressing her hands against both temples. Her head felt like a cage of trapped birds: ideas darted in and out, whirring and pecking, striking each other, falling in mid-flight and springing up again. She forced herself to a careful review: Pomp had found John alone in his officc holding a loaded pistol that he had lacked the courage to use. At least no one but Pomp and herself, and now Genia, knew of his speculations. The important thing was to act quickly before word got out.

Pomp could be trusted to stay with John and keep him quiet.

"Get him home—get him out of sight!" she had instructed

when the two of them had appeared at Cedarhaven's back door a few minutes ago. A few minutes? It seemed hours had passed, but common sense told her there'd been little more than time for them to reach the Tower home.

She could imagine what faced them there: the cold stove, the sour-smelling ashes gray in the fireplace, the tumbled bed—its sheets now cold—that Genia had quitted. Perhaps she should have let Genia go to her husband—but no! Genia's impulsive kindness, at once her best and worst trait, could not be trusted. On the spur of the moment she might commit herself to any absurd position. Keep her here. Keep her away from John till some course was settled upon.

Pomp—trustworthy Pomp!—would get the fires going and the coffeepot on, warm the house, insist on John's eating something. For the moment, John was in the best possible hands. What she must do now was to find Eric.

Firmly she opened the door and went into the diningroom where Lainie and the Newton family still lingered over the breakfast table. The boarders had left for work. Papa was sleeping in.

With an effort, Darrie made her tone casual: "Cheecha's taking care of you, isn't she?"

Belle frowned. "We're all right. But what in the world is going on? Such a lot of running up and down stairs and chattering in doorways!"

"It's nothing, really. With such a household I'm bound to be a sort of Mother Confessor."

Belle said, "Oh, Darrie—that sounds so Popish—please!" and Howard said, "It's only an expression. Darrie doesn't mean anything by it."

While they pursued a mild discussion of Rome and its evil influence, Darrie went on into the kitchen. She took a shawl from its hook by the door and went out the back way.

Obscurely, the feeling that she must hurry diminished when she was on her way. The old switchback steps had been replaced with a board sidewalk set at dogleg angle to provide a grade. At the turn a rough bench gave a climber a chance to rest and recover breath. Darrie paused there. She did not sit down—the plank bench glistened from the recent rain—but she stood by it for a few minutes looking downward.

The sun had shone but briefly. Again, mist drifted across the harbor and softened the wooden geometry of the town's business section. Down there, in the town, she was going to meet Eric.

In the five years since he had come back to Port Townsend they had almost never seen one another. Their rare meetings had been no more than a distant bow and nod. But awareness of Eric as a factor in the town, the thought of him sleeping somewhere within a few thousand feet, of his waking to the same burst of winter sun that flung its crimson path across the harbor, hearing the same news, feeling the same gusts of boisterous wind, seeing the same tender veil of green drift across spring-wakened thickets in the town's vacant lots—all this was a sustaining factor in her life. She could, and did, writhe in humiliation over her memories, she could say "I loathe him!" but she could not cease to share his world. His simple existence changed the climate of her life.

And now, with the most legitimate and urgent of reasons, she was on her way to see him. The moment was too tremendous to be rushed into carelessly.

She pondered what she would say. Would she be practical, speak of a loan to John as a business venture? "The town is growing," she might say. "It's full of promise. If John is helped past this bad time, he'll pay you back." Surely this was true. Why, right now there were four ships in the mist-filled harbor, three bare-masted and at anchor, the fourth at the dock where only yesterday those two poor men—but she didn't want to think of that, so dreadful in itself, as well as cause for John's dilemma. Enough to say that Port Townsend was again a seaport of consequence. At table yesterday Papa had said, just before the holiday spirit had been shattered by that messenger, "The men who have confidence in Port Townsend will be wealthy in another ten years." He had said the same thing ten years ago, when they had first come here. But this time, she told herself, it well might be true. But she wasn't going to give Eric a lecture on economics. He was making money. Who could know better that, with luck and a little help, someone else could do the same?

But if he did not see a loan to John as an investment . . .

Darrie might be forced then to confide the truth of Genia's marriage. The words she would use came tumbling into her mind the more urgently for having been held back: "There is this terrible thing in Genia that draws men, and that *draws her*—I *had* to get her safely married, for her own sake. You see that, you understand it, don't you?" She put her fingers across her lips; almost, she had whispered Eric's name at the end. He'll understand, she told herself, if only because he loved Genia once. Here, at last, was someone with whom she could share the burden of her heart.

An ecstasy of relief flowed through her. She pressed her knee against the bench for support, forced herself to calmness by long slow-drawn breaths. By the time she could trust her legs to carry her forward, she had determined the course of the coming talk. Never mind the idea of a loan—it had been ridiculous at best. Let this be the meeting of two minds filled with good will for Genia. It was even possible to imagine Eric saying, "You have been a good sister to her, a wise counselor." And she would divert this praise, even while savoring it, by saying, "You *do* see the marriage must be saved. Without John, Genia will be lost . . . lost. . . ."

Eric's office was on the first floor of his own Bond Building, with an entrance from the street. Darrie seldom made a trip downtown without passing it, her eyes carefully straight ahead. Now she found the door ajar, Eric leaning over the wood-burning heater with a match in his hand; he must have just come in. He straightened to stare at her, but not with the complete surprise she had anticipated.

"Come in."

She closed the door behind her. Her carefully rehearsed speeches had vanished. "We are in—" She broke off, and began again, "Genia is in trouble. I didn't know where else to turn for help."

Eric nodded. "The only thing I have that could help you is money. So that's what you want." When Darrie started to speak, he held up his hand. "Let me go on guessing. I've kept a close eye on John Tower and his investments. His bad investments. Months ago I suspected he was borrowing from Peter to pay Paul, and getting it back to repay Peter. Eventually he had to dip into Redfellow funds. Our exalted Keeper of the Wampum is now up against a double insurance claim, and no wampum to pay it. Is that right?"

Darrie put her hand toward a chair back, and drew it away again, ashamed of her weakness. But Eric had noticed the gesture. He led her to a chair. The room was filled with the crackling sound of paper and kindling taking fire. Eric crossed, with his slightly uneven step, to close the damper on the stove. Back at his desk, he picked up a ruler and flexed it in his strong hands. He has to be doing *something,* Darrie thought. All that energy pent up, all that strength . . .

He said, "Genia's husband is faced with prison unless someone makes up the shortage. You had no one else to turn to. This hasn't been easy for you." He looked directly at her as he said this, as if she were a person and not a messenger. "You've changed a bit yourself, haven't you?"

"I . . . I have?"

"Of course! You must know that! Good God! Do people go through their days being tried and tortured, getting tough enough to kick back at life, and not feel the change, inside themselves? You've learned to go after what you want. Most women never do."

"If I'm different . . ." If I'm different . . . if I'm more nearly what you want . . . now that Genia's gone from your life, it's not too late yet, is it? The heart dies slowly, Eric Bond. . . . Her thoughts could not reach him. Nor had he said that strength in a woman was the desired trait. Papa had told her men did not admire a strong-minded woman. Oh, Eric, if I only knew what you wanted—I could be *anything.* . . .

The ruler bent in Eric's hand. He'd break it—she waited for the crack of splintered wood. Then he set it down gently on the desk. "When I left Port Townsend Genia was a child." He turned away. When he spoke again, Darrie thought she must have imagined the break in his voice. "When I came back, she was married—and to John Tower! So weak, so clearly headed for trouble! What she ever saw in him! But then, a young girl, completely innocent of life . . ." He paused. "Well, I've watched, I've waited for the blow-up. Now it's here. You expected to surprise me. I was ahead of you all the time. I have my answer ready."

Darrie had to remind herself this was what she had come for. She put a gloved hand across her eyes to shut out the sight of Eric. You've grown tough, he'd said. And it was true. She was here to save Genia, at any cost. She said, "You'll help her?"

"On my conditions."

"And they are?"

"I'll make up the Redfellow shortage. I know exactly what Tower's supposed to have in that fund. It was announced when they made him Redfellow of the Year six weeks ago."

Darrie had the hysterical impulse to burst out laughing. Redfellow of the Year! But Eric was too much in earnest to notice the irony of the title.

"I'll make that up—nothing more. That's where he's criminally liable. As for the bad debts—God knows what they amount to!—he can declare himself bankrupt."

"His reputation will be ruined, and Genia's with it."

"Are you suggesting I prevent that by paying his debts? He'd only turn around and get in debt again. Next year we'd have the same thing to go through."

"You mentioned 'conditions.'"

"Yes. Tower will leave town. His desertion will be grounds for Genia to divorce him."

"He adores Genia! He won't go!"

"He's a weakling—he'll go. It's that or prison."

The little stove was doing its work; the air was close and warm. And there was the pressure of Eric's contempt. For John . . . ? Only for John . . . ? Darrie lowered her shawl. She was exhausted, giddy. But Eric had agreed to help. That had been her mission. She could leave. Something as yet unsettled nagged at her still. She said, "You insist on divorce?"

"I do."

"Genia may not be willing."

"Without that, no money."

"But—why?"

"It should be self-evident. She must be free to remarry."

Darrie looked up to find Eric's expression altered, softened. The word "fatuous" came to her mind.

"She needs protection and . . . and love." The last word must have stuck in his throat, but he got it out. "I intend to marry her, to take care of her from now on."

Darrie's impulse to escape was strong. She gathered up her shawl and started to rise. But she forced herself back. "Has it occurred to you that, over the years, Genia might have . . ."

"Well?" His voice defied her.

"Might be different from . . ."

"Go on!"

"That she might not precisely need protection?"

"You don't want me to marry your sister?" It could be a simple question, or a rough hand poised above the never-quite-healed wound. It was an effort for Darrie to say, "Genia was only a child when you knew her. Time makes a difference."

"She is still a child at heart. Innocent! Untouched!"

Darrie got to her feet. The hands that once more drew the shawl about herself were shaking. Unsteadily, she said, "I must get home. You should—talk yourself—to Genia—"

"You can give her my instructions. I'll have the money by afternoon."

He held open the door and Darrie passed through it.

CHAPTER 20

Belle didn't know which was the more shocking news in Darrie's letter, that John had declared himself a bankrupt and left town, or that Genia was divorcing him. The latter fact was the excuse for the letter. Darrie actually had the audacity to suggest that Genia ought to get away from Port Townsend for a while; it would be appreciated, she wrote, if Belle would ask her for a visit after Christmas and—in Darrie's own words—"Genia could be with you then when her divorce comes up before the Territorial Legislature in January."

Ordinarily Belle did not disturb Howard when he was writing his sermon, but this news would not keep. "It's shameful!" she cried, thrusting the letter before him. "Oh, I've begged Genia, and John too, to lead more Christian lives. They don't go to church six times a year. And now see what's happened!"

"Now, Belle, dear, it may not be as bad as you imagine."

"Not as *bad*! My own sister being *divorced*? Well, I'll tell you one thing—she won't live under *my* roof while she's doing this shameful, wicked thing! I won't have it!"

Howard was frowning. "Have you stopped to think, all this can't be exactly pleasant for Genia? She must be pretty unhappy about—"

"She should be unhappy!"

"And John—I find myself thinking of him. How utterly miserable he must be! I wonder if there isn't—"

"John indeed! He caused all this disgrace. Oh, just imagine how people must be talking!"

"I can well imagine. But all the talk in the world won't change the facts, will it? And John must be a pretty desperate fellow by now. When we pray about this, I think we should ask for special leniency and compassion for him, don't you?"

Belle could bring herself to no better response than the dark prediction that John "would be punished."

"I'm sure he's already being punished. John is essentially a kind and generous man. He is suffering now, you may be sure."

"You certainly aren't condoning—"

"No, of course not. As for the divorce—well, we must do our best to persuade Genia against this. The Church's position is plain: marriage is a covenant of God and cannot be dissolved. Unfortunately, the laws of the Territory allow it. We are working on that—but never mind that now. Genia is our concern at the moment."

"She's *not* coming here."

"Before you decide that, Belle dear, think of the opportunity to reason with her. We might be able to prevent her making this terrible mistake."

"What would your congregation say if we had her in this house?"

Howard considered this, ruffling the back of his head as he did so. Usually Belle found the resultant tousle rather endearing, but on this occasion she was too annoyed to admire it. "Well," she persisted, "what would they say?"

"I don't know. But *I* will say to *them,* 'My little sister-in-law—whom I dearly love, by the way—is staying with us. And while we disapprove of what she is doing, still it is her affair.' "

"Hmph!" It was impossible as well as un-Christian to stay angry with Howard. If Belle could find a fault with him, it was his easygoingness. Even Christ had taken a whip to the money-lenders, hadn't He? But as her annoyance subsided she could see reason in his argument. Events often vindicated his passive attitude. Perhaps they would again. Perhaps here in this truly devout household Genia would see the error of her ways. Aloud she said, "You will promise to dissuade her, won't you? You'll talk with her—pray with her?"

"As much as she'll allow. I wouldn't be doing the right thing if I didn't make my convictions clear to her."

It was left at that. Belle kissed Howard and left him to finish his sermon. When they had Genia here in this Christian atmosphere they would—a phrase came readily to Belle's mind—begin the battle for her soul.

The Christmas visit to Cedarhaven was brief, and unsatisfactory. Both Papa and Darrie refused to discuss Genia's plans with Belle. There was, it seemed to her, almost a conspiracy of silence. When they were back in Olympia, new obstacles appeared. For one thing, the little Newtons adored their aunt and were always clinging to her. Even Howard, who had always been eager to go off to school, wept on the day vacation ended and he had to leave the younger children in possession of their Auntie Genia.

"I don't in the least *mind* this," Belle confided to her husband that night after they had gone to bed. "But I'm afraid it teaches the children to be irresponsible."

"I wouldn't worry. She's teaching them to laugh. That's important too."

"I hadn't noticed they were unduly sober."

"I didn't mean they were. But Genia finds such joy in living. Isn't that a good thing for them to see?"

"Surely not as good as a sense of duty."

"My dear, I trust they are getting that from you."

Only partially mollified, Belle said, "Except that Genia is too simple to do such a thing, I'd believe she was using the children as a shield. We don't have a moment alone when we could talk confidentially. I'll have to make an opportunity."

Rather sleepily, Howard said, "Forbearance is a virtue. She's only been here a week."

Belle waited a few more days, during which Genia continued to be carefree and uncommunicative. Then one evening when the children had been put to bed and Howard was away at a church meeting, she brought the issue into the open.

A basket of socks and stockings sat on the parlor table between the sisters. Genia smoothed the stockings, sorted them into pairs, and laid aside the ones that needed darning. She said, "This is simply endless! Anyone would think you were raising a family of centipedes."

"I'm grateful to the good Lord they're well and strong enough to wear out their stockings." Belle squinted to thread her needle, and pulled through a length of darning cotton. "My children are my greatest earthly joy. It's a pity you and John never had a child."

"Do you think so?"

"It's God's purpose in marriage!"

"I don't think God had much to do with John's and my marriage."

"That was your fault then. Marriage is a sacrament."

"I'm not sure ours was."

"*Howard* performed it."

Genia had the poor taste to laugh at this, though she quickly recovered and said, gravely enough, "If anyone could sanctify a marriage, I'm sure it would be Howard."

Belle shook the darning ball out of a sock, and laid the mended one, with its mate, on the table. "I trust you have given up this wicked idea of divorce."

"Well, no. Any day now I expect to hear that Lawyer Tripp is ready to present my plea to the Legislature. I wonder if they'll have me there—ask me questions. My toes simply curl with excitement when I think about that."

Belle had an instant and shattering vision of her little sister—a pastor's sister-in-law—standing up before the Legislature and prattling about— She gasped, "You don't mean you'd actually appear—in public—!"

"Lawyer Tripp said it might be effective—that's the very word he used."

"*Have you no shame*?" Belle had not meant to be so dramatic, but pain and outrage squeezed her voice into a whisper hoarse enough to make Genia raise her head sharply and stare at her.

"Why—why, Belle! You're so excited—"

"Excited! I'm filled with disgust!" The word had a nasty tongue-shriveling taste.

Genia's hand, encased in a brown stocking, made a little gesture toward her—pawlike, placating, "Belle, honey, don't be mad at me. I know you wouldn't do such a thing. But I'm different. I'm sort of—well, light-minded."

"Divorce is not light-minded. *It is a sin.* Can't you understand that?"

"I know you say so—"

"It's not what *I* say. It's in the Scriptures, in simple black on white. It's in the marriage service: 'Wherefore they are no more twain, but one flesh. What therefore God hath joined together let no man put asunder.' Those are God's own words. How can you go against them?"

"I suppose I shouldn't, really, But it was the only way—" She left that unfinished and said defensively, "Darrie thinks it's all right."

"Darrie is wrong. *I* am quoting Scripture to you. It's plain enough."

Tears, filling Genia's amber eyes, made them look large and tremulous. When she shook her head a tear spilled out and ran down her cheek in a glistening line. "I wish you wouldn't be so mad. I've got to do it—truly, I do. It's been—well, all arranged."

"What do you mean 'arranged'? Surely John didn't agree to it?"

"Yes, he did. He gave Lawyer Tripp a letter saying he was leaving me for good, that he'd never, ever come back, and that I needn't count on a penny for support. Mr. Tripp says the letter will be what he calls 'adequate and sufficient grounds.'"

The letter was an ugly surprise to Belle. Not that it affected the fundamental wickedness of divorce, but imagine all of them —Papa, Darrie, even Genia—knowing these details and not telling her! She fell back on Scripture. "This is a sin—maybe all the worse for John's conniving in it. The Bible is clear enough on that! You can carry out God's precepts, or expect eternal punishment. Hell is full of divorced women."

"Maybe it's already too late for me to get to heaven."

"It's never too late! That's the beauty and the wonder of the

Christian faith! Don't you understand, Christ died on the Cross for *your* sins? Accept him, repent, and you will be at His side through eternity."

"Then I reckon I'll wait and repent after the divorce."

For a moment Belle was too shocked to speak. Then she stood up and said, with her voice shaking, "You may go to your room, Genia. I will not tolerate such an attitude in my presence."

Genia's expression showed surprise. If it hadn't been too fantastic to believe, Belle would have thought it showed relief as well. In silence, Genia lighted a candle at the fireplace and left the room. Belle could hear her footsteps on the stairs and, after a time, the bed creaking under her weight.

For a time after she had dismissed Genia, Belle tried to keep on with her darning. But the depths of her sister's depravity had been so shocking that her own hand trembled and made work difficult. When a darn in Marian's stocking became hobnailed with knots, Belle gave up the attempt to work, and knelt by her chair.

At first she prayed incoherently for self-control and the clearing of her own mind. Miraculously, peace came to her. She could actually feel the presence of God. "Guide me in bringing this child to the light of Thy presence. Help me to show her the way. . . ."

A revelation seemed close at hand when she heard Howard's step on the porch. Clearly, he was the instrument. She remained on her knees, and raised her face to her husband. "You have come in answer to my prayer," she said. "You will know what to do."

Howard's immediate reaction was fright. His face paled. "One of the children—?"

"One of God's children." She had hoped he would kneel beside her. Instead he drew her to her feet.

"Tell me about it. Then we can pray together."

The conversation, repeated, shocked Howard less than she had expected. "There's a sort of childish logic in Genia's reasoning," he said, "It would be normal coming from Marian or David. The blessed grace of Christ's atonement isn't grasped on an instant, and I doubt if Genia has given much thought to it."

"Then you must make it clear to her. The idea of deliberately planning, first to sin, then to take advantage of Christ's death on the Cross!"

"It is childish. I'll talk to her."

"Right away!"

"Oh, I don't think I'll wake her up for it! But first thing in the morning."

"How can she be sleeping, with such a conscience?"

"If she is lying awake, why don't you go in and kiss her goodnight? If you want to convince her of God's love, what better way than to show your own?"

"You're right, Howard. You're always right. Oh, if Genia had a husband like you—"

Howard stopped her mouth simply and directly. In his arms their love—their God-given love—flashed through her in pure flame. This would be one of the nights when they reconsecrated themselves. For a moment she almost regretted the necessity of leaving him, even briefly, to go to Genia.

As it happened, there was no real delay: Genia was sleeping as innocently as Marian, with whom she shared a bed. They lay on their sides, facing each other, each with a hand clasped under a cheek, each with the shadow of a smile on her lips.

*

Belle woke with a throbbing headache and a lassitude of limb. It was no wonder, she thought, after what Genia had put her through the night before.

Looking at her sister's face—bright and cheerful across the breakfast table—she could hardly hold back her angry words. But the children were beaming fatuously at Genia, and making excuses to touch her.

The moment Howard finished his coffee, Belle told him, "You were going to speak to Genia."

"We-well, after a bit—"

"Now!" It must be the headache, Belle thought, that made her teeth clench on the word.

Howard gave her a look of surprise, but got to his feet. The children watched big-eyed as their father and aunt went into the parlor and shut the door.

It was a long session. Belle got Howard off to school, dressed Jonathan, put some clothes to soak, washed the breakfast dishes, and had started cutting vegetables for soup when she heard Genia go upstairs. She immediately went to Howard. She closed the door behind her; this was no discussion for the children to hear. "Well?" she asked.

Howard looked shaken. He got up from the "sermon desk," took a turn up and down the room, and sat down again with the heaviness of the physically weary.

"*Well?*"

"Sit down, Belle."

"Tell me what's happened."

"This whole thing is much worse than we suspected."

Belle groped for a chair and sat down. Her hand was pressed against a painfully quickened heart. What could be worse than she already knew? Adultery? Oh, no! That she could not believe—not her own sister!

Howard passed a hand across his forehead. "It appears this whole thing—paying John's debts to the Redfellows, which we knew nothing about, the divorce, a remarriage—it's all been planned from the start."

"Remarriage? You mean John intends—"

"Not John! He simply doesn't count any more. He's like a worn-out coat. Get rid of it! Give it to charity! Burn it up! John's *gone*. No one's concerned about John. Eric Bond paid off the Redfellows to avoid criminal action, with the understanding—cut and dried as a business contract, if you please!—that John clear out and leave the field to Eric. As soon as Genia's free they'll be married."

"We won't allow it!"

"We can't prevent it."

"That woman leaves my house today! I will not have her here, associating with my innocent children. Why, do you realize she is *sleeping* with Marian?"

"I don't really suppose that's hurting Marian."

"Genia is no better than a . . . a woman of the streets!"

Howard raised a protesting hand. "Now wait a minute! I don't approve of what Genia is doing. I consider it highly immoral, and told her so. But she's still your sister, and she's still an essentially innocent young woman."

"Innocent? Planning to marry one man while she is still married to another? You call that innocent?"

"In spite of all that, there is an innocence, a childlike quality that—"

"Shut up!" For the first time in her married life Belle was thoroughly angry at her husband. In other cases where they had disagreed it had been her pleasure to concede to his superior judgment. But this—! To uphold Genia in such utter depravity! To call her childlike, innocent! Why, even when they had been girls together at Cedarhaven there had always been that . . . that *something* in Genia that deceived men, that made men want—

Howard was at her side. "Belle, dearest, are you ill? Let me—"

She struck off his hand. "Don't you dare touch me! Oh! To have you side with her, against me—your own wife—oh, oh!" There was room in the tumult of her mind for one thought: This must be a heart attack. Nothing else could explain such a frightful pounding of hot blood within herself, such a throbbing, smothering, bursting violence of feeling.

The far wall of the room came toward her, then receded. She reached toward it, and knew that she was falling.

There was a cool floating period when the doctor seemed to be there often, when children distant and small as dolls peered at her through an open door, when Howard's eyes burned with anguish, when Genia's hands—more gentle than she could have imagined—bathed her face and brushed her hair, brought trays of food and coaxed her to take a bite—"Just one, to try it, dear, I used your own recipe." Imagine little Genia, the child, pretending to such maturity!

Then, on a crisp January morning, Belle wakened clear of mind. She had been ill—very ill. Her body felt now as if composed of old cotton wadding. Her head was light, and filled with the faint whispering that can be heard when a seashell is pressed to the ear. She called out weakly and found Howard at her side.

There were a hundred questions to be asked, but he hushed her and she slept.

Another day or two drifted by. Genia fed her like a child. She remembered now that Genia was a wicked girl, that something must be done about it, but that would have to wait till she was stronger.

Although her illness seemed to have lasted a lifetime, she learned, when she had recovered from it, that it had lasted less than two weeks. And it had not been a heart attack, which would have been so apt a punishment for Howard, Genia, Darrie —all of them—but a particularly virulent case of the grippe which, according to the doctor, had been prevalent in the community. The two older children had had lighter cases of it during her own illness.

Beaming, Howard said, "I don't know what we would have done without Genia. The way she took care of all of us—"

Marian said, "I helped. I set the table, and even dried dishes—till I got sick myself."

"Of course you did. You were wonderful. But the brunt fell on Genia."

From her nest of pillows on the parlor couch, Belle gave Genia a sharp glance. The girl did look tired and pale, where usually she had the fresh coloring of a wild rose. It was impossible to forget the care she'd had at her sister's hands, but Genia was the last person to whom she would choose to be beholden.

Later in the day, talking alone with Howard, she was shocked to learn that while she had been ill—helpless was the term she used in her mind—the divorce had been granted. Too late now to prevent that. The only hope was to keep Genia from the sin of remarriage. "Bring me my Bible," she ordered, and Howard was pleased to obey.

When Genia next returned to the room bringing a tea tray, Belle sent the children out. She had her finger in the pages of the Gospel of St. Mark. "Listen to this, Genia: 'I say unto you that whosoever shall put away his wife save for the cause of fornication, causeth her to commit adultery; and whosoever shall marry her that is divorced committeth adultery.' "

"I know, dear," Genia soothed her. "Now let me take that heavy old Bible off your hands and pour you some tea. Look, I have some raisin cake, too. You know, you have to build your strength back."

Belle kept a firm hold on the Bible. "My strength is unimportant compared to your immortal soul."

"But the Bible said 'put away his *wife*.' And you know John didn't divorce me."

"You are both equally bound. *You cannot remarry.*"

When Genia poured the tea and put a cup on the stand at Belles' side, the cup chattered in the saucer all the way. "Please," she begged. "You make me feel bad—truly you do."

"Then give up this sinful plan."

"I don't think Er—Mr. Bond would let me. Not now."

"Let you indeed! He can't marry you by force!"

Genia lifted her eyes. They were brilliantly golden, as if a fire burned behind them. "Can't he? After he's waited all these years?" A scarlet tongue-tip touched her lips. "He'd kill me if I refused him now."

"Oh, what nonsense! He—" But suddenly Belle was exhausted. The Bible slipped from her hands, and she lay back on the pillow, her eyes closed.

"Oh, Belle! You haven't had a relapse, have you? Oh, dear—"

She sensed that Genia knelt by the couch. There were soft touches on her wrists and her forehead. She spoke with an effort: "I only want to *save* you."

"I know, Belle, honey. Only I'm not worth saving—truly I'm not."

Conscience urged Belle to go on fighting, but her strength was gone. Even to lift her lids was an effort. Her sister's face, warm with concern, was close to hers. Piercing her exhaustion was an arrow of awareness that Genia's presence would have adorned the halls of heaven. But it was all too late. Too hard. Too . . . somehow impossible. Genia was already damned.

CHAPTER 21

Going home alone on the steamer, Genia could not free herself of the notion that Belle was still with her. If she sat in the cabin she could feel Belle's presence on the bench behind her. If she took a turn on deck, she expected Belle to appear around a corner of the deckhouse. And always in her sister's eyes that look of—what was it? Disapproval? Dislike? Or something more cruel, more unnatural, than either of these?

Genia hated to leave Belle so soon after her illness, but it had been made plain she was not wanted. Even crueler had been Belle's efforts to keep the children away from her. Oh, dear! She was not all that bad, was she? But perhaps she was. Belle had made such a study of what was moral and what wasn't. She ought to know. Still, who was harmed by her divorcing John? It would do him no good to be legally bound to a woman he had left behind him. As for marrying Eric . . .

When she thought of Eric, icy shivers ran across her flesh. How much he must have wanted her, to wait all this time and to pay John's shortage as price for having her at last! In all the romantic novels she had read she had not come across a situation so dramatic. Why, she could write a story about it herself! How did one go about that, she wondered. Someone must write all the stories that appeared in books and magazines. Perhaps the writers even got paid for them. Well, no need now for her to earn, with Eric's means. If she'd had some way to make money when she and John—but, no, John wouldn't have wanted her to earn. That was his privilege. All he had wanted from her was—what it was impossible to give: love, and response to his love.

It had been truly dreadful that last afternoon before John had taken the boat to Victoria, when Darrie had allowed him to come and say goodby to her. He had wept, with his face in his hands and tears slipping out between his fingers. She had ached with remorse to see him so broken, and had wept too. Dabbing clumsily at his tears and her own, she had cried, "I'll go with you, John! We'll go somewhere far, far away—to Australia or . . . or to Portland—if only you'll stop crying!"

Darrie must have been standing just outside the door. How else would she have known the exact moment at which to re-enter the room and say, "Now you *must* say goodby! You know it's all been settled—and it *is* best, for both of you." Darrie had looked quite distraught, but her presence had been enough to stop John's tears, get him on his feet and out the door.

The parting might have been different without Darrie. Was it possible that, without Darrie, it might not have been a parting?

Genia tried to imagine what John would be doing now, what it would be like for her to share the meager hand-to-mouth existence that seemed his probable fate. Well, even under happier circumstances their marriage had been dull as ditchwater. She hadn't really wanted to go on with it. Except that she had, at the end, hated to see him suffering. If only that could have been avoided. . . . Remembering the parting, tears returned to warm her lids. She fumbled in her muff for a handkerchief, touched it to her eyes, and became aware that she was being watched.

She looked up with caution.

From a seat across the aisle a well-dressed gentleman rose, as if the flicking of her eye upon him were a prearranged signal. He bowed at her side. "My dear Mrs. Tower—"

Close at hand she realized the delicious boldness of his glance. His nostrils flared like a stallion's. Oh—! How dared he—! "I don't believe we are acquainted."

"Unfortunately, no. I recognized you from having been in the Senate Chamber when your divorce petition was presented."

"Oh?"

"Forgive my speaking to you now. But I see you are distressed. If there is any way I can be of service—"

Genia was looking down now—it was necessary in order to

escape the heat of his regard. Belle had said—among other things—"No decent person will respect you as a divorced woman." Belle could not be in the seat behind her, looking on . . . could she? A furtive glance behind her revealed an empty bench.

"You must think I'm forward. But a lovely woman in distress—"

Genia said, rather faintly, "Sir!"

"May I sit down beside you?"

They had the attention now of other passengers. Common sense came to Genia's rescue. What would they all think of her? Besides, wasn't she on the way to be married? She drew herself up. This time her "Sir!" rang with outraged virtue.

The stranger drew back, looking first startled and then amused. His "Excuse me!" was almost mocking.

Genia was aware of approving nods from the other passengers. A masher put in his place, they would be telling themselves. How well she had behaved, she thought. Why, even Belle would have approved!

When the man left the cabin, her imagination spun out a picture different from what had taken place: The stranger's bold approach, but without an audience . . . where? A lonely road, perhaps. One with a grassy bank—dear heaven, where was her fancy taking her? She thought of Eric Bond waiting for her, his passion mounting with the passing days. A sort of giddiness came over her. The cabin air was stifling—she must get on deck.

Outside, she leaned against the rail and breathed deeply of the chill air.

She had not known the stranger stood nearby . . . or had she truly and deeply known he was precisely there, his eyes waiting for hers, his breath drawing in the same salt wind that stung her nostrils. . . . She raised her muff, looking at him through the blurring of its furry edge as if peeping from a thicket. Behind this shield her lips were smiling. Their eyes exchanged awareness. Her heart was a trapped bird beating on its cage when, at last, she let her lashes fall and turned away.

They both knew, perfectly, what they were leaving untouched.

Papa was waiting at the dock to meet her. "Gentle Genia," he greeted. "We've all missed you."

It was a pleasant contrast to the attitude at her sister's. Restored by her father's obvious pleasure at seeing her, she clung for a minute to his arm, pressing her forehead against his shoulder. His coat sleeve smelled of tobacco and bay rum, with an overtone of perspiration: a man-smell. "Dear Papa! I've missed you, too!" The words were muffled against his sleeve.

"Why don't you just stay on at Cedarhaven with us, be my little girl again?"

They were blocking the way of other passengers. Someone brushed against her and she looked up to meet the bold stare of the man who had spoken to her on the steamer. He raised his hat—"Excuse me!"—and was gone.

"Bounder!" Papa said.

Genia smiled and took his arm. "We're in the way here. Come along."

Stay on at Cedarhaven? There was no need to answer. Life waited to be seized. And to seize . . .

Darrie insisted that, for appearance sake, a certain time must pass before remarriage. And, for the same reason, the wedding must be quiet, a civil ceremony. Judge Swan's office would be suitable. So it was that on a May afternoon, dressed well but not ostentatiously, Genia, holding her father's arm, walked toward Judge Swan's residence-office. Behind them, walking with equal sedateness, were Darrie and Lainie. Eric would meet them at the Judge's, with Pomp to serve as witness.

During this period of waiting, Eric had been allowed to call upon her perhaps a half dozen times, each visit taking place in the parlor of Cedarhaven, strictly chaperoned by some member of the family. Eric had been, on each occasion, a model of self-control, treating Genia with a disciplined respect that gave no hint of turbulent passions held in check. But tonight—today, perhaps—! For might not his need be so urgent—

"Genia, my dear! Did you stumble? These wretched wooden sidewalks—"

"No, Papa, it was nothing."

"I thought you clutched my arm."

"Of course not!" She pressed his arm now for reassurance. "Maybe I was thinking about leaving you—all of you—"

Papa's pace slackened. "You needn't go through with this. I've had my doubts—"

"You know it's all settled."

"But if you don't *want* to—"

"I do! Truly, I do!"

They were moving forward again, though perhaps more slowly. Papa patted the gloved hand on his arm. "You haven't had a chance to get really acquainted with Eric. How can you be sure—"

"Why, Papa! Eric lived right with us, at Cedarhaven."

"That was years ago. You were a child."

"Not such a child." In a burst of confidence she added, "I'll tell you something funny, but sort of sweet. Long ago—the day Victor Smith came back and took the Custom House, you remember?—I met Eric on the street. He was on his way to join the Army. He said then he was coming back to marry me."

"Really? And you a little thing with your hair down your back! Well, that is romantic! And, I must say, he seems a fine young man. But then so did John. Things have a way of turning out . . . hm. . . . What I mean is, I'd hate to have you marry someone you didn't—someone else you didn't—"

"Now don't you worry, Papa. We're in love, and we're going to get along just fine."

After a few more steps taken in silence, Papa said, "If only your mother had lived—"

"I don't want to talk about her!" Genia sensed in her voice a strident tone unsuited to the occasion. She forced her mind to this moment in time, this morning in May, herself a bride, young—yes, and beautiful! Tongues might lie but mirrors did not. A bride on her way to her waiting bridegroom. The girl who had married John Tower had been only a shadow of herself. There had not been then this heightened awareness of the world, and of herself within it, precious as a pearl within its coarser shell. Oh, how Eric must value and need her! She felt her fingers tightening on her father's arm, and forced them to relax. "It's a beautiful wedding day, isn't it, Papa? Can you smell the wild roses? The hedges are thick with them."

"Lovely!" he agreed. "Lovely! Happy is the bride the sun shines on. For your wedding day you have a sky as blue as heaven itself."

"My, you are poetic!"

"Don't laugh! I wrote a bit of poetry back in my salad days. I've always felt that, given a chance, I might have done something in the literary world."

"I'm sure you would have. Oh! Oh—!"

They had turned a corner. Eric, with Pomp beside him, stood outside the door of Judge Swan's office. He was resplendent in dark broadcloth and a tall beaver hat. His look, meeting Genia's, was a cable drawing her inexorably toward him. Her heart, responding to this demand, rose and swelled in her throat. Instinctively she drew her scarf closer to hide the throbbing that she felt must be visible to Eric at the distance that still divided them.

There was a mannered ritual to be observed. Pomp and Eric stood aside, their hats removed. Papa's hat was lifted with his free hand as he guided Genia across the threshold. The men bowed as they passed. Through the corner of her eye, Genia saw Darrie bowing as she followed through the doorway. Lainie's bright curls bobbed beneath her hatbrim as she curtsied.

When, after they had entered, Eric came into the room he brought with him a fire that drew the very oxygen from the air. Genia struggled for breath and wondered if she might be going to faint. She dared not look into Eric's eyes, but forced her attention to the room and to Judge Swan rising to greet them, a stocky badger-whiskered little man in a frock coat worn thin at the seams, and a string tie.

There was handshaking among all the men, a desultory conversation: "The license? . . . Ah, yes, Mr. Ryan! . . . And the ring . . . Who gives the bride . . . ?" The words were no more than leaves floating on the meager air, unrelated to her, requiring no attention. Nothing had reality except the time that had to pass like ribbon slowly reeled onto a spool. Time growing shorter . . . shorter. . . . Its passing was too exquisite to be borne. She had meant to find refuge in . . . what? Ah yes! The room. She willed her mind to its details: a stuffed bird on the shelf, fish spears leaning in a corner, drying starfish tacked to the wall—it all reminded her of something. Had she lived through this moment in time before? No, her memory saw not this room but another like it—the Agency at Neah Bay, carrying, after Judge Swan had left, the stamp of his occupancy. Neah Bay . . . She had long pretended the place had no existence. Those rain-swept winter days of waiting—a tale she'd heard of someone else's misadventures. Not hers. *Not hers. . . .*

In the close room, Lainie had slipped off her hat, swinging it back and forth by its ribbon band. Her hair was bright as sunlight in the fusty room. Looking up she met Genia's eyes. At once her lips parted in a smile that showed the badge of her age: a missing tooth. "Is Auntie Genia married yet?"

A gust of laughter greeted this, and Judge Swan said, "Young lady's right—we'd better get on with the ceremony. Take your positions, please." He cleared his throat, and thumbed through a worn leather-bound book.

*

Coming out of the shadowed office, Genia looked up into the burnished blue-and-white of a cloud-flecked sky. From the field below the Judge's office a meadow lark's song spiraled upward. A flowered yard nearby filled the air with the scent of honeysuckle. The world was drenched with summer sweetness. Thus the last day of life might be honed, Genia thought, the sweetness sharpened to an edge so exquisite that one longed for the dulling touch of death.

During the plans and preparations for her wedding Genia had taken the passive part. Darrie had thought this, and that. Eric preferred so, and so. Bemused by expectation, Genia had allowed arrangements to be made.

By Eric's preference they went now, directly after the ceremony, to the house he had bought years ago. It had, she knew, been redecorated and furnished for her. A hired woman had been found to manage the housework, this luxury accomplished by the offering of wages too high to be refused.

This woman, the widowed Letha Morrison, met Genia at the door of her new home.

"Come in, ma'am! Let me take your wraps. I hope I've got things fixed to suit you, but if not it won't take me long to catch on. I surely aim to please you—Mr. Bond will vouch for that."

Genia looked at the woman without curiosity; she was there, like the furniture, on the periphery of this new existence whose fiery core was Eric and herself.

The woman chattered on: "I've got a tray of tea, and a nice cake ready to be cut, if you'd like a bit of food. I could serve it anywhere you like, in the parlor, maybe? Oh—and the bathroom's upstairs, ma'am. First time I ever see such an arrangement. Comes to that, first time I ever took care of a house *with* a bathroom. Seems almost too elegant, if you ask me. But like I said, it's upstairs if you wanted to freshen up. Or you could use the kitchen sink. Just suit yourself."

It became necessary to look at this woman with whom Genia would share her roof: leathery, middle-aged—the sort who would inevitably be described as a "good worker." Obviously a chatterbox. Or was it something else? Genia's attention was caught and held by some quality of eagerness and waiting. She thought, with surprise, She's nervous! She's afraid she won't please me—poor thing! She smiled and laid her hand on the woman's arm. "Don't worry, Mrs. Morrison. Everything will be just fine. I appreciate your being here."

Color rose into the sallow cheeks. "Oh, thank you! And may I say, Mrs. Bond, you are *the* prettiest bride!"

"Mrs. Bond!" That was Eric's voice. "It's the first time you've been called that. Why don't you go upstairs and freshen up, Mrs. Bond, my dear? Then we'll have our cake and tea in the parlor?"

"I didn't light no fire in the grate. It come on so warm. But seems now like it would of been cozier. . . ."

Ascending the stairs, Genia passed beyond the sound of the servant's voice.

In the bathroom, so well described as "elegant," she looked around her: a bathtub on curving legs, a washbasin set in marble, a water closet beneath a massive flush tank. She ran her hand along the inside of the bathtub. The copper had been polished to a satin finish. She had never lived in a house with a real bathtub. At Cedarhaven, and even in the new Tower house, they had used a tub brought into the kitchen and filled by the bucket- and kettle-full. But this—! Why, she could lie out full length, the water flowing along her naked body . . . shivers of delight followed the imagined caress. She closed her eyes. She had not supposed Eric would wait *at all*, that he would be able to curb . . . Obviously, he did intend to wait till bedtime. It might be better so. The hours of velvet dark ahead of them, the house quiet, that woman gone to—wherever she did go. She did not, Eric had told her, "sleep in."

Genia washed her hands, letting the cool water flow across her wrists, dried on one of a row of linen towels, and went decorously downstairs to tea.

Little was left of the afternoon. Eric took her on an inspection tour of the house and garden, explaining what he had done, what he intended to do. Mrs. Morrison served them an excellent dinner. As the woman cleared up, Genia played, at Eric's request, some of the tunes she had played as a girl at Cedarhaven. Of course she didn't have her music; that, and her own inattention, made her fingers stumble on the keys. When she let her hands fall from the keyboard, the house was quiet. Mrs. Morrison must have finished her work and slipped away. They were alone in the house.

Eric rose, came to the piano, and took her hand. "I have to keep telling myself you are actually here, actually my wife, after all this time. . . ."

A tremor ran through her. She felt her hand quiver in his.

"Come," he said gently, "let's sit here together on the sofa. There's such a lot I want to say to you."

When they were seated she stole a look at him. What iron control he had! The full underlip that spoke of sensuality was firmly held in. The solid lines of his face must be a mask to hide the passionate need that would be surging through his blood.

He took her hand again. It lay small and helpless in his. When he closed his fingers over hers she noted again the little islands of fair hair. Her hand moved convulsively. At once he released his hold. "I've frightened you," he said, "and that must never happen."

He moved, to put a little distance between them on the sofa. "We've had an odd courting, you and I. You know I've been in love with you for years. There's never, really, been anyone else."

Something in the way his voice fell away made Genia look quickly at him. "But you have—there have been—other women?"

"I wish you hadn't asked that. I won't lie to you. But you've got to understand men are—well, they're not like women. In the best of men—and God knows I never pretended to be that!—there is an animal-like lust. It's something you would never understand. A decent man hopes to keep his wife from ever being . . . touched by that side of life. If you had not been married to that—to that—" Now, at least, emotion revealed itself. A muscle tightened at the corner of Eric's mouth like a thread pulling through the flesh. His face seemed to darken with angry blood. "I could kill him!"

"Oh, Eric, please! I never really loved him! I give you my word I didn't!"

Control came back. Eric composed his features. He even smiled at her. "I hope that's true. At least I know he didn't—he couldn't!—feel for you what I do."

"What do you . . . feel, Eric?" She reached out to lay a hand on his knee, and was rewarded by a tensing of the muscles beneath her fingers. Instantly he removed her hand and held it in his.

"You see, you have a kind of childish innocence in spite of your—" The word gave him trouble, but he got it out: "—your marriage. Believe me, Genia, I'd cut off my right hand before I'd destroy that quality in you. I want, above all things in the world, to keep you the sweet warmhearted child you are now." For the first time his voice was less than steady. "I'm ready to devote my life to that."

Genia turned her face to him, and lifted her lashes slowly, slowly, until their gazes met. Words slipped like honey across her tongue: "Eric, don't you . . . want me . . . as a woman?"

Eric was on his feet. Her hand was flung aside. He took a step or two away from her, whirled to stare, then strode to the piano and put the cover down over the keys with force that set the strings to vibrating.

Genia's heart began to beat hard, sending blood into her breast and throat.

Over his shoulder Eric said, "I think you know—even in your innocence you must have guessed—how much I want you. But you needn't—you *need not*—" He raised a clenched fist for emphasis; "—be afraid of me. I will have, for your sake, infinite patience."

Genia was on her feet. "I'm going upstairs. When I call you—"

By the time she reached their bedroom the beating of her heart was suffocating, the quickened blood suffused her whole being in a rosy mist. Premonition was there, like a tiny fog bell ringing far off in the swirling mists of her own emotion. It was there, but she could not believe in it.

Darrie had seen to it that her necessities were here. In a room barely shadowed with summer twilight, she pulled out the white nainsook gown with its embroidered yoke and virginal little collar. Genia looked at it, and flung it aside. She took off her clothes and stood naked before the mirror. How could he *not*—when he saw. . . ? Her hands enclosed the rosy-tipped breasts, lifting them. She saw, in the mirror, a flushed face, parted lips that pulsed with quick-drawn breath. Trembling fingers tore at the combs and pins that held her hair, and it fell in a drift of dark gold about her shoulders. She put cologne on her palms and brushed them on her throat, her breasts, her thighs. Then she turned down the bedcovers to leave a smooth expanse of undersheet.

On arched feet—a cat would walk so, she thought—she went to the head of the stairs and called, "Eric?"

There was a sound in response. She did not wait to hear what it was but flew to take her place on the bed. Eric's step was on the stairs. In a single glance, consuming as flame, he would see the perfection of her body. He might talk of patience, but she knew his need. The total rallying of her strength would not suffice against him! There was no longer room above her racing heart for breath to come and go when Eric stood, frozen for one eternal second, in the open doorway.

Then he was gone. From the immaculate and elegant bathroom she heard him retching, retching, as if he would never empty himself of loathing.

CHAPTER 22

Darrell Starkweather died more quietly than he had lived. One morning he complained of not feeling well. "Must have caught a little cold," he told Darrie when she came to his room. "It's hard to breathe."

She went out to bring him coffee and toast, as she had done on many other mornings. When she returned he was resting against the raised pillow, his lips curved in secret triumph. He had slipped away from a world which, in spite of the best effort he could muster, had never yielded him the treasure he suspected it held.

Darrie was shattered by his death. If only she had had some warning, she thought; if he had been ill, if she had seen him failing, but this—! One moment he was there representing the complex of problems created by the breadwinner who does not win bread, nor the jam nor butter for it, nor coal, nor shoes. The next moment he was gone, the problem solved by default.

Perhaps she had half believed his repeated assurances about the up-coming position, the soon-to-be-improved finances. Now all she had was remorse for the weakness of her faith. Now their relationship would never be set right.

Pride kept Darrie from dissolving into ready tears, as Belle did when she arrived from Olympia. "Poor Papa! Dear Papa! Do you think he truly found Christ before he went?"

Terse from an intertwining of annoyance with Belle and the discomfort of her own held-back tears, Darrie asked, "Can't you trust Christ to find him?"

"Please—! At a time like this! Christ is always there. We are told, 'Underneath are the everlasting arms.' But we must seek and accept Him. It's all He asks."

Genia's "Poor Papa! Dear Papa!" was more convincing. She was truly grief-stricken. In her twenty-six years no shadow had ever fallen between Papa and his adored Genia. Now, crushing herself to Darrie, she sobbed, "Losing him like this—I never dreamed! I can't stand it!" Her whole body shook with a child's abandonment to grief.

Presently she found a way to dull the razor's edge. Her sodden, swollen face became even more blurred, her expression more vague. During the funeral she sat in the back parlor between her husband and Darrie, on her lips a little half-smile as if she had learned some secret unknown to the other mourners.

"When I'm gone," Papa had told Darrie more than once, "you'll be comfortable. I've taken care of that. Insurance, you know. The poor man's estate."

It was no surprise for Darrie to learn that he had borrowed to the hilt on his insurance. The amount she received did not take care of the numerous small bills he had left and the cost of his funeral. Even at that, she doubted that all the merchants presented their just claims. The suspicion galled her. She paid for a notice in the weekly newspaper: Anyone with a claim against the late Darrell Starkweather should present it for payment to his daughter, Miss. D. Starkweather. No claimants appeared and she was obliged to let the matter drop.

There was, of course, Cedarhaven itself. It was mortgaged, as any property owned by Darrell Starkeather would be. But it had supported them before. It must continue to do so.

On a morning of harsh realism, Darrie got out her worn account books, locked the door of her bedroom, and assessed her position. Cedarhaven would be hers. Papa's will had made no distinction among his daughters, but Belle and Genia were willing to quitclaim their rights. Perhaps they had not cared for the alternative of having to support her and Lainie. At once she recognized this as unfair. Belle and Howard could barely keep themselves and their growing family afloat. More than once Darrie had tapped "board money" for a pair of copper-toed shoes, or a necessary dental bill. With Genia and Eric it was not a financial problem. Yet obstacles as solidly tangible as a rock wall made it impossible for Lainie and her to join that household.

In fairness, either of her sisters might have demanded, on firm legal ground, that Cedarhaven be sold and the equity divided equally among them. Genia's temperament would not have allowed this. As for Belle, perhaps God—or Howard—had spoken to her. In any event, neither sister had made such a suggestion. The house was Darrie's. Morally it had been hers from the day it was built. Now it would be so legally, except for the bank's claim which, with interest faithfully paid, was no present threat.

Darrie had not realized, until presented with the risk of losing it, how much Cedarhaven meant to her. Now, sitting at the desk in her bedroom, she closed her eyes and let her mind inventory the four walls within which she had her life: the gracious double parlor with its marble fireplaces, the warm red-papered diningroom, the ugly but familiar kitchen from whose windows one could see the spar-filled harbor, the spacious bedrooms—doubly important since they were her source of revenue.

It was a lovely home. If it could be just that—a home for Lainie and herself, with the faithful Cheecha slipping in the back door in the early morning to kindle fires and start breakfast. . . .

This was daydreaming with a vengeance.

Darrie opened her eyes, drew the account book toward her, and studied the past month's entries: coal, an assessment for that wretched city water system that as yet had come to nothing and probably never would, wages for a carpenter to replace a broken window pane (Papa had meant to "get around to that" but never had), Cheecha's wages and an extra dollar and a half when she had allowed herself to be taken to the dentist with a painful and swollen jaw, groceries . . . groceries . . . groceries. . . .

On the credit side were the few neat entries: Mr. Beale, $30; Sam Coos $15; Pomp Ryan, $40.

This month, of course, there had been no entry of Papa's earnings. They had never been large—a few dollars here for copying a brief, a few there for "tending office" for a friend. While Papa had been alive Darrie had not taken his earnings seriously. She had even resented secretly the offhand way in which he handed over the small sums with instructions to "buy some little trinket for yourself or Lainie." He must have known as well as she did that the "trinket" would be a sack of potatoes or a cord of firewood.

Now, looking at the pages of her account book, Darrie put from her a temptation to go back over the last twelve months and see what total her father had contributed. It really didn't matter. She had not depended on his earnings, but his presence had been a bulwark. She had never been a woman alone against the world. Now she was. The knowledge chilled her.

On an impulse, she left her desk and opened the bureau drawer where she had put away Papa's few personal treasures. She had covered them with a seldom-used shawl so that she would not see them and be reminded. Now she took them out, examining them, holding them in her hands. Here were his onyx cufflinks, his pearl stickpin, his penknife, his watch in its time-smoothed case, and—in a well-worn satin box—a locket that had been Mama's. When Darrie pressed the spring a ridiculously young-looking Darrell and Cynthia Starkweather smiled at her from the facing heart-shaped frames.

For the first time since her father's death Darrie gave way to tears. Once she had allowed them to flow, there was no damming possible. Sobs wracked her body. Tears soaked her handkerchief, wet her sleeve, ran down onto the dress, and still flowed as if they came from some perpetual spring within herself. She could not have said whether she wept for the loss of her father or for some deeper and more dreadful loss disclosed by the locket's picture. Papa, elderly, pretentious, undeniably selfish, had been one person; Papa young and hopeful, eyes full of dreams and love, was another. This was the measure of a life, then: expectations, soaring dreams—and in the end a handful of trinkets hidden beneath a shawl.

After a time, when she had ceased to fight them, her tears dried.

She had been wrung out, drained, emptied of all feeling. There was nothing left. It was the same sensation she had when the pain of a sick headache finally ceased. There was this same feeling that the unbearable had been borne. She had survived somehow. It was time now for a fresh start.

That January, in spite of the most painful counting of pennies, the most stringent economy, Darrie could not cover the annual interest on the mortgage. Fifty dollars had to be added to the face of the loan against Cedarhaven. This meant that, next year, the interest would be even harder to meet. If, each year, the indebtedness mounted, nibbling away at the narrow margin of safety with which she clung to Cedarhaven . . . Darrie said that she would not think about it, but it was never out of her mind.

When Mr. Beale shipped out on a steamer bound for the Orient and left the front corner room vacant, Darrie was close to panic. Then Sam Coos introduced a friend who was looking for a place to board. There was something about Si Booker that Darrie instinctively disliked. His small eyes were deepset and wary and—she thought—too close together for honesty. And he had a thin cruel mouth.

"Are you in business here, Mr. Booker? I ask that because I like to get permanent people in my rooms."

He cut his eyes at her and said, "I'll be staying here. I'm a shippers' agent."

That explained his acquaintance with Sam Coos, the chandler's clerk. Still Darrie hesitated. Then she decided to let fate settle it. "That's a very nice room. I'll have to have $45 a month, in advance. With full board, of course."

To her surprise he agreed at once, pulling out his wallet and handing her the bills. "I'll move in tonight."

It seemed to Darrie that, with the advent of Si Booker, the atmosphere of Cedarhaven subtly changed. To offset this she became even more formal than before. She took care to be in the diningroom early enough that none of the men could find an excuse to be seated before her. To emphasize her wishes, she nodded permission after she had taken her place at the head of the table: "Please be seated." On a warm evening when Si Booker came to table in his shirtsleeves, she said, with lifted brow, "We'll excuse you while you finish dressing." That mistake was not made again.

She tried to exact the same respect for Lainie that she demanded for herself, but it was impossible. Lainie, at ten years of age, was endearingly gay and good-natured. She gave deference rather than expected it. In spite of Darrie's best efforts the child would come to table late and out of breath, apologizing to everyone and explaining that she'd had to feed a seagull in the backyard, restore a lost puppy to its mother, or free a robin from one of the house cats.

The men, knowing her penchant for tending wounded creatures, called her "Dr. Elaine," and brought her sweets which they gravely insisted were for her patients. She was such a lovable child, and the men were so obviously fond of her, that Darrie was obliged to accept a certain informality between them. To counteract this, she talked firmly to Lainie in private. "Never forget you are a lady. There must always be a distance between you and—well, such men as board here."

"You don't mean *Uncle Pomp*?"

"Well, perhaps not Uncle Pomp. But the others. Always—always!—think of a space between you. Don't let them reach across it."

Lainie, after such a lecture, was apt to hug Darrie ardently and say, "I'll remember, Auntie. Truly I will."

She was a child who took joy in pleasing.

This was all right, Darrie thought, if the person to be pleased was herself. The possibility of Lainie trying to please someone . . . someone . . . Why was it always, in her mind's eye, a masculine someone? Yet who was there around Lainie but men? The next time Darrie had a room vacant, she told herself, she would wait until she could get a woman boarder in it. Even as she planned this she recognized the financial disaster of such a prolonged vacancy: women were still scarce in the Territory, unattached women looking for a place to board were scarcer still.

It was the unexpected expense that always betrayed Darrie. Cheecha let a kettle of hot fat boil over on the stove. It caught fire. The flames spread to the window curtains, scorching the window frame and damaging the wallpaper. The following month a branch torn by the wind from one of the cedar trees fell across a dormer window, and the carpenter had to be called again.

These crises had barely been surmounted when Belle and Howard returned to Port Townsend to live: the local church had finally reached the point of having a full-time pastor, though they were not quite ready to pay him a full-time salary.

Darrie said, "Belle, how will you manage? Five hundred a year—really! And with four children."

Belle gave her a look of serene confidence. "By fall it will be five little ones. But the Lord has seen fit to bring us back here, where there is such a great need for Howard's influence. I'm sure we can trust Him to provide for us."

Darrie, as usual, found it difficult to argue against Belle and the Lord. She helped her sister and brother-in-law settle their meager household furnishings in the little board-and-batten house the church had provided. She sorted out a couple of dresses from Lainie's wardrobe for her cousin Marian, and made a coat that Pomp had discarded into trousers for little Jonathan. The family got along somehow. Perhaps, Darrie thought, Belle was right: the Lord—or someone!—did provide.

Durand, the Newton's fifth child, was born in September. From the first Darrie saw a striking resemblance to her father: this infant had the same wide-set eyes, the same sweet mouth that had, in Papa's case, gradually drooped into weak petulance, the same finely modeled forehead.

When Durand was a few months old it became apparent that he had a deformed foot. At first his parents refused to concede this. The foot merely turned inward, as all infants' feet turned toward each other. "When he gets to standing," Belle said, "he'll be all right." Howard agreed. "He's such a sturdy little fellow—there can't be much wrong."

Darrie made it a point to consult Dr. Madden and was told that Durand did indeed have a congenital defect. He would, the doctor told her, be lame at best. He might have to use a crutch or brace. But the doctor also told Darrie that a surgeon he had known and worked with during the war, a man now practicing in San Francisco, had performed several near-miraculous operations on similar defects. There was a good chance, the doctor thought, that Durand's foot could be corrected, especially if he could be taken, while still an infant, for the surgery.

"But San Francisco!" Darrie protested. "Howard and Belle can't afford that. And this doctor would charge a fortune, wouldn't he?"

"If I wrote him explaining the situation, I expect he'd trim his fee. In any event I'd want to send him my opinion of the child's condition, and get his own ideas, before there was any traveling done. It would be spring before it would be worked out, like as not. Maybe they could find the money by then."

Find the money, Darrie thought, when she had come out onto Water Street. As if it were under a rock somewhere, waiting to be turned up! Why, a trip like that cost hundreds of dollars, even with the fee "trimmed." It was impossible.

Still she could not put out of her mind little Durand's twisted foot, the projected image of an older Durand hobbling along on the outskirts of a group of playmates who ran, climbed fences, skated, danced. A life so set apart would inevitably dwindle into failure. In her mind's eye she saw another old man, when the futile years had slipped through his fingers as they had through Darrell Starkweather's, standing alone and sour-mouthed at the end of life. No! She could not let this happen. Something had to be done for Durand.

Belle and Howard came to agree with this, though not till after a sharp lecture from Dr. Madden and the black-and-white facts of his correspondence with San Francisco.

"We'll pray over it," Howard said. And Belle, her pretty eyes full of tears, said, "Yes, surely the Lord will show us a way."

Si Booker seemed an unlikely emissary of the Lord. Darrie herself did not immediately recognize him in the role when, after breakfast one morning, he asked for an interview with her. "A private interview," he said. And he added, "I can put you in the way of making a little money."

Darrie looked at him, her dislike and distrust quarreling with the magic of those last words. "Come into the parlor," she said, "and tell me what you want."

It was quite simple, really. He wanted her to buy a certain building downtown, using money he would advance to her. The building housed two enterprises, a tailor shop and a box house known as Anchors Aweigh. The location was ideal, on the corner, with a vacant lot on the other side that went with the property. The recent owner of the Anchor had been killed in a street brawl. His widow would sell the business reasonably, since she couldn't operate it herself. Si Booker had splendid notions of improving the place, booking in talent through "connections" in Portland and Seattle, making it, in his own terms, a real little gold mine. In time, a store or rooming house could be built on the vacant lot.

Darrie tried to follow his reasoning. "What have I to do with this?"

"It's the property's ownership that sticks me. The businessmen in this town are a pack of mangy dogs, the way they set on any newcomer to tear him to bits. Want to keep the goody all to themselves. Well, this Allie McMann, the widow, she and I understand each other. We've shaken hands on our deal, but her lease comes up for renewal in three months. And I happen to know the owner of the building—he's one of the pack of old dogs—won't renew it for me. It's buy the building, or let go the whole proposition."

"Who is the owner?"

"Your brother-in-law, Eric Bond."

Darrie sat perfectly still, determined not to show by the quiver of a lash that the name meant anything to her. She spoke casually: "Mr. Bond wouldn't sell to me any quicker than to you. Anyway, he'd know you were back of it, since you've already talked to him."

Si Booker nodded approvingly. "I knew you were smart first time I set eyes on you. You get down to tacks like a man. But you're *not* a man and that's the nub of it: he *will* sell to you."

"Why?"

"The way you'll put it up to him. Now, honest, Miss Starkweather, does he know all about your finances? You're not that thick with him, are you?"

"No."

"If you told him you'd saved and scraped and got together, say, $300, he'd believe you, wouldn't he?"

Darrie laughed. "He might be fool enough."

"All right, that's your pitch. Lord God! you tell him, how you need a good investment for your bit of savings! Now you've found out I want to lease the Anchor and improve it, and you can see that Monroe Street building is the gilt-edge investment you've been looking for. You're a woman, you're his sister-in-law, you're asking a favor that won't take a pinprick of skin off his nose. Of course he'll sell it to you."

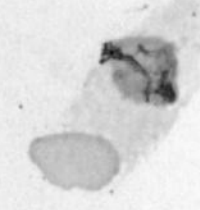

"He'll know you are putting me up to it." The statement,

which seemed to have spoken itself, made Darrie realize she was actually considering this fantastic scheme.

"Not if you're foxy. And I think you can be. If I'd thought there was anyone else could pull it off, I wouldn't have come to you."

"You're frank."

Si shrugged. "Nothing to lose by it. If you bring it off, you and I are ahead by a country mile. If you fail—" He shrugged again; "—I'm no worse off than I was before. I can't dog it alone—not in this town."

When Darrie didn't answer—actually he had given her so much to think about she didn't know what to answer first—Si whipped out a pencil and a well-thumbed notebook and began to quote figures: the property was worth $5000 but she ought to con Eric out of it for $4500; Si would put up the down payment, she to return her half of it to him from profits—"Won't charge you interest, either—that's the kind of partnership we'll have." The tailor paid $25 a month for his shop, the Anchor $65. In a few years they would own the building free and clear, as equal partners. "Offer Bond $300 down—I'll go higher if I have to—and hold the interest to 5 per cent. He'll do it for you."

"Doesn't it bother you to deceive him? To ask me to deceive him?"

"Not a pinch! He's a shrewd operator. Many's the poor sucker he's had by the ears, and squeezed out their last drop of blood in some business deal. Look at it this way, girlie, we're not cheating him, we're just not telling him the whole truth."

For him to call her 'girlie' pointed up the sordidness of their discussion. Darrie liked no part of it except the possibility of making money. How she did need that!

Si might have sensed her weakening. He leaned toward her. "What have you got to lose? It's my money. I'll tell you something else too. You're more woman than you know you are. You're too icy for your own good. You go in there, give Bond a bit of lovey-dovey stuff, and you'll have him eating out of your hand."

No poison arrow could have had a more vulnerable target.

Darrie sat frozen for a moment, then got up quickly. "You've said enough. I want nothing to do with your nasty schemes."

"Now wait a minute—"

"There's nothing more to say." She was already in the doorway between the front and back parlor.

"Wait—wait!" Si ran after her, caught at her sleeve. She shook off his hand. "Don't make up your mind so quick! Take twenty-four hours—forty-eight! What can you lose? Please, Miss Star—"

The swinging kitchen door cut off his plea.

Darrie got a cup and poured herself some coffee. Her hand was shaking so badly some scalding drops spilled onto her fingers.

"What's matter, Miss Darrie? You sick, huh?"

"No, Cheecha, I'm all right."

She sat at the kitchen table, holding the coffee cup, trying to think. It was an utterly outrageous proposition. She had been out of her mind to listen to Si Booker. Of course she wouldn't involve herself in such a venture. Why, Anchors Aweigh was a notorious place even now! Under Si's management it would be worse rather than better. No—no! She wouldn't dream of getting into such a partnership even if it would work, and it probably wouldn't. Eric was too shrewd to be taken in by such a subterfuge . . . wasn't he . . . ?

All day she thought about the proposition, telling herself the arguments against it. Si's voice kept repeating in her mind the arguments for, thus producing an endless and tiring debate.

In the evening when Si tried to speak to her, she evaded him. "I'm very tired. Please—I'm going straight upstairs."

In her room she went over the painful figures in her account book. There was no changing them. Every year, every month, *every day* she was slipping a little farther behind.

When she thought she had heard all the men go out, she came downstairs again. She found Pomp alone by the hearthfire. He drew up a chair for her. "Sit down, my dear. You're looking fair beat out tonight. And where's our Lainie—she's the one can always make you smile again?"

"At her cousins'. It's Jonathan's birthday."

"You should have gone with her."

"I'm too worried."

"Is it something new you have to worry about then?"

"No, the same old thing—money, or lack of it."

A lump of coal fell from the grate. Pomp got out the tongs and tried to pick it up. Without looking at Darrie he said, "You know I could always loan you a little something. You could take your own sweet time to pay it back."

She knew he had very little saved; every month he sent money to his family in Ireland. The Irish were supposed to be flighty, but Pomp was as steady as a rooted tree. And like a tree he would never do anything out of character. He was simply there, to be relied on.

He had asked her several times to marry him. The first time had been while the wound of Eric's rejection still burned with a fresh and bitter fire. Out of her pain she had cried, "No! It's impossible!" and had seen Pomp's face wither in hurt pride.

Later, after the winter in Neah Bay, he had said—this time half-joking, half-serious—" 'Tis a father for Lainie you're needing now more than a husband. Do I look better to you in that light?"

Compassion must have deepened within her by then, for she had been grateful for his offer, and thanked him for it.

"But it's still impossible?"

"Yes, Pomp, it is."

Again, soon after Papa's death he'd said, "It is any use at all then for me to wait and hope?"

And she'd said, "Pomp, you're like a dear, dear brother. But —no!"

It had taken only seconds for these memories to flash through her mind. Pomp was still lifting the coal back into the grate, still avoiding her eyes as he had when he offered her the loan. She said, "Thank you, Pomp. But it would have to be paid back sometime. That's the point."

"Not necessarily." The coal was in place. He stood up so that she had to lift her head to look at him. When she did so, she found his gaze so intent she had the feeling he had taken physical hold of her. "I'd still like to marry you." His mouth twisted.

Then he laughed. "That sounds lukewarm. I'm anything but that."

Darrie felt color coming up into her cheeks. "I appreciate your offer, but you know I can't marry you."

"You can't—or won't—marry me. I understand that."

"Not just you, believe me. Anyone."

"Sure I'd like to show you how wrong you are. 'Tis a man's part you've been playing since you were thirteen. A good job you've made of it, too. But you've got a woman's body—"

She started to get up, but he stepped in front of her so that it would have been awkward. "No! Let us finish for once! Any man could teach you you're a woman, and better off you'd be for knowing. There's that side of it, and there's the plain, practical side. You wouldn't have to keep up this eternal scratching to make ends meet. 'Tis understood at home the money quits if I have my own home here. I'd be that proud to support you and Lainie."

She shook her head.

Pomp stepped away from her then, and went back to his own chair, where he stood with his arms resting on its back. "I suppose you'd be offended at some straight talk. Or at least embarrassed. A woman seldom wants a man the way he wants her till they've been married—or together. The polite ideas are all wrong—man loving like an animal, woman all ether and moonbeams. In fact, 'tis quite the other way around. The woman loves by touch. By some man possessing her she's captured for good. There's no explaining otherwise how women stick to men the way they do, and all. You've seen it—a self-respecting dog would leave. A wife hangs on. But with a man—"

Darrie waited. When he did not go on, she said, "How is it with a man?"

He straightened up. One fist struck softly into the other palm. "Men are the true great fools," he said. "They're the dreamers. Do you know what holds a man the tightest? You ought to, God knows, but do you?"

"No."

"The woman he never got! He dreams about her when he's

ninety, warming his scrawny shanks by the fire, gumming an old pipe. By God, he's still wishing he'd had the one he missed."

Darrie knew the conversation was indelicate, but it was fascinating. With tightened breath she said, "A woman's a fool to marry then, isn't she?"

"She is! But a greater fool to pass it up. She's stuck with only men to choose from, more's the pity! Man's a polygamous devil at best. A smart woman knows that, and holds to him, and makes the best of it."

"And overlooks his . . . transgressions?"

"If she can't prevent 'em, yes! They don't mean much to him. They would to her. Because touch, to her, *is* love. A man can lie with a woman and by morning forget what she looks like. His wife, if she only knew it, hasn't so much to forgive."

Darrie felt the conversation had gone far enough. She stood up and said, "I've heard of strange proposals, but this is queerer than most. Surely you don't imagine you're making marriage sound attractive."

"The truth is always a compliment, if there's sense to receive it. Oh, Darrie, girl, we could have a fine life together. You've a brain on you like a steel trap. I admire that, though few men would. But not to the exclusion of your lovely body. There's times I'm fair sick with thinking how that's being wasted."

Darrie's response frightened her. She bent her head to hide the warmth she felt pressing upward from a fast-beating heart into pulsing cheeks. "Marriage is out of the question," she said.

"Will you for once tell me why, then?"

She could have said, with truth, I gave my heart once, and now I've nothing left to give. Or, with equal truth, I have been—as you so aptly put it—"touched." And you are right to say one is captured for good. Or bad. Neither would have been quite the whole truth, yet both were part of it. When Pomp spoke of love, Eric filled her mind. And there was no escape from that.

The blood was still hot in her cheeks. She pressed her palms against the warmth, willing it to subside. Pomp was looking at her, but without hope. When she turned toward the hall, he made no move to stop her.

Darrie had thought she would lie awake for a long time. Instead, she closed her eyes and fell instantly to sleep. She wakened at dawn to the tentative grace notes of birds in the cedar tree outside her window. Quickly, daylight strengthened their song to a triumphal chorus.

Decision had formed in Darrie's mind while she had slept.

She got up, dressed hurriedly in the morning chill, and went downstairs.

It was early; even Cheecha was not here. Darrie started a fire in the cookstove, and then stood for a few minutes on the back porch. It was a windless morning, softened by a fine mist so that the sleeping town and the harbor beyond it seemed to lie beneath a sheet of silver gauze. Darrie counted the ships in the harbor: a schooner, bare-masted and at anchor with a deckload of yellow lumber; a barkentine high in the water, waiting to be laden; a sleek clipper ship bearing, even with her sails furled, a look of bird-like eagerness; a stolid square-rigger . . . that was four, and two more in the cove . . . was that a seventh just visible beyond the shoulder of land? On some days there were more ships than this, and seldom less.

Port Townsend lived on money from these ships.

That was why places like the Anchor made money. That was why every other door on Water Street was a saloon. People were getting rich downtown, while she sat here on the hill like a blind woman and grubbed for pennies.

Cheecha appeared on the walk below her, came wheezing up the steps, and greeted Darrie. "Hanh! You up?"

Darrie could laugh at the pointlessness of the question.

"You look good. Strong. Ha!"

It was true. Last night's distress was gone. There was a way to have money, and she had found it.

When breakfast was out of the way—again Darrie avoided any private exchange with Si Booker—she went upstairs to change from her percale work dress into something more impressive. There was not much choice—she had never spent money on herself—but she weighed the black watered silk with its close-fitting bodice against the newer brown alpaca, and chose the black.

There was the black bonnet to go with that, its brim lined with shirred green velvet. "It makes your eyes look like emeralds," Lainie had told her. Studying her reflection—another luxury she seldom allowed herself—Darrie thought her eyes did look rather bright, and greener than they actually were. A startling idea came to her: she was better looking today, as a mature woman, than she had been as a girl. How could that be? At her age a woman was settled, out of circulation, on the shelf. But as a rule she'd had children, too, and lost her figure. Pomp's conversation last night, shocking as it had been, had put ideas in her head. . . .

Standing off from the mirror, Darrie eyed her slim waist and high little bust. She supposed she'd been too busy to get fat. Why, she told herself with genuine astonishment, Belle looks years older than I do! As for Genia . . . if someone were to look at me and compare me with Genia . . . Someone! That was a euphemism! There was only one person who would make the comparison. And loyalty if nothing else would color his opinion.

She must be out of her mind, speculating on what Eric might think of her! She ought to know. His attitude had been demonstrated every time they were together: it was complete indifference. That was why she could, in clear conscience, go to him with a business proposition. It hardly explained her own excitement. . . .

For a moment she was swept with panic, but only for a moment. Her days of grubbing foolishness were past. She was on her way.

Eric was in his office, and alone, but Darrie had been so sure of Fate's direction she would have been surprised at the slightest obstacle to their meeting. He looked up, surprise showing on his face, then got to his feet.

"Well! I seldom have this honor. Come in, sister-in-law. Sit down."

He waited for her to be seated, then went back to the chair behind his desk. Darrie noted that he still had the trace of a limp. She thought, Genia ought to bathe his leg and massage it. But in the picture behind her eyes it was not Genia who knelt. . . .

"What can I do for you, Darrie? Are you in trouble?"

"Financial trouble. It's chronic."

"I told you, at the funeral, I would be glad to help—"

She raised a hand. "No! I don't mean to be ungracious, but not that."

He was silent, looking down at his hands.

The hair at his temples was whiter than it had used to be; he was graying, as blonds often do, by a gradual lightening of his hair. Soon he would be silver-headed, and handsomer for the change, she thought. His thick eyelashes had the old endearing trait of curving upward into lighter tips. It was the only trace of boyishness left in him, for now a web of lines fanned outward from the corners of his eyes, his mouth was hard, the fullness of lower lip gone completely. To think she had once pressed her own hungry mouth—

When Eric lifted his head and looked at her, Darrie felt stripped of the hearty assurance that had carried her this far. But Eric only smiled at her with the mechanical kindness he might accord one of the squaws who sold baskets on Water Street. "Don't be afraid to ask what you want, Darrie. We're family, aren't we?"

"I need your help."

"I'm yours to command."

It was only a polite phrase, but Darrie let her mind savor it before she asked, "You own the building that holds Anchors Aweigh, don't you?"

His look was pure astonishment. "Yes."

"Will you sell it to me?"

He turned a pencil in his hand, and considered it thoughtfully, before he said, "You know—you must know—Si Booker wants it?"

"I know."

"He sent you here?"

"He asked me to come. He wants me to buy the building with his money for down payment, and we'll be partners in it."

Distaste soured Eric's mouth. "You don't know what Booker is really like. You couldn't be his partner. If nothing else, he'd steal you blind."

"I don't want to be his partner."

"But you said—"

"Thats what *he* wants. *I* want to buy the building and give him a lease on the Anchor."

"You buy—" Eric's mouth stood open in astonishment. He shook his head. "My God! With his money!"

"It's simple, really. He wants to—what is the word, manipulate?—you and me. Why should we let him? Why shouldn't we manipulate him?"

When their glances met, she thought, I'll get nothing from him that he doesn't want to give me. I could kneel here on this wooden floor and beg, and he'd not turn a hair. But if *he* decides—

The swivel chair squealed a protest as Eric rose; the very upthrust of his stocky body spoke of energy leashed and disciplined. He walked across the office and back again, his step vigorous in spite of that slight unevenness.

"A man likes to think the . . . women of his family are above certain things. A man likes to think . . ."

If I could see inside his mind, Darrie thought. Or he in mine! Instinctively she raised a gloved hand as a shield, then self-consciously arrested the futile gesture.

The chair cried protestingly again. Eric drew a pad toward him on the desk and made slashing, angry pencil marks across it. "I'm sure you know I wouldn't refuse you anything within reason."

"You wouldn't?" It was a whisper. Darrie cleared her throat and said, more firmly, "I know you wouldn't. You've been very good to . . . us." For him to be concerned, to serve her, was a twisting visceral anguish of need. It was why she had come here really, wasn't it? The mute need beneath what could be admitted —but not just that! She began to speak quickly, over shortened breath: "I think Si Booker will let me have $500. He doesn't want to, but he will."

Eric gave a barking laugh. "You should have been a man! Yes, you can squeeze that out of him. I suppose you know what kind of place he'll run?"

"It's a box house—"

"And all that implies—crimping, women, drunks getting rolled in a back room—oh, it's a pretty business!"

For a moment Darrie studied her gloved fingers. She could say, Oh, I didn't understand! I wouldn't want to be mixed up in—

But that was where the money was being made. She said, "The 'best families,' " her voice made quotation marks, "are getting rich that way. Besides, I won't be running his business, just renting him space."

Eric shrugged. The pencil that had been slashing dark lines across the pad was making figures now. "Call it $4000—and that's dirt cheap—at 4 per cent interest. Cheap too. Five hundred a year, take you about eight years to pay it off. You can do that out of Anchor rent, and have the tailor shop rent for profit. The Anchor will cover your taxes and some of the upkeep."

"I'll have it in the lease that Si Booker does his own repairs."

The pencil stopped. Eric looked up at her. "You'll get along," he said.

Darrie waited until the papers were signed before she told Si Booker she intended to keep title to the building.

He looked at her then with anger and respect mingling in his little close-set eyes. "So you euchred me?"

"As you pointed out, you're no worse off. You'll get your lease. And I'll pay you back the whole $500 instead of half."

"Might I be so rude as to ask when?"

"There are other . . . obligations that come first." No need to tell Si Booker about the operation for Durand. "Anyway, the receipt I gave you is for 'funds in trust,' It doesn't say how I have to pay it back."

By an odd coincidence, Si used the very phrase Eric had. "You'll get along," he said.

"Thank you."

Si pushed back his chair and got up from the breakfast table. "You know, since you're going to be my landlady downtown, I think we'll see enough of each other. I'll move my things to a hotel."

Darrie shrugged. "As you like."

A month ago she would have panicked at the idea of a vacancy. Now she knew she'd manage. The ingredients for making money had always been here; she simply hadn't known how to use them.

CHAPTER 23

With Si Booker out of the house Cedarhaven should have recovered its old atmosphere. It didn't. Pomp, Darrie told herself, was partly at fault. He should have been pleased that she'd got her hands on a good investment, instead of acting so cool and virtuous. If he would be his old sharp-tongued good-natured self Cedarhaven would return to normal.

She would be glad, she thought, to have his advice and help with little problems that arose in her new business venture, if only his attitude were more cordial.

Then, only a few months after she had taken ownership of the Monroe Street property, an emergency came up which frightened her so thoroughly she turned to him without thinking of his attitude.

Markie, the tailor who occupied the shop next to the Anchor, failed to pay his rent. After a week of indecision, Darrie called on him and was met with an almost idiotic indifference: "So I haven't got the money. Bussiness is bad."

"Business generally is very good, Mr. Markie."

"Generally has nothing to do with Markie." He adjusted some pins in a band of canvas that hung about his neck. When he looked up again Darrie caught the scent of liquor on his breath.

"Are you sure you have been attending to business?"

"Maybe you'd like to take over management of my shop?"

"I'm only suggesting *you* manage it efficiently. And I shall expect your back rent within a week."

She marched out, her head high, while Markie looked after her with an expression of sullen resentment.

Passing the entrance to Anchors Aweigh, Darrie not only kept her head high but averted it slightly from the heavy brass-studded door and the windows obscured by red velvet curtains. At this time of day the Anchor looked as quiet and innocent as a Sunday School reading room, but it was not the sort of entrance about which a respectable woman cared to linger. At least, Darrie thought, Si Booker paid his rent. As for that wretched little tailor —but he would simply *have* to pay. She'd given him an ultimatum, hadn't she?

Within a week Markie was gone, leaving behind his simple furnishings: sewing machine and cutting table, bookkeeper's tall desk behind a green baize curtain. On the desk top was a penciled note: "Yor wellcome to these in loo of back rent. Anyhow I couldn't pack them off. I don't like to gip a woman but I don't like to rent from one neether."

Gone was the income, over and above contract payments, that Darrie had come to count on. It simply couldn't have happened like that, without warning, but it had.

She almost ran to the Bond Building, but Eric was out of town. When she had recovered from this added blow, she realized she had no real excuse to bring her problem to Eric, and was grateful she had not been allowed to humiliate herself by going to him.

She sought out Lawyer Tripp and was advised there was nothing she could do. Markie had left town. To pursue him and attempt to collect would cost more than the amount involved.

Feeling angry, defeated, and more than a little frightened, Darrie climbed the steep side street to Cedarhaven.

This time, sleeping on her worries brought no solution. Rather, the problem was larger and uglier in the cold light of morning.

After breakfast, when Pomp started for work, she followed him out of the diningroom. "Pomp, have you a minute, please?"

"Only that. The Baron admires promptness."

This was ridiculous! Pomp had become, over the years, Rothschild's right-hand man. He could name his own hours. It wasn't an auspicious opening, but she decided to go on. "I only wanted to ask if you had any suggestion about . . . about my building.

Markie, the tailor, is gone. Maybe you knew that. Anyway, I can't afford a vacancy."

"I should imagine not."

"You aren't being very helpful."

"What is it you expect, then? Shall I rent the place and set up shop myself?"

"Of course not! I just thought you might have some—some suggestion."

"If you'd asked me earlier I'd have had a suggestion right enough. I'd have said, 'Keep out of that dirty business.' "

"You call owning a building a dirty business? It was simply an investment."

"An investment, is it? Well, now you're talking like a blessed capitalist. No, my girl, you've done more than buy a building. You've got those pretty hands of yours deep and dirty in the filth of this precious little town. And now you've had a taste of the way the dear boys run things."

"I don't know what you mean. To lose a tenant—"

"That's how simple it is to you, then? And why do you think you lost him?"

"He got to drinking."

"That he did! With a connecting door between his shop and the Anchor, and with Si Booker saying every few minutes, 'Come in, me bucko, and have one on the house,' why wouldn't he get to drinking?"

"B-but why—?"

"God in heaven, need you ask why? So that what has happened would happen, exactly. And Booker laughing fit to kill himself over how he got rid of your tenant for you. Did you expect, then, he'd be pleased with the trick you played on him?"

"Why didn't you tell me—"

"So you could do—what? Say to Markie, 'Don't you drink that naughty man's whisky!' A great help that would have been!"

She cried, "You could have warned me!"

Pomp took his hat from a rack by the door and said, "You have an advisor, I believe."

"If you mean Eric—"

"You named him, not I."

"I haven't talked to him since the papers were signed—not once!"

"Maybe you should have then. If you had wanted my advice—and clearly you did not—you'd have accepted being a woman, and all that goes with it."

"If you mean get married—"

"An offer was made."

"I'm not that desperate—yet!"

Pomp's hand was on the doorknob. "If you should reach such straits, let me know. I may hear of some poor silly chap that's looking for a wife to wear his pants."

The door closed after him. Darrie stared at it, blind with rage.

She was still empty and shaken when Lainie came downstairs. Hers was the last breakfast, served on the kitchen table.

"Have you had your breakfast, Auntie? Eat with me!"

"I'm not hungry."

"Are you getting one of your headaches? You look kind of greenish. May I rub your forehead before I go to school?"

This was so endearing a gesture, so like Lainie, that Darrie stopped her work to stand behind the child, a hand on the chair-back. She wondered what Lainie would say if she told her, "Your 'Uncle Pomp' and I have had a quarrel. He may leave Cedarhaven. . . ."

He couldn't. It was unthinkable.

As it worked out, Pomp didn't leave. There were a few days of awkward stiffness between them, and the matter was forgotten—or at least left unmentioned. But the problem of the empty tailor shop remained to be solved.

Darrie took her keys and went, one morning, to inspect the premises again. Dust was gathering on the floor and furniture. Darrie opened the desk drawer (it was locked, but the key stood in it) and found a few receipts and the yellowed clipping of an advertisement for "Markie's Tailoring and Dressmaking Business, Olympia, Washington Territory."

The whole place was quiet as death.

Darrie went to the connecting door of the Anchor and listened, with her ear close to the panel. There was no breath of sound there either. On an impulse, she tried the door. It gave in her hand, and she found herself in a dusk-filled hallway.

She moved cautiously toward the front of the building.

The corridor opened into a large shadowy room with curtains drawn. She could see the watery light of a mirror above the bar and, along one side, a stage where a piano stood ankle deep in scattered sheet music. The opposite wall was lined with two tiers of private boxes, each large enough for a small table and two or three chairs. Some of the crimson velvet drapes that protected these boxes were drawn, some thrown open. Midway in the upper tier a curtain had been pulled loose and now hung over the railing of the box. Between boxes and stage was a scattering of larger tables, the chairs around them every which way, one even on its side. The tablecloths were pulled askew. Empty bottles lay about. In the half light the room gave an air of having been abandoned weeks ago.

The silence was complete: not a sound penetrated from the outer world. Yet the air seemed filled with evil whispers, echoes, stifled cries, smothered laughter. The life that had gone on here had left its mark: the room smelled of stale smoke and cheap perfume and liquor dregs, of flesh unhealthy and unwashed.

Darrie's feeling of security in owning the building—or an equity in it—had already been shaken. Now she speculated on what would happen if Si Booker moved out. Suppose she had this joyless and unlikely "place of entertainment" on her hands too. Then, instead of money coming in she would have it all to pay out on her contract.

A sound from overhead scattered her gloomy thoughts. She had not supposed the bedrooms upstairs were occupied. Quickly she retreated through the hallway and into the tailor shop, locking and bolting the door behind her.

Money. . . . She had to make it, somehow, out of this dusty empty space.

She put her hand on the cutting table and willed Markie to come back, reopen his dressmaking shop, pay her his back rent.

Dressmaking shop . . . ? Where had that phrase come from? She remembered then the clipping in the desk drawer. But the words had come to her with the impact of a message from the spirit world. Port Townsend needed a dressmaking shop: Mamie Van Hoffen had left town months before. Here was the space and the equipment. Only days ago Howard had told her about a young woman from his congregation, an orphan, who had a real talent for sewing but who was handicapped by a harelip: Cissie Latham. "If someone could set her up in a shop," Howard had said, "Get her started. . . ."

The solution had been here all the time, Darrie told herself, and she had been too stupid to see it.

Cissie Latham was pathetically grateful for someone to take over and manage her meager life. She had been working as a hired girl out in the country. Darrie kept her at Cedarhaven until housekeeping rooms could be found for her over the hardware store. Her defect made her timid, and complaisant, but she did have a talented needle. Within a short time a small but steady profit began to come from the dressmaking shop, a profit over and above the rent, which Darrie now paid to herself, and the wages she paid to Cissie.

Another hurdle had been passed.

CHAPTER 24

Durand Newton was edging toward his third birthday before Darrie was entirely satisfied he would have no limp. He had been nearly two before Belle had taken him to San Francisco; it had taken that long to save the money, even with the added income from the dressmaking shop.

Now that the operation was over, a success, and paid for, Belle said, "We prayed, and the way was made clear."

While Darrie admitted both these facts, she did not regard them as cause and effect. She knew only too well how the money—that bright and glittering essential of life—had been garnered, a few dollars at a time.

Money made the difference between controlling one's life and being a mere puppet in any capricious change of fortune. The knowledge came late, but not too late. It was a pity, she thought, that Papa had not lived to see his predictions come to pass: Port Townsend was the leading seaport of Puget Sound. Even he might have prospered in today's business climate. From her kitchen window Darrie could look out any morning to see the harbor full of ships. When she went downtown she brushed shoulders with seamen from every country: swarthy Hindus and pigtailed Chinese from the British ships, Malays from the Dutch and French vessels. She saw Hawaiians, Negroes, Spaniards—there was no use to guess at the races represented or their varied results in mixed blood. There were white seamen too, plenty of them. They were the most likely to jump ship, their race and knowledge of the language giving them the hope, at least, of mingling with the Territory's changing population and escaping notice. The dark-skinned seaman who decided to end his voyage in Port Townsend was quickly routed out and returned to his own ship or sold to some other shorthanded skipper. No ship, it seemed, left Port Townsend with as large a crew as its captain would have liked.

Max Levy was the acknowledged shanghai king of Port Townsend, but there were those who said Si Booker ran him a close second. He was coining money at the Anchor, as he had said he would. After a year, Darrie raised the price of his lease. He protested, but he paid. He could afford to.

Some instinct, as strong as it was undefined, made Darrie keep what she called her "downtown business" separate from Cedarhaven. Soon after Cissie was established in the dressmaking shop, Darrie had moved her account books there. Behind the baize curtain, the tall desk at which she could stand, or sit with her feet hooked over the rungs of a high stool, gave her a feeling of power. When she left the "office," as she called it in her mind, she could lock the drawer on her records and tuck the key in her purse. That she was putting money aside now from time to time was no one's business but her own. Every penny of it was a bulwark for Lainie's future. If the child should have a serious illness —but she would not allow herself to think of that. Better to let her mind explore the possibilities of two or three years at some finishing school, a lovely wardrobe, perhaps a formal coming-out party, trips she and Lainie would take together. Lainie deserved the best of everything. Everyone adored Lainie, as they had adored Genia. . . .

There were areas of Darrie's thinking that offered no comfort, but gave, instead, the sharpest sort of warning. Genia's life would have been different if there had been money, if they had not needed to turn to Eric. At least, with the magic of money on her side, the mistakes would not be repeated with Lainie.

A hundred times a day Darrie told herself that Lainie and Genia were as different as sugar and salt. If there were moments when her heart stood still at some trick of turning head, meltingly sweet smile, or slow-lifted lash, she put it harshly from her mind. It was coincidence. It was coincidence also that Lainie's chief fault—and virtue—was her tender heart. Her childish concern for the wounded bird, the starveling kitten, extended now to anyone less fortunate than herself.

Cissie, with her harelip, aroused a flood of compassion. With no more positive outlet for her concern, Lainie gave deference to Cissie's dressmaking talent, gravely asked advice about doll clothes made from the shop's odds and ends, or said, with wide-eyed sincerity, "Cissie, your hands are the smartest—and prettiest!—I ever saw. Honestly they are!"

At first it had been a pleasant thing to have Lainie drop in at the shop after school, exchange comments with Cissie, and walk home afterward with Darrie. But in time this had to be forbidden.

One afternoon as Darrie was putting away her books the bell above the entrance door tinkled its warning of a caller or a customer. Darrie was astonished at the conversation that went on beyond her sheltering curtain.

"Good afternoon." This was in a strong firm voice. Darrie made a mental note to instruct Cissie to speak first when a customer came in.

There was an awkward pause, then a reluctant "Afternoon."

"I seen you were opened up here. I was thinking of getting a couple of dresses made. Something real nice for—well, for evenings, you know."

Darrie gulped, almost audibly, and put a hand to her lips. A *couple* of dresses! What a windfall! She thought Cissie must be as stunned as she was herself, for her reply was slow in coming. When it did come, Darrie could hardly believe her ears.

"I'm sorry, but I'm pretty busy. I . . . I couldn't tackle it."

In one motion Darrie slammed shut the desk drawer and swept aside the curtain. "We can manage it nicely. Suppose you tell me what kind of dresses you were thinking of. Cissie does beautiful work—I know you'll be pleased."

The usually compliant Cissie gave her an angry look and went back to her sewing machine. Darrie saw that the girl's hands were shaking. She turned her attention to the customer, offering a Lady's Book for her consideration. "Here, look at this costume in brown velveteen. It would become you." Having said this automatically, she made a closer inspection of the young lady whose head was now bent above the fashion book. Darrie could not remember having seen her before, but that was not surprising; she went about so little. The woman had an assurance unusual in one so young, but she wore no wedding ring. Obviously she could spend money on her clothes, for she wore a fur jacket.

She looked up now, smiling, from the fashion magazine. "This here's too plain," she said. "When you entertain, you got to hit 'em in the eye. Now if it was red velveteen, say, and the neck cut out here, pretty low, and with lace along the edge. . . . Could your girl do that, busy as she is?"

There was no mistaking the irony. And now that the woman had lifted her head and was looking directly at Darrie, there was no mistaking the rouge, the painted lips, the too-strong sachet. A picture flashed suddenly into Darrie's mind: a woman in a rose satin wrapper standing in a doorway saying—what was it?—"Scat out of here, as fast as you can trot." For a moment Darrie's legs went as weak as if she had indeed been trotting. She felt herself sway, and took hold of the counter. But it was only for an instant. Then she heard her own voice saying with silky calm, "Of course we can do it. Now about the material. . . ."

When the doorbell had tinkled its farewell to Miss Violette La Fontaine, as she had carefully spelled her name to Darrie, Cissie came up to the counter. "Do you know *what she is*?"

"Of course I do."

"And you expect me to work for her?"

"It wouldn't help if she went around naked, would it?"

"But she's wicked!"

"Do we usually ask for a character reference before we make a dress?"

"It's wrong! She hadn't ought to come here. You hadn't ought to bow down to her."

"I was courteous, that's all. She's a customer. Her private life is her own business." It was amazing how readily the words came to her tongue. Had her mind been organizing them while she had talked to Miss La Fontaine? But Cissie's next words pierced her complacence:

"The nice women won't come here any more if they find out."

Darrie temporized. "Maybe they won't find out. You keep your mouth shut and they won't. You hear me?"

It was not quite that simple. Miss La Fontaine proved to have friends. Moreover they had more money, and parted with it more readily, than the respectable women on the hill. For a time the situation hung in delicate balance. Then Mrs. Whiteson came face to face with one of the shop's new clientele, turned an ugly purple, and swept out of the door without so much as a goodby.

Word spread quickly. Belle came storming to Cedarhaven, and left weeping. A new women's club was being formed in Port Townsend, the Key City Culture and Science Society; she had hoped to be a charter member, but "with my own sister actually consorting with *low women*—oh, I don't see how you can face yourself!"

Darrie's answer was simple: "The shop is making twice as much money as last year."

"To think you'd soil your hands with it!"

"It seems to buy as much flour and beefsteak as any other."

"When I think of Lainie—that *innocent* child!—putting into her mouth food that—that—" Belle was unable to finish. She left Cedarhaven muttering tearfully of eternal punishment.

She had, of course, put her finger on the sore spot: Lainie was no longer allowed to visit the dressmaking shop. Sometimes in the night Darrie wakened, her palms wet with sweat, from dreaming that Miss La Fontaine or one of her friends had been chatting with Lainie or laying her hand on her cool young flesh.

Her fears came into sharper focus with a call from Genia. Such visits, which had once been commonplace, were rare now. Genia seemed to be immersed in the lassitude of a life peculiarly her own. She almost never went outside her home. It was a surprise when she dropped into Cedarhaven one fall afternoon.

Cheecha's dark eye beamed through a crack in the swinging door while Darrie poured tea at the diningroom table. "Two lumps as usual?"

"Yes. And don't tell me I'm getting fat and ought to cut down."

"You may have gained a few pounds. . . ." Darrie's voice trailed away. Genia seemed not so much heavier as softer, somehow. Undisciplined . . . that was an odd word to come to mind. She said, "I'm glad you found me home. I'm often downtown now in the afternoon."

Genia gave her slow sweet smile. It had lost none of its heart-pulling magic. "I hear you keep Cissie busy."

"Yes."

"Tell me about some of your customers. That's why I came over, really. I've been hearing such gossip. Even Eric made a nasty face when I asked him about it. Oh, don't look so startled! Men are all stuffy. All the lovely wicked things they do—as if by divine right, mind you!—and roll their eyes and look so shocked when their lily-wives turn out to be human. I declare I'm sick of all the pretending that goes on. Aren't you?"

"I hadn't thought about it."

"Well, I have! And I think some of those women you make dresses for are smarter than we are. Now come on, honey, tell me what they're really like. What do they talk about, the men they've had?"

"I don't know what you mean. I have no idea what my customers do outside the shop. It's none of my business."

Genia laughed and said, "Come off it! I'll bet they tell you all sorts of tidbits that you're too straightlaced to share. They tell me there's a big red-headed woman downtown that whips men for money. Does she come to you?"

Darrie's lips felt as if they were frozen. She had difficulty in forcing out the words: "That's disgusting! For you to *talk* about it—"

Genia shrugged. "It's what I've heard. And, you know, I kind of understand. Don't you?"

"It's loathsome."

"Is it, really? Maybe life is loathsome."

"Don't talk that way! I've never seen you in such a mood!"

"No? Perhaps we've grown farther apart than you imagine."

Before Darrie could think of an answer to this, Lainie came in from school. She embraced Aunt Genia warmly and kissed her before she came to offer a cheek to Darrie. And why not? Genia was the guest. Darrie had taught the child good manners.

"Aunt Darrie, can I have cambric tea?"

Cheecha must have been listening at the door, she was there so quickly with the cup of hot water. While Darrie added milk and sugar and a coloring of tea, Lainie gave Cheecha a grateful squeeze.

At first Darrie had been glad of the interruption to their talk, but her gratitude was short-lived. Genia continued to be difficult. She found her opening when Lainie, teacup in hand, said, "Aunt Genia, it was *so* nice to find you here. You hardly ever come any more."

"Your Aunt Darrie would as lief I hadn't come this time."

"Oh, that can't be true, is it, Aunt Darrie?"

"Of course not."

"We all love you, Aunt Genia."

"There's disapproval in some quarters."

Darrie said, "Genia, I think you're forgetting yourself."

Lainie put down her teacup to stare at first one and then the other. A little frown appeared between the delicate golden arches of her brows.

Now Genia brought war into the open. She turned her head away from Darrie to look directly into the girl's face. "Do you ever visit your Aunt Darrie's shop any more, Lainie?"

"W-well, no, I don't."

"Why ever not? You used to have such fun, when it opened, getting scraps for your doll clothes, and talking to Cissie."

"I really don't play with dolls any more. I'm thirteen, you know."

"Are you really? Almost a young woman! But is that the only reason you don't go there?"

"That and—well, Aunt Darrie doesn't want me to go."

This had gone far enough. Darrie broke in: "There are any number of reasons why Lainie shouldn't go there. It's not in a good part of town, and Cissie is busier now and shouldn't be bothered."

"That's two."

"Well?"

"You said there were any number of reasons."

"The two I've mentioned are enough."

"I thought maybe there were things you didn't want Lainie to know. . . ." A half smile tugged at the corner of Genia's lips. "About the shop, maybe, and . . . well, other things. . . ."

Darrie felt as if a cold hand had closed around her heart.

Genia chatted on: "Everything comes out sooner or later, I declare it does! Sometimes I think it's better to just *out* with the *truth*!" She made a wide gesture that rattled her cup in its saucer, and made her catch at it to keep it from overturning. "Whoops! Did I nearly spill something?"

Darrie stood up. "If you have to go, Genia, I'll see you out."

In the hall Genia put a placating hand on Darrie's arm. "Don't be cross. I was only teasing."

"You deliberately tried to set her against me."

"I was vexed because you wouldn't talk to me. You're always so right, Darrie. So damnably right! No one has a chance against you."

She was in the doorway when Darrie caught her back and held her by the shoulders. "Genia! Oh, Genia! What is wrong? You've got *everything*. . . ."

Genia simply looked at her. The golden eyes revealed nothing. She slipped out of Darrie's hold and went on.

When Darrie went back to the diningroom she thought she saw antagonism in Lainie's eyes. It must be her imagination. There had never been a child more eager to please, unless . . .

"Why can't I go to the shop any more, Aunt Darrie? It was always such fun. And I wouldn't bother Cissie."

"I told you why."

"You gave a reason, yes. But Aunt Genia didn't think it made much sense, and neither do I."

"It isn't like you to be saucy."

"I don't mean to be saucy. I just want to know."

The idea had been forming in Darrie's mind for a long time. She had refused to set a date, since the thought of being separated from Lainie was almost too cruel to be borne. But now the words came quickly, spoken from necessity recognized. "It won't matter really, because you're going away to school."

"Going away? From Cedarhaven? From you?" Lainie's transparent skin had paled. Her dark eyes were enormous. A death sentence might be faced with just such an expression.

Darrie refused to look at her. "Yes. There's a good boarding school in Tacoma. I'll take you there this weekend."

"But—but *why*? Because I was saucy?"

Darrie waited, while hope stirred in her heart, for Lainie to say, "I won't be saucy again. I won't ask about the shop. I won't pay any attention to Aunt Genia." With such promises there might be a reprieve. But no promise was offered. There was only silence. She made herself look back to Lainie. A subtle change had taken place. Shock and pain were still there, and surprise. But the soft lips that, in babyhood, had dimpled as prettily as Genia's had straightened now into a defiant line. Their very silence seemed to say, Send me away! Kill me if you will, but I won't give an inch.

For a brief moment a stranger, tough and unyielding as the cedar roots that enmeshed the earth beneath them, faced Darrie. A thought she seldom allowed herself struck through her mind: Who was her father? What was he like?

She made herself speak carefully, without emotion, "My mind is made up. Get a tray from the kitchen and clear away the tea things."

Darrie made her way upstairs. A hammer of congested blood was striking its warning note at the base of her skull. Cedarhaven would be nothing—nothing without Lainie. She could not let her go. But Lainie was aroused now, and curious. . . . Darrie dropped to her bed, pressing her temples between shaking hands. What had possessed Genia? A new thought stabbed her: Genia must have been drinking. There had been nothing on her breath, but weren't there ways of masking the odor of alcohol? Genia had been so clumsy with her teacup at the last, as if the innocent tea had revived some earlier and more potent drink.

She had not heard Lainie come in the room, but she felt a warm young hand laid over hers. "Oh, Auntie, you're getting one of your headaches! Poor darling! Cheecha and I will manage supper. You get into bed."

"Maybe I'll have to."

"You must! and take your headache wafer. I'll run get a hot salt bag for your feet. It helps draw away the blood."

She was soon back. Her hands were gentle, arranging the warmth of the heated bag against Darrie's clammy feet. A wet towel cooled her forehead. Its edge cut across her vision so that when she opened her eyes, Lainie's face was shadowed. The child was on her knees beside the bed. She pressed Darrie's hand to her cheek, kissed the palm. "Oh, if only I could *do* something. . . ."

Nothing had changed between them, Darrie thought. Nothing could change. She is the core of my life. Everything I do, every penny I earn, is for her. When I'm over this pain and can think clearly again, I'll explain why she has to go away—for a time, at least. She'll understand. She has always put my wishes first . . . always. . . .

The headache followed its familiar pattern: the tempo of pain mounting, mounting, as if her head would burst. Then nausea, and retching that tore her very flesh apart. Exhaustion had its way at last. First she drowsed, then drifted into the small death of leaden sleep.

In the morning she awakened to the familiar aftermath of a headache: airy weightlessness, a feeling of having been broken into fragments, washed by scalding waters, and cast up on the shore of life, reborn, weak and spent, but as freshly alive as if she had never drawn breath before. It was an interval of exquisite peace. Nothing mattered. No threat existed to her, or to those she loved. She recalled as vaguely as she might remember a page from ancient history that she had planned to send Lainie away. What nonsense! She could not live without Lainie beside her.

It was very early, scarcely daylight outside, but she could hear a distant rattling of stove lids. Cheecha was already here.

Darrie crept downstairs to be given breakfast at the kitchen table. The toast was delicious, the coffee as nectar-sweet as if it had assuaged man's first thirst. But all men's yesterdays were hers, and all her yesterdays waited beyond the little circle of lamplight wherein her hand reached for the enamel coffeepot and where butter glistened like pale gold on the darker toast.

"Cheecha," she said, "this afternoon we will get all Lainie's clothes ready and pack them in Papa's little leather trunk. On Sunday I am taking her to a school in Tacoma."

"Why?"

"It's better."

"School is here too. No good?"

"No good for Lainie."

"This house stone-cold with Lainie gone."

That would be true, Darrie thought. Lainie was the flame at which they all warmed themselves. But she said, "She has to go. It's for her own good."

Cheecha was in the dusk-filled area beyond the circle of lamplight. Darrie had to move her head to catch the dark gleam of her eyes. "Don't you say one word against this to Lainie. You hear me?"

Their eyes held, hot and angry. It was Cheecha who turned away, making a necessity of tending the cookstove. "Bad woman!" she muttered.

"I do what I have to do."

The steamer trip to Tacoma was strained, almost silent. Darrie and Lainie shared a basket lunch packed by Cheecha, though neither did more than make a pretense of eating. In the school office, which they had reached by hansom cab, the headmistress looked down a haughty Roman nose at lack of "references" and "recommendations" and "advance correspondence," but when Darrie showed willingness to pay a year's tuition in advance objections were waived. It was further proof that money was the final arbiter.

A girl was called to take Lainie to her room. Somehow Darrie had not visualized a parting so abrupt. She could not get a steamer back to Port Townsend till the next day, and had imagined being invited to have dinner at the school, meeting some of Lainie's classmates and, in general, getting a picture to take back with her of Lainie's new life. But Miss Morford stood up, and the interview was ended as decisively as a ribbon snipped off by Cissie's big shears. "Mary, you take Elaine upstairs. I'll have her trunk carried up later. And now goodby, Miss Starkweather.

You'll have a monthly report by mail. And of course Elaine will write to you weekly."

Darrie and Lainie looked at each other across perhaps three feet of floor space. Darrie had the absurd idea that beyond this abyss Lainie was bleeding to death from an invisible wound. If they had been alone she would have put her arms around her and found some words to make matters right between them before they parted. She had always meant to do this. But dissolution trembled in her blood, tears pressed hard against her will to hold them back. She dared not touch the beloved flesh. Almost, she dared not speak: "Goodby, Lainie. You'll be happy here." That, and no more.

"Goodby."

Darrie thought she saw tears quivering in the child's eyes before she turned to follow Mary from the room. But she could not be sure when her own anguish flowed between them like a mist.

She spent the hours between leaving the Seminary and taking the Port Townsend steamer pacing up and down, or trying to sleep, in a cheap hotel room.

CHAPTER 25

Lainie Starkweather came awake slowly at first. She realized she was not in her room at the Seminary, with Louise Bolton a solid lump in the bed across from her, wondered for a moment if she were dreaming, then—suddenly—was wide awake, her mind singing with the knowledge that she was home at Cedarhaven for the Christmas holidays and for her sixteenth birthday.

She sat up in bed and hugged her knees.

A distant clattering of pans indicated that Cheecha was already in the kitchen though winter daylight was no more than a gray blur at the window. Last night Aunt Darrie had said, "Sleep in—you need the rest." But who would want to waste any part of these wonderful holidays? This day, especially, was not to be diminished by sleeping. It was Christmas Eve. And tomorrow would be Christmas, and her birthday.

She slipped out of bed and patted, barefooted, to the bureau drawer where she had hidden the presents. Here was the Angora-yarn hood she had crocheted for Cheecha. The sides could be drawn forward to cover the scarred face. Cheecha never mentioned her scars, but she was always turning to hide them. This gift had still to be wrapped; last night it had received its final brushing.

Cissie's present, already wrapped in tissue and tied with bright ribbon, was a blue collar-and-cuff set, blue to match Cissie's eyes. Lainie had spent hours embroidering roses on it. Beneath Cissie's gift was the package containing Aunt Darrie's knitted silk gloves. No one could imagine the difficulty of making fingers! She had done one glove over at least six times, but Miss Wells, who supervised the needlework, had said, "It must be perfect!" And so it was, finally.

Lainie shivered. The floor was dreadfully cold on her bare feet. She rubbed one foot behind the other ankle, but it helped very little. She decided to dress and run downstairs for breakfast in the warm kitchen. It would be just like old times before she had been sent away to school.

She pulled her woolen union suit on underneath her nightgown. It was warmer—and more reserved. Since she had been a child bathed in the kitchen by Aunt Darrie, no one had seen her body. Perhaps some time—oh, years from now!—there would be someone. . . .

Miss Morford said woman's noblest ambition was to be the wife of a virtuous man and mother to his children. Lainie did not doubt this but she found it impossible to picture. It was easy to imagine a suitor. At school the girls were always describing the knights who would tilt at life in their behalf and win them against frightful odds. Lainie's own dream had the clarity of a steel engraving: a tall man, romantically dark, with a tiny clipped mustache. Sophisticated, of course, and very rich. In her daydreams she saw him in various circumstances, rescuing her from a runaway horse, pulling her from a burning building, being himself rescued and gently ministered to—"I never dreamed human hands could be so cool and sweet! Promise you'll never leave me. . . ." While the picture varied, it always framed the same darkly handsome central figure.

Intimacy beyond the misty bridal veil and the murmured "I do's" was an image Lainie could not manage. It belonged to some distant time far removed from woolen union suits pulled on beneath a high-yoked nightgown.

The gown could be put aside now. She reached for her corselette. A whiff came to her, distant put penetrating, of frying bacon. She hurried with her stockings and garters. Again the phrase, "Just like old times" came to her mind but with less authority. It was not the same. Each vacation at home was a treasured interval, but it was not childhood recaptured. It was a suspension of school life, and school life was a suspension of the old sweet days at Cedarhaven. The whole world was changing, and she was a rootless speck within it, floating without direction or destination.

For a little time Lainie stood quiet as stone, a shoe held hard against her breast. The heel, cutting into her flesh, made her loosen her hold. How silly! There were tears in her eyes. She was as bad as Aunt Belle! She must finish her dressing and go downstairs. But not to old times. They were gone forever.

Aunt Genia and Uncle Eric did not come to Christmas dinner that year. It was understood Aunt Genia was not well. The Newton family came, and gifts were bestowed, but they left soon after dinner with murmured excuses of "church work."

The pleasantest part of the whole holiday, Lainie thought, was New Year's Eve. They stayed quietly at home, and Pomp sat with them in the parlor watching the old year of 1882 go out and 1883 come in. Aunt Darrie served wine and biscuits, and just at midnight they all three joined hands and sang "Auld Lang Syne." Lainie had not realized how pleasant Pomp's voice was. When she complimented him he said, " 'Tis an Irish tradition—we're all fine tenors and great lovers."

"But your voice—isn't it baritone?"

"Ah, you've put your finger on it!"

Lainie thought there was a look exchanged between him and Aunt Darrie that excluded or was meant to exclude her. But it was gone so quickly she could not be sure. She knew only that this was a happy, comfortable time, and that there had not been many of them during her vacation.

Because she was so nearly a young lady now, and because the trip was familiar from having been so often taken, Lainie was allowed to return alone to Tacoma after the holidays.

On a storm-swept morning after the New Year, Aunt Darrie put her aboard the steamer, with her valise on the seat beside her to discourage unwelcome companionship. When the warning whistle sounded and Aunt Darrie had to go ashore, Lainie went to stand at the railing and wave goodby. Sheets of rain whipped between steamer and dock, so that her aunt's figure was quickly lost. The town itself, Lainie thought, was dwarfed by the rain; the cliff separating the hill from downtown seemed foreshortened, as if both parts of the town huddled together for comfort. The whole effect was depressing, and Lainie was glad to get back into the cabin.

When the steamer reached open water beyond the protection of Point Hudson, it began to roll. Lainie knew from experience they would soon be past this stretch of water; moreover, she was a good sailor. A woman in the seat in front of her, accompanied by a little girl, did not do so well. She began to dab her forehead with a handkerchief. The little girl whimpered, "Mama, I don't feel good!"

At this point a young man presented himself on the scene. He took off his hat and bowed—his manners really were charming, Lainie thought. "Ma'am, I beg your pardon for speaking, but I'm a doctor. I'd suggest you get out on deck. The air in here isn't helping you."

The woman looked at him without moving.

"If you have smelling salts—"

She shook her head.

Lainie leaned forward. "Excuse me, but I have some." She held out the crystal phial which had been among her Christmas gifts. "No lady travels without one," Aunt Belle had said.

The sick woman thrust the offer aside. Suddenly her expression of distress changed to one of acute alarm. She jumped up, pushed the doctor aside, and headed for the lavatory.

The little girl set up a wail. "Come back, Mama! Come back!"

"Let's get her in the fresh air," Lainie suggested. "I know a sheltered spot on the after deck. Come on, honey."

"No! I want my mama!"

The young man told her hopefully, "You'll feel better outside," but it was the promise that, on deck, she might smell Lainie's "pretty bottle" that did the trick. She gave a hand to each and they made their rather awkward way around the deck into a refuge from the wind. The young man took off his coat to spread on the damp bench, and they sat down with the child between them.

Fresh air, and a few sniffs from the bottle of lavendar salts, were enough to restore the child. Soon she was chattering like a little sparrow: her name was Mary; she lived in Victoria; next year she would go to school; she had a kitten named Boots. And what were their names? Where did they live?

Lainie, who had been secretly admiring her companion's narrow rather overserious face, smooth-shaven except for the golden feathers of sideburns, was glad to find out about him: Dr. Adam Coates, newly come to Port Townsend from Philadelphia, now on his way to Olympia regarding his license. She could have applauded when Mary asked forthrightly, "Have you got any children, or a wife?"

His amused glance met Lainie's over the little girl's head. Lainie noticed before she looked away that his eyes were a steady, friendly blue. Blue eyes are the truest. . . .

"No family at all." When he added, as an afterthought, "Not yet," she was unreasonably saddened. That must mean he was promised. . . . Something in her mind was adding hours: three to Seattle, an hour and a half to Tacoma. If only she too were going on to Olympia—oh, don't be silly! He doesn't know you're alive.

A great deal can be accomplished in a few hours. Ideas can be exchanged, and ideals. "You'll laugh at this—you really will! But when I was little I was always rescuing hurt animals and patching them up. The men . . ."

"The men?"

For the first time in Lainie's life she didn't want to speak of Cedarhaven as it was. She looked into the blue eyes . . . blue as the sea, the sky . . . blue eyes are the truest. . . . "My aunt," she said, "she's like a mother, has boarders—men boarders. I'm proud of her."

Blue eyes are the kindest too. "I'm sure she's very proud of you."

"They—the men—used to call me 'Dr. Elaine.' It was a . . . sort of joke. But I always thought being a doctor was the most wonderful thing in the world." Had that been too bold? But he looked pleased.

"To think you might cure people, to study and be ready to help them—well, yes I . . . I guess I'm glad to be doing that. It sounds conceited, doesn't it?"

"Oh, no! No!"

In a few hours so much can happen, and they can be so soon past.

On the dock, in Tacoma, she said, "I can't believe the trip is over!" Then, aghast at her boldness, she looked down, aware of the warm color coming into her throat and cheeks.

He had carried her valise ashore for her. "Someone ought to meet you."

Did he feel—could he feel—that she should be protected—looked out for? It was a sustaining thought. She said, "I usually take a hack."

"I'll find you one."

"You mustn't miss the boat." Of course if he did—

The sun had come out at last and was reflected in the rain-soaked planking of the wharf. Stevedores rushed about with hand trucks. Passengers were greeted, and bade farewell. Standing, an island of quiet in this confusion, Lainie thought, Is this the end of it? A goodby, and he's gone? But what did I expect?

Dr. Coates had whistled and held up his hand. A hack drawn by a sway-backed white horse approached. The driver climbed down and took Lainie's valise.

Now this was the end.

She held her hand out formally. "Thank you so much. And goodby."

"Wait a minute!"

Her hand had been engulfed in his—warmer and stronger than she had imagined any hand could be. She was bereft at losing it. But he was getting a notebook and pencil from his pocket. He wanted the address of the Seminary. He would write. "Would they let you have a caller?"

"If Aunt Darrie approved. You wouldn't—couldn't—?"

"Call on her when I get back to Port Townsend? Don't think I won't!"

It wasn't really happening this way—it couldn't be. She missed the iron step of the hack and would have fallen if he had not been there. The driver had no time to waste. The whip snapped over the white sway-back. The hack lurched forward. She twisted for a final glimpse through the cracked isinglass of the back window. He stood where she had left him, bare head yellow in the sunshine, hand upraised.

When the hack turned off the dock and rounded the corner of the warehouse, she leaned back in her seat. The long-awaited dark, romantic stranger had been swept from her horizon. He had never existed.

"I'm in love," she whispered. And pressed the words back with her fingertips, afraid to trust even the air with so fragile a secret.

CHAPTER 26

On a February morning of false spring when the sun was bright as May though certainly less warm, Belle came to Cedarhaven in great agitation. "I've got something *terrible* to tell you."

Darrie smothered a sigh, and said, "Come on in the diningroom. The breakfast coffee is still hot."

"We oughtn't to talk there. Cheecha might be listening."

"Nothing goes on that she doesn't find out anyway."

In the diningroom there was a short disapproving silence. Darrie could guess her sister's thoughts: Making your living by associating with evil women, disgracing us all, your own brother-in-law a minister of the Gospel. It must be a serious problem that would bring Belle running to her for help.

When Belle looked up there were tears in her eyes. "It's about . . ." she faltered, "about Genia. It's so awful—to think *both* of my sisters! And with Howard's reputation to think about." Two large tears slipped down her cheeks.

Darrie thought, She's really suffering. She said, "Tell me—whatever it is."

"You know how much Eric is away, though I don't know what you'd expect from a marriage like that—"

"Oh, Belle, come to the point!"

"I am! But I have to explain. Well, Mrs. Dunlap's back bedroom window looks out on Genia's side door. She's not one to gossip—"

Darrie gritted her teeth but kept silent.

"—and she's absolutely truthful, so when she says she saw what she saw—"

"Belle!" In spite of herself Darrie's hand shot out to grasp Belle's wrist.

"She saw a man! A man, coming out just at daylight. And you *know* Eric is gone."

Darrie's mouth felt dry. She let go of Belle's wrist.

"Well, what are you going to do about it? You're the only one with any influence on her. And a fine example you've set her, I must say!"

"I don't know what can be done. Genia's a grown woman. She doesn't care what we think."

"You could always keep her out of . . . of difficulty when you tried. The last few years you've just let her *go her own way*."

Belle couldn't possibly know why it had been necessary to discourage intimacy with Genia. Nor what loss of Genia's companionship, sporadic as it was, had meant to Darrie. But she persisted in her demands: "We ought to go to her right now. We ought to get down on our knees and beg the dear Lord's forgiveness for her. And you might put in a word for yourself!"

Darrie put a hand across her eyes. She had never let herself say, before this, I don't like Belle. But the words stood out sharply in her mind. She supposed it was because Belle was always virtuous, while she was—but, no! I am not bad! I've always done the best I could for all of them, never anything for myself. So then how could things turn out so badly? Now this latest news about Genia . . . Face it—you're not really surprised.

"Darrie—! I asked you a question! Will you go with me to Genia?"

Decision had been forming painfully in Darrie's mind. She said, "No, I'll go alone. Wait till I tell Cheecha. Then we can go to the corner together, and I'll go on to Genia's."

After the kitchen door had swung shut, separating them from Belle, Cheecha made a gesture of spitting on the floor. "She talk bad about our Genia—old dog-bitch!"

"Ssh!" Darrie put a hand across Cheecha's mouth. The spitting had been more than a gesture: the Indian had saliva on her lips. Still, Darrie was brightened by the defense of Genia. There must be good in her sister to earn such loyalty. Papa adored her too, she thought. God knows I love her. And John . . . there had been no lack of love on his part. As for Eric . . . but this was the imponderable, the great enigma.

She rang Genia's doorbell and waited.

Presently she rang again and, after a short time she heard Genia's step on the stairs. The door opened narrowly to reveal a head of tumbled hair, sleep-flushed cheeks, a robe held together at the throat.

"Why, Darrie, honey! Whatever are you doing so early? It's hardly daybreak!"

"It's nearly ten."

"Is it, really and truly? Well, I declare—"

This was a trick left over from childhood: Genia, caught out in some difficulty, reverted to a Southern treacle of speech no longer natural to any of them.

"Can I come in?"

"Things are in such a mess. I'm afraid I've overslept but—oh, you won't mind! Come on in, do."

There had been a moment of conviction that someone else

was in the house, a moment that produced, in the pit of Darrie's stomach, the sensation of a dropped stone. Silently she followed Genia into the disordered house.

Mrs. Morrison had reigned briefly, and left. Following that, Genia had had a series of unsatisfactory "girls," between intervals of struggling with her own work. Clearly this was such an interval. A film of dust lay on the furniture. Ashes spread outward from the hearth. Magazines, papers, a piece of mending, an empty teacup were distributed at random about the parlor. Darrie thought, I should have sent Cheecha over; I didn't realize things were so bad.

"Isn't this awful?" Genia ran about raising window shades, straightening pillows on the couch, picking a magazine off the floor. When that was done she looked despairingly at the cold hearth, drew her robe closer, and said, "Would you mind if we went into the kitchen? Then we could make a fire, and have coffee too?"

"That would be better."

The kitchen was less disordered than the parlor. Darrie suspected that when Eric was away Genia's cooking consisted of sandwiches and tea; she was probably in the kitchen seldom.

It was Darrie who took over the building of a fire. The coffeepot was full of grounds. She washed it and started a fresh pot while Genia was making a half-hearted attempt to clear the worktable of soiled dishes and bits of leftover food. Once, turning quickly, she caught Genia leaning across the table: her robe had fallen apart; beneath it she was naked. On the white flesh above her breast a bruise stood out lividly.

Nausea rose in Darrie's throat. "Go get dressed!" she said.

Genia gave her a startled look that changed to one of appeal. "W-why, Darrie, honey, don't be mad! I know this kitchen's a regular mink's nest—" She had drawn the robe together, unaware of what the previous moment had revealed.

"Go on upstairs."

"All right, if you say so."

It was the old habit of authority and acceptance. Where did I go wrong, if the authority was mine? Oh, dear God, where did I go wrong?

She was standing in the middle of the kitchen, palms pressed to temples, eyes screwed shut. This wouldn't do—there was work to be done. Blessed work to fill the hands: heat the teakettle, gather soiled dishes, bring in wood from the entry, cram it in the stove, get a broom—oh, this floor! It really needs a mop!

The hands take refuge, but the mind has no escape.

The kitchen had been restored to passing order when Genia came back downstairs. Her hair, darkened now to bronze with threads of gold, had been brushed and pinned into a knot on top of her head. She was wearing a fresh cotton dress of pink and white stripes, buttoned up the front to a standing collar ruched in white—the very picture of the respectable young housewife. But Darrie's imagination saw the dark bruise burning through the innocent fabric, just there, above the tender curve—oh, Genia, my love. . . .

Her heart had spoken, not her lips.

Genia was smiling happily. "It's so nice to have you run in this way. You know, you hardly ever come any more. But then I know you're busy. Mmm! That coffee smells good. I'm starved."

"There's no bread, but I found a box of crackers."

"Oh, I love crackers with coffee. Now you sit down, and I'll pour." Serving Darrie, where she was seated at the worktable, Genia bent her knee in a mock curtsy. "Coffee, Madame?" Her dimples flashed.

Delightful, bewitching, *wicked* Genia—what could be said to her?

Genia seated herself across the worktable, sipped her coffee and ate her crackers with evident enjoyment. Presently she turned a little, drew up her knees, and hooked her heels across a chair-round. With the cup nested between her palms she looked ten years old. An elfin child . . . an evil child. . . .

"Genia—"

"Well?"

"I've got to talk to you."

"Oh, Darrie, it's such fun to have you here. *Don't* be serious!"

"We must be serious. Ive heard something terrible about you."

Genia made a delightful moue. "Probably from one of Belle's old Culture and Science tabby-cats. They're jealous of me."

"Have they any reason to be?"

Genia's golden eyes widened. "I reckon Eric's the richest man in town."

"And at home the least."

"Well, business . . . you know how that is." She brightened. "I could go with him—I suppose."

"Why don't you?"

"Oh, I don't know. . . ."

Darrie thought, Be truthful, Genia, he doesn't want you. Until now her mind had been filled with the present moment. Eric was a shadow on its periphery. Now his presence walked into the room. She saw him, eyes coldly appraising, face set in controlled indifference, well-brushed beaver hat set at a slight angle, carpetbag in gloved hand. Goodby, Genia, I'll see you in two weeks . . . three weeks . . . a year . . . never again. . . .

Genia said, "You're biting your knuckle."

Darrie lowered her hand and looked at the indentation left by her teeth. "How can I talk to you, Genia? There's so much—so much—" So much that never can be said, was that what she meant? Where Eric is concerned, so much wickedness in my own heart—but I've paid for that! Ten thousand empty nights washed in an oceanful of tears. Ten thousand days with memory eating its ugly way like a secret cancer. Oh, I've paid!

She said, "Don't you think you owe Eric anything?"

Something changed in Genia's face, something as elusive as smoke blown into the wind, but a change: a secret had been threatened, and was guarded—no more than that. She said, "Eric has all he wants of me."

"Doesn't he want loyalty—*decency*?"

The word was out. All the time it had hung unspoken between them, like a faint but ill odor in an unaired room. Now it had been said.

Genia's lower lip trembled till she caught it between her teeth, and steadied it. She whispered, "I can't stand it for you to be mad at me."

"*Then why do you—*" It started as a shout. Darrie forced control on herself, but there was nothing to say in the moderate voice of everyday exchange: Pass me the sugar, Genia, and don't sleep with strange men. Or, It's warm for February, and you are destroying yourself and Eric. Yet once she had found the voice to say, "Marry John Tower or I'll tell Papa." And, later, "Send John away and marry Eric." She had been so sure . . . so wrong. . . .

"Genia!" she cried, "Oh, Genia!" She sensed, too late, a dreadful dissolution. Tears burst from her, the very tissue of her being ruptured by the flood. Her head went down on the table. Sobs racked her body. She was broken, dissolved, destroyed.

When she could sense, at last, the existence of life outside her own anguish, she felt a warm and trembling hand caress her cheek, heard a shaking voice say, "Oh, please, Darrie, please! You never cry! Nothing matters that much. Don't—don't—don't cry!"

So it was Genia who consoled her, Genia who held her, crooning small sounds of comfort, Genia who finally brought a cool cloth and bathed her eyes.

She walked home through the unseasonable February sunshine with all the words of admonition and advice still locked within herself. Perhaps, she thought, Belle would have done better after all.

A few days after the visit to Genia, Darrie went carefully over her account books. There was money in a Portland bank; a mortgage on Pete Halleck's Fuel Yard that could be converted into cash; a substantial sum of actual cash recorded in the books but kept in a locked strong box on her closet shelf at home. It had taken a long time and a lot of pennypinching to amass this over and above Lainie's school expenses.

But the school expenses were over now, and the Monroe Street building paid for at last. She would have, now, a steady and substantial income. Why, she thought, I won't even have to keep boarders! The old dream of Lainie and herself alone at Cedarhaven with only Cheecha coming in to wait on them was no longer a fantasy. Except that the perfection of the image was dimmed by this new concern for Genia. Shattering as it would be to part with Lainie, perhaps the girl would be better off to marry someone from another town, and move away. We could visit back and forth, Darrie thought. Lainie would be safe that way. Nothing mattered now as much as Lainie's safety.

For the last two years Darrie had been thinking of a trip to Europe. It would add the final luster to Lainie's education, and it would give her a chance to meet the sort of person she ought to marry. Not a European, of course; Darrie didn't want her that far away. This very fall—it would take that long to arrange it—was the time to go. Darrie could almost taste the pleasure of leisurely weeks alone with Lainie, no intrusion of boarders or family, all made possible by the money whose neat symbols stood on the pages of her account books. As she closed the ledger, she let her hand run caressingly along the binding. Then she drew a sheet of paper toward her and, in a firm hand, wrote "Thomas Cook and Sons" at its head.

The weather continued fair. One morning Pomp astonished Darrie by announcing that she was pale, obviously suffering from a touch of spring fever, and that he was going to take her for a drive into the country.

"Why, Pomp! The Kentucky Store will fall apart without you!"

"Fall it must, then."

"And Cedarhaven will collapse without me."

"Disaster will be complete. But risk it we will, and no back chat from you, my girl! Now if you'll be leaving instructions with your handmaiden, along with your last will and testament, I'll go get the finest rig in the livery stable and be back for you." He clapped his hands. "Get busy, woman! And be ready to leap aboard when the chariot flies past the front door."

Putting on a warmer dress—and by chance her most becoming one—Darrie wondered if Pomp wasn't planning another proposal. It had been months—more like years, come to think of it! —since his last one. She would say "no" of course, but the chance of saying it again made an interesting prospect. And she had been oppressed lately by her worries. Pomp had been shrewd to see that. A day in the country would do her good.

Anticipation must have shown in her face, for when she came downstairs, Pomp, waiting for her in the hall, said, "Ah, the very notion of a drive has brought roses to your cheeks. Come along then, Madame, your carriage awaits."

"Madame. . . ." Genia had called her that, curtsying, with the coffee cup in her hand.

"Now what have I said to make you frown?"

Darrie forced a smile. "Nothing, Pomp. Come along!" She laid her hand on the arm he offered her, and they went out to the hired rig.

At the edge of town, Pomp turned the horse toward Happy Valley. The road here led past fields rough with winter fallowing, and rail-fenced pasture land. Log cabins and shake-covered barns sat back from the road. Farm horses, shaggy in their winter coats, raised their heads and whinnied at Pomp's sleek livery stable nag. A dog ran after them, barking, and a man came to the door of his cabin, waved a greeting, and whistled the dog back.

Then, abruptly, the road led to higher ground, and to forest. The change was like going into a cold and unused room. The road, which had followed survey lines, now wound among trees whose tops made a dark ceiling. The sun did not penetrate here except for occasional narrow rays livened by insects and by floating particles of vegetation.

Darrie drew her scarf closer against the sudden chill.

Alongside the road last year's ferns lay soaked and rotting, filling the air with a strong yet not unpleasant odor. The underbrush—salmonberry and elderberry, and bush willows—was bare of leaves. The forest was still in the grip of winter. It was a relief to come out once more into sunshine, and the open clearing above Keymes' Landing.

Pomp did not drive down the last steep quarter mile to the landing itself, but pulled off the road at the hilltop which commanded a view of Discovery Bay and the Strait.

"Get out and stretch yourself."

Darrie found that her legs tingled as she stepped down, with Pomp's help, and walked toward the edge of the hill.

To the left, across the Bay, a plume of white smoke from the Discovery Mill drifted upward against the cool majesty of the snow-covered Olympics. On the still air, the whine of the saw rose and fell, and rose again to a crescendo—then silence. To the right, in the open water of the Strait, a square-rigged ship beat its slow way southward, its great sails barely distended in the light wind. Beyond it, the coast of Canada was no more than a low purple cloud on the horizon.

It all seemed splendid, and peaceful, and far removed from Cedarhaven and other problems.

Pomp said, "You're shivering. Is it so cold as that? I'll give you my coat."

"No—no, thanks! It was just a passing chill. The sun is quite warm."

"That it is, for February. We'll drown in March to make up for it. Still and all, 'tis a magnificent climate, isn't it? When we can have a week or two of summer in February, and look down on water as blue as heaven."

"Discovery Bay is blue, isn't it? It would be nice to live out here, away from town . . . and its troubles."

There was a pause before Pomp said, "The ground is wet for all the sun. Your little boots will be getting damp. Shall we sit in the buggy and invite our souls? Perhaps I'll even try to hold your hand, under cover of the robe."

She shot him a startled look, and met his lopsided, brow-quirking, teasing grin. What was he leading up to? With only slight trepidation—she could always handle Pomp!—she allowed him to help her back into the buggy. There he tucked the robe about her respectfully—and left it at that. But he did say, "There's a thing I want to talk to you about. I know someone who'd buy your building from you. He'd give a fair price. You'd clear a little something."

"But I don't want to sell it."

There was a brief silence while Pomp looked out over the Bay. Then he said, as if there were some connection, "In a few months

Lainie will be coming home for good. If 'good' is the word to use."

Did he imagine she hadn't been thinking, almost exclusively, of that? She said, "I'm quite competent to plan for Lainie."

"You're sure you understand her?"

"Of course I do!"

"You know then how easily her heart would break?"

"Really, Pomp! Has the bachelor become an expert on child raising?"

She had spoken too quickly, but Pomp did not take advantage of the opening to ask if an old maid could do better. Instead he said, "There's always been that lovely compassion in Lainie. She wouldn't hurt a fly. And she could be broken to see it hurt."

"I don't know what you're talking about."

"I think you do. Oh, I'll say nothing about your dressmaking shop and its fine-feathered customers! I suspect they're what worry you. But that's your blind spot. I'm worrying about Si Booker and his filthy business."

"I've nothing to do with his business, and Lainie knows it."

"Oh, come off it, Darrie girl! You slipped in like a knife and bought that building with the special purpose of being Si's landlord—knowing full well the sort of place he'd run."

"I had to have money—I *had* to!"

"And never let it be said greed is not an endearing feminine trait."

Darrie caught her breath and turned to look at him. "It wasn't for myself—you know that! Lainie had to be educated. And there was Durand's operation. There was always something—and something more to come around the corner. No matter how I scratched and struggled, the board money was never quite enough."

"All right—the past is past! You needed money, and you made it. Now you can sell and get out before it causes trouble between you and Lainie."

"Nothing can come between Lainie and me. Anyway, I have plans. . . ." She hadn't meant to speak of them.

"What plans?"

"I'm going to take Lainie on a tour of Europe. Then she'll marry someone away from Port Townsend. So you don't need to worry about her living here and being upset about . . . about anything at all."

Pomp was looking at her with an expression she took to be surprised admiration. " 'Tis already blueprinted then, our girl's future?"

"There's only one future suitable for her—a *good* marriage. And I intend to see she gets it."

"Have you reckoned on love, at all?"

"Of course I have! But with Lainie's looks, and the advantages I've given her, and will give her, she'll have men buzzing around like bees at a honey pot. She can choose an eligible man, and still have love."

"I see."

Pomp sounded so unconvinced that Darrie felt impelled to offer proof: "She's already had a suitor—child that she is! But I sent him packing."

Now there was no mistaking the surprise on Pomp's face.

"Yes, that young doctor—Coates, his name is. He scraped up acquaintance with her on the steamer—imagine the impertinence! He actually came to see me afterward and asked permission to call on Lainie at the Seminary."

"And you said. . . ?"

"I told him absolutely not. He hasn't a dime to his name and probably never will have. I could tell in five minutes' talk that he was a visionary, wanting to vaccinate everybody—free, mind you!—and close up certain kinds of business in town."

"He might even object to Anchors Aweigh, is that it?"

"There's nothing wrong with the Anchor—I keep telling you that! It's a place of entertainment."

"Would it be presumptuous of me, considering our long acquaintance, to ask what you really know about the Anchor? Have you ever visited it in action? Have you ever been near it after dark?"

"Of course not!"

"Oh, 'Of course not!' in a tone of outraged virtue! But you

own it. You help make it possible. You ought to spend an evening at the Anchor—yes, and take Lainie with you, why not? You can have a few drinks—well watered down for the price you pay—and you can watch the girls dance with as few clothes on as the law allows."

"Oh, stop it! You sound like one of those street preachers—what do they call themselves? The Lord's Firebrands! They want to burn out half the businesses in town. This kind of entertainment goes on—you can't stop it."

"Entertainment you call it! And is it entertainment when some fellow gets to feeling his liquor, or the drops that have been slipped in it, and disappears. He's sold—quite literally sold—to some crew-hungry captain in the harbor."

Darrie found she was having trouble breathing. She said, with an effort, "The most respectable people in town make their money that way."

"They do indeed. That's the charm of Port Townsend. But you can't keep the line drawn. Sooner or later the innocent ones—like Lainie—get pulled across into the filth. Clear yourself of it, for God's sake, while you have this chance!"

He waited for an answer, but Darrie only shook her head. It was ridiculous, of course, but his face actually seemed to grow older. "To be frank with you," he said, "I was hope's fool for thinking you'd listen to me. Everything has to run its course, whether 'tis folly or wisdom. And you've still a way to go."

She said, "You just don't understand. If everything you said was true—which it isn't!—then I need more money than ever to keep Lainie safe."

"Where Lainie is concerned, you have a blind spot big as a barn door."

"I have made my life around her."

"That you have. And I hear you speak of it with pride instead of terror."

Again Darrie said, "You don't understand. Lainie simply mustn't be allowed to—" She was suddenly aware of where her words were leading her: "—allowed to repeat Genia's mistakes." This had been at the top level of her mind, but she had no sooner caught back the words than she realized that beneath them had been another and more jealously guarded thought: I mustn't repeat the mistakes I made with her mother. This idea, once it had been acknowledged, thundered so loudly at her inner ear that she began a denial: "Lainie is not at all like—" The words, in her own voice, truly frightened her. There was a weighted pause before she stammered, "N-not like a silly child, to be upset by . . . by . . ." The words were lame indeed.

Looking from the side of her eye, she found Pomp's gaze fixed shrewdly upon her. She had said too much. She was a fool. He would imagine all sorts of things. That upper lip of his was a foot long when he pulled it down in speculation. Well, why didn't he *say* something?

He said, "I'll be getting you home. There's a chill in the air when the sun gets low. Reminds us the days are short after all."

"Yes," she said faintly. "Yes, we should get home."

She was safe in her own bedroom, taking off her bonnet, before she thought, Pomp never mentioned marriage! That omission had been lost sight of in his ugly and unreasonable attack on her. But now it returned as a small stinging gnat of—surely not disappointment. Surprise would be all.

Hanging away her coat, she let her hand run along the smooth side of her cashbox on the closet shelf. The touch of its cool solid steel was reassuring after the disquieting day.

*

As Pomp had prophesied, March was a drowning month. Darrie was depressed by the rain and by an elusive feeling that somewhere something had changed color or shape or position and, in doing so, had threatened the whole structure of life. But spring came, as it was bound to do. The frail sunshine of April coaxed out primroses in a front yard too shaded by the cedar trees to be truly productive. In May the lilacs bloomed. Their lavender plumes almost covered the little back yard privy that might, when Darrie's finances had recovered from the European trip, be replaced by an inside bathroom.

As the days slipped by with that quick transience they seemed to have only in spring, Darrie began to have more confidence in her plans. Genia seemed to be behaving—if not morally, at least discreetly. The "European Fund," rather than being depleted by emergencies—the common fate, Darrie had found, of saved money—actually had been added to. Schedules and itineraries arrived from Thomas Cook.

Not only was this trip essential for Lainie's good, it would be the first holiday Darrie had ever had. She had worked hard all her life—how she had worked! Now for the first time she would relax and enjoy the fruit of her labors. Enjoy it with an adored and adoring Lainie, a compliant and grateful Lainie.

They would visit France, England, Switzerland, Italy. She pictured the two of them in some modest little pension, Lainie arranging for their rooms in a pinwheel burst of Seminary-taught French; Lainie standing beside her in the Louvre studying the old masters; Lainie with her in London. Reading had produced in Darrie's mind a montage of ancient buildings, gray stone bridges, the grandfather of all clocks, its hourly booming muffled by a warm and romantic fog.

What a vacation they would have! And home by Christmas. Celebrating Lainie's seventeenth birthday in the traditional manner, around the Christmas tree. Except that Lainie would be sophisticated by travel, those dark eyes opened wide to what the world could offer, that eager mind ambitious for a really worthwhile marriage. . . .

CHAPTER 27

For the first few days of summer vacation, Darrie allowed herself the uncomplicated pleasure of having Lainie in the house, of hearing her laughter trill through the rooms, of looking up to see her standing, unexpectedly, in a doorway. Her plans became more precious as she hoarded them, yet as her pleasure grew she needed more poignantly to share it.

On one warm June afternoon she could wait no longer. She and Lainie sat on a bench that ran from trunk to trunk of the two cedar trees. Cheecha had brought them lemonade. Moisture ran down the side of Darrie's glass. She set it on the bench beside her, and wiped her fingers on her handkerchief. "In France," she said, "they sit at sidewalk cafes and drink their lemonade while they watch the world go by."

"Lemonade, Aunt Darrie?"

"Why not?"

"At school Mlle. Dupres says everyone in France drinks wine."

"Then we'll drink wine!"

Lainie look puzzled, and only mildly interested. "When?"

"When we get to France."

"Whatever are you talking about?"

"About us going to France. And England. And Vienna, maybe, or Rome."

"My goodness, Aunt Darrie! Are you going to marry a millionaire?"

"Of course not!"

"You're talking like a rich woman."

Darrie was not getting the response she expected. She took up her glass, stared at it, and said, "I've no intention of marrying anybody. That's not the—"

"I suppose you've waited too long." Lainie turned to smile at her, her expression free of malice. It was simply youth speaking to a maturity that, in her eyes, must verge on senility.

In Europe, Darrie had been told, men found maturity in a woman attractive. She might merit some attention there that would open Lainie's eyes. Of course that wasn't her purpose in going, but it might be an accidental dividend. She said, "I'm not quite on the shelf, in spite of what you may think. And there are worse things than not being married."

Lainie's eyes widened. "What's worse, Auntie?"

"Oh, for heaven's sake!"

"No, I mean it! I can't imagine anything worse than *not* finding someone you could adore, and having him love you in return."

"You must think I cut a rather pitiful figure."

"Oh, Aunt Darrie, I wasn't thinking about you—"

"Obviously not."

"I didn't mean to hurt your feelings. I know you could have married if you'd wanted to."

"Thank you!"

"Oh, I have been clumsy! Honestly, I'll be satisfied if I'm half as alluring as you are when I'm your age."

"You're not improving matters."

Lainie looked so remorseful that Darrie's heart softened. She said, "I don't know how we got off on all this. I had some wonderful news to tell you. That's why I was talking about the outdoor cafes—France—all that. We really are going to see them. This fall you and I are going to Europe."

The effect of this statement, now that it was clearly understood, was electric enough to suit even Darrie. Lainie's mouth opened into a round O. She looked, for the moment, almost simple. Then she swallowed hard and said, "How could we afford such a thing? Why, it would cost hundreds of dollars!"

"I have hundreds of dollars." She made the statement simply, over a wild boiling up of pride. "We'll leave in September. That gives us the summer to get ready—Cissie will make clothes for both of us—and we'll be back by Christmas."

Lainie turned the lemonade glass in her hands. She did not meet Darrie's eyes.

"Lainie, don't you *want* to go?"

"Actually, Auntie, at some other time I'd adore it. And I think it's just wonderful of you to offer—truly I do."

Darrie was stunned. "At some other time . . . ." A wonderful "offer"—by implication not to be accepted. Her impulse was to say, "You'll go! I've made up my mind!" But she held the words back and forced herself to cool thinking. The child was simply too uninformed to realize what she'd been offered. Or the offer had been too abrupt. Lainic would want to go when she really understood.

Meantime, this astonishing reluctance. . . .

With a young girl one thought at once of heart interest—but this was nonsense! There was only that penniless doctor. He had not been allowed to call. His name had not been mentioned. Still, who else . . . ?

Darrie took another sip of lemonade. Lainie, she saw, had drained her glass. But now Darrie imagined her own drink tasted bitter and unwholesome. She held the glass, looking into it as if it were a sorcerer's crystal. Presently she said, keeping her voice carefully level, "You've been home over a week. What have you been doing, except to see your cousins and your old friends here?"

"Not much of anything."

"You haven't been . . . bored?"

"Oh, no!"

Darrie thought, Well, this hasn't produced anything.

The girl moved slightly on the bench, enough to let her back rest against the thready bark of the cedar tree. When she tipped her head back and looked up into the branches, her lips curved almost imperceptibly; it was less a smile than the shadow of remembered sweetness. The annoyance that Darrie had felt only moments before was swallowed up in a passionate flood of protectiveness and love. Lainie was so young, so untried, so vulnerable. Her mouth was wide and generous—a giving mouth. The expression came out of memories long dormant: Mammy Scofer's thick sweet voice describing one of Mama's friends. "She got a giving mouth, she has." But Lainie has nothing to give, Darrie thought. She's only a child. It's I who will give to her. Yes, it was a child's face—eyes wide apart and innocent, skin translucently clear but already touched across the short tilted nose with half a dozen freckles that would multiply with summer into a drift of rusty flecks. Even her hair was pulled back carelessly like a child's, and held off her temples by a band of yellow ribbon. "It's so warm," she'd said, only a short time before, leaning backward and tying the ribbon any old way to hold the weight of hair. Still, a few tendrils had escaped to soften the line of her temples. Here in the shade her hair was the soft tan of undyed leather, but Darrie—knowing in her heart every detail and variation of detail in Lainie's appearance—knew the sun could turn it into a blaze of gold.

Lovely child . . . head tipped back, eyes dreaming. Tender child, lost in reverie. To be guarded from all hurt and sorrow. . . .

"Aunt Darrie, do you know what I'd like?"

"What?"

"I'd like to be a nurse. There are places you can learn—hospitals that train you."

"You'll be no such thing!"

Lainie's head jerked straight. Her eyes spread wide, stared their astonishment.

"Of all things for a well-brought-up young girl to think about! Handling people with—with diseases you don't even know about—and shouldn't! Having to see men—exposed—!" All this came out without Darrie stopping to think. Now the surprise and hurt in Lainie's eyes made her speak more carefully. "You're simply too innocent—and thank goodness for that!—to realize what you're saying. A nurse's life is ugly, coarsening. Why, do you think any decent man would want to marry a woman who—" The pictures in Darrie's mind were graphic enough, the difficulty lay in conveying them to Lainie.

There was a pause. Lainie could have said something, but she didn't. She seemed to have shrunk back against the tree trunk. Perhaps it was the shadow of overhanging branches that made her look pale, that turned the few freckles into penciled dots. The notion came to Darrie—it was fantastic, of course—of a wood nymph shrinking away from intrusion. But—good heavens! —it was this very delicacy she wanted to protect. She said calmly, but with firmness, "I forbid you to think any more about this. The matter is closed."

For a moment Lainie made no answer. She seemed to be collecting her forces. Then she said, with astonishing self-possession, "Aunt Darrie, I'm afraid you can't order what I think."

She got up, picked up her lemonade glass, and walked into the house. The last glimpse Darrie had was of narrow ramrod-straight shoulders, a head arrogantly high.

It was the first time the child had ever defied her. What had happened? Darrie found that she knew, though she would have liked to reject the knowledge. Dr. Coates, whose name had not been mentioned, had been a third party to the whole conversation. The notion of nursing—that mad, ridiculous, stupid notion —had hardened Darrie's earlier suspicion into certainty. Lainie must have been seeing him. It was unlike her to be sly. Darrie saw that she must proceed with extreme caution.

When she got up from the bench, it was an effort to raise her body. For the first time she thought of herself as growing older—indeed, growing old. The heedless remarks Lainie had made earlier came back to her now: ". . . you could have married . . ." That damning use of the past tense! At the time it had stung. Now it made her angry. After all she had done for Lainie, she deserved better than this.

Stepping up onto the porch she was aware that her own back was stiff, her own head high.

CHAPTER 28

Darrie no longer had any doubt about the direction of Lainie's folly: the child had been romanticizing about that doctor. She was precisely the sort to throw herself away on some penniless dreamer—unless she was protected from herself. While he was out tilting at windmills she would be having a houseful of children, tending a potato patch in the back yard, and cooking clams and beans.

There had been enough of that in Darrie's own first years at Cedarhaven. Good heavens! How many times she'd contrived a meal around the clams bought for two bits from some crony of Cheecha's! Lainie was not going to repeat that kind of life.

She planned numerous conversations with Lainie in which she made her own position clear, and forbade Lainie to think again of Adam Coates. She was held back by the memory of Lainie saying, with a cool and unexpected disdain, "I'm afraid you can't tell me what to think." (What had they taught her in that school, anyway?) There must be a better way to take care of it. Darrie decided to call on Dr. Coates. No kid gloves would be needed to handle him.

Adam Coates had a grubby little office above the feedstore. Darrie reached it by wooden stairs on the outside of the building, and found herself in a waiting room furnished by half a dozen kitchen chairs and a homemade bench. Several of the chairs were occupied by rough-looking men, not one of whom got to his feet when she came in. It demonstrated the sort of practice Dr. Coates had—in fact, was bound to have. One of the men pointed to a sign on an inner door, and obliged her by reading it aloud: "Hours nine to twelve. Please be seated."

After Darrie had taken a chair, he asked, "You come for a shot?"

Darrie said, "No," without understanding his question; but when one of the other men went into the private office and popped out in less than five minutes, she began to suspect. At her turn, she entered the private office.

Adam Coates did get up. He was in his shirtsleeves, and he made a further gesture toward the amenities by putting on his coat. He had looked very young without it; now he was blushing like a boy. Darrie wondered why she had thought of him as a threat: he was a Nothing.

"Won't you sit down, Miss Starkweather?"

"What I have to say won't take long. I am not a patient."

Adam Coates had recovered a little of his composure. He smiled at her and said, "I've been giving vaccination for small-pox—free. I'd be glad to oblige you."

This was beneath her dignity to answer. She said, "I'm sure you know why I'm here. I did forbid you to pay attention to my niece—my ward."

He looked at her without answering.

"But I suspect you have been seeing her."

There was still no answer.

"Well, *have* you been?"

"Why don't you ask Lainie?"

"It happens I'm asking you."

"And it happens I'm not answering."

Darrie was not used to insolence. She had thought she could tell this young man, in the plainest possible terms, to keep away from Lainie. But he was making this difficult. "Are you aware that Lainie is not of age?"

"I am."

"And that I could take legal steps to control her—and you?"

"Do so, if you like."

The interview was not going as she had planned it. Suddenly another approach occurred to her. It was so obvious she should have used it first. But perhaps she had needed to see the squalor of his office, and his "free" practice. She smiled at the young man. "May I sit down after all?"

"Please do." He continued to stand beside the battered roll-top desk that he must have bought second- or third-hand. She let her eyes turn over it, and move on to the medicine cabinet with its cracked glass, the clumsy folding screen that hid God knew what other makeshift.

"You can't be doing too well here, Dr. Coates."

"I'm not getting rich."

"Actually, your coming here was a poor choice. I don't know who advised you . . . ?" She paused, but he was not going to help her. "There's really no more practice here than one doctor can handle. And naturally people turn to Dr. Madden. He's been here a long time. His wife is one of the Norton family."

Darrie waited for Adam to say that Dr. Madden was getting old, occasionally careless, and addicted to the bottle. But he said nothing.

"So, really, there are other towns where you'd have a better chance to build up a practice."

She saw that some mental process had commenced behind the clear blue eyes. He really was not unattractive, physically. Even a fastidious child like Lainie might be attracted. But he was weak, unambitious, everything that was wrong for a husband. He had got around to saying something, at last: "It just happens I've spent what money I have in getting settled here."

"That's a pity. But if you had a little capital, to pay office rent somewhere, and tide you over . . . ?"

"It would take quite a bit. Wouldn't I have to visit some other towns, look the ground over? Make sure the next move was the right one?"

Darrie was surprised at how easy it had been, "I'll be frank with you," she said. "I'll be happier with you gone—no need to go further into the reasons for that. I'll give you enough to pay three months' office rent somewhere else, and, say, $200 to get yourself moved. You'd be better off, much better off!"

"Mmm . . . let me see. I'm paying $22 a month here. Say I

figured on $30 somewhere else. Call it $100 for rent. That would add up to $300, wouldn't it?"

"I won't haggle over a few dollars."

"It does take a while to get patients coming in, you know. I'd have to eat and sleep. And—be honest with me now, Miss Starkweather!—don't you think I need a new suit? First impressions, and all that."

Darrie had not expected quite this degree of calculation. It was very nearly blackmail. But how thoroughly it vindicated her judgment of him! She looked away from Adam to hide the contempt in her eyes. "I'll give you $350. *When* you leave town."

"No more than that? Not a penny more?"

"That's generous!"

"Generous . . . ? Hm. . . . That's not the word that came to my mind. But is it your absolutely top figure? Suppose I said, 'I'll go—I'll stay away—you'll never see me again! But it will cost you $500'?"

Five hundred dollars! Why, the difference between that and three fifty would pay their fare to Europe! Families *lived* on five hundred a year. The man was absolutely unprincipled—which made it all the more necessary to get rid of him. Pay him five hundred, then, and go to Europe next year! It would be worth it to keep Lainie out of his filthy, money-hungry clutches. She said faintly, "You'll have to sign an agreement. . . ."

"But you would pay me five hundred?"

"Yes! Yes—to be rid of you!"

"Miss Starkweather, I'm sorry, but you've failed to convince me."

"Convince you? But you said—"

"I asked you what you'd pay—I didn't say I'd take it. I wanted you to prove something, and you did. You love your niece. You want her to be happy. You're a women of means. And you offer $500 for her happiness. I haven't any money, but if I had a million dollars and Lainie's happiness was for sale for that, I'd buy it. You've convinced me, you see, that Lainie's happiness means more to me than it does to you. I don't think it's in her best interests for me to get out of town. And if *you* had the million dollars, and offered it to me, I wouldn't go."

Darrie felt as if the breath had been knocked out of her body. She closed her eyes against a sudden giddiness and a suddenly blackening world. She could not faint here, in this creature's office. Never! She would get up in a minute and sweep out of this dingy hole. Perhaps, before she went, she would find words cruel enough—some way to punish him.

But he was the one with words: "Lainie thinks the world of you, Miss Starkweather. She's really very dutiful. Very devoted. If someone were to tell her that you are domineering, ruthless—yes, cruel!—she wouldn't believe them. You're lucky. For her sake as well as yours, I hope she never sees you as you are."

Darrie managed somehow to get up and get out of the room. In the outer office she sat for a few minutes gathering strength to tackle the stairs and the street.

*

Darrie was not used to defeat. She could not believe that this penniless upstart had defeated her. He had tricked her into a momentary embarrassment, that was all. If it were not for the formless suspicions that already troubled her, that notion, ridiculous but persistent, that the current of her life had changed direction, she would have been sure that that was all.

It was more urgent than ever to get Lainie away from the influence of Adam Coates. Half formed in her mind, not looked at directly but sensed as a possible last resort, was the use of force. But that would not be necessary. Lainie was obedient—and sensible at heart. She would get over this nonsense about Adam Coates. By spring they could be on their way to Europe. Perhaps early summer would be a better time to go—more expensive than winter, but more romantic.

On an August evening, when Lainie was visiting with her cousin Marian, Darrie got out pencil and paper to calculate just how much more a summer trip would cost than the one originally planned. Needed information was in her desk at the shop. She would have to wait till morning.

She walked around the empty house. Pomp had gone off somewhere. Dutton, the new young boarder, was seldom home in the evening. He had shown a tendency when Lainie first returned from the Seminary to lurk about the parlor after supper, but Darrie had soon frozen him out. Now she almost wished he were here, or Pomp; it would make someone to talk to.

The house was sultry. This had been one of Port Townsend's few hot days; the heat lingered on in the closed rooms. Darrie stepped out onto the back porch. Below her the lights of the town glowed softly. Pinpricks of light on mastheads in the harbor trailed yellow ribbons of reflection. Footsteps drummed on a board walk and died away. A door opened to release the tinny sound of a piano, and was closed again. The town was quiet tonight, quiet enough for her to run downtown and get the information she needed. A respectable woman didn't go out alone at night, but it would take only a minute. She stepped back into the kitchen to take her keys from a nail by the door. She needn't bother with a wrap: the night was warm, no one would see her.

The steep board walk was deserted. It was only a block after that to Monroe Street. A saloon had to be passed, but Darrie crossed the street to avoid it and came back again at the corner. There'd been nothing to it—she hadn't seen a soul.

Inside the dressmaking shop, she lighted a lamp and carried it to her desk.

The racket going on in the Anchor was amazing: the piano was being banged as if a blacksmith were playing it; a woman's voice caterwauled in words too muffled to be understood; there was applause. Feet, stamping in rhythm, shook the dressmaking shop. Darrie was grateful the door was bolted.

At first the noise distracted her, but she found the letters she wanted and the folders from Thomas Cook. She copied the needed figures, did a little addition and subtraction, and closed the desk.

She had blown out the lamp and was at the door when she

became aware of voices close at hand. Pulling the shade aside she peeped out. Several men stood by the door. They were debating—a few words reached her—about going into the Anchor. She stepped back and waited for the issue to be settled. When time passed, and the voices went on, she looked out again. Now two of the men were sitting on the board sidewalk. A bottle was being passed back and forth.

Darrie was growing nervous. Lainie's cousins would be bringing her home. Mr. Dutton might have returned. There was another way out of the shop, though it was seldom used: a back door that opened onto a delivery court shared with the Anchor. She would go out that way, and up the alley. It would be dark, deserted. But it was better than facing those drunken men at the front door.

She was disgusted to realize she was trembling. This was ridiculous—even Lainie would not be so childish. But Port Townsend's alleys were no place for a man after dark, let alone a woman. She should not have come downtown. But here she was, and she had to get back to Cedarhaven.

She let herself out the back door. The delivery court was pitch-dark. She couldn't find the keyhole. As she fumbled for it, she heard the door of the Anchor open behind her. She whirled about. In the sudden flood of lamplight, a jumble of empty barrels and packing cases loomed shoulder-high. Instinctively, Darrie crouched, and flattened herself against the wall.

A voice said, "Chris' sake he's rummy! Can't even walk." Another answered: "We're lucky. He'd give us a tussle if he knew."

The door across the court closed; it seemed darker than before.

"Where's the runner?"

"By Pearson's Dock. He'll have a boat there."

"Well, come on! Get 'im between us." The voice altered as it said, "Come on, you bastard—move your feet!"

A third voice, thick and slurred, said, "W-where we goin' . . . eh?"

There was a laugh. "We're gonna meet the girl you was drinking with, remember? She sure took a shine to you. Wants you to spend the night. So come along—leg over leg, like the dog went to Dover, eh?"

The other voice said, "This fresh air's dynamite. He'll come to."

The sound of shuffling steps was coming closer. Darrie pressed her back to the wall so hard she might have been part of it. She sensed rather than saw the huddled group pass from behind the shelter of packing cases and toward the alley on her side of the court. At the corner of the building a change took place. The third voice, less muffled now, said, "Hey! Lemme go!"

"Aw come on, feller! We're gonna see the girlies, aren't we? We're just helping you."

"No! Lemme alone! I don't know you guys."

"Sure you do—we're your friends."

There was a scuffling of feet. He's getting away from them, Darrie thought. Then came a sound, unmistakable, sickening, too dull to be the blow of flesh on flesh. They had struck him with a blackjack, or something like it.

There was a moment of silence. She heard someone breathing hard. Then a voice said, "Chris' sake, you've killed him!"

"He's just knocked out. Let's get him to the boat."

"I can't carry him—not with my bad back."

"Aw, he's just a kid! Help me pick him up."

"No. We better get Si out here."

"He'll be mad."

"If you've killed the kid, Si sure as hell will be mad. Remember, it was you done it."

"Come on. We'll get Si."

There was a fanning out of light across the brick-floored court as the door to the Anchor opened, darkness again when it closed.

Darrie's every instinct said: Run! Run while you can! But her flesh refused. Her legs, shaking with terror, took her to the building's corner. She groped toward a sprawled bundle barely to be seen against the dark ground. Her hands when she touched it were wet and sticky, and she wiped them on her skirt. She pressed her palm against thinly fleshed ribs. He was no more than a boy! She felt a heart beating. She thought, You fool! You can't move him! But she groped for his legs and started dragging him the few feet toward the door. She got him inside the shop, locked the door, and leaned against it with her heart thrashing against her sides. Strength ran out of her now that he was safe. She sank to the floor beside him, and waited till her heart slowed and her breath came back. Then she crawled on hands and knees and found the lamp. The glass was still warm. In that lifetime while she had crouched outside the door, the lamp had not had time to cool.

In the lamplight, she made herself look at the boy. His shirt was pulled up across his head. She straightened his arms and pulled down his shirt, wondering why she hadn't strangled him in her haste. But he still breathed, shallowly. Blood was smeared across his face, and continued to well from a swelling knot above a barely slitted eye. He was not dead, not yet, but he might be soon.

Darrie forgot that she had been afraid to go out on the street. She opened the front door, saw the huddled group still there, and called out, "One of you run quick and get the doctor. There's a man hurt here." She didn't wait. She was used to being obeyed.

One of the men followed her back into the shop. Together they got the boy onto the cutting table when it had been cleared, by one sweep of her arm, of scissors, pincushions, and patterns. She got a basin of cold water, and put compresses on the wound above the boy's eye. She thought the eye itself was injured. If Dr. Madden would only come!

But it was not Dr. Madden who came. There was a stir at the door and Darrie looked up to see Adam Coates. Darrie's anger spurted up. "Who sent for you?"

The man behind him spoke. "You did, ma'am. You said, 'Fetch the Doc,' and I did. This here's the Doc."

Adam was paying no attention to her. He bent over his patient, felt for a pulse, lifted the compress. He looked grave. "We'll get him to the hospital. Round up a stretcher, will you?"

The man seemed relieved at having something to do, and set off on this new errand.

For the first time, Adam Coates looked directly at Darrie. He was a competent, assured stranger—someone she had never seen before. He said, "Did you do this?"

"Me? Are you insane?"

"He might have broken in, or tried to attack you."

"And you think I would have done *this*?"

She had never faced such a lack of respect in any human eyes. "Yes, I did."

"You're a fool!"

"Then how did it happen?"

Darrie thought how she had saved the boy, how she had dragged him in from the alley—it seemed impossible now, yet she had done it. Now she was being almost accused of his murder! She turned her back.

"Well, what happened?"

Without turning she said, "He came from the Anchor. I had nothing to do with it."

"Except, of course, to own the place."

"Only the building—if it's any concern of yours!"

He didn't answer.

Into the silence came a new and raucous burst of music from next door, and a cackling laugh. The boy could be dead for all Si Booker cared. But that was not her fault.

The man and a companion were back with a canvas stretcher. Adam helped them put the unconscious boy on it. He said to Darrie, "I'm sorry I can't see you safely home. But perhaps one of these men, if they are friends of yours—"

She looked at them and saw two of the anonymous riffraff of the downtown streets. But one stepped forward, his eager smile showing broken teeth. "I know who Miss Starkweather is," he said. "I'd be glad—"

"No! I don't need anyone's help!"

They were leaving. She followed them, and at the door stepped in front of Adam. "You have no right—"

He looked at her.

"You seem to think—"

His eyes were cool. Was it contempt that chilled them? She had saved the boy. . . . "How can you know anything—as young and untried as you are—" She knew her voice was shrill, but she could not control it.

"I have to go with my patient, Miss Starkweather. If you'll excuse me." He was actually brushing her aside.

Pure rage drew a veil of red between them. "I'll drive you out of this town! You and your sanctimonious—"

But he was gone. She was speaking to the empty air.

As the late summer days went by, memory of Adam Coates' contempt corroded Darrie's mind like a slow acid. She had thought, with pleasure, about destroying him. Now she had the feeling he would destroy her. There must be some way to get him out of town, if she could only find it. . . .

It was ironic that wherever she looked for help she found only obstruction.

Genia had a birthday in September, and Lainie insisted on having her at Cedarhaven. "Uncle Eric is off somewhere—he always is! We can't let Aunt Genia spend her birthday alone. Cheecha and I will bake the cake. It won't be any work for you."

"I don't mind the work. It's just that . . ."

"Aunt Genia hardly ever comes here any more. I'm sure she's lonely."

"She has her own friends."

"But we're her *family*!"

Darrie's real objections were better not voiced. Genia was invited, and she accepted. "And of course Pomp will be here. Oh, I love parties!"

The Newtons were, as usual "occupied with church work." Lainie's earlier delight was clouded. "Here it is September, and Aunt Belle has only been here once since school was out. I just don't understand this family any more."

"Nothing is the way it was when you were a child. You can't expect that."

"N-no, I suppose not."

On her birthday, Genia was almost like her old self. It was amazing how she had kept her looks in spite of everything. Nothing had quenched in her the flame at which anyone who passed might warm himself with delight and gratitude. As for her family —Lainie, Pomp, and Darrie herself—Genia charmed them with the lifting of a finger. Laughing like a child, she blew out her candles and cut the cake. Cheecha lumbered in with a tray of coffee, was given the first slice of cake, and retreated to the kitchen swollen with pride.

Darrie thought she had not seen Lainie so happy all summer. The evening would have been a great success if Adam Coates's name had not come up.

Genia could hardly have done it deliberately, unless Lainie had been confiding in her, but that was too unlikely. It had to be sheer stupid coincidence that made her sister say, "Have any of you got acquainted with Dr. Coates? I declare, no one in his right mind—or *her* right mind, anyway!—would consult Old Doc when that sweet young man is around."

Darrie saw that Lainie had come to instant attention, and, as quickly, gone on guard.

Pomp joined in the conversation, though he should have known better: he knew how she felt about Adam Coates. "You won't be alone, Genia, in feeling that way. Old Doc is frothing at the gills. To hear him talk you'd think the young man was undermining the town's health instead of putting out pills to cure gout, or asthma, or whatever."

Stung by the unique cruelty of knowing precisely what was going on in Lainie's mind, Darrie said, "The man's a fool!"

"That he is! At his age he should be glad to cut down his practice a bit—"

"I don't mean Dr. Madden."

"Don't you? Who, then?"

"I mean *him*. That—that—"

"Ah! 'Tis Adam Coates you don't like, then?" Pomp looked across at Lainie. An eyebrow quirked up wickedly, an eyelid flickered with conspiracy. Darrie saw that his part in the conversation had been deliberate. She could not trust herself to speak.

But Genia chattered on: "Isn't he a lamb? I can hardly wait to get some dreadful illness like smallpox or diphtheria, and have him fetched to cure me."

Lainie was looking at Genia with an expression of idiot pleasure.

Darrie said, "You'll have to hurry, Genia. He won't be in Port Townsend long."

"Oh? Why not?"

"He'll never build a practice. Why, he was vaccinating people for nothing!"

"Oh, yes!" Pomp agreed. "That caused a bit of talk in a town where nothing's free but poison and black eyes."

Genia's laugh rang out, silvery as a child's. "You know, the greatest joke of all was that people who *could* afford it went and got their vaccination free."

"And back to Old Doc next day with cash in hand for a sprained ankle, I've no doubt."

Darrie forced herself to speak calmly: "That's exactly what's wrong with giving people something for nothing. They despise you for it. He'll end up being run out of town."

Pomp was looking at her with an odd expression. For a searing instant Darrie was reminded of Adam Coates standing over the cutting table in her dressmaking shop. "You really think he should be driven out, don't you? No doubt you'd help do it."

"Give a man enough rope and he'll hang himself."

"Especially if friendly hands prepare the noose."

Genia interrupted: "You two are getting cross at each other over something. I can't believe it's that innocent young doctor. Darrie, give me a touch more coffee, will you, dear? Yours is always so good."

The coffeepot shook in Darrie's hand, and drops of coffee ran down the outside of Genia's cup. She said, " 'Innocent' is hardly the word for Adam Coates. He's . . . he's sly as a fox."

"Why do you say that, Aunt Darrie?" The tone of voice was a danger signal. And Lainie's freckles stood out on an almost waxen pallor.

"Because he—because I—" It was impossible to describe the scene in Adam's office where he had deliberately tricked her into offering— She said, "You've only to talk to him!"

Lainie was pushing aside her plate with its partly eaten cake. She was standing up. "I'm sorry, Aunt Darrie, but I can't listen to you talk like that. If you'll excuse me . . ." She started toward the hall and stairway, her eyes as distant as those of a blind person. At the door she turned, "Aunt Genia, could I get my nightgown and go home with you?"

Genia stared at her and at Darrie. Her lips parted. She swallowed, visibly. "If . . . if your Aunt Darrie—"

"Lainie will not leave this house."

Lainie's voice was as small and cool as the tinkling of broken ice. "I'm going. With Aunt Genia, or alone." She ran up the stairs before there could be an answer.

Pomp and Genia should have supported Darrie. By now her pride was too white-hot to beg, but they owed it to her. Instead they made light of it.

"To stay with her own aunt—after all, why make a great thing of that! Genia'll take good care of her."

"Of course I will. Now don't you worry! By morning Lainie will want to come back—she adores you."

"I told her she was not to go!"

"But she's in such a pitch, what with you baiting her—"

"*I* baiting *her*? You were the one, Pomp Ryan! You and Genia—"

"Well, the milk's spilled, no matter whose hand tipped the cup. Short of locking her in her room, you can't keep her."

"She's never spent a night away from Cedarhaven—"

"Listen to her now! And the girl just back from three years away at school!"

"I mean here, in Port Townsend—"

" 'Tis time she did then. While I'm walking her and Genia to the Bond house, you get hold of yourself. You'll be down with one of your headaches if you're not careful."

Darrie fled to the kitchen. She would not stand in the parlor and watch Lainie walk out of Cedarhaven.

Cheecha was gone. The kitchen was deserted. Presently Darrie heard the front door open and close. Lainie hadn't even come to say goodnight.

Darrie spent an almost sleepless night, dozing off finally toward daylight because she had convinced herself that Lainie would be back in the morning.

The forenoon passed and she did not come. She would be there by supper time, then. But she was not. "I'll do the dishes, Cheecha," Darrie said. "I want you to take a note to Genia's house on your way home."

"What's wrong? We got nobody here."

Darrie wrote: "This has gone far enough. I want you home. Be sure to come before dark. You mustn't be on the streets alone after nightfall."

Cheecha trudged off. Twilight closed in. There was no Lainie. But tomorrow morning, certainly . . .

Darrie tried to convince herself it was all for the best. There had been this reserve between them all summer. A quarrel was unfortunate, but it did clear the air. When Lainie got down off her high horse and came back to Cedarhaven, she would be in a chastened mood. She might even be ready to take the trip to Europe.

From the exhaustion of last night's sleeplessness, and the comfort of these thoughts, Darrie slept well.

Another day went by. It was Sunday morning, and the house was empty. It was necessary to speak to someone, to confide, to ask advice.

When Pomp came home from Mass and she had served his breakfast, she said, "Have you a few minutes?"

"Always! What's on your mind?"

"Let's take your coffee into the parlor. I'll have some with you."

When she had filled their cups she left her own on the tray and leaned back in her chair. Now that she had set the stage for their conversation, she found herself unwilling to start it: there was a fragile and momentary feeling of peace in the situation: she could sense the autumn sunshine against the louvred blinds without facing its brilliance; she could sense Pomp regarding her affectionately from a few feet away. She could watch through half-closed eyes the delicate spiral of steam rising from her cup, with its fragrance of fresh coffee overriding the faintly waxy, faintly dried-rose-petal scent of a well-kept parlor. She could imagine this was some other autumn Sunday with Lainie safe at school.

But it was not that. It was nothing safe and comfortable. Suddenly the words were torn from her, shattering the moment. "How can I get Lainie back? I sent her a note and she ignored it."

"If I could think of a way to help—" Pomp shrugged.

"She's not of age, you know. I could *make* her come back."

"Could you now?"

"I'm her legal guardian." Darrie had used the phrase many times. It always seemed true. Now the words had become a monstrous lie. Lainie is with her legal mother, her blood mother, she thought. Between them, after all these years, they have made me nothing. But this was the precise and secret reason Lainie could not be with Genia. "Pomp, you don't understand, she *can't* stay at the Bonds. It mustn't be allowed."

"I understand you hate it. But Genia loves the girl. And she wouldn't hurt a fly. Why not let things work themselves out?"

"No—no! Genia will . . . she'll drink! She'll *tell* Lainie . . . things—lies!"

"Can't you trust Lainie to know truth from lies?"

"No! She's too young, too inexperienced. She has to be protected."

"Chiefly from Adam Coates. That is what really sticks in your craw, isn't it? Lainie's smitten—and why not? If not Coates, she'll find someone else to pin her dreams on. You can't change that. You're fighting life itself." Pomp was actually red in the face, and only a few minutes ago he had been looking at her so kindly.

Darrie said, "You know as well as I do, I want only one thing: what's best for Lainie."

"And you've not the slightest doubt you know what's best."

Darrie saw no irony in this. "Of course I do! I know that child inside and out. She's far too young and inexperienced to make a choice for herself."

For a while Pomp said nothing. He continued to study Darrie thoughtfully. Finally he said, "The one single thing that makes it possible to go on loving you is that you're really sincere. You do want the best for Lainie, though you've a queer way of showing it."

Darrie only half heard the last sentence; her attention had been caught by the phrase, "Go on loving you." A warm and weakening confusion trembled through her, an almost girlish confusion, it seemed. "Pomp, you said . . ." She faltered; "Did you say—?"

"Yes! Yes, the saints have pity on me, I still love you!"

She waited for him to go on. Surprise, and this disturbing sense that she could not, by herself, manage the situation with Lainie, were having their effect. Besides—and this too she acknowledged with surprise—suddenly she was tired. She had driven herself relentlessly. She was no longer young. It would be pleasant to let someone else, someone strong and loving, take over. "You could have married," Lainie had said. The words still stung. Well, Lainie would find out it was not too late yet!

Now Pomp did go on: "Long ago I gave up asking you to marry me. 'Twas part your callous trampling on me poor heart, part maybe the pure convenience of having a home, female companionship, and no strings attached."

With Pomp's words, the impulse to yield herself, so alien to Darrie's nature, had begun to diminish. She should expect better of a man in love.

There too Pomp set her right. "There was a time, Darrie, when I was mad for you. Enough to keep me on here when good sense was plainly telling me to get out while I could. But nothing so feverish lasts for long. You die or you get well. And, you see, I'm healthy." He flexed an arm, regarding it ironically.

"But you said . . ." Darrie's lips were stiff. She gave up the effort to speak.

"I said I'd gone on loving you. So I have, but in a different way. Once, with the twiddling of your finger you could have made a fool of me. Now I think we could marry and rub along. And both of us be the better off. But if it's a final 'No,' well, I'm not cutting my throat."

"Are you seriously asking me—like this?"

"To be my wife? Yes. I hadn't started out to make the proposal, but there it is. And mark this—" Something in his tone made Darrie look directly into his face. A subtle hardening of the features had taken place. His blue eyes were brightly cold, his expression deadly serious. "This is the last time, my girl. I've come to a turning point. So have you, though you may not know it. You can have your life, shared with me should it please you, or you can knock your brains out playing God with someone else."

Emotion, which had been slowly forming in the yeasty ferment in some lower level of Darrie's mind now bubbled upward in the heat and violence of anger recognized. "This is not a proposal, it's an insult!"

Pomp's shoulder lifted in the suggestion of a shrug. It was more infuriating than any statement.

Darrie pressed on: "I won't dignify your offer by—" This was not going to be scathing enough, and she abandoned it. "Playing God, you call it! Is that your name for decent concern over your family? What would have happened to this place—to all the family—without me? You don't know a fraction of what I've had to do—"

The various triumphs over fate pounded in her mind till she was dizzy: this house itself. Papa—what would he have done without her? Durand, walking—yes, and running!—on two sound feet. And a hundred other times she'd found ten dollars, or fifty, or a hundred, for Belle's family. Genia and her marriages—well, leave that. Lainie with an education equal to any girl in the Territory. She'd done it all, hadn't she? Managed it somehow, by tooth and toenail, no thanks to anyone.

Her heart was pounding in her breast heavily and with pain.

Pomp had got to his feet, and managed to take hold of her

hand though she tried to keep it from him. "I'd no intention of hurting you so badly, Darrie, my dear. It wasn't a romantic proposal, maybe, but it was a sincere one. I've a bit of money put aside. Now you do respect that! We could take that trip to Europe for our honeymoon. I'd show you my old village in Donegal, and show my village you—with pride. 'Tis not too late yet for us to share a life, and a good one."

The fool didn't know what he'd done to her. She pulled her hand away. Strength was coming back. She steadied her voice to say, "Should I thank you—for less than nothing? I told you years ago, there's someone else."

She looked up to meet the final searing of her pride: Pomp was regarding her with pity. As if he knew as well as she did that she lied. "Get out!" she cried. "Out of my house! Out of my sight!"

When she set the table for dinner, she had regained control of sorts. She had, by this time, gone upstairs, patted cologne on her temples, and lain down. Now, downstairs again, she told herself this was no different from any other autumn Sunday, with the blinds drawn against the sun, with the sparrows twittering in the rosebush outside the diningroom window, and with enticing smells wafting in from the kitchen. It was any Sunday, except it was *the* Sunday when she had quarreled with Pomp. Ah, but he had said such dreadful things! The terms of his proposal, his suggestion that they might "rub along" together, was bad enough. But to say that she was playing God . . . Someone else had said that long ago. The memory teased, and emerged: Edward Lord at Neah Bay. What a lifetime ago!

She wondered where Edward Lord was now. Perhaps he was dead. If he were alive, he would be an old man.

Standing, with a knife and fork in her hand, Darrie realized she had been motionless for several minutes, staring at the wall without seeing what she stared at. She could not think whether to set the table for Pomp. The wallpaper, its fleur-de-lis design rising in endless columns against its red background, gave her no answer. She shook her head, but ideas continued to press in like stinging gnats. Papa had been so proud of this wallpaper, brought on special order all the way from San Francisco. Only near the doorway was there a trace of fading. She had always taken care the sun did not strike it, and had brushed it gently on cleaning days. Papa would have been pleased to see how it had lasted.

Suddenly the silver in her hands felt heavy, though it was not a burden. The true burden was some inescapable pattern in her thoughts: Papa . . . Edward Lord . . . Pomp. . . .

Beyond the closed blinds the twittering of the sparrows became shrill, then dissolved in a sudden whirr of wings. Lainie's cat must be lurking beneath the bushes.

His eye is on the sparrow. . . . If there really were Someone who cared, who would take care. . . .

Pomp did not come back for dinner. On Monday he had his trunk taken to the hotel. His board was paid for another week, but he said it did not matter.

"Maybe 'twas our misfortune the word "money" ever passed between us. Maybe—but no matter now. Let us at least part friends." He put out his hand, and she took it.

"Goodby, Pomp."

"Goodby."

Goodby. . . . It was only after the door had closed and she was alone in the quiet house that she realized how much she was saying goodby to.

CHAPTER 29

Lainie too slept badly on that first night of separation. She had gone forward into a dimension of anger unfamiliar and isolating. Aunt Darrie, after a summer of covert cruelty, had attacked the very center of her being, the secret chamber where she kept bright the image of Adam Coates—honorable, without flaw or fault.

That night in a strange bed, a strange room, her body sang with wakefulness. Her mind soared, and spun, fell heavily into despair, and rose again in remembered anger.

Toward morning she slept. When she wakened the house was silent, her aunt's bedroom door was closed. Lainie got out of bed and knelt at the window sill.

Where Cedarhaven looked toward the harbor, the Bond house faced Kah Tai swamp with its majestic background of Olympics. This morning the mountains seemed almost within reach. They were a dozen shades of rose and lavender in the morning sun, their glacial veinings bright as quartz. Against Lainie's lightly covered flesh the morning air was cool as flowing water. She drew her arms across her breasts and leaned on the sill. Somewhere, far beyond those mountains, on the seaward side of the Olympic Peninsula, was Neah Bay, where long ago a Spanish ship had been wrecked and—so she had been told—she had floated ashore lashed to an empty cask. From that time on, Aunt Darrie had stood as father, mother, protector, guardian.

Only once before this summer had Lainie doubted the perfection of her aunt's concern; now the old hurt of being sent away to school throbbed freshly beneath the newer one. Lainie thought, She never really cared for me. It was a pretense, all these years. She was doing her duty by the "Spanish orphan," no more than that.

There had been, in the past, a certain romantic glitter in the term "Spanish orphan." When she was loved and cherished, her history had drama and mystery. Rejected, her role became a mockery.

Speculation, which in times past had drifted light as thistle-down across a carefree mind, now pierced her whole being with a poignant need. Who were her true mother and father? Who was *she*? This casing of fragile and articulated bone, and flesh chilling in the morning air, what were the secret sources that had supplied its inner self?

"Mother. . . ." She whispered the word: "Mother. . . ."

A door opened behind her. "Lainie, honey, you'll freeze to death!"

Startled into sudden hurtful awareness of the present, Lainie stumbled to her feet and pulled down the window.

Aunt Genia, rosy with sleep, her eyelids heavy with dreaming, came to touch Lainie's arms, her shoulder. "You're cold as ice—and up so early! And—my goodness!—didn't I just sleep! Now I'm going to get you one of my own pretty negligees and we'll fix us a nice breakfast."

Occasionally, in the past, Aunt Genia had urged that Lainie visit her; Aunt Darrie had always declined on the ground that Aunt Genia was not well. Aware of this, Lainie was determined not to be a burden. As a house guest, her least obligation was to be cheerful and helpful.

Cheerfulness was an attainable mood in Aunt Genia's company.

By the time they had fought their way through an accumulation of dishes and got their breakfast onto the kitchen table, both Lainie and her aunt were weak with laughter. Everything was amusing—their shared clumsiness in household tasks, the crank falling from the coffee grinder and being scrambled for beneath the table, the dropping of an egg on the floor—each incident was more hilarious than the one before.

When they were through breakfast Lainie would have set to work immediately on doing the dishes, but Aunt Genia pushed her back into the chair and refilled her coffee cup. "Tomorrow we can be housewifey. Anyway, it'll be Friday, won't it? Or Saturday? And Loretta Pape promised she'd come clean house. Don't worry about it."

Lainie had always found irresistible the slow sweet smile, the tender play of rosy lips, the crumpling of flesh into a lopsided dimple that gave youthfulness to a face no longer young, the radiation—directly toward the person smiled at—of unique concern. It had always seemed to her that any man within the radius of that smile would melt at once into abject slavery. If she could smile that way at Adam . . . dear Adam . . . lost Adam . . .

"Now, now!" her aunt said, reaching across the table to draw moth-light finger tips across Lainie's cheek. "You're looking sad again. You mustn't, you know. We're going to have fun together. I'm going to keep you right here with me till you get married you hear me? There's a very, very special reason for us . . ."

Lainie waited for her aunt to go on. "Yes, Aunt Genia?"

"A special reason. But we'll talk about it another time. Another time . . ." For a moment her face was old and sad. She pushed back her chair. "I always take a little medicine after breakfast," she said. "Excuse me. It's on the buffet. . . ."

Lainie did not believe in Loretta Pape. On that first day she worked as hard as her aunt would permit on putting the house to rights. It was a comfort to keep busy. There was satisfaction in the very violence of shaking rugs, the strain of carrying bedding outside to air in the back yard.

That evening, when Cheecha brought the note from Aunt Darrie, Lainie glanced at it, tore it into scraps, and threw the bits into the kitchen fire.

They had been getting their supper. Cheecha was urged to join them, and sat sipping coffee, her scarred face turned to one side.

"You come home pretty quick, huh?"

"No, Cheecha." Lainie was surprised at how firmly she could say this.

"The woman, she's not mad any more. Feels bad, bad, bad. House no good without you."

Aunt Genia laughed, and reached across the table to pat Cheecha's arm. "Don't begrudge my having Lainie for a while. It's my turn, isn't it?"

Slowly Cheecha's head lifted. She turned, unmindful of her scars, to face Aunt Genia. "You lose your turn. Forever. Don't forget."

Aunt Genia's eyes widened. The two women stared at each other. Something meaningful and exclusive passed between them. Then Aunt Genia laughed again, shrilly. "Nothing is forever, Cheecha."

Cheecha too had changed. The lids slid down over her polished eyes. Her head tipped forward. "Kalakala kopa otelagh," she said.

Aunt Genia's voice caught. "Oh, Cheecha! *Dear* Cheecha."

When the Indian was leaving, Aunt Genia kissed her cheek. "You know, don't you, that in heaven *you* will be the 'bird in the sunshine' and I—if I were to get there at all!—would be so old and ugly you'd spit on me as you went by?"

Cheecha looked at her a long time. It was, Lainie thought, as if the woman wanted to memorize her aunt's face in last detail. "Never spit," she said. "Never, never, never. . . ."

Cheecha's visit left a shadow.

As the days slipped by, Lainie realized more fully that her aunt was ill. She varied between moods of gaiety, of drowsiness, of lassitude. The "medicine on the buffet" was liquor. Lainie's knowledge of drinking was bounded on one side by Aunt Belle's rabid strictures against the very mention of the word, and on the other by the occasional glass of wine served at Cedarhaven. She did not know if liquor was the cause of Aunt Genia's trouble, the result of it, or unrelated to it; but she suspected a connection.

Certainly Aunt Genia was disorganized, her household neglected. Lainie did what she could to produce material order, over her aunt's languid protests and without her assistance.

Actually, Lainie was grateful for work to occupy her time. There were enough hours, as it was, when she and her aunt sat and talked aimlessly about everything, and nothing. Everything except Adam Coates. Lainie still had a deep-rooted feeling that she must not speak of her feeling for Adam until he had dignified it with a proposal, or a statement. But with Aunt Genia the topic was skirted. Aunt Genia spoke of marriage in general, and of love. "Have you never been—well, kissed and made love to, Lainie?"

"No, Aunt Genia."

There was a gesture of annoyance. "Don't call me 'aunt'!"

"But—but—"

"Oh, I know! It's just that—well, we're not *so* far apart in age, are we? Call me Genia—as if we were friends."

"I'll try."

"Now what were we talking about? Oh, haven't you *wanted* to make love?"

"I—I don't know." Was this the specific relationship she wanted with Adam, or only a part of it? She did not know herself.

Her aunt stared into a glass of liquid the same dark gold shade as her eyes. A small smile curved her lips. "I guess making love is the most important thing in the whole world. But it's got to be *right.*"

"You mean getting married, of course."

For a moment the smile was gone. Then it came back, and Genia raised her lovely eyes to Lainie. "It ought to be the same thing, now it truly ought." She asked an odd question then: "If you could have picked someone to bring you up, to—well, *be* your mother, you'd have picked Darrie, I suppose?"

Six months ago Lainie wouldn't have hesitated. Now she struggled against a sense of ingratitude, and said, at last, "She's the only mother I've ever known."

"Yes . . . yes . . . well, you've been happy. That's what matters. Do you think, Lainie, if I'd had a daughter, she would be proud of me?"

There was no hesitation when Lainie said, "Genia, she would have adored you!"

"Do you really think so?"

"I'm positive."

Genia was smiling now. "But you were . . . safe . . . at Cedarhaven, you know? There's no place in the world so—so *solid* as Cedarhaven." She lifted her glass in salute, saw that it was empty, and put it down, hard, on the marble-topped parlor stand. "Cedarhaven doesn't change, Darrie doesn't change. She doesn't need to. She's always right. She's even right about your being here."

Startled, Lainie said, "Oh—! Well, if I'm a trouble—"

"No! No, it's not that." Genia was moving toward the diningroom with her empty glass. On the way she stopped behind Lainie's chair, just stopped, and stood there. Then she suddenly bent and kissed the top of Lainie's head. "I love having you here. It's just that I keep thinking I'll tell you something. . . ."

"You mean a secret of some kind?"

"It's not important."

Her aunt moved away and seconds later Lainie heard glasses clinking on the buffet. She was quite sure her aunt should not drink so much. It couldn't be good for her. Later, perhaps, when they were more used to each other, she would mention it. . . .

When Lainie had been with her aunt for almost a week, they had their first caller except for the essential visits of the grocer's boy.

They had finished the supper Lainie had prepared and served in the diningroom. They lingered over after-dinner coffee. The set of belique china, the cups as small and fragile as eggshells, was Lainie's especial delight. She had, a few days before, washed an accumulation of dust from them so they could be used. Genia was casual about the set: "Eric picked it up somewhere. I suppose it is quite nice. . . ."

Doesn't Uncle Eric ever . . . I mean, is he usually gone so long?"

Genia shrugged. "He comes and goes. He has business everywhere, you know. He's a rich man."

"I know. . . ." It was impossible to put into words the concern that had been growing with each day she stayed here: did Uncle Eric care at all about his wife, his home? Didn't he honor Genia with the slightest knowledge of his whereabouts? Looking across the table at her aunt, Lainie wondered how Uncle Eric—or any man—could fail to be enchanted by a woman so obviously made for love.

Meeting Lainie's glance, Genia smiled. Her golden eyes kindled to affectionate warmth, her dimple flashed and was gone. "Don't look so worried. Eric and I understand each other. He has his money, and I have my . . . friends."

"But I haven't seen—" Lainie bit back in time the tactless statement that she had seen no friends. She finished rather lamely, "—any tea parties here."

"Why, darling! I should have been having people in for you. I never thought of it. And you've been working so hard too. The house is ready for a party, isn't it? We must do something about that."

"No—no! I didn't mean it that way, honestly!" In spite of herself, Lainie had the quick vision of a party going on in the now-presentable rooms, with Adam as one of the guests. . . .

"Let's see, who are some of your friends? Of course there's your own cousin Marian, but Belle takes such a narrow view of me she might not let Marian come here. Well, we must get our thinking-caps on and plan something very nice."

Genia looked so pleased, smiling to herself and staring into her little cup, that Lainie didn't protest further. She suspected the project would soon be forgotten anyway. "More coffee?" she asked.

"No, thank you, dear." Genia set the cup back in its saucer with a tiny but decisive click. "Let's just leave the dishes. I'd like to have brandy in the parlor. I don't suppose you would—or perhaps I shouldn't suggest—No, I'm sure . . ."

"Not for me, thanks. But I'll do the dishes while you have yours."

"That's not right. *Leave* the dishes."

They would be there in the morning, with the food dried on them and flies droning about. Her aunt apparently never looked that far ahead. Lainie had the notion, and not for the first time, that she was the older person and Genia was the child. She said, "I don't mind doing them. You go on in the parlor. I'll be with you in no time." Passing behind her aunt's chair, she leaned down and pressed her cheek to Genia's.

The dishes had been washed and put away and she had joined her aunt in the parlor before the doorbell's purring wakened the stagnant twilight of the shuttered room. Perhaps because no one else had rung the bell, the summons seemed charged with meaning. Lainie saw her aunt's lips part with excitement. Under the ruffling of lawn at her throat, Genia's breast rose and fell with quickened breath. "Who . . . ?" she whispered.

"Shall I go?"

"No! I will!" She flew light-footed toward the hall. Lainie heard voices, and moments later Genia returned followed by a man dressed in the blue serge of a ship's officer. Lainie had the impression of youth, of strength, and of some less pleasing quality—arrogance, perhaps, or ruthlessness. She got to her feet.

"This is my niece, Lainie Starkweather," Genia was saying. "And this is Mr. Herbert, First Officer from the *Cyrethra*."

The young man bowed toward Lainie with no pretense of interest.

"Would you like a brandy, Mr. Herbert? Lainie, dear. . . ?"

"Of course. I'll get it."

Lainie took her time about carrying the balloon-like glass to the kitchen to polish it with the teatowel before she poured the liquor from its cut glass decanter. Then she looked for a tray. All the while she heard the point and counterpoint of voices from the parlor: the tinkle of a silver bell, the response of a plucked bass viol.

The young man rose at her return and thanked her absentmindedly. His hand on the glass's fragile stem was enormous—weathered and muscular. A half-forgotten phrase came to Lainie's mind: Every finger a marlin spike, every hair a rope's yarn. But

First Officer Herbert's hair was as black, as glossily waved to his head, as the pelt of a water spaniel.

"You're not joining us, Miss . . . ah . . . ?"

"No, thank you."

Did he mean joining them in a drink, or joining their company? Lainie was about to sit down when the latter thought occurred to her. She hesitated. Genia said, "Do sit down, dear." She was not unwelcome then, or was she, to the young man? But this was ridiculous! Her aunt was a married woman. Even as she told herself this, she fought off the impression of something quite removed from innocence.

As if Genia might have sensed this doubt, and intended to dispel it, she smiled now at Mr. Herbert and said, "It's odd, your coming here, a stranger—oh, not that you're not welcome!"

"Yes, ma'am. Like I told you at the door, this skipper from an English ship, we got to talking in a . . ." His eyes went to Lainie; she noticed they were meshed about with the minute wrinkles that come from long watches at sea. This gave him a look of calculation, of penetration. One could expect little mercy, she thought, from eyes so coldly green, so deeply set in weathered flesh. She looked away from him.

When their glances had broken, he spoke again to Genia. "Well, we met, the way sailors ashore will. Anyway, he told me about . . . visiting you. . . ."

Genia's head had been tipped forward, eyes on the few drops of brandy left in her glass. At Herbert's words she looked up quickly. It would be possible to think she was frightened. Then she gave a small self-conscious laugh, and held her glass toward Lainie. "Please, dear . . . ?"

Lainie thought, She oughtn't to have any more. She really oughtn't. On several nights during the past week Genia's pretty cheeks had flushed with unnatural color and her tongue had grown unruly. This man—this stranger—could easily get the wrong impression. "Oh, Aunt Genia—!"

The young man was on his feet. "Let me." he said.

Lainie's revulsion to his making free of the house was sudden and violent. She almost snatched her aunt's glass and carried it to the diningroom. There, away from this strangely unwelcome visitor, she took her time about pouring. There were several decanters on the buffet. She touched one and another, though she knew quite well which one held the wanted brandy. When she moved one decanter, taller than the others, she found herself staring into the buffet mirror. Her face was pale, unnatural looking, eyes shadowed into caverns of concern, mouth trembling. Before she could assess the change in herself, real or imagined, she saw beyond her mirrored shoulder the portieres between diningroom and parlor. Framed in their crimson velvet her aunt and the young man leaned toward each other, half rising from their chairs, their separate bodies straining across the space that divided them.

A crash of glass struck Lainie's tautened nerves like a blow. She had let a heavy cut glass stopper fall through her fingers to the sideboard.

"Heavens, Lainie! What are you up to?"

"Nothing. I dropped a stopper, that's all." Her hand shook as she poured her aunt's liquor. A few drops fell onto the mahogany. Lainie wiped them off with her cuff, wondering in the next instant how she could be so slovenly.

Back in the parlor she knew beyond any doubt that she was unwelcome. Yet when she said, "If you'll excuse me—" Genia's "Don't go!" was a command. Or a cry for help? In any case, not easily refused.

A conversation that must have begun in her absence now went on.

"I guess I made a mistake to come. If I owe you an apology—"

"Please don't apologize! The situation might have been . . . different . . . don't you see? When your friend was here."

"My *friend*? I told you, I met him in a—"

"I know! But since he told you . . ." Lainie felt more than she saw Genia's eyes fleck toward her and away again. "Perhaps you'll be in port again. Another time. . . ."

He gave a short ugly laugh. "I'm not a guy likes to be made a fool of. Not twice anyway. I thought at the time this guy was pulling my leg. Only I'd heard something else once that made me think—well, no matter now. I'm obliged for the drink."

"Must you go so soon?" Genia's voice was slightly thickened, as if her throat had swelled with tears, or with this need for pleading. Don't! Lainie thought. Oh, *don't*!

"I'm not going to spend my first night ashore talking politics. I've been at sea two months."

"Oh? So long a voyage?"

"From Melbourne. And trouble every foot of the way. I want to get its taste out of my mouth."

"Ah! You do deserve that. . . ."

It had become impossible for Lainie to continue a third party to what was so obviously a dialogue for two. She stood up and said, "I'm tired, Genia. Please excuse me. And—" She gave their guest the briefest of nods; "—good night, Mr. Herbert."

Upstairs she leaned, trembling, against her closed bedroom door. The need to know what was going on, and the fear of knowing, tore her apart.

She had gone to bed but not to sleep when Genia tiptoed into the room. "Lainie?"

"Is he gone?"

"Not yet. I think he'll stay a while—oh, just a little while!—and talk. He's lonely, you know."

"Send him away, please—*please*?"

"That wouldn't be hospitable, now would it?"

"But there's something so ugly—"

Genia smoothed the sheet across Lainie's breast. Her pale face floated in the shadowed room, disembodied, expressionless in the half light. She said, "Don't say that. It isn't kind. He is what he is. No one can help that. We may be sorry, but we have no choice."

Genia, please! Please listen to me—"

"I must go down now. He's waiting. I have no choice."

"Genia!"

"No . . . No. . . ."

It was no use. There was nothing Lainie could say to reach her. Her aunt leaned forward for a goodnight kiss. Her perfume was a teasing sweetness, her lips butterfly soft on Lainie's cheek.

Her whisper was so soft that Lainie might have imagined it: "Forgive me for . . . everything."

The wraith of her aunt's face drifted away. Her figure was a shadow at the door. Lainie started to get out of bed.

"No! Don't get up! *Don't leave this room!* I mean that!" There was the faint click of the doorlatch.

Straining her eyes toward the darkened corner, Lainie cried, "Genia? Aunt Genia?"

Silence.

A dreadful sense of illness took hold of Lainie, as if mind and body were dissolving under some corrosive acid. She thought, If I'm ill—very ill—I'll have to call out. I can't stay here. She slipped out of bed and to the door, but some inner injunction stronger than her aunt's warning kept her from opening it. She sank to the floor, half leaning against the solid paneling of the door.

The distant sound of voices was no more than a whisper: a soft low whisper, a harsher one, a tinkle of laughter. Footsteps—she could more nearly feel than hear them. The sudden creaking of a stairstep under pressure. A door closing. Sounds of breathing, heavy as an animal's. A little cry. A laugh.

Oh God! Lainie thought. Make it not be! Make it be a dream! She ground her hands against her ears and felt her blood pounding in the pressure between them. Even thus, with her ears stopped, she heard and felt the crash of something striking the floor; a chair, perhaps? The stand by her aunt's bed? She dropped her hands and listened, her breath held in the desperate need to hear—to know. Then a shrill high laugh—her aunt's—shut off as quickly as if a hand had stopped her mouth.

Lainie crawled on her knees across the floor and into bed, and pulled the covers across her head. The darkness smothered her, and the close air. But most of all the knowing, the awful knowing.

After a time the house grew quiet. To breathe, to live, she had to press back the weight of covers. And, cringing against the sounds she might hear, she heard nothing.

Presently it seemed to her the silence became so palpable a

thing it moved upon her in waves like the ocean's surf, closing in only to roll away again with a suction so monstrous that she was drawn with it. Out . . . out . . . out, and rolling back again, floating in space. Drawn out . . . and floating back. Floating . . . floating in sleep. . . .

She woke to a cool autumn dawn. Outside her window the sleepy twittering of birds sounded rudely loud in comparison to the silence of the house itself. But Genia always slept late. . . .

For a time Lainie made herself lie silently in bed, but hunger put out little claws of need to twist her flesh. She got up, dressed herself, crept past the closed door of her aunt's room, and went downstairs.

At mid-morning, when she had been able to put aside her worst fear—that her aunt was not alone—she put coffee on a tray and carried it toward the stairs. *Act as if nothing had happened.* The voice within herself was silent but wise. No one can help being what he is, Genia had said. Genia was what she was, no less endearing, no less lovable because of some dark and dreadful need.

Making her way carefully up the carpeted stairs, an eye on the stairs but attention, too, on the brimming cup, Lainie wished that she had put her arms around her aunt last night and said, "I love you. Nothing matters—I love you." But she would say it now. She would put the tray down, take her aunt in her arms, press the bronze hair back from sleep-bemused eyes, and say, "I love you."

She tapped on the door, the tray precarious in one hand. Then, quickly, lest she spill the coffee, she turned the knob and pushed the door open with her toe.

That was not Aunt Genia—that creature sprawled naked and unlovely across a tumbled bed. Not Genia's that purpled face, mouth gaping, eyes rolled upward, her throat swollen and mottled with black fingers of bruise. And, from all this hideous distortion of once-tender flesh, no whisper of sound, no stir of breath.

A scream shattered the silence and echoed in scream upon

scream. A crash of cup and silver tray. A brown stain widening on the pale carpet.

Lainie could only run and leave it all. Run down the stairs, run out the door and along the quiet street. But there was no escape. The screaming went on in her ears, the nightmare vision burned in her eyes. She could not run against the solid flesh of someone holding her. She felt her hands clinging to the rough fabric of a man's coat before it was all blotted out, vision and reality dissolving into the nothingness of unconsciousness.

CHAPTER 30

From the back parlor, through a narrow opening left between the sliding doors, Darrie could see the corner of Genia's coffin. There was a steady rustle of people being admitted and finding seats. Sometimes the aperture between the doors was filled by decent black broadcloth or billowing dark skirt.

Papa's coffin had stood precisely there in the front parlor, perhaps on those same sawhorses now decorously covered with black cloth. How long ago—five years? Six? A lifetime? Why was she thinking of that now? The thing she must cling to was that, at long last, Genia was *safe*. Nothing more could ever hurt her. And she could hurt no one. But I didn't mean to think that—as if her death would protect anyone. Her *awful* death . . .

Someone close to Darrie had made a small sound of pain. Someone's fingers were across her lips. Someone's? Her own. In black gloves.

This was part of the absurdity: black gloves, inside the house, ready for the drive to the cemetery. Outside, mellow with autumn, was a world of which Genia was forever deprived. When was it she herself had first noticed this change of direction, this warning that the world, that life itself had betrayed her? Only at the beginning of this now so sadly ending summer? Only those few months ago when the name of Adam Coates, so carefully not spoken, had echoed louder than a thunderclap? Was that the beginning of it?

Lainie is all I have left now. I will protect her. I will keep her safe.

They shouldn't expect Lainie to be here, to sit through this. She was too thin, too pale, too wounded. But she had said, "I'm quite all right," and had turned away from comfort. During these last days she had lain silent on her bed upstairs, obediently drinking the potions Old Doc had mixed. "They'll quiet her," he'd said. But she needed no quieting. Still, she was back in this room where she belonged, this room she should not have left. She would have been safe here. This dreadful thing would not have touched her here. Would it . . . ?

"Let me see her, please, just for a minute? To know how much I care that she's been hurt." It was Adam Coates who had said that.

"I can tell her that. She's not to have visitors. The doctor's orders." Darrie had emphasized the irony of that: You pretending to be a doctor, with your silly free practice—don't you know enough to leave my child alone?

"Will you surely tell her I've come? It's very important." Standing there at the door of Cedarhaven, begging. . . . There should have been more pride in turning him away. If only she hadn't weakened, at the moment of his turning, to slake her own curiosity: "That young man—that boy—at the dressmaking shop? He—he was all right?"

"He lived."

"I saved *his* life, you know." Yes, she had actually offered this, as if a nameless young man, alive, made up for Genia. . . .

"He may not thank you. He's blind."

Blind!

In the front parlor a chord was struck on the piano. Someone began to sing. Oh, God! They shouldn't sing. Darrie bowed her head. I will not cry. Not for the blind, nor for the dead. I will not cry.

That was Howard's voice: "I loved this woman."

Only last night Belle had said, "I don't know what Howard, with all his godliness, will find to say."

"I loved this woman."

There was a whisper of turned pages. "We are told, 'Judge not that ye be not judged.' How wise is this provision, for no man knows what is in the heart of another. That is for God alone to know. That is why God alone may judge."

In the little silence, Darrie stole a look at Lainie, sitting as still as if carved from ice. Only her eyes were alive, begging for comfort.

Howard said, "For my sister, whose earthly body lies here, I shall read from the Epistle of Paul to the Romans. 'Owe no man anything but to love one another. . . . Love worketh no ill to his neighbor: therefore love is the fulfilling of the law. . . . Now it is time to wake out of sleep: for now is our salvation nearer than when we believed.' "

Behind Darrie, Belle whispered, "He left out part of it."

"Be still!" That was Eric's voice. "He read all that mattered."

There was a stirring now. It was time to go. Time for that drive to the cemetery through the last desperate sweetness of the autumn sunshine, the sunshine that would never again warm Genia's flesh.

The sheriff had been forestalled for a while in his questioning of Lainie. Darrie would have kept him from ever speaking to her had that been possible. But in the evening, after the service for Genia, he came to Cedarhaven.

Darrie was not sorry that Eric insisted on being present. They sat in the parlor, the four of them, as if this were some grotesque social ritual in which each must play out his part—the sheriff bluff and self-assured, Eric tight-locked in his secret thoughts, Lainie a cool wraith of herself. Her pallor, Darrie thought, could come from the bleaching of my own heart, as if we all were part of one another. As I bled to death when Genia died. . . . Genia, whose coffin had been just there, before the window. She said harshly, "I hope you will be brief, Mr. Nolan. My niece has been through a great deal. And, as I told you, she saw nothing—heard nothing."

"I'll be as easy as I can. Now, Miss Lainie, you'd been with your other auntie—with Mrs. Bond—all week?"

"Yes, I had."

"I suppose she had callers?"

"No one."

"Not even on that day?"

"No."

"One of her neighbors saw a man on the porch. Pretty soon after suppertime, she thought it was."

"Aunt Genia did go to the door. Maybe it was a peddler. She didn't buy anything."

Darrie felt the child's careful lack of expression in the muscles, stiff and cold, about her own mouth, felt the lies on her own tongue. Doesn't he know she's lying? Doesn't Eric know?

The sheriff said slowly, "It figures out then—what you're telling me—someone you never seen got in after dark. A burglar, say."

"It could have been."

"But the doors would have been locked, wouldn't they? There'd be a broken window to show?"

Eric's hand flicked downward, caught the sheriff's eyes. "My wife," he said, "was rather careless at times. It would not surprise me if the door had been left unlocked."

"Mmm . . . And you, Miss Lainie, you slept all night? You didn't hear anything out of the way?"

"My door was closed."

The sheriff cleared his throat and looked at Eric. "I've talked to Mr. Bond, of course. Not that he had any information, getting back to town when it was all over, so to say. But to see how he felt about . . . well, about the investigation. Around town here we think a lot of what he—well, anyway he's the one most concerned."

There was an exchange of freighted looks between the two men.

"There is some cases that is just a waste of public funds. I mean, who wants you to spend the time and money when you know ahead of time it won't come to nothing?"

Eric spoke in a tone of indifference. Or was it contempt? "We are lucky to have a public official who understands this."

"Yes . . . well . . . I'm elected to serve the people—I don't forget that."

Darrie sensed the interview was over, if it had been an interview at all.

In parting the sheriff took Lainie's hand. "It was a terrible thing for you—terrible, finding her that way. You try to put it out of your mind now and be your sweet happy self again."

Lainie rubbed the hand he'd freed against her skirt, as if the rough fabric might have some cleansing effect. Rubbed and rubbed. When the sheriff had left she said, "Excuse me—I'm going to my room."

Darrie watched her mount the stairs, her back as straight as if it were a lighted candle carried against the wind.

In the parlor Eric was still waiting, standing by the mantel, as he had done throughout the sheriff's visit. In the two days since he had returned to Port Townsend to bury his wife he had not shown a flicker of emotion, unless it had been to silence Belle at the funeral this afternoon. Now he said, on a note of pleading, "Could I stay a while with you, Darrie?"

Once she would have given the live beating heart out of her body to hear these words. Now they were nothing more than dried autumn leaves blowing on the wind. Her lips were dry. She touched them with her tongue. She felt light and dry all through, as if she might float away like ash. She thought: We are both burned out. The old racing of hot blood that had drawn her to him was like a story read so long ago its details could not be remembered.

"Well?" he said.

"I'm sorry, Eric. I must have seemed rude. Yes, do stay. Please sit down. Can I get you something—coffee, tea, a glass of wine?"

"Nothing, thank you."

Vaguely Darrie was grateful that effort was not required of her. She did not know what state the kitchen was in: with Genia's death, Cheecha had left Cedarhaven, had disappeared like a stone dropped into her own Indian world.

Eric had been waiting for Darrie to be seated; now he sank into a chair. He must be exhausted, as she was. She thought, We are both old and spent, and empty-handed. Anyone else in the world might comfort him; anyone but Eric might comfort her. But they had nothing for each other. She groped for the special reason that made this so, but it eluded her.

Eric said, "This has been an ugly thing for Lainie. I hope she can put it behind her."

"Are you concerned for her?"

"Very much so."

"Why?"

"For herself. She's well worth concern. And because she's Genia's daughter."

Darrie felt herself leaning toward him, felt her breath ebb away. It was a time before she could whisper, "You knew that? Only Genia and I, of all the world . . ." She knew at once this was not true. Cheecha had always known, though no word had ever passed her lips to prove it. And there was Edward Lord, and the Armstrongs, and Ubatsk, that ugly devil with his squaw's blood on the hand that trailed across Genia's cheek. . . .

She realized she had covered her eyes. She let her hand fall away so that she could look at Eric. Lamplight caught his hair, turning it to silver, but his eyes were shadowed, hidden from her. "How did you know?"

"Once, when she'd been drinking, Genia told me."

"Do you think she told other people?"

Eric shook his head. "I doubt it."

Darrie had to moisten her lips again. The inner fire blazed like a fever. Soon there would be nothing left to burn. She asked, "Do you think she told Lainie?"

"I'm sure she didn't. She never wanted to hurt anyone."

"I know . . . I know. . . ."

Eric's hands were clasped between his knees, his head was bent above them as if he were studying the detail of finger, joint, and nail. "There never was anyone who wanted so much to be loved. And yet, to her, to love was to be destroyed." His fingers closed on each other and trembled with the intensity of his hold. "When I finally understood that, it was too late."

"But you loved her, Eric?"

"God knows I did."

"I, too. Now that it's too late, by years, I wonder if we . . . if I . . . had let her alone. . . ." Once, a woman resilient with youth, and—yes, now it could be said—flushed with beauty, had walked through the rain to Eric Bond's office to hear him, out of all the world, say, "You were a good sister." And by his silence she had been made nothing, her youth and beauty withered. Now he was simply here, no more important than the parlor stand, the firetongs. Now he said, "You were a good sister." And it was a lie.

What else could I have done? Where did I go wrong? The questions spoke in her mind, but it was no use to ask them.

Eric was saying something. Once words in his voice would have been hoarded like precious stones. Now she had lost a phrase before she heard, ". . . something alike, you and I."

"Are we?"

"You know that." He smiled at her. For a fleeting moment, in that smile, he was a younger man, innocent and full of hope. But he turned his head and the lamplight struck silver from his hair. "We share the terrible danger of being strong."

"But I *had* to be strong! They all depended on me—needed me! Without my strength—without all I did—yes, I wore myself out doing for all of them! You know that! What would they have done?"

He looked at her with pity. "They would have found their own strength."

Eric was getting to his feet. He moved like an old man. "I've been selfish, keeping you. I'll go now, and let you get some rest. You need it."

"You're going back?"

He shook his head. "I'll never go back there."

Darrie followed him into the hall. He took her hand. It was years since his flesh had touched hers, and now it was as if one dead hand clasped another. She thought, The heart dies slowly, but it dies at last.

He was gone. The door had closed behind him. His step on the board walk, his not-quite-even step, grew fainter till it too was gone. Perhaps I will never see him again, she thought. But it no longer mattered.

CHAPTER 31

Lainie had not chosen to return to Cedarhaven, she had simply found herself there. It was as good a place as any.

In time she learned that pain too harsh to be endured *was* endured because it could not be escaped. A fact had taken place. A life was ended—snuffed out like a burned match—and something that had made the world richer and sweeter was gone forever. In the emptiness she reached out, groping for a warm and living hand to clasp, but others too were locked in their secret grief. Hands did not touch.

Yet life went on. Lainie tried to pick up the broken pieces of it and make a pattern. She forced herself to help Aunt Darrie with the housework, now that Cheecha was gone. She began to make an elaborate piecework quilt, setting tiny careful stitches in the small squares and diamonds of cloth. She visited her cousin Marian. A thousand times she thought of seeking out Adam Coates, but pride held her back. Adam had not come to her. She could not, in decency, go to him.

On one October morning Aunt Darrie had been helping her cut quilt pieces from gingham Cissie had brought from the dress-making shop. The dining table had been cleared of cloth and silence cloth, and the paper patterns laid out on it. When the hall clock struck eleven, Aunt Darrie straightened up from her steady click-clicking with the shears. "That'll keep you busy for a long time," she said. "Now I have to start dinner. Mr. Dutton will be home."

The pose of her aunt's head, or some trick of light from the window behind her, made Lainie realize how thin she had become. The flesh about her eyes was bruised with weariness, or secret tears. She had loved Aunt Genia, Lainie thought. When the name was spoken in her mind she felt the old tired tears press against her own lids. She blinked them back.

Only the corner of the mahogany dining table separated her from her aunt. Was she stretching out her hand across it? Was she saying, Let us forgive each other, take me back, help us to comfort one another? But on the table's dark waxed surface she saw the unmoving reflection of her own hand, fingertip to fingertip. And the only sound was the heavy ticking of the clock.

Aunt Darrie folded the unused pieces of cloth and put them in the workbasket. Purposefully brisk, she said, "The sun seems to be coming out, at last. It wouldn't be October without morning fog, though, would it? Why don't you go for a little walk before dinner?"

Not caring, except to be amenable, Lainie said, "All right," and folded her own sewing. In the sad sea-change that had come over their lives she and Aunt Darrie had nothing for each other.

For lack of better purpose, Lainie directed her steps toward the Newtons'. She would look in on Marian and Aunt Belle. She had passed the corner by the Rothschild house when she came face to face with Adam Coates.

"How are you, Lainie?"

"I'm well, thank you." She was not. An inner trembling had seized her and she could barely stand.

"You look pale."

"It's nothing."

Adam moved to take her arm, but she moved away lest he should feel her trembling. "Please, Lainie, sit down for a minute. You don't look well." He gestured toward a low rock wall, whipped out a handkerchief and spread it on the stones. "Please?"

Her weakness was reason enough for complying. Seated, she clasped her hands together and willed them to be quiet.

"You know I came to see you?"

"No!" was squeezed out of her, a thread of sound.

"Your aunt didn't tell you?" For a moment silence hung between them, but no answer was needed. "She said you weren't well enough to see anyone. That I was not to come again. But she would tell you—she promised that." The words tumbled out in disorderly earnestness.

Lainie, who had been afraid to reveal herself by looking at Adam, now raised her eyes. He seemed tremendously tall, standing above her. When their eyes did meet, at last, the concern in his was a palpable thing. Her clenched hands relaxed as if, in a moment now, she might take hold of this assurance.

"I can't argue against what your aunt says, you know. Right is all on her side. You're so young! And she intends to do a great deal for you. She pointed out—and God knows it's probably the truth!—I'm the sort who'll never have two dimes to rub together."

He seemed to have run down at last. His face was palely serious above her. Then suddenly he smiled. The warmth of it blessed her. He sat down beside her on the stone wall, neglectful of dust on his good broadcloth trousers. A doctor had to be careful of appearances. If someone cared enough to brush and press his suit . . .

He said, "My God, how good it is to see you—talk to you! It seems like a thousand years."

"Adam! Oh, Adam!" She did not know that she had moved, nor notice that he had, but their hands were clasped together with hurting intensity. "I wondered if you really cared. . . ."

"Cared? Don't you know *I love you*?"

"Oh, Adam! Adam!" It was all she could say. Tears flooded her eyes, silly tears, releasing tears, tears that would not be stopped. Laughing and sniffling together, she pulled her hands away and groped for a handkerchief.

"Here—use mine." He slapped an empty pocket. "Lord, you're sitting on it!" He was laughing too as he took her handkerchief to wipe her cheeks. Then it was against her nose. "Blow!" he told her.

She took the handkerchief from him. "You can't blow unless you hold it yourself. A doctor—and you don't know that!"

The sky was still overcast, but a lovely iridescence seemed now to surround them, as if the air had taken on the shimmering nacre of a seashell's lining. The world was right again, and sweet, and safe.

"Adam, are we . . . promised?"

He pressed his hands together—those lovely long-fingered doctor hands. "I have no right to ask you to promise anything. But I am promised—yes! Committed for life. When you're eighteen, if you've waited—"

"*If* I've waited! I won't do anything *but* wait every minute of every day till then."

They talked a little longer, exchanging the tremendous trifles of lovers' words. Then Adam stood up. "There! I've done the very thing I promised your aunt I wouldn't do—to pay you court. I shouldn't have, but I'm glad I did. So now—well—goodby!" He almost shouted the word. Without waiting for her to reply he stalked off down the street.

Oh, dear Adam—stiff-necked, delightful, stubborn Adam—he

had cared all the time. Nothing else mattered against that.

Presently Lainie rose from the rock wall, lifted and shook out his handkerchief, folded it carefully, and slipped it inside her dress above her heart.

CHAPTER 32

The days of Indian summer slipped away. Darrie clung to the conviction that matters somehow would be set right between Lainie and herself. Nothing had really changed between them; she had spoken a few careless words about a virtual nobody and Lainie, acting quite out of character, had rushed off to Genia—but Darrie would not allow her mind to explore that path.

She found that while waking thoughts could be controlled, dreams could not. Genia came and went at night, flitting through the corridors of imagery, laughing, teasing, cajoling. In the morning Darrie would find her pillow wet with tears. At times a formless specter, faceless except for eyes filled with blood, intercepted her dreams of Genia. She wakened, exhausted from her dream-filled nights, and forced herself to the essential tasks of the day.

She had been neglecting the dressmaking shop. She realized this with a touch of panic when Mr. Dutton gave her notice. Cedarhaven would be without income for the first time since

Pomp had walked inside the front door carrying his worn valise. How angry Papa had been! How odd that she should remember that now.

"Miss Starkweather, did you hear me say I'd be leaving on Saturday?"

She brought her attention back to Mr. Dutton, saying, "Oh, yes, I heard you. I'm sorry. Are you leaving town?"

"No, ma'am."

She forced a smile. "Not getting married and setting up housekeeping?"

"Oh, no!"

Curiosity floated to the surface of other and more consuming emotions: she set an excellent table; Cedarhaven was immaculate; boarders, once here, stayed on. She said, "Why are you leaving, Mr. Dutton?" When it was too late she realized the question was rude.

Perhaps it surprised from him a bald reply: "I'm sorry, ma'am, but the place is too gloomy these days. I like a bit more life, if you know what I mean."

Darrie bowed. "You're free to go, of course."

Now the Monroe Street building was her only source of income. She must get back to keeping a closer eye on that, see that nothing went wrong there.

"Why, Miss Darrie! You haven't been here hardly at all lately. Of course I know about your trouble, and all. It's not that I'm complaining. My, you look so thin! You haven't been sick, have you?"

"Of course not. I'm never sick—except for my headaches. How have things been going, Cissie?"

"Oh, fine! I've kept busy. You haven't got some time to help out, have you? I got two dresses on the make. There's a hem, miles around, to cat-stitch by hand. If you was of a mind . . . ?"

"Certainly I'll help." Darrie got out the box in which she kept her own thimble and needles, while Cissie took a red velvet dress from the rack of hangers and laid it across the table, the table where the boy with the blood-smeared face had lain. "Show me what to do!"

"What's the matter, Miss Darrie? Are you mad?"

"Of course not."

"Well, all of a sudden you sounded—"

"Don't be silly! Show me what you want."

"The hem's basted already. But the handwork takes time. You know how crawly velvet is."

For a little time they worked in silence. Then Cissie said, "That Miss Allie Lee, she works in the Anchor, these are for her. That red velvet and this plum-colored street dress. My, she's got a cute little figure! I don't wonder that Si Booker's crazy about her."

"*The Anchor!* Cissie, you haven't had that door open? You haven't got mixed up with—"

"Oh, no! That's a wicked place! Believe me, that door is bolted all the time, and a chair under the doorknob for extra. Look for yourself! Oh, I'm scared of *that* place!"

"I should hope so!"

"Yes, ma'am!"

For a moment Darrie had been really alarmed. The sort of corruption applied to Markie had been so patently unsuited to Cissie that Darrie had never considered it a possible threat. Cissie was prattling on; her slurred speech made close attention necessary.

"She come in by the front door, Miss Allie Lee did. She sort of manages the shows they have there. And you better believe she manages Si Booker too! Well, they sleep together—she as good as told me that."

"Cissie—what are you saying?"

"Just the truth, Miss Darrie. If it comes to that, she's like our other customers, you know."

"And have you got around to approving of that?"

"W-well, not approving, no. . . ."

"I remember very well when Miss La Fontaine came in here the first time, you were furious at having to work for her."

"I guess I was at that. But you can't stay furious—not all day, every day. It turns out they're just people, you know. They can be as folksy with you, or more so, than our old customers."

"We can sew for them, Cissie, but we aren't friends with them. Remember that."

"Yes . . . well, it's kind of hard to draw the line, sometimes, isn't it? Miss Darrie, do you hold with them Lord's Firebrands? The ones that keep talking about how they'll set fire to the saloons and these other places?"

"Certainly not! There's nothing worse than destroying property."

"No, I s'pose not. It's all talk anyway, I guess. And those women, they got to make a living some way, don't they? I guess you wouldn't call it hard work. Not as hard as treadling away on that sewing machine anyways."

"Cissie! What's got into you?"

"Nothing. Except sometimes I get to thinking, well, they do have pretty clothes, their underthings, and all. So frothy and frilly. And someone gets to see 'em."

Darrie looked up. An expression both curious and hungry had come into Cissie's eyes. "Do you suppose, Miss Darrie, them women *like* what they do, and get paid for it too?"

"Now you stop that kind of talk, Cissie Latham! No decent woman would even think of—"

"No, ma'am, I guess not. I don't really think about it. Wouldn't do no good. There's the way I look and all."

Cissie's hand had come up to cover her deformed mouth. Her wounded eyes looked out above the prison bars of outspread fingers.

"Oh, Cissie . . ."

"Oh, I'm all right, Miss Darrie. I'm the way I've always been. I *know* that. Well—" She picked up her sewing again. For a minute she stared at her hands holding the plum-colored fabric. Then she smiled. "Miss Lainie always said I had the prettiest hands she ever seen."

Darrie found it impossible to control her needle; she ripped out stitches and did no better on a second try. She could take the red dress home and work on it this evening, but she didn't want that garment in the house where Lainie was. She said, "I'll come back tomorrow. My eyes are getting tired."

"Oh, that's all right, Miss Darrie. I'd get it done anyway. Don't you worry."

Putting away her workbox, Darrie looked again at the door to the Anchor, the bolt in place, the chair solidly fixed beneath the knob. She had felt Cissie was quite safe here. Now a thought flashed through her mind: not only had Cissie not been safe, it was too late to save her. The idea was gone before she could weigh it.

Darrie's visit to the dressmaking shop freshened her memory of the injured boy. Adam Coates had no doubt lied about him. Probably he was quite well by now and on his way to some distant port. A sailor went to sea, by choice or by necessity, didn't he? Was the method of his going so important?

Darrie knew that some of the townswomen visited the Marine Hospital with food and tobacco for the men. She had never had time for such nonsense, but decided to go now and set her mind at rest.

An attendant took her through the wards. She distributed her offerings to half a dozen mariners beached here by one ailment or another, mostly old men or men made to seem old by rough usage. As she had suspected, there was no blind boy. Then, as she left the ward, a blond youth turned the corner and walked directly into her. He had an ugly scar on one temple. His eyes were vacant and fixed.

"Careful, Buddy," the attendant said. "We told you not to wander 'round."

"Hell, I can't just sit all day."

"Watch your language. There's a lady here."

"I'm sorry." With his hand against the doorframe he began to feel his way past them. His face—if it was the same—she had seen only once, smeared with blood. . . .

"Wait a minute—please! Where did . . . this happen to you?"

"Right here in this town, this—" He used an expletive that made the attendant wince. "Shut up! I told you she's a lady."

The malevolence of the blind boy's look was the uglier for having no focus. It was hatred, unvarnished and unrepentant, directed at the world. He slipped past them and groped his way along the ward, directed by voices saying, "This way, Buddy!" or "Hard aport there—that's Mickey's bed."

Within the safe walls of Cedarhaven, Darrie huddled in her room. Presently she realized she was lying on her bed, still wearing her jacket and hat. Putting them in the closet, she brushed her hand against her cashbox. It was cold as ice. The money in it had been no good: Lainie had refused to use it. Was that because, as Pomp had suggested, it came from the Anchor? Perhaps Lainie's coolness to her was not entirely, after all, the result of those few careless words about Adam Coates.

Adam Coates! Ah, there was something solid for her anger to take hold of! "Did you do this?" he had said, his eyes cold and contemptuous across the cutting table. No doubt he had been talking to Lainie, meeting her on the sly, filling her mind with lying nonsense about the Anchor and her own connection with it. Suddenly Darrie saw that Pomp had been right. Her ownership of the Anchor could be distorted into guilt. She should have severed all connection with it long ago. Perhaps Pomp knew where to reach that long-ago buyer. . . .

She got her hat and jacket out again and hurried to the Kentucky Store. It was humiliating now to ask Pomp for help—and it was too late. The buyer had left town.

"Are you ill, Darrie? You look bad. Let me get a hack to take you back home."

"No, no, I'm fine! I must go see Lawyer Tripp. He might know a buyer."

Lawyer Tripp agreed to keep his eyes open. But buyers didn't grow on bushes, he pointed out. It would take time.

"I don't *have* time!" Darrie told him. "It has to be done quickly."

Obviously he didn't understand; he ushered her out as if he were glad to be rid of her.

The afternoon was ebbing away, the streets were shadowed as Darrie went to the dressmaking shop. From the desk she got out the copy of the lease drawn up between Si Booker and herself, studied it word by word, and found a clause that permitted the lessor to cancel the agreement if leasee "indulged in unlawful enterprise on said premises." Vaguely she recalled Eric's having advised this wording. "You never know," he'd said. "Better to be safe."

Exultantly she took the document to the sheriff. He was getting ready to lock up his office and go home for supper. "This won't take long," she said, and showed him the lease. "I *know* they shanghai men from there. That makes it very simple. You must arrest Mr. Booker. When he's tried and found guilty, I'll cancel his lease."

The sheriff pursed his lips and studied the paper. "We don't want to hurry into anything," he said.

"Oh, but we do! I mean, we must hurry!"

The sheriff folded the lease carefully, running his thick fingers along the fold as if to satisfy himself the crease was perfect. Darrie had not noticed before how flat and stubborn his face was, like a head carved from a too-flat block of wood which forced the artist to foreshorten his work. "Miss Starkweather, you know we can't just run out and arrest people on someone else's say-so. It ain't legal."

"But you know—you must know—"

"I dunno's I've ever had a complaint about Si Booker."

"Nor one about Max Levy?" This was indiscreet. She saw the sheriff was angered where before he had been merely annoyed.

"I don't stick my nose into a crime unless I see it committed. I got to think of everybody's rights, not just what one or two folks might want. You know I've gone out of my way—pretty far out, some folks might say—to accommodate you. Not that I wanted to raise a stink about your sister. . . ."

He had cunningly cut the ground from under her feet. When

he handed the folded lease back to her, she took it in silence.

He was more affable now, with the prospect of getting home to his supper. He said, "You're tired out and upset, Miss Starkweather—the trouble you've had and all. You need a rest. Why don't you and Miss Lainie take a nice trip? You've done well—you can afford it. When you come back, everything'll look different to you."

When Darrie reached Cedarhaven she was exhausted. She sat for a while slumped over on a kitchen chair. She ought to start supper, but what did it matter? There was only herself and Lainie now. And neither one ate more than a bird.

A dreadful sense of dissolution had come over her. She had always known how to manage her affairs. The knack for this—once as solid in her hand as a tool shaped from long use—had slipped away from her.

After a time she climbed the stairs. Lainie's door was closed. She tapped gently and when there was no response opened the door cautiously. On the wide bed Lainie lay on her side. Her cheek was pressed against one hand on the pillow. In sleep, her face was like that of a child, smooth and expressionless.

Tiptoeing close, Darrie drew a coverlet over her. She let her hand brush soft as a breeze across the tumbled hair. She leaned over, wondering if she dared, by barely touching it with her lips, kiss that flushed cheek. She saw then that something was clasped tightly in the hand beneath Lainie's other cheek. She touched it. It was a man's handkerchief, carefully folded.

She recoiled in shock. It was like coming onto nakedness asleep, unable to cover itself.

She backed out of the room, closed the door, and went into her own bedroom. Along the back of her neck, a little hammer struck experimentally on taut muscles. From the washstand drawer she took her bottle of headache wafers, dropped one in her drinking glass, and added water. When the wafer was soft and swollen she lifted the glass and swallowed the sticky mouthful. The water was stale and tepid—it had stood all day in the pitcher—and she made a face against its flat taste.

Darrie slept briefly and wakened at dawn. Pain still throbbed its warning, soft but persistent, at the base of her skull. She dressed and went downstairs.

From the back porch she looked out over the still-sleeping town. The late fall world was quiet as death, held breathless and immobile between the warmth of summer and the chill of winter. The very air waited in suspension as if, at the slightest sound, it would echo like a bell.

Darrie caught herself listening with painful intentness as if she were part of that vacuum of stillness that ached to be set ringing. But there was no sound. There was nothing. The town below her might be not simply sleeping but dead and forgotten for a thousand years, preserved in the still autumn air as the ancient dead lie perfect in their tombs. But she had heard that once the airless crypt was broached the body disappeared in a puff of dust. Port Townsend would not so vanish. Soon it would begin to stir. It would resume its business of drawing a living from the ships that entered its harbor to lower their sails like the wings of seabirds weary from long flight. The quiet morning air had, if one waited for it, a sting of cold, faint but tangible as the scent of snow from the nearby mountains. Darrie went inside and started the breakfast fire.

As she went about her work she felt again the warning throb of pressured blood at the base of her skull, a needle of pain across her temple. Perhaps she ought to lie down. But no! She would not give in to it.

It was amazing how much of the daily work Cheecha had done. Perhaps, Darrie thought, she noticed the added load because she was growing older. But she was not that old! Not forty yet—not by a good two years.

Lainie came downstairs for a late breakfast. Her eyes were clouded, the flesh about them darkened by tears or sleeplessness.

They always ate now at the kitchen table; it was too much trouble to set places in the diningroom, and the long empty table was a reproach.

"Lainie, if anything is bothering you . . . if there's something you want to tell me . . . ?"

"There's nothing, Aunt Darrie."

"We used to find a lot to talk about."

"Yes, didn't we?"

"Why don't you go visit Marian today?" As soon as the words were out, Darrie had an image of Lainie meeting Adam Coates at the Newtons'. It would be like Belle to connive at such a meeting. She'd always been underhanded. At best Belle would talk against her to Lainie—she probably had already done so. She said, more loudly than she had intended, "No! I don't want you to go."

Lainie looked up, her dark eyes wide with surprise. "All right, Auntie. I didn't intend to go anyway." She smiled faintly. "It's small of me, but I get tired of hearing about Marian's wedding plans."

"Wedding plans! I didn't know—"

"It would have been announced officially, except for—" Lainie steadied herself with a visible effort, and said, "except for Aunt Genia. But they will be married in the spring—Marian and Robert Ball."

"Marian is too young to marry."

"She's as old as Aunt Belle was."

"That was too young."

"It seems to have worked out." It was impossible to know if this was irony, impossible to know anything that went on behind those now-secret dark eyes. Genia, at least, had been open. Genia . . .

"What the matter, Auntie? Are you getting a headache?"

"I'm afraid so."

"Why don't you go back to bed?" Darrie waited for the warm-hearted offer of the salt bag and the cold compresses. None was made.

I've lost her. Her heart has gone to Adam Coates. In a little time she will be eighteen. She'll marry him. I'll never see her again.

Darrie got up and stumbled over the corner of the woodbox. She hadn't seen it. She could be blind, as that boy was blind. . . .

The day crept on, empty and savorless. Darrie went listlessly through the motions of housework. The air continued still and heavy. It was unnatural: the wind blew sometime every day in Port Townsend, and sometimes all day. Now it seemed necessary to leave doors open in order to breathe. Or perhaps it was her mounting headache that made Darrie feel she was starving for air.

If I could escape, get free now of the Anchor, keep Lainie safe here, away from that Adam Coates—get rid of him! Get free! The thoughts were formless but insistent, part of that throbbing of heavy blood inside her head.

Darrie and Lainie were still at the supper table, where Darrie had been able to force down only a few mouthfuls of food, when they heard the firebell ring. Both raised their heads, listening. A single brazen stroke quivering with that peculiar urgency evoked only by a firebell, a pause, another stroke. The sound seemed to be in Darrie's head, beating against her skull for escape. A pause. another stroke; the repeated pause, and stroke. The fire was downtown in District One.

She and Lainie went out onto the back porch. Above the lower end of town the sky was crimson. Occasional billows of dark smoke rose to obscure the color, and bright tongues of flame leaped upward.

Lainie said, matter-of-factly, "It must be the cribs."

Darrie had not supposed the child knew they existed, much less what to call them. But she was right: the fire was obviously among the cribs, or close to them. Darrie thought, the shop has some money due down there, and was astonished she could think of anything so small and personal.

Lainie caught at her arm and cried, "Look! There's another fire at the Point—where the Chinese live!"

The new fire, and the swelling flames of the earlier one, shone like stage lights on two anchored ships invisible before. Brass fittings winked in the light, and bare spars gleamed as if waxed.

Above the continued tolling of the firebell, shouts could be heard. The volunteer firemen must be gathering by now. The clanging of metal suggested the forming of a bucket brigade.

Abruptly the bell stopped. In the comparative quiet Darrie heard a new sound: approaching Cedarhaven from the street above was a chorus of voices chanting "The Battle Hymn of the Republic:" ". . . He has sounded forth the trumpet that shall never call retreat,/ He is sifting out the hearts of men before His judgment seat./ Oh, be swift, my soul to answer Him! Be jubilant my feet!"

In a moment shadowy figures appeared on the board walk, moving toward town. There might have been a dozen men, their heads covered with what appeared in the poor light to be pillow-cases. Breathlessly, for they were hurrying, and in poor time, they continued to sing: ". . . let us die to make men free/ For God is marching on!"

Darrie had been puzzled by the two fires. Now everything was clear. The Lord's Firebrands had started their purifying flames. She felt no surprise. It was almost as if she had known, in the morning's first eerie stillness, that the day would end like this, that it was right to end like this.

She started down the back steps and across the grass, with the dew wetting her ankles. Lainie was close behind her. She thought of telling Lainie to go back in the house, to lock the door and stay there in safety. But an inner knowledge told her the girl would not obey. She saved her words.

There was magnetism in the fire: Darrie found herself hurrying on the board walk, her breath catching, her heart pounding like a live thing that, on its own, must hurry toward the lure of the flames. She thought of the time so long ago when she had run through the smoke and ashes of Kah Tai's burning, the day she had found Cheecha. But Cheecha had never cared for her, nor been really grateful. It had always been Genia that Cheecha loved, and now Genia was gone. Cheecha was gone. Lainie was gone. . . .

She become aware that Lainie was indeed gone. Darrie was at the Monroe Street corner, but she was alone. Everyone in town seemed to be beyond her, hurrying toward the fire. Lainie had slipped away from her.

The door to the Anchor stood open, the room behind it empty.

Even Si Booker's entertainment could not equal a fire in the cribs, or at the Point.

Someone was pushing a hosecart down the street. Darrie turned into the alley to avoid it and, after a few quick steps, realized she was standing at the very spot where the boy had been struck down. She pressed her hands to her eyes for a moment, then ran on down the alley. At its end she came out into a crowd of milling people. Two or three hundred feet ahead of her she saw two of the wooden cribs reduced to a jumble of charred and smoking timbers framed in a welter of smoke and steam. The smell of burning wood and cloth rode the air.

Here the fire was controlled: the bucket brigade must have done its work well. But a block away, across vacant lots, some of the Chinese shacks were burning furiously. The hosecart that Darrie had avoided was being wheeled into place here, and a bucket line was already forming from the beach to the burning shacks.

Darrie heard the sound of hysterical weeping, and peered through the crowd to see a scantily-clad woman being comforted.

Someone touched her own arm. She turned to find Pomp at her elbow. He was having trouble with his breathing. "I'm blown," he said, and took a deep gulp of air. "Let the younger ones take over."

She looked at him in surprise. He did look old, and tired. His shoulders had begun to stoop. His hair had receded above his uneven black brows. Someone should have taken care of him. Someone . . .

"God, how we pitched in when the fire started! And fighting those blathering idiots in pillowcases all the way!" He stopped again, breathed deeply, and said, "They've likely killed Old Doc. Hauled him off to the hospital a bit ago. To my eye he was already a goner."

"Killed him? How?"

"He was on a ladder to the roof, and one of the reform laddies pulled it down. Doc's no youngster, to go falling into a pile of rocks." Pomp looked around now that he had his breath, and said, "Where's Lainie?"

"I don't know. I've lost her."

"Get back to Cedarhaven. This is no place for you. I'll hunt for Lainie and bring her home. Please!"

"Yes . . . all right. . . ."

Pomp moved away in the crowd, but Darrie did not turn back.

A roof on one of the Chinese shacks fell in with an upward burst of flame and smoke. A concerted sound, half-moan, half-cry, rose from the onlookers. For a few fiery moments the whole area was lighted: painted buildings were brilliantly white; windows shone like flame; the anchored ships stood out in bold relief. Then the flames died down. There was the loud hiss of water striking live coals, and a column of white steam rose.

A little group of people were moving toward Darrie, at their center a bowed and mute Chinese woman in her native dress of trousers and coat. The few Chinese women from the Point were never on the street; Darrie had no sense that she had seen the woman before, but as a victim she was familiar. The Oriental, her head bowed almost to her breast, the scantily clad prostitute, Cheecha crouching terrified in the swamp grass . . . why did an image of Genia join them in her mind's eye . . . or was it Lainie? Or a blond boy with blood running across his eyes? It was always these weak ones who got hurt, the very ones she had tried to protect. While the strong ones . . . what was it Eric had said about the terrible danger of being strong? Yes, a terrible danger, for she was broken too. Despoiler and despoiled shared a common anguish. It was so clear now that Darrie could not believe she had not always known it.

Her head was pounding cruelly. She must get home. But there was something she had to do. Something. It eluded her for a frustrating moment, then came clear again. She went back along the alley, turned onto Monroe Street, and reached the corner.

The door to the Anchor was closed now. Although he had lost his patrons, Si Booker must have come back to put out the lights and lock his door against possible looters. It didn't matter. Darrie had her keys. She unlocked the door of the dressmaking shop. Inside, she groped her way through the dark to the connecting door. She took the chair away from underneath the knob, and slipped the bolt. The door resisted her. Si Booker, that hateful and hated creature, must have installed a bolt on his side. Fumbling in the darkness, Darrie located the chair she had put aside and brought it with all her force against the door. The chairlegs stung her hands. She struck again and again and was rewarded by the sound of splintering wood. Her questing fingers found an opening in the door. She reached through and touched the cold steel of the bolt.

Inside the Anchor she moved forward, hands outstretched, groping her way along the hall. Who was it moved this way. . . . ? She would remember later. Now there was something she had to do.

The smell of stale cooking grease led her to the kitchen, the stove's warmth was a guide to it. She opened the door to the firebox and found a bed of coals. If they had not been there, if she had had to search in a strange place for matches, she might not have been able to do what she knew she must do. But the live coals were there waiting for her, as she had known they would be. With that for an omen, she knew she would find paper, shavings, oil from a lamp. . . .

When she was through, she went back through the dressmaking shop. Someone had said, here in this room, that property should never be destroyed. What nonsense! When she let herself out onto the street, she could see, through a crack between the Anchor's window curtains, a bright tongue of flame.

Walking quickly, at times running, she went back to where she had spoken to Pomp. He was not there, but Lainie was. She was, in fact, part of an unbelievable tableau made up of the dispossessed prostitute, wrapped now in someone's shawl; Adam Coates, who was giving the woman something in a glass; and Lainie, who was holding the woman's hand and urging her to drink. Others stood about like the minor and almost invisible supporting actors at a moment of on-stage drama. The shawl-wrapped woman was no longer crying. She had spent what emotion she had.

Lainie was stroking her hand and speaking to her soothingly. Approaching, Darrie heard the girl say, "Dr. Coates has arranged for you to have a room. Come along, we'll take you there."

Close to the woman, Darrie realized what she had not before: she was one of the shop's customers. A few months before they had made what the woman herself called a "street custom" of green broadcloth. It must be ashes now. We'll make her another, she thought, and not charge her for it. Doubt nagged her: there was a reason they would not be able to, but it eluded her. She imagined herself putting her arms around the woman, kissing her cheek, saying, "You poor creature! I'm sorry—so sorry this has happened." The prison of habit made the gesture impossible. She turned instead to Lainie and said, "You shouldn't be here—it's not decent." She did not know where the words had come from. They were not what she had meant to say.

"I'm with Adam," Lainie said, as if that explained everything.

"You must come with me."

Lainie ignored her. She seemed not so much rude as beyond the sound of Darrie's voice. "Come along," she said to the prostitute. "I know you must feel dreadful, but it's not far. The Doctor and I will help you."

They had her between them now. Clumsily they moved away together, as if Darrie did not exist. She followed them without knowing why. They didn't need her. Lainie did not need her. The knowledge throbbed against her skull, part of the mounting pain of her headache. Perhaps Lainie had never needed her. . . .

She might have gone on stumbling after the oddly assorted trio of figures, but a great shout rose behind her. "The Anchor! My God, the Anchor's burning!"

For one wild disoriented moment Darrie wondered how that could have happened. Then she remembered. Strength ran out of her. She leaned against a doorway to keep from falling. A medley of shouts and of pounding footsteps came from the Point. One voice, above the others, yelled, "Get on a roof across the alley! We can keep it from spreading!"

After a few minutes Darrie realized she could walk, not firmly but well enough to reach home. As she climbed the hill she saw the windows of Cedarhaven were blood-red with the reflection of the flames, but she did not look back to the fire itself.

Inside the house, everything was dark, cool, orderly, and deserted. The blinds were drawn at the windows, and she left them that way. She had no desire to look out on the activity below. After a time she realized she was chilled to the bone. She lighted the fire that had been left laid on the parlor hearth. The flames rose and danced, but crouching near them she could feel no warmth.

The wind had risen at last. It screamed around the corners of Cedarhaven and shook the walls. Was it true, she wondered, that a fire created its own wild wind? Now, on its fitful gusts, the shouts of the firefighters were carried to her. They seemed to come from another world. This was her world, and she was alone in it.

She did not know if she had been told, or knew without being told, that Old Doc was dead. This meant that Adam would take his practice. He would be in a position to marry—he would marry. Lainie would be gone. Every day would be like this: an empty house, a lonely hearth that no amount of fire would warm. . . .

Someone was ringing the doorbell, pounding the door. No one would come—she must be imagining it. But the demand went on, the pounding a part of the unendurable pressured throbbing in her own head. It must be stopped! She ran into the hall and unlocked the door.

Pomp came in and closed the door behind him. "I found Lainie, but she wasn't ready to come home. She's not alone, though. You've no need to worry."

"I know who she's with."

"Ah! 'Tis all right then."

Perhaps it was all right. . . . Darrie put her hand to her forehead as if to test in that way the amount of pain. She took a deep breath and said, "I've lost Lainie for good. I know that."

"When you really know it, you'll have her back."

Darrie steadied herself with a hand on the newel post. She thought that when Pomp had delivered his message he would turn and go, but he did not. "Will you come in by the fire?" She wanted it so much she hardly dared to ask.

"Thank you. I will. I've some bad news for you. 'Tis better you sit down to hear it."

She could not imagine any more bad news. Lainie was safe. "Is it Belle, or Howard? Or one of the children? Tell me, Pomp!"

He waited till she was seated, and said, " 'Tis about your property."

"Oh—that!"

"You knew it was burning?"

"Yes."

"With your permission, *I'll* be sitting down!"

She saw the astonishment on his square Irish face, and thought how much more astonished he would be if she told him. One day she might. He was the one person—had always been the one—that she might have confided in. He would not have said, "You've been a good sister." No. More likely, with a wild uprising of crooked brow he would have shouted "You've been a fool!"

Perhaps, she thought, that's what I should have heard. The idea was an alien one. Humility was not her habit. She said, "Pomp, I've never had the heart to rent your room."

"Haven't you, then?"

"No. It's empty. And I wish you would . . . come back to it."

When he didn't answer she made herself look at him. She remembered having thought, years ago, that in Pomp she was seeing for the first time the storied "Irish eye": brightly blue and with a dancing quality as if lights stirred deep within them. Unquenchable eyes. But now inscrutable. She could not guess what was going on in his mind.

He shook his head. " 'Tis a polite offer. Thank you for making it. But my mind was made up when I left Cedarhaven. I would not live here the way it was between us, and I'd not ask you again to marry me."

She knew, then, what was going on in his mind, and turned away from the knowledge. She stared into the fire. Coals sang in the grate. Writhing pennants of flame whipped upward and were snapped off in the wind-swept throat of the flue. The flames would be dying down now in the Monroe Street building. Those wooden structures went quickly. Tomorrow she might feel regret, but not now. Not tonight. It had been necessary to make an ending.

"Pomp," she said, "you told me once that everything has to run its course, even folly."

"I believe that's so."

"Could you believe that tonight was the end of mine?"

"It would tax me, I'm obliged to say."

"You don't want to believe it."

"More like, I don't dare."

It was deeply important that he should believe. Darrie thought, He will, in time. Words, unplanned but urgent, burst from her: "We haven't a lot of time left, Pomp. I've made us waste too much."

"That you have." He stood up. "I'll be getting back downtown. Likely I'm the only man in town who's not there now, though there's nothing left to do but wring our hands."

When Darrie went to rise, Pomp drew her up and held her in the circle of his arm. It was strange—that painful throbbing in her head had stopped. She floated, feather-light, in the new-made world that always waited beyond pain. The unendurable had been endured. Life flowed on. " 'Tis a cruel hard time you've had, Darrie girl. My heart has fair withered for you. But you'll manage."

She laid her head on his chest, and felt his arm tighten about her, felt her own flesh relax against the solid strength of his. There had been, almost lost in memory, a fusing of flesh in molten need. But never in her life had Darrie leaned, weak and suppliant, on a man's greater strength.

Peace touched her, a passing breath, but the promise of something attainable.

"Yes," she said. "Yes, Pomp, we'll manage."